LUCIFER'S ARK

Recent Titles by Simon Clark

BLOOD CRAZY
HOTEL MIDNIGHT
THE NIGHT OF THE TRIFFIDS
VAMPYRRHIC
VAMPYRRHIC RITES

LONDON UNDER MIDNIGHT *
LUCIFER'S ARK *

available from Severn House

LUCIFER'S ARK

Simon Clark

This first world edition published in Great Britain 2007 by
SEVERN HOUSE PUBLISHERS LTD of
9–15 High Street, Sutton, Surrey SM1 1DF.
This first world edition published in the USA 2008 by
SEVERN HOUSE PUBLISHERS INC of
595 Madison Avenue, New York, N.Y. 10022.

Copyright © 2007 by Simon Clark.

British Library Cataloguing in Public

Clark, Simon
  Lucifer's ark
  1. Horror tales
  I. Title
  823.9'14[F]

ISBN-13: 978-0-7278-6580-9   (cased)
ISBN-13: 978-1-84751-039-6   (trade paper)

Except where actual historical events and characters are being
described for the storyline of this novel, all situations in this
publication are fictitious and any resemblance to living persons
is purely coincidental.

All Severn House titles are printed on acid-free paper.

Typeset by Palimpsest Book Production Ltd.,
Grangemouth, Stirlingshire, Scotland.
Printed and bound in Great Britain by
MPG Books Ltd., Bodmin, Cornwall.

FIRST TRACT

One

Choir-Moore Abstracts look after their own. You might call them comrades-in-arms, but it goes deeper than that. If there's a problem they don't turn to anyone outside their team for help: they fix the problem themselves.

This afternoon the problem presented itself as the piece of crap in Holding Cell D. The Crap in question might eat, drink, make utterances, take naps, wash the blonde spines of its hair in the sink, but to the men and women of Choir-Moore Abstracts the occupant of the six-by-ten room is still 'a Crap'. And 'a Crap' it would remain for the rest of its life.

Two guards chatted casually as they entered data into a laptop. 'Crap in Cell D is washing its hair again.'

'Got to be the tenth time this afternoon.'

'Smears shit into its hair, works it into spikes then washes it all over again.'

'Got an endless supply of shit.'

'But you could hardly call it bottomless.'

The other guard smirked as he sipped his coffee. The pair were dressed in jeans and sweatshirts. People who didn't know any better would assume they worked in the docks nearby. Apart from a suggestion in the guys' manner that they were ex-military there wasn't much to differentiate them from the crane drivers or cargo handlers. For the pair this was a routine shipment. The Craps were heading out on a one-way ticket. Where, they didn't know – come to that, they didn't care.

'That stink again.'

'What the hell has it been eating? Stinks worse than the boiled cabbage I got at school. Blast. I've entered the time in the wrong box.'

Both men stared at the screen with its columns of text that frustrated them on a daily basis.

'Keep hitting back-space until you rewind to box eleven.'

The guard who operated the keyboard hit the back-space. But his eye wandered to a batch of video screens bolted to the wall. The one marked 'Cell D' revealed a rear view of a naked figure running slick brown fingers through blonde hair, coaxing it into stiff spikes. Seeing the hands spike the hair with excrement only made the stink more noticeable.

'We need more extractor fans,' the guard grunted. 'Got it. Departure time: eighteen hundred.' He tapped keys.

'What's the one in D being shipped out for?'

'Killed a couple of kids.' He flipped back a page on the screen. 'Two confirmed . . . three probable . . . suspected of more than a dozen assaults, but insufficient evidence for conviction.'

'Busy bastard, eh?'

The figure on the screen cupped one hand beneath its buttocks. Then it squatted so it could empty its colon.

Grimacing, the other guard opened a drawer to fish out two blister packs of pills. 'What do you think, Rob? Yellow or green?'

'Two of each. Knock it out until they ship it.'

The guard snapped the tranquilizers from the pack. 'Does our friend speak English?'

'Not according to this. ID unknown. Nationality unknown. Language unidentified. For all we know it floated up the U-bend.'

The guard with the pills crossed the holding bay to the steel door of Cell D then flipped down a hatch that was maybe a foot long by four inches high; the effect was of an elongated letter flap in a house door. Inside, the creature groomed itself in its own unique way – a creature that was stateless, nameless and refused to speak. Not that this was unheard of. Plenty that came through here had burned their passports and pretended to be mute in the hope they'd wind up in a cozy psychiatric ward rather than the everlasting fun land that is maximum-security prison. 'Hey, blondie. Stop that. Come and swallow some happy tabs.'

Later, the guard would admit he was careless. The emaci-ated thing inside, with its hair stiffened into spikes with its own you-know-what, appeared three-quarters lifeless, a skeleton of a human being that no longer had any interest in life, or possessed any physical strength come to that. It devoted what little energy it had to defecating, coaxing its blonde hair into spikes, then washing it clean again in a sink that was little bigger than a construction worker's hardhat.

When the lightning bolt of pain hit, the guard he knew he'd been lax. The creature had no possessions in the cell, not even clothes, but he dealt with the kind of prisoner who hid shards of glass inside their foreskin, or could store needles from hypodermic syringes under the flesh of their scalps or in groins, anywhere tufts of hair might conceal a tiny entry wound. These would be extracted later at the prisoner's leisure to inflict injury on themselves or others. This time the prisoner had drawn a sharpened implement, probably a toothbrush, from where it had been secreted in its anus. The plastic shaft had been honed to a tapering blade of near surgical sharpness.

The guard saw it punch clean through the palm of his hand. The pain caused him to flinch so violently he cannoned backwards into the wall.

'Damn it, Rob!' He clutched the hand that had been skewered by the toothbrush shaft. 'Look what the bastard did!'

'I'll buzz the doc.'

'You'll do no such fucking thing. Call in the rest of the team. Tell them to bring in a bottle of bleach – make sure it's one of the big ones.' The injured guard smiled despite the pain in his hand. 'And tell them one of our guests is as thirsty as hell.'

In the next cell Sami heard the guards crash through a door to beat up the occupant. Cell beatings composed their own kind of symphony. First came the opening bang of the door. Then a tumultuous overture, lots of fast sounds one after another, crick, thud, snap, pop, slam. Then a pause. *Check the prisoner's still breathing . . . good, they are . . . they can take some more . . .* Then a slower, more controlled rhythm of sounds as guards took it in turns to kick the prisoner in the guts or beat their head against the wall. Sometimes it would go quiet for whole minutes. Time to rest before the finale. Then the guards finished with a crescendo of pounding.

This time Sami heard someone shout: 'Hold the head! Tip

the bottle up, get it into their mouth!' A bit of silence now.
'Don't get that stuff on your own hands – it'll burn your skin
right off.'

After the treatment was over Sami heard the noise from the
next cell, but thought nothing of it. Vomiting is a common
sound in prison. So are muffled choking sounds. Then, through
the wall, came a yell. This sounded different to the screams
that Sami regularly heard in jail. This one sounded as if the
screamer's vocal chords were burned. There was something
else about the sound too. It contained notes that weren't
entirely pain – a kind of ecstasy, a joy, an electrifying peal
of triumph.

Sami curled into a ball. The yell became a nitric rasp. It
filled his head with so much pain he wanted to kill himself.
But that sentiment wasn't unusual either: Sami was on suicide
watch. He was figuring how to die before the ship left port.

Two

Airport departure lounges bustle; delayed passengers run
for planes; the electric buggy that carries the disabled
hums along concourse routes with the orange warning light
whirling. Conversely, the departure lounges of ships are stagnant. They tend to be full of men, women and children who
wait, stare into space, and don't move about. There's no sense
of urgency. No one's in a hurry to do anything because the
ship is tethered in the dock. It doesn't have to dash to make
an air-traffic controller's precious departure window.

That's usually the case, thought Tanya Rhone as she gazed
out of the departure windows at the *Volsparr*. The vessel
dwarfed the warehouse buildings on the quayside. The ship,
tall as a six-storied apartment block, waited there on a freezing
December afternoon. An afternoon already dark because of
heavy cloud running from the north to engulf the port of Hull
here on England's east coast. Tanya saw her own reflection

in the glass. A twenty-five-year-old with short dark hair, casually dressed in jeans, a sweater and shoes that made her imagine that if she were in a TV commercial the voiceover would purr, 'Tanya Rhone, loves footwear that declares to the world: I work hard but I can be sexy too.' She bit her lip to stop herself grinning at her reflection. Boredom did that to her. She'd find herself slipping into whimsy where she'd picture herself as the subject of a TV documentary or an advertisement. *Does everyone do that? Or am I just two stops away from the asylum?* Now she couldn't stop the smile reaching her lips. Quickly, she popped a mint into her mouth to disguise her amusement.

Normally the embarkation lounge would have held passive travelers, but perhaps because it was so close to Christmas there was a sense of restlessness. Frustration snapped on the warm, airless atmosphere. Too many people crowed into too small a space without enough seats.

Tanya sat in seats with a view of the ship. Lights blazed from the darkness, like buds of silver fire erupting from the superstructure. Did she glimpse snow? A phantom strand of white darted by the window.

A boy of around eight had been playing with a toy gun, but now challenged his mother. 'We should have flown there. Why didn't we?' Tanya recognized a Texas accent through the whine.

'They can't use the airport in the winter.' The mother spoke without lifting her eyes from a wad of travel documents she examined with grim determination.

'Why not?'

'Ice.'

'They have ice in Chicago; it didn't stop us flying out.'

'Well, it's worse in Russia, Billy.'

'Dad should have come home.'

'He can't; he's busy at the mine.'

'I won't go to no damn Russia.'

'*Billy.*'

'And I don't want to go on *no* damn ship!' He aimed the dart gun at his mother's eye.

'Not now. I can't find the visa.'

'Good.'

'They won't let us in if I can't—'

'Damn good. I hate Russia.'

'We'll have Christmas with – ' she pushed aside the gun muzzle that threatened her right eyeball – 'Dad. You haven't seen him since August.'

'He should come home.'

Mom sighed. 'I told you lots of times. Daddy has to work this Christmas.'

'Will I still get presents?'

'Of course you will. Ah, here it is. Thank the Lord, I thought I'd . . . never mind. Put that gun away, Billy.'

The PA chimed. 'Will passengers please remain in the departure lounge. We will begin embarkation at seventeen hundred hours.'

Tanya glanced at the TV monitor. *Volsparr.* Departure: 1800.

Hurry up. I want my cabin and a shower. I've endured six hours on a train that couldn't have been any more overcrowded. I've had my toes stomped on, a stranger fall asleep on my shoulder. I want hot food . . . The litany in her own head made her sigh. It wasn't helping. Instead she tried to blank out her mind so she could spend the next thirty minutes here in a state of Zen-like calm. Only it didn't work. Billy climbed over her seat to retrieve an orange dart. A pair of women sitting by the bureau de change coughed endlessly as an infection tormented their throats. A man at the kiosk demanded to change Euros into Rubles.

'We can't give you Rubles here,' the cashier told him.

'But I'm going to Russia. I need Rubles for the cab.'

The cashier endeavored to explain. 'The part of Russia where you're going, there's not much call for Rubles. Dollars, Euros and Sterling are accepted – in fact, they're preferred.' The businessman marched away, his face scarlet with anger.

Meanwhile, the boy fired an orange dart at the Christmas decorations hanging from the ceiling. A foil angel fell to earth. At the information office a woman with a crimson headscarf had her own agenda.

'I need to board the ship now.' Her red lacquered fingernails tapped the desk to the rhythm of her words. 'It's important. Let me on to the ship.'

'Madam, I'm sorry. We can't board until—'

'There's something I need on there. It's vital.'

'You can't board yourself yet, but I could ask a member of crew if—'

'No. I need to retrieve it myself.' The woman's dark almond eyes had the same quality as portraits of Persian princesses. 'Tell the boarding gate to admit me.'

'I can't do that. I'm sorry,' the clerk explained. 'The captain won't allow us to board yet.'

The fingernails tapped harder. 'But I need to collect something from the ship.'

'If you can tell me what it is you need . . .'

'No. I can't do that.'

'Then I'm sorry, madam. I can't help you any—'

Another dissatisfied customer stormed across the lounge, eyes flashing with anger. She trailed an exotic perfume of almond oils.

Another woman of around thirty sat beside Tanya; she had wiry red hair decorated with strips of green ribbon. Her perfume still had a raw power, as if she'd sprayed freely in the bathroom to hide the odors of a long journey. Tanya wondered whether she should do the same. She ached for that shower. Hot food. A cozy bunk.

When the redhead's phone sang she answered it with a groan when she saw the caller's ID. 'Hi, Mom.' She took a deep breath. 'Bad news, Mom. Very bad news.' A pause as the redhead listened to the inevitable question. 'I won't be home for the holidays.' Tanya heard the mother's cry. The redhead flinched. 'I'm sorry, Mom. Doug's not coming for Christmas. Why? Because he's working over frigging Christmas, that's why.' The redhead's apologetic tone turned to anger as her mother began to interrogate. 'I told you a month ago that the mining company had fallen behind. If they don't meet the quota by the end of the year they have to surrender the lease back to . . . I don't know, whoever owns the land. That's right, but it's not Doug's fault. Guys are pulling sixteen-hour shifts, so— No, Mom, I can't cancel the trip. I'm at the ferry port now, in Hull . . . Hull? It's a seaport in England . . . No . . . Mom, I couldn't tell you earlier because you— Mom, will you listen? I can't come home now. I haven't seen Doug since August. If I miss this trip it won't be until April . . . and there's no frigging airport in use either until— Fine, that's just fine!' A pause, then the redhead pressed her fist against her forehead. 'Mom, don't you cry. I'm warning you, don't you cry. I'm going to spend Christmas with Doug!' Cell phone bubble syndrome. Even though fifty people were crowded into this corner of the departure lounge, the redhead no longer cared. She could have been arguing with her mother long-distance from an empty room.

Tanya Rhone allowed her gaze to rove across the faces of the waiting people. Their eyes had that faraway look that came when identifying with someone else's plight. *Yeah, we're all in the same boat*, Tanya though with grim humor. *Or we soon will be. Boson Eumericas has to meet its extraction quota by New Year's Eve; either that or surrender a ninety-nine-year mine lease that's as lucrative as a dozen oil wells. If the lease is yanked then Boson Eumericas goes bust, its workers lose their jobs, then their cars, homes, possibly spouses – the entire package.*

The redhead had fire in her voice now, daring her distant mother to criticize. 'So this is the only chance we get to see our husbands for months . . . No, I don't know if they have turkey in Russia. But I do know they don't have Santa Claus.'

Billy picked up the terrible news. 'Mom! The lady says they don't have Santa Claus in Russia.'

The mother smiled, albeit grimly. 'They do have Santa Claus, only they call him Father Frost.'

The PA chimed. 'Passenger announcement. All passengers please proceed to embarkation point. Take care when boarding; the cold has made the entrance passageway slippy underfoot.'

Tanya joined the line for embarkation; a shuffling, generally tired line. Here were men and women who were making the most of what promised to be a poor Christmas. A seventy-two-hour journey through freezing temperatures to an island in the Baltic Sea. One that should ensure they met loved ones who made their living tunneling into the bedrock of Russia. *Deal with it,* she told herself. *Make the best of a bad thing.*

The boy fired his toy gun, then disappeared between the legs of passengers to retrieve the dart.

His mother despaired. 'Billy . . . Billy, where are you?'

The line moved forward in a subdued shuffle, like deserters plodding toward a muddy field where a firing squad waited with loaded rifles. Tanya wasn't normally prone to such gloomy thoughts, but this time the situation demanded it. Here she was boarding a ship that loomed darkly above the dock with all the sinister air of a prison. Cranes towered over wharves, iron guardians of the underworld. The River Humber that would carry the ship into the North Sea swirled with a blackness you only find in the deepest of tombs. *Tanya, face up to this. You've got news for Jack that can only be told face-to-face. Come hell or high water, you've got to make this trip.*

By now Billy's mom had gripped him by the wrist. Grimly, she dragged him toward the embarkation gate. Then, inexplicably, a terror gripped the boy as if an evil prophecy had been whispered into his ear. 'Mom! I want to go home. I'm frightened. Don't make me go in there. *I'm frightened!*'

Pressing her lips together, as if preparing herself to sacrifice her first-born to gods who reveled in bloody tortures before death, the mother hauled her son up the walkway, then into the iron belly of the ship where his screams finally died.

Three

The execution is always efficient. The execution of the deed of transfer, that is. Prisoners to be carried by the *Volsparr* to their overseas prison were wheeled in cages not much larger than those used to transport family dogs on airliners. When the men putting you in the cage are as professional as those employed by Choir-Moore Abstracts, it is surprising how even the most ample human frame can fold up into the most compact steel box. Not that anyone on the quayside would be able to see into the secure transit compound anyway. If they had, they would have assumed that the steel caskets, with a small grille at either end, would have contained either live animals or goods requiring ventilation. The cages were delivered into the hold of the roll-on-roll-off vessel by forklift, then transferred to a man-hauled pallet truck. After that it was a short trundle to specially prepared cells at one end of the former car deck – the one reserved for the floating 'prison bus'. A bulkhead separated the deck from the ten cells but the twin doors were large enough to admit the cages. The cages were then fixed by steel pins to the mouth of a cell door. The door opened inward, allowing the occupant of the cage to crawl out into their own private cell without the slightest opportunity for these dangerous individuals to attempt a dash for freedom. From transit cell to cage to secure holding cell onboard: these pieces of living evil never took a single step.

They knew they were on a non-return journey, so understandably even the craziest of psychopaths refused to leave their mobile cage. But the guys from Choir-Moore Abstracts have a wonderfully inventive array of techniques for decanting even the most reluctant prisoner from cage to onboard cell. A small opening at the rear of the cage called the glory hole admitted all kinds of prisoner-shifting appliances: broom handles, stun batons, compressed air nozzles, blow torches, fire – when it comes to wild beasts, fire is always effective. Psychopaths tend to be no exception. When a living flame licks the bare soles of their feet they move – really move. Problem solved.

This pod of cells in the ship's stern formed a U-shaped room. The floor had been painted red, the walls silver. Slung beneath the ceiling was the usual array of insulated pipes found on car decks. Above this level were another four levels that included passenger cabins, crew's quarters, galleys, restaurants, bars, a cinema and a casino.

Turrock rose from his desk in the pod's center. From it he could see all ten cell doors. On the desk a monitor showed the interior of each cell in turn. At the moment all were empty of occupants. The screen showed that each cell contained a single bunk bolted to the floor, a steel lavatory bowl and a steel sink. There were no windows, blankets, shelves or cupboards. Prisoners were transferred without possessions. That included clothes. If the prisoners wanted to hide their flesh they could don the white paper coverall that formed a pale blob on the foam mattress.

Wheels clattered on steel beyond the double doors. When they opened they admitted icy air blasting through the ship's doors that gaped open to elements. Turrock saw snow driving past the lights of dockside cranes. In teams of three they wheeled in cages to the cells. Choir-Moore Abstracts employed personnel who moved with rehearsed precision – cages slammed against cells, steel pins slotted into hoops, a technique similar to transferring lions from transport cages to their zoo compound. All the men were casually – even anonymously – dressed. They could mingle with other dock workers in the bars after the shift and not be noticed as anything unusual. At the moment, however, all the guards wore black rubber gauntlets, surgical masks, and the kind of goggles lathe operators use. Prisoners could still spit, flick body fluids. Turrock had even seen a guard darted by a guy who'd fashioned a blow pipe from a drinking straw and half an inch of hypodermic needle.

'Mr Turrock, chief guard, I presume.'

'Mr Clements, transit guard?'

The men's military backgrounds allowed them to fall easily into habitual formalities. They even awarded each other the courtesy of a relaxed salute.

Turrock eyed the cages being trundled into his domain. 'I'm expecting ten.'

'They're all present and correct.'

'Anything I should know about?'

'Nothing out of the ordinary.' Clements handed Turrock an envelope. 'The one in C cage is having a nap.' He smiled. 'It got cranky so we popped in a couple of tranqs.'

'Any diabetics or medication requirements?'

'Who gives a damn?'

When the cell doors opened most prisoners shuffled out of their claustrophobic transport box into the roomier territory of the cell. It was hardly a palace but they could stand, take a piss, slip into their paper jumpsuit and pretend to be Elvis. Or they could roll their beady eyes in the direction of their own TV behind toughened glass.

'I need to go through the transfer schedule,' Turrock said, sitting at his desk.

'Be my guest.'

'We don't usually carry so many at once. What's more, I'm down to one guard.'

'We can't take any back. You don't get these beauties on approval.' Clements drew a stun baton from his belt. 'There's no sale or return.'

'I'm aware of that.'

One occupant of a cage decided an ocean voyage wasn't for him; he was staying put. Clements thumbed a switch on the side of the stun baton, which resembled a long flashlight coated in black rubber. Instead of a light at one end a pair of metal contacts flashed blue as a high-voltage charge snapped across them.

Turrock studied the schedule. 'It doesn't say if any of the prisoners speak English.'

'You'll find they're not the kind you'd want to spend the evening chatting with anyway.' Clements thrust the cattle prod into the glory hole at the back of the cage. Something like blue lightning seared the shadowy interior. With a howl the occupant made like a jack-in-the-box. The monitor on Turrock's desk showed a naked figure explode from the mouth of the box in a whirl of limbs. A moment later it lay face down on the floor cell as it rubbed its left buttock. The man had a body shape that reminded Turrock of a toad. The man was all torso, belly and head – no neck to speak of, while the arms were almost nature's afterthought.

Turrock scowled. 'Ten is more than I want when I've only one assistant.'

Clements grinned. 'The crossing's only three days. Drop bread down the feed chute then leave them to it. They're not going to write letters of complaint to the papers, are they? We're sending Crap to be buried alive in some stinking jail God knows where.'

'What I'm driving at is if a problem arises with a prisoner; I need more manpower.'

'You've done this job long enough, Turrock. You know the score – if one croaks, or looks like croaking, leave them to it. You're guaranteed a death certificate that says in nice bold letters **Cause of death: natural causes**. Everyone's covered, everything's legal. And nobody on this damn planet will shed a tear over these pieces of excrement.' To emphasize the word he jabbed the stun baton into another cage. A piercing yell followed by a sobbed '*No-no-no-no.*'

'What I need, Clements, is you to assign one of your men for the crossing.'

'You are joking?'

'I need more guards for the delivery. The company will pick up the bill.'

'Turrock, what are you forgetting?'

'I'm forgetting nothing.' And he meant it.

'In four days it's Christmas Eve. These men need their holidays. Partners will skin them alive if they aren't home tomorrow with their pay checks.'

'You served in the front line. You know what happens to soldiers when there are cutbacks in personnel.'

'You're carrying canned shitheads to Russia. What's the worst that can happen?'

'What's the worst that can happen? Damn it, Clements, are you trying to put a curse on me?'

By this time the guards were trying to empty the last cage. Trying, but having no luck.

'Allow me.' Clements applied the instrument through the glory hole. The contacts discharged five hundred thousand volts into bare flesh but the prisoner didn't so much as squeak. He tried again.

Turrock's eyes narrowed. 'You brought me a corpse. Take it back with you.'

'This is the one that's napping. We had to sedate it.'

'You've done a bloody fine job. If you can't wake them with that lightning rod of yours then they're as dead as a door nail.'

One of the guards checked through the bars at the far end. 'Still breathing, Mr Clements.'

'Use the broom handle.'

Choir-Moore Abstracts employ men who can easily cram fully grown adults into these compact boxes; they're equally adept at expelling them again. As a plunger drives liquid from a hypodermic so two men shoving hard with a broom handle through the glory hole managed to evacuate the prisoner. Again, there was no noise from the interior.

This was more brute force than finesse, which prompted to Turrock to object. 'Not so hard.'

Clements reacted with some surprise. 'Afraid we'll bruise the goods?'

Covering up the angry outburst with a shrug, Turrock grunted, 'Hurt them too much and they puke or piss themselves. It'll be me mopping the floor when you've left.'

'They're safely in, sir,' reported one of the guards.

Clements checked the desk monitor. 'And sleeping like a

baby. You worry too much, Turrock. Ever do a tour of duty in sniper country?'

Turrock didn't answer.

'It leaves its mark, doesn't it? Little things make you anxious.' Clements handed Turrock a pen. 'If you sign my delivery docket we'll be off. Date and initial each page. Cheers.' He folded the sheet. 'Have a good trip. We're heading out for Christmas cocktails now. And the company's picking up the tab. We'll have one for you.' Turrock nodded. As Clements followed his men out of the secure pod he banged on a cell door. 'Bon voyage, chaps. Don't forget to send post-cards home.'

The twin doors of the pod closed on the guards as they strolled, laughing, along the car deck in the direction of the ramp that would return them to dry land, and no doubt a cozy bar. In Turrock's mind's eye he could see the off-duty guards spilling in through the doors ready to drink the place as dry as the Gobi Desert. No doubt there'd be girls wrapping themselves round their shiny dance poles, too. One guard would down a whiskey. 'Here's to Turrock. I can't say I envy him. Three days at sea with a bunch of crazy folk.'

'I'm not drinking to Turrock. Damn weirdo.'

'Have to be for that job.'

'But have you ever shaken his hand? Later, you find yourself looking at your palm as if something comes off him and sticks to you. It's like the black spot. Turns your blood cold.'

Once the doors were closed the icy breeze that swept along the river had gone. Within seconds the atmosphere of the pod became still. Turrock sniffed. His nostrils picked up a scent that wasn't there before the doors were opened. He glanced at the monitor that showed the interior of cell six. A blonde figure lay still on the floor where the broom handle had shoved it.

'Damn.' Turrock tapped in the cell's key code. 'The bastards . . . the incompetent bastards . . .'

As he neared the cell the raw stink of bleach grew stronger. By the time he unlocked the steel door it made his eyes smart.

'Fytton, bring the kit. Hurry.' He only hoped his assistant was close enough to hear otherwise he'd have to do this himself. When Turrock swung the door inward he saw the bloody mess the shore guards had made of the prisoner. Boot prints showed on the naked stretch of back where they'd stomped the prisoner down. The stench of bleach was choking. It was an old trick. Force a pint of bleach down a trouble-maker's throat, then treat it as suicide. Meanwhile, the prisoner spent the next two hours writhing in agony as their guts bathed in the caustic fluid until they liquefied. Frequently the poisoned individual would die as they squirted blood from both ends of their body. As deaths go bleach poisoning is as painful as you get.

When Turrock turned over the blonde-haired figure he started back in surprise.

What he'd expected to find on their face wasn't there at all. In fact, what he did see was so unexpected he recoiled through the door in absolute shock.

Four

Tanya Rhone's heart sank. The cabin-door key didn't work. *This is all I need.* She longed for a hot shower. Quite frankly, she needed the toilet too, thanks to all those coffees she'd drunk to kill the time on one hell of a train journey. She eased the strap from her shoulder. The bag thumped harder than she intended on the floor of the passageway. *Damn. Please don't let anything be broken.* Tanya had bought Jack an expensive present as a peace offering. If he unwrapped fragments of Rolex rather than a whole watch it would only make things worse. *Work, blast you. Work!*

Meanwhile, her fellow passengers surged along the passage. They longed for their cabins, too. They craved to kick off shoes, unpack, shower, change. Every few moments a suit-case scraped her leg, or a shoulder bag caught her arm. Tanya swiped the card through the sensor again. No satisfying click, no welcoming green light flashing on the lock. Only unblinking red. *Ouch!* A terrific blow in her back knocked her face forward against the locked door. Tanya regained her balance in time to see what had struck her. It was the woman in the scarlet headscarf, the one with the Persian empress looks, the same one who had demanded to board the ship before everyone else. The woman sailed with majestic grace down the corridor as if nobody and nothing else mattered but her seemingly God-given quest.

'Oh, please, do excuse me,' Tanya snapped, then hissed under her breath, 'for being in your majesty's way.'

Next, this infuriating, self-appointed empress bumped a child who'd been standing patiently by her mother. The five–year-old girl bounced as she hit the floor. The mother had been struggling with the door key too. As she tried to help the child stand she emptied a bag full of possessions on to the floor – wallet, keys, comb, phone, camera, toys, documents all spilled on to the carpet.

Tanya's blood boiled. She darted along the corridor to snarl at the empress of loutish manners but four men speaking in a foreign tongue were hauling cartons the size of washing machines into their cabins, and arguing how best to do it. They effectively barricaded the way, leaving Tanya to fume at the woman's back as she swept away along the corridor.

Too enraged by the woman's behavior to remain silent, Tanya shouted to her, 'You better learn some manners! Hey you! Did you hear me?'

Apparently not. The woman vanished. Two of the men stopped wrestling the cartons through the door. They smiled at Tanya, asked her something in a language she didn't understand. Grinning, they gestured for her to enter their cabin. She shot them a withering glare then returned to help the mother and child. The girl sobbed softly to herself as she rested a finger against the red dash where her cheek had struck the floor.

'I'm so sorry,' the mother said, thinking that Tanya wanted to get past. 'Jo, move back, let the lady by.'

'No,' Tanya said, 'let me help. Here, you hold the bag. I'll put these back.'

The girl's mother had the washed-out expression of someone running on their last reserve of nervous energy. Her hands trembled. When she spoke her voice never rose above a timid whisper. 'Thank you . . . it's been a long day.' She managed a smile despite being close to tears. 'I've never made the crossing before . . . It's . . . well, *frightening*, isn't it?'

'It's not so bad. I've done it a few times . . . Oh-ho.' She smiled at the girl. Her blue eyes were still full of tears. 'This will be your ship, won't it? Make sure it doesn't sink.' She handed her a miniature replica of the ship they'd just boarded. Minute white letters on the black hull spelt *Volsparr*. Her mother must have bought it in the departure lounge. *Make sure it doesn't sink? Tanya? What were you thinking, telling the girl that? Why am I getting so morbid about this trip?* After helping mother and child into their cabin Tanya headed back to reception. Here the lights were brighter. She could discern a scratch – well, more of a gouge really – through the magnetic tape on her keycard. A dozen people queued for the reception clerk. Most scowled at faulty keycards. The urge to find a lavatory became more uncomfortably pressing, but Tanya decided not to yield to the urge as she'd find herself at the back of the queue again. She focused on a wall-mounted TV to distract her from the discomfort. An information program disgorged facts about their ship. '*The* Volsparr *was built in Hamburg to the highest specifications. This vessel boasts fifty passenger cabins, all of which are en-suite and enjoy sea views, television with bespoke programming and public address system to provide you with up-to-date inform-ation . . .*' Ten minutes later Tanya Rhone still stood in line. Ahead of her the man in the business suit asked why he couldn't convert his cash into Rubles. Through the observa-tion window the lights of the docks flickered as snowflakes streamed on the night air.

The PA chimed. 'This is a passenger announcement. We regret that the departure will be delayed by approximately four hours.' Passengers groaned. 'In the meantime, please make yourselves comfortable and enjoy the facilities of the ship. The bars will open at seven o'clock as usual.'

Beyond the window, gales came roaring from the north to push the ship against the dockside. In Tanya's mind's eye she saw all those steel cables binding the *Volsparr* to the main-land with her on board. It seemed as if forces conspired to trap her there for ever. Fate itself didn't seem to want her to meet Jack again after all this time. Even the surge of river waters thrust themselves at the ship. The currents, the winds, the steel hawsers held her back. This notion produced a spasm of claustrophobia that pressed down on Tanya like a physical weight. *I'm never going to see Jack again. My parents don't want me to go. Work wouldn't give me leave so I pretended I was too sick to go into the office. Now this . . . Nature is holding the ship prisoner here.* Her imagination conjured images of a huge clot of dirt oozing through the fuel pipe to kill the ship's engine. Failing that, navigation charts would be blown from an open window; the captain would break a leg. She was certain the ship was doomed never to leave. Gloomily, she asked herself, *Whatever can go wrong will go wrong . . . it's inevitable.* Meanwhile, the pressure in her bladder meant she had to fight hard to stand still. *What a night. What a hell of a rotten night. Knowing my luck this is just the start . . .*

Five

'**L**isten,' Turrock told the woman in the cell, 'I'm not going to let you die. Do you understand me? *You will not die.*' He turned his head. 'Fytton! Bring the kit. And all the milk we've got. Poisoning – bleach poisoning! Got that?'

The assistant guard called that he'd heard.

'Well, hurry up. I'm not going to lose her!'

Turrock held the woman so that if she vomited it wouldn't drain back into her lungs. The sodium hypochlorite in the stuff would turn her lungs to gel. Meanwhile, the stench of bleach struck his face. The transit guards had beaten her bloody then drained a bottle of it down her throat.

'Bastards,' he hissed. The injustice scalded him.

What had shocked him so much when he saw the woman prisoner wasn't that she was naked, or that she'd been kicked – if anything, it was unusual for a prisoner to reach the ship unmarked and clothed. Black eyes, cut lips, flesh burns from stun batons, all were commonplace. It was what Turrock saw when he turned the woman over. She looked up at him with a dreamy smile on her face, as if he'd made love to her a few minutes before. The smile had been radiant. Her brown eyes, with flecks of brilliant amber in the iris, were breathtaking. This was a woman who bathed in the focus of the most intensely satisfying pleasure imaginable. Even though the bleach must have blazed through her gut she gently stroked her bare belly from ribs to pubic hair. She could have been enjoying the afterglow of the best orgasm of her life; a climax of surreal intensity.

Turrock recovered from his shock. 'Must be acute mental dysfunction. You flip sensation one hundred and eighty degrees, don't you?' He stroked her hair from her face. 'Pain is the nicest sensation of all . . . Stay with me, sweetheart. Don't fall asleep! Fytton!' He rubbed her arm. 'Keep looking at my face. Listen to me. My name is Turrock. I'm going to keep death away. You're going to live. Those men shouldn't have done that to you. Think about them. Think how you'd like to get revenge.'

'Boss.' Fytton, a burly man of fifty-five, handed him the first-aid pack. His face bore a dozen triangular scars from a grenade blast. One piece of shrapnel had sliced through both his top and bottom lips, which left it pinched into an odd-looking cupid effect, as if he was always puckering his mouth in the expectation of a kiss. His eyes were dulled by far too many experiences of brutality as a mercenary. They seemed to say *Nothing you can ever do will surprise me. I've seen it all.* When Fytton ate steak he never cut it into pieces. Instead he picked it up in one huge paw of a hand and tore chunks off with his teeth. But whenever he passed a fiberglass statue of a little girl at the entrance of the ship's café, Turrock noticed the man's eyes always swiveled to lock on to it. The model of the girl incorporated a slot in her open palm that accepted coins for a children's charity. Fytton couldn't pass it without his stare fixing on to the fiberglass face with its hopeful smile. Then, as if held by an invisible force, he'd carefully ease a coin into the slot in the palm. *Fytton's bribing a ghost*, Turrock told himself. *Proof positive of a guilty conscience.*

'Give me the milk first, Fytton.'

The naked woman should have been howling with pain. Bleach burns lips, mouth and oesophagus as it's swallowed by the victim. Right now, her stomach should feel like someone had dumped burning plastic in there. Yet still the woman smiled. An expression of ecstasy lit her face. Waves of pain reached her brain as surges of pure pleasure. Some brain defect had screwed with her nervous system, transmuting agony into bliss. This was the psychological equivalent of the medieval alchemist turning lead into shining gold.

'She's going to die, boss,' Fytton uttered in a bass rumble with its middle-European accent. 'Got all da symptoms of a belly load of bleach. See how red her eyes are? Boy, oh boy, you could light a cigar off of those – like hot coals they are.'

'Fytton, get the tube down her throat, then help me pour the milk down.'

'Milk's gonna do no good if she imbibed too much. Milk helps kill da bleach but you need charcoal for antidote; we don't have no charcoal.'

'Listen to me, Fytton. I'm going to save her. We'll get the milk down her then use the fire hose.'

'Really?' His face only registered mild surprise. 'You're da boss, boss.'

Fytton had served ten years with Choir-Moore Abstracts. Like all his colleagues, Fytton didn't have a squeamish gene in his body. He also lacked any empathy with other human beings. The thick muscle that sheathed his bones made his movements slow, yet they were somehow unstoppable. He was a battle tank of a man. Once he decided to move in a certain direction there weren't many men who could stop him. Slowly, deliberately, yet with ponderous force, he reached down with those giant fists of his, grabbed handfuls of the spiky blonde hair and hoisted the naked woman up into a sitting position. Then, clamping her forehead with his thick fingers he used the other hand to force open her jaw so wide Turrock heard the joints crack, a sound like snapping pencils.

The woman gurgled with pleasure. Anyone else would have collapsed under the onslaught of pain. *This is fun. She's loving it.* Even so, the whites of her eyes were becoming a fiery red as the poison roared through her body. *Kill or cure*, Turrock thought. Then he went to work. He drove a rigid tube down her throat, like it was some perverse sword-swallowing trick. That done, he spun the top off the milk bottle and watched the white liquid glug down the pipe. If you don't have charcoal to hand then milk is the best antidote to bleach. At this stage it was too dangerous simply to make his prisoner vomit the poison. It was too concentrated. Once he'd got a few quarts of milk inside her to dilute the astringent fluid, then she could puke. Then and only then. Of course, after all this she still might die. London's prostitutes in the nineteenth century often used bleach to kill themselves when poverty broke their will to survive. It is brutally effective stuff . . .

There was something hypnotic about pouring milk down the plastic pipe that protruded so rigidly from the woman's mouth in her upturned face. The whites of her eyes blazed red as she gazed into his, as if in they were in the midst of a deeply passionate act. There was a submissive quality there. It made his spine tingle. *Did I say submissive? Those eyes are permissive. They're saying, 'You can do anything to me. That's all right. Anything you want. Go ahead; do it.'*

Turrock had left the army at the age of thirty-five. He'd been ready to re-enlist but his sergeant had introduced him instead to Choir-Moore Abstracts. The company had offices in Detroit, Liverpool, Marseille and Kiev, all big centers of population in areas where people had to work extra hard for their money. Turrock had visited the offices in Detroit. They occupied a modest suite in a nondescript building on a business park. The name Choir-Moore Abstracts gave no clue as to the line of business. The people who delivered mail and stationery supplies to the office wouldn't be any the wiser, either. From the appearance of the twenty or so clerical workers at functional desks, visitors might suppose the company specialized in sanitary ware for commercial premises, or handled wage payments for a restaurant chain. Something so deeply unglamorous as to render the offices anonymous. Long ago, companies that hired out mercenaries had stopped using such a controversial word. After all, mercenary always appears to scream blood and mayhem, whether written in capital letters or in delicate copperplate. Operators that provide armed personnel describe them as 'Security Contractors', or an equally friendly sounding 'Domestic Watchmen'. Turrock's old army buddy had given the recruitment manager an irresistible sales pitch and they offered Turrock the position of 'Maintenance Operative'. Turrock took the job. He'd loved the army, and apart from the lack of a uniform this was largely the same; although Choir-Moore paid him far more than the military salary. His first assignment from Choir-Moore found him guarding a fuel depot in central Africa. He'd expected lush jungles, elephants, attacks by fanatical guerillas. Instead, the depot sat high on a hillside in its own cool microclimate that was more alpine than African. The biggest animals he ever saw were the rats that gnawed through the steel floor of their refrigerator like it was made from cheese. The view from the accommodation bungalows took in a ravine. The only thing that grew there were trees with four-inch thorns that resembled sharks' teeth. Spanning the ravine, a footbridge provided the vital link between two places that could be described as 'nowhere in particular' and 'the town that God forgot'.

The posting provided a good opportunity for contemplation. There was nothing else to do. Come to that, nowhere to go. On the second week Turrock sat on the timber porch in front of the bungalows to watch the sun go down. He sipped a can of beer from the fridge that the rats invaded nightly. Even the can had twin dimples at the bottom where the rodent had tried to score a free drink. A couple of his colleagues had sauntered up with hunting rifles.

'What do you say to a Quilp Hunt, Turrock?'

'You'll have to give me a minute to get my boots on.'

The men had laughed as they opened cans of beer.

'Quilp Hunts don't need much in the way of walking,' the red-haired man had told him.

'Make you lazy, make you fat. Fun. Plenty fun.' The second man didn't speak much English. Turrock figured him to be Vietnamese. The man, however, insisted his name was Woolworth. F.W. Woolworth. Nobody disagreed. Most people who worked for Choir-Moore Abstracts used assumed names. Even the company name, Choir-Moore Abstracts, was nothing more than a meaningless assembly of words.

'So,' Turrock had asked, 'what's a Quilp? And where do we hunt it?'

'Quilp is anything you want it to be.' The red-haired man shielded his eyes as the sun flooded the chasm with red light. Dogs bayed somewhere nearby. 'In fact, here come some tasty specimens right now.'

The dogs began barking. A pack must be roaming nearby. Turrock had seen these before. They weren't a naturally wild species. These mutts once lived in the villages nearby but had become feral when the government burned the houses down.

Officially, the ministry had re-homed the population. Turrock, however, had seen human skulls sitting there as smooth, creamy domes in the ashes, so he guessed that was one story that didn't have a joyous ending. Now the villagers' dogs begged for scraps or chased rats that had grown fat on fridge food.

Woolworth loaded a rifle. A grin formed a glittering U-shape at the bottom of his face. 'Quilp Hunt. Bang-bang dat Quilp!'

Turrock scowled. 'Why shoot the dogs? They're the only animals that keep the rat population down?'

'Dogs?' The red-haired man smirked.

'Dogs!' Woolworth screwed up his face he laughed so loud. 'Dogs! He say dogs!'

Turrock wasn't stupid. A moment later he saw what Quilp were. Four people strolled across the footbridge high over the gorge. They were maybe a hundred yards away. Four herdsmen maybe, or poachers. One undersized due to years of malnourishment. *So, this is Quilp?* Turrock sipped his beer. He would have preferred a Scotch and ice but beer is all they had. He was thinking about Scotch whiskey when his two colleagues started firing. They were good shots. High-velocity rounds popped heads like water-filled balloons.

Jack Daniels would go down smoothly right now. Just one. OK, make it a large one. This beer tastes metallic. It's probably been sitting in a hot stockroom for months. If I switch duties so I drive the truck on the grocery run tomorrow I'll be able to pick up some whiskey in the town. It'll cost a fortune though. Certainly for a recognizable brand.

'Got Quilp,' Woolworth sang out. He reloaded.

'Want to try?' The other man held out the rifle.

'Do you know where I can buy whiskey?' Disinterested in the hunting game, Turrock gestured the rifle away with his beer can.

The red-haired man shrugged as he chambered another round. 'You go blind drinking the local stuff. They say it's made from the piss of old sows.'

'Taste blah!' Woolworth added helpfully.

'You might try a place called the Ocean Hotel.'

'What ocean?'

'Exactly.'

'Ho! Ho!' Woolworth shouted. 'Little Quilp running . . . running *whee* fast.' He fired. Missed.

The silhouette of a figure sprinted back along the foot-bridge. Behind him his associates lay with parts of their heads missing.

'Sure you don't want to bag some Quilp?' the red-haired man offered.

'I'd rather have a Scotch.'

'I know, but we just have to do the best we can – substitute entertainment and all that.' He fired the rifle. The bullet struck the diminutive figure in the hip. The force of the bullet slapped the guy sideways over the rail. He plunged silently into the thorn trees twenty feet below.

'He dead?' Woolworth asked.

In the gully the pack of wild dogs suddenly began an excited barking. A moment later thin screams – human screams – wailed like a siren on the evening air.

'No.' Woolworth gave an exaggerated shrug. 'He not dead.'

'But he soon will be.' Smiling, the redhead cupped his hands to his mouth before calling out, 'Enjoy your supper, boys. But leave room for rat dessert, eh?'

'Dem puppies love their Quilp meat.' He patted the red-haired man on the shoulder. 'Dis a good guy, hmm? He look after dem puppies like he love dem.'

That became the pattern for the next five years. A splendid salary yet pretty much a dull life. Many of his colleagues livened it up by casually victimizing the local population. Invariably the authorities ignored such activity. Foreign investors were far more important than the men, women and children who were unlucky enough to be in the wrong place at the wrong time. Turrock would still be guarding installa-tions if he hadn't slipped down a step during the monsoon rains. Even the most expensive procedures couldn't fix a torn cartilage so he'd quit front-line postings for a position as a prison guard. He thought he'd hate the work, so he promised himself a year of it to build up enough cash to buy a Harley-Davison then see if he could ride from Alaska to the tip of South America (he secretly hoped he'd die trying). But being a prison guard wasn't what he expected at all. He found a job that he loved. No, more than love. It became his passion. This was a reason *not* to die. When he wasn't at work here in the cell pod that's all he thought about. He lied, schemed, cheated, swindled rosters – anything to avoid taking holidays. Being a prison guard lit up his bones inside. When he took charge of his realm of ten cells on the converted car deck, life roared through him again. It gave him his heartbeat back; it filled his lungs with the oxygen of existence. When he wasn't on duty he lay on his bunk to watch the hands of the clock until they told him it was time to begin his shift. And nobody would take this away from him. *Nobody*. And nobody would take away *his* prisoners before he delivered them at the destination port. His colleagues had beaten this woman, then poisoned her, but he wasn't letting her go.

'Think she's had enough, boss?' Fytton asked.

By now the blonde woman's stomach looked pregnant, there was so much milk in there. She gurgled with ecstasy. Her mind had dissolved into an ocean of pleasure.

Fytton sounded insistent this time. 'Boss. She's had plenty. Gonna pop her guts all over if you don't stop pouring.'

'I'll tell you when she's had enough.'

Fytton had amused himself with prisoners plenty of times until Turrock had put a stop to it. Now Fytton used the office computer to find the kind of video footage that tickled his pleasure zones. Not porn. Fytton had been a mercenary, too. Employees of Choir-Moore Abstracts generously uploaded their Quilp Hunts to the web. Just this morning Fytton had called his boss over to watch a team of 'maintenance operatives' riding a train through some plantation in south-east Asia. A bunch of youths ran alongside the slow-moving carriages, cheering when the men threw chocolate out to them. More gang members joined them to sprint through the long grass as the hot sun shone down. Off camera a voice announced, 'Quilp Hunt.' A fist moved into shot. It gripped a hand grenade.

Fytton had been ecstatic. 'Hey, boss. Take a look at those bandits. Ha! They don't know what's gonna happen to them. Hey, boss, keep watching. Any second now. Boss, why aren't you watching this?'

The sight of milk bubbling from the woman's nose drew Turrock from his reverie.

'Reckon she's full to da gills, boss.'

'She can take the rest.' Turrock emptied the bottle down

the tube. Stretch marks appeared on the distended belly as the volume of milk forced the muscles outward. 'OK. Empty her.'

In his stolidly methodical way Fytton dropped her to the steel floor. Then he picked her up by the ankles. When she hung upside down, her blonde hair swishing his feet like a broom, he shook her. He could have been emptying dregs out of a cup. When the milk rushed out of her it came like a dam burst.

'She's not going to make it, boss. Nobody can take this punishment. Want me to get a body bag?'

'This woman isn't dying. I won't let her.'

Fytton didn't answer. All he did was roll his eyes a little, which was the most expressive he got when showing surprise.

Five minutes later Turrock used the fire hose. At full pressure he blasted the interior of the cell walls. The milk, curdled by stomach bile and bleach, gurgled down the drain holes set in the floor. He left the woman sitting on the floor with her back to one wall. He directed the torrent at her, too. Its force pummeled her. Her breasts shook. Concave depressions formed in them and her naked torso as the water struck, its power as bruising as a punch, yet the water swept away the dirt, the blood, all the crap, along with remnants of bleach that would have blistered her pale skin.

An hour later the cells were quiet. Fytton had mopped the woman's cell, and Turrock had rubbed her body dry with towels. Whether exhausted, dying or merely passive he hadn't known. The woman had simply lain there, her eyes shut, while he worked the towel across her skin.

Now he had the opportunity to read the reports on his prisoners. He took his time, savored them; reading them generated a warm glow in his stomach. It flowed in a tide of rich satisfaction throughout his entire body as he digested the information about his charges. Names, ages, nationality (if known), life history compacted into two hundred words of diamond-hard fact. Then, best of all, the narrative concerning the crime they had committed. It always contained more detail than necessary; maybe that was intentional. The full-blooded account of these creatures' vicious acts ensured that the prison guard would never feel any sympathy toward them. Come to that, to read these descriptions of staggering cruelty would render any guard incapable of believing the prisoners even half human. That was the intention anyway. Turrock read each word as if it released its own unique flavor, one that infused his body with a sense of well-being. But he'd barely begun to savor the blonde woman's report when the telephone rang.

'Turrock,' he announced. 'Suzanne? I thought you'd be home by now.'

The female voice was breathless. 'I was halfway back to the car when I saw the sailing had been delayed.'

'Until ten.'

'Want some company?'

'You're onboard?'

'Oh, you know me. I can get where others can't.'

He licked his lips. 'And you're a very, very naughty girl.' As he spoke he allowed his fingertips to stroke the case history of the blonde in cell six.

'I am a naughty girl, Mr Turrock,' the voice continued. 'And you've such a stern, stern face. Can I meet you in your cabin?'

'Suzanne, afraid not. I'm on duty.'

'You talk just like a soldier. C'mon, I won't see you again for three weeks. Why don't we make the most of this time, hmm?'

'I can't. This is my shift.'

'Think of it as Santa Claus giving us an early Christmas present. C'mon, the ship doesn't sail for hours yet.'

He made a decision. One that sent a thrill down his spine. 'I can't come to the cabin,' he said crisply. 'So why don't you come down here?'

Six

Tanya Rhone would have been astonished that three decks beneath her there existed another world. One comprising ten steel cells in a partitioned section of the car deck. She'd made this journey five times before. As far as she knew, the *Volsparr* was part cargo vessel, part company passenger liner, its sole purpose to serve the mining operation on the Baltic island. Not in a million years would she suspect it was also part prison transport.

At long last she had succeeded in gaining access to her cabin; she'd showered, changed her clothes, then made her way to the ship's restaurant to beat the rush, only tonight she saw there would be no rush. Information monitors on the corridor walls apologized for a reduced level of service due to the reduced number of passengers on the sailing, and asked passengers to note that the *Volsparr* would be served by a skeleton crew. *Figures*, Tanya thought; *it's Christmas day on Monday. Who in their right mind wants to spend three days sailing through the Baltic only to arrive at a Godforsaken mining station on Christmas Eve?*

The restaurant only held a dozen diners so far. Most of the dining area had been roped off, the chairs having been stacked at one end of the restaurant. The tables looked downright disturbing. Even morbid. There was no escaping the impression that the tables appeared to support a human body covered by a sheet. An impossible thing to happen, but Tanya shivered as she stared at corpse-like forms beneath the white sheets. Every table looked like a cadaver.

The businessman who'd complained about the lack of Rubles also noticed the man-shaped forms beneath white sheets. Grim-faced, he leaned over a plush barrier rope to lift the shroud. His habitually grim face broke into a smile of relief as he saw piles of table linen beneath the sheet. He noticed Tanya had been shooting nervous glances at the tables, too.

'Thank God for that.' He smiled. 'For a moment there I thought they'd turned the place into a morgue.'

As he headed to grab a tray for the self-service counter Tanya saw more diners enter the room, then immediately stop dead as they saw the array of cadaver look-alikes on the tables. More than one took a peek under a sheet only to laugh with relief when they saw that a stiff didn't lie there, waiting for a funeral.

Tanya took her tray with a plate of goulash and boiled potatoes to a table that allowed views through the observation window. Snowflakes whipped by outside, lending the cranes on the dockside an other-worldly appearance. She could have been gazing out on to an alien world where huge menacing robots lay in wait for unwary travelers.

The goulash ran spiky flavors across her tongue. Surprisingly, it was good. It made her realize how hungry she'd become. To compensate for the reduced menu a waiter handed out complimentary bottles of wine. The moment Tanya poured out a large glass of ruby merlot a triumphant voice struck her like a slap.

'Ah-ha, the lovely Tanya. Shall we continue where we left off last time?'

'There's nothing to continue, Philip.'

'Mind if I join you?'

Before she could snarl *no!* he bounced down into the seat opposite. 'Snap. We've both chosen goulash. The food of lovers, no?' He beamed at her. He was just as she remembered. Well groomed – even prissily well groomed – he wore a pale blue suit and a yellow shirt with a bright red tie. He must have spent most of the evening blow-drying his hair into crisp waves.

She thought, *If someone asks you to picture a lounge-bar pianist then Philip De-Fray has to be the walking cliché.*

'Tanya? More wine?'

'No, thank you.'

'You are beautiful, by the way. Really beautiful. I looked across the room and saw you shining here like a jewel. A beautiful, precious jewel.'

'I'm expecting someone to join me.' A lie, but worth the attempt.

'You pretended to forget about us.' He waggled a scolding finger. 'Now, I don't believe in being coy. Life's too short. Why not come right out and say what we want?'

'Philip . . .'

'And what I want is to continue where we left off.'

'Philip, I already told you, there is nothing between us and so nothing to continue.'

'Ah-ha, my lady, that's where you are wrong. Listen carefully, while I remind you what we did . . .'

In cell four many feet beneath the restaurant the air bore the hot, greasy smell of the ship's engines. The monstrous pistons throbbed beneath his naked body.

Sami had planned to kill himself. He'd spent a month working on the plan. The psychologists anticipated it. They'd put him on suicide watch but he could outsmart them. Only something had happened to change his mind. When he'd been in the transit cell in the docks he'd heard the guards beat up one of the inmates. Nothing new there; that's as common as corned-beef hash for dinner.

Now as he sat on the floor of the cell, his naked buttocks transmitting the vibration of the ship's engine into his spine, he knew it had started again. The desire to continue his life's work, which had been so cruelly halted by his arrest.

Sami watched the TV screen behind the armor-plated glass. It distracted him from the dull gray walls of the cell, and lights that cast a glow the same sickly yellow as jaundice. He even ignored the white paper suit on the bunk. It shouldn't be there, of course. The guards had left it by accident. After all, that was to be the instrument of Sami's suicide. That is until his calling had returned.

Eyelashes obsessed Sami. He stroked his own as he watched a children's cartoon on TV. Human hair is the atrophied remnant of the hide of our reptile ancestors. Eyelashes have a different quality to other body hair, however. Nature has formed it into curving member. It is flexible, yet rigid enough to return to its bow-like curve. Each hair has its own memory to do that. They provide a subtle guard to their neighbor, the eye. If other body hair is the mutated remains of reptile skin then the eyelash must have been something else on the creature. Yet it still performed the vital task of protecting the eye. Many extinct dinosaurs had an eyelid of tough, armor-plated horn. One hundred million years later these hard eyelids that were impenetrable to predators' teeth had become eyelashes. Sami preened his eyelashes. To touch them made his nerves tingle. If only he was free to touch the eyelashes of other people again . . .

The TV screen cut from the cartoon to a man's face. 'Good evening. My name is Mr Turrock. I am the chief guard. I am in charge of you for the duration of this journey. In two hours food will be delivered to you through the chute beside your door.' The man on the screen loomed closer. Briefly he glanced sideways as if to check he was alone, then in a lower voice he said, 'You will find me different to the other guards you've met in the past. Quite different. If you need to speak to me one-to-one press the red button. You'll find it set above your bunk . . .'

Sami wanted out. He must begin his mission . . .

Turrock looked directly into the camera lens embedded in the top of the computer monitor. The screen revealed ten thumbnail images of the occupants of the cells. The woman poisoned with bleach lay naked on the bunk. She smiled dreamily as she stroked her stomach. The others sat or stood in their cells. For now they seemed lifeless. None chose to move, or even say anything. That tended to be the effect of transportation. New surroundings tended to paralyze these individuals. Turrock glanced back again to make sure Fytton hadn't returned from his cabin. When he saw he was still alone he murmured into the mic, 'I want you to look at your television screen. Remember my face. You are looking at the man who now rules your lives. I'm in charge. I have the power of life and death over you. You know that's the truth. But with a new master comes a new regime. Forget what happened to you in prison before you came onboard. Your lives will be completely different now.'

In one of the clutch of passenger cabins that had been allocated for the guards' down-time, Fytton watched the laptop screen. He'd logged on to his favorite website. Now he trawled through the latest uploaded videos.

'Ah,' he murmured. 'Quilp Hunt.'

The videos were variations on a single theme. Most showed his front-line colleagues in Choir-Moore Abstracts having fun. The camera's point of view revealed an open car window in some dusty street. He guessed it might be North Africa, but then it could equally be the Middle East. The (unseen) driver slowed the car when he saw pedestrians.

A male voice called out, 'Quilp? Quilp?' to a middle-aged man pushing a bicycle. When he looked into the camera a gun muzzle swung into view near the lens. The man had just enough time to widen his eyes in shock before the gunman shot him in the face.

'Tenth Quilp of the day,' announced a satisfied voice as the driver accelerated away to find the next target.

Fytton glanced at his watch. When Turrock went off duty, that's when Fytton would go hunting. *Some mighty fine Quilp down in the cells. Time I bagged a couple.*

Seven

As Turrock ushered Suzanne in, he muttered, 'You do realize that between them, these prisoners have killed more than fifty people?' Turrock couldn't stop the sentence coming out of his mouth, as if he were announcing one of the wonders of the world. But then these were no ordinary people inside these cages.

Suzanne's eyes widened as she stared at the cells that ran in a U-shaped bay around the room. 'I hope all those doors are locked.' She didn't say this lightly. She meant it with all her heart.

Turrock smiled. Civilians always reacted in the same way. A physical flinch backward, their eyes widening in shock. He couldn't say exactly why it was that he liked that reaction, but he did. It sent tingles through every nerve in his body.

Suzanne Lynch, twenty-eight, worked as a clerk for a shipping agent in the precincts of the port. It demanded acute mental dexterity because she had to monitor thousands of containers flowing through the wharves. She also had an eye for anomalous transport patterns that earned her praise for alerting customs to illegal drug shipments. Standing close to six feet tall, her body had a taut, whip-like quality. She wore tight jeans with an equally tight black sweater that made her appear even taller. Suzanne's dark hair shone beneath the brilliant lights, while the uncompromising illumination made her olive skin appear paler than usual. Her cherry-red lips not only dominated her face but became the most noticeable feature in the room. A milk-white scar that ran from her right ear lobe to nearly the tip of her strong chin formed a permanent reminder that her choice in boyfriends hadn't always been wise. Turrock knew that the ex who'd punched her through a plate-glass store front still prowled the streets of Hull. The law could be thicker than mule poop sometimes. So these days Suzanne felt herself attracted to men who wielded power. That aura of force drew her into what became for her a protective envelope. Turrock knew her appetite for men who exercised control over others was something she couldn't suppress. Waving his hand at the cells, Turrock gave her a tour of his kingdom.

'I've got ten killers in those cells. In cell number one is a man who believed his neighbors were werewolves. He killed four members of the same family and shaved their heads. In cell two is someone who ate certain choice parts of his boyfriends . . . after he'd electrocuted them while they slept.'

'My God . . .' Her eyes were held by the cell doors. 'They can't see me, can they?' She gave a nervous laugh. 'I mean . . . just thinking about them looking through some peephole at me is enough to make me need the lavatory.' Though her cherry-red lips formed a wide smile her eyes flashed with fear.

'It affects most people like that first time they pay us a visit.'

'John, I mean it – they can't see me, can they?'

'No. We can see into the cells; they can't see out.'

'Thank heavens for that.' Relief made her heave her chest so deeply her breasts rose. 'Just knowing they were watching would have freaked me.'

'Take a look at my charges.' He rested one palm on the desk as he tapped the keyboard. The monitor switched from the Choir-Moore Abstracts logo of a simple circle enclosing the name, to video images of the cells' interiors. It revealed one at a time – a three-second shot of cell number one before moving to cell two, and so on. As Suzanne watched with a morbid fascination, John Turrock talked about the people and the terrible things they'd done.

'Experts categorize them as psychopaths. But often that's just a convenient catch-all label. Most of the people you're seeing now don't have mental conditions that a psychologist could diagnose. Something has gone wrong with their mind, something that makes them do wrong. The woman with blonde hair lying on the bunk doesn't feel pain, her sensations are reversed. If you hammered a nail through her arm she'd smile and tell you how nice it feels.'

'Then she's a masochist.'

He shook his head. 'Masochists feel pain. They want it to hurt. For them pain titillates. The woman in cell six is not only incapable of experiencing pain, but for her the sensation is converted into pleasure. Torture her and she'd laugh all day.'

'She's naked . . . and look at her body. It's covered in bruises.'

'Transportees don't need clothes; the temperature's maintained to keep them comfortable. She attacked one of the guards before she arrived at the ship. They will have retaliated.'

'I expected them to be like caged beasts. You know, snarling, clawing at the doors.'

'In reality most psychopathic killers exercise more self-control than we do. Normality is their mask. If you spoke to them you'd be surprised how gentle they are. They'd seem friendly, modest, good-natured. You couldn't believe they've committed such evil acts. Some visitors even describe prisoners as being saint-like.'

'I'm only glad that they can't get out.'

Turrock smiled. 'Movies about psychopaths are full of fallacies. They depict them as leering, menacing creatures – in reality you'd find them gentle as kittens.'

'Until they caught you in an alleyway at midnight.'

Turrock glanced at the screen, which revealed the toad-like man, his plump face the image of serenity. 'Some might follow you into a quiet lane then kill you. But most in there would consider it unthinkable to murder a stranger.'

'Really?'

'The fact is that lots of psychopathic killers don't kill strangers. They'd no more kill a stranger than you'd kiss the first person you find in a street. They get to know their victims, they groom them and go to great lengths to form a close emotional bond before they attack.'

'Why?'

'Essentially, their minds are unknowable. But often when they open up to you they tell you how surprised they are to be treated like criminals. Often they believe they've made a great discovery that will benefit humanity. You see, if they eat a piece of a victim's skin, for example, it might make them feel ten times stronger or ten times more intelligent than before. The man in cell eight – the guy with the odd body shape – he never held down a job for more than a few days; he lived in hostels for the homeless. Then one day he killed a man and kept his heart in a jar. After that, he knew he could do anything. He became super-confident. He changed his appearance, got a well-paid job, bought a house. It turned his life around.'

'Keeping a heart in a jar?' Suzanne shivered.

'You know that business executives power-dress, people wear make-up, they buy sports cars. Those trappings make them feel more powerful. The psychotic empower themselves by taking trophies from their victims – hair, genitals or whatever. Or they drink human blood. Or bury the body in a place only they know. Knowledge of the grave's whereabouts gives them strength. It seems bizarre to us – we don't understand exactly what's going on inside their heads – yet it suggests an extreme version of what we do ourselves when we indulge in retail therapy, change a hairstyle, or buy a Ferrari.'

'So this is your world?' Her brown eyes roved across the steel walls. 'Do you actually like it?'

'It's a living.' He glanced at his watch. 'The ship leaves in just over an hour.'

'It's a pity you're on duty. We could have had some time alone in your cabin.'

'We're alone here. The doors are locked.'

'*Here?*'

'Our friends in there can't see or hear us.'

'Really, *here?*' She smiled as the erotic potential of the place sank in.

'This is my kingdom. I'm in charge. Those prisoners have killed more than fifty people, and yet . . .' He kissed her on the lips. 'I have the power of life and death over them.'

'That's right, you do, don't you?' The notion thrilled her.

'As far as they're concerned I'm their god.' He stroked her arms; he could tell she was becoming aroused. Her eyes sparkled; they had that melting quality when they met his. When he unbuttoned her jeans she took over, slipping them off her long legs, then kicking them away. She pushed aside the computer keyboard. By the time she sat on the desk she breathed hard as she unbuckled his belt.

'Promise you'll make it last the full hour,' she murmured.
'I want an early Christmas present.'

'Take your sweater off. Everything off.'

Once she slipped off her bra she lay back. Her naked body
gleamed under the savage light. He stroked her brown nipples,
then kissed her hard on the mouth. When he pressed her head
down against the desk with the force of his kiss she closed
her eyes. Without her seeing, he pressed a button on the
keyboard. The screen scrolled through images of the cells interiors. Now the prisoners no longer watched a children's
cartoon. Instead they saw that on a desk in a room with steel
walls their guard made love to a naked woman. In cell after
cell faces loomed closer to the TV screen as they absorbed
every detail of the naked bodies.

'Come on, come on.' The woman arched her back as she
lay on the desk. 'Give me something to remember.'

The silent figures in the cells watched as their guard did
exactly that.

Eight

Tanya Rhone decided to wrestle this particular bull by the
horns. The bull in question was Philip De Fray – an implau-
sible surname, she'd always figured – who played piano in
the Moonlit Bay Lounge of the *Volsparr*. It occurred to her
to avoid the bar completely, but that would mean staying away
for the three-day voyage, which would effectively confine her
to cabin. The ship served the Boson Eumericas Corporation
mine on its Baltic island, which meant that many passengers
knew each other, or were relations of the mining personnel,
and so often the cruises had the air of a floating club house.
Tanya wouldn't imprison herself when it was Philip De Fray
who'd deluded himself that they were romantically entwined,
just because on a summer crossing she'd allowed him to stroll
with her on deck then kiss her, a lapse that she blamed on

too much champagne at a party. Of course, just being in the Moonlit Bay Lounge sent out the wrong signals. The bar was far quieter than usual since there were so few passengers. It boasted thick carpets and low tables topped with smoked glass; the soft lighting was easy on the eye. Behind a long bar, with lots of polished brass, racks of wine and mirrors, a lone barman set out bowls of savory tidbits. Tasteful Christmas decorations adorned the walls.

Tanya sat with a glass of white wine for company, and endured twenty minutes of Philip playing gentle melodies on the piano while trying to catch her eye, then smiling at her as if to say, *I knew you'd come.* When he took a rest from playing she'd zero in so she could tell him in terms he couldn't possibly misunderstand that there was no romance, that there was nothing between them, and that he shouldn't even think about following her with love-struck eyes.

'You're my kind of people,' he told his audience as they sipped their drinks. 'Ships, moonlit oceans, voyages to meet faraway lovers . . .'

Dear God, we haven't even left the port yet. She glared at him. *No, don't look his way; he probably thinks I'm making eyes at him.*

His fingers rippled across the keys. 'I want to play this tonight . . . for a special lady.'

God, oh God, don't say my name out loud.

'And that special lady's name is . . .'

God, don't. Tanya gripped the glass stem so hard it was in danger of snapping.

'Her name is the *Volsparr*, the good ship that carries us safely to meet friends and those who we love, and who we haven't seen for so long.'

Tanya kept her face down as if examining a mark on her dress. The relief at not being sung to in public by Philip De Fray made her shake inside. Even so, his cheesy line in sentiment curled her toes.

'That's right,' Philip said as piano chords swelled, 'you're my kind of people.' Then he began to sing.

Has he really written a song for the ship? It wouldn't surprise her. A career as a bar pianist on a ferry must skew your perceptions of not only the world but yourself as a person. She noticed the lights on the wharf move, the pace agonizingly slow, but the ship performed its convoluted waltz as it turned in the dock prior to slipping out through dock gates into the river, which took them to the North Sea some ten miles away. Leaving this port required endless delicate maneuvers for the massive vessel, and it would take thirty minutes to exit the dock. From this angle she looked down into a road just beyond the security fence. Young people wended their way through the cold night air to bars. Girls wore short skirts, skimpy tops and most had adopted seasonal head gear in the form of plastic reindeer antlers decorated with tinsel.

As the ship worked through its dance moves to free itself of the dock, people in the bar said hello then exchanged a few pleasantries, mainly along the lines of, 'We must be out of our minds taking this trip so close to Christmas.' But each had their own special reason for leaving home comforts for a voyage through the freezing Baltic Sea to a mining town that would be battered by blizzards. A luxury destination it was not.

'Oh, what a night. What a night!'

Tanya had been gazing wistfully at a couple walking hand in hand along a quayside road so the voice caught her by surprise. That voice belonged to the stranger with the red headscarf who Tanya had seen trying to board the ship first, then barging by her and other passengers in the corridor like they didn't exist.

'Hello.' Tanya kept her voice neutral. *Do I know this woman?*

The woman sat down at the table as if she'd known Tanya for years. She carried a glass containing tomato juice with a dark blotch of Worcester sauce floating on the top. Those dark, exotic eyes of hers flashed with nothing less than pain. The haughty expression had been replaced by one of sorrow.

'I don't believe it.' The words tumbled out. 'It's not fair what they did to me. It shouldn't be allowed.'

'What did they—?'

'I arrived just five minutes late at the restaurant. They wouldn't let me eat. "Get out," they said, as if I were a dog. I haven't eaten at all day.'

'That doesn't seem right at all.' Tanya wondered if she'd misjudged the woman. After all, anyone can have an ogre of a day that leaves your nerves so raw you just want to—'

'They wouldn't sell me food at the store. They said they're

closing, too. Now I have no food. Only a glass of tomato juice.' Her voice bore a faint accent but Tanya couldn't identify it. Greek? Russian? When she saw that Tanya wore an expression of sympathy for her she smiled. 'Don't worry, dear. I'll find food. I'm Armenian. We're survivors. My great-grandmother crossed Turkey barefoot. All she had to eat was the bark of trees.' Suddenly, she shuffled sideways along the sofa so she could sit hip to hip with Tanya. 'Granny Uska would show me these.' The woman pointed at her own exposed incisors. 'She wore these teeth away gnawing bark. Her sister and her brother died on the march to the coast. But if they didn't keep moving, bandits would carry people away to rape and murder them.'

'I'm sorry. That's dreadful.'

The woman's voice rose as if she was about to weep. 'Just a month ago my mother died.'

Tanya didn't have to find any words of sympathy for the woman suddenly changed tack. Smiling, she said, 'I have my own business. Armenians are born making deals. I have money now. Not when I was young. Then the man who collected our rent would tell my mother if she slept with him he'd halve the money. My mother told him to go to hell, tore off her apron, then beat him down to the ground with her two fists. Listen to this . . .' She softly sang a verse in a foreign tongue that seemed to rhyme with hush and tack. 'That's an Armenian song. The army threw my family out of their home and they had to walk five hundred miles to the coast so they could escape to Greece. My people sang that song all the way. It gave them strength. What was left of our family – those who hadn't been murdered – were evacuated. The Greeks didn't screw the Armenians over. Take this advice, always trust a Greek. They are beautiful people.'

'I will.' Tanya tried to catch Philip's eye. Now she *wanted* him to come over. At best this woman was eccentric . . .

'At last the ship's moving. I thought we'd be here all night.' She didn't sip the tomato juice, just sniffed it, then set it down again as if she enjoyed the act of possessing the beverage and had no intention of actually consuming it.

'I said I'd meet a friend for—'

The woman leaned closer. 'Listen. I want you to help me. Come to my cabin. What I have to tell you is very important;

no one else knows about it. Then I need you to do something
for me.'

Tanya Rhone glanced across the bar at Philip as he played
the piano. Right at that moment he seemed a million miles
away.

'Come.' The woman took Tanya's wrist. 'Come to my cabin.
I will tell you something that will make your heart feel as if
it will burst! You won't believe your ears! Come . . . *Come!*'

SECOND TRACT
Nine

'Quilp . . . Hiyo, Quilp.' At the start of Fytton's shift he shuffled into the cell pod. Ever since he was a young child he combined the greetings 'Hi' and 'Hello' into a mutant combination of the two. His parents thought it cute. Now he was fifty-five a psychologist would vouch it a symptom of arrested emotional development. And a little boy's emotional musculature in an adult's body can be a dangerous thing.

'Hiyo . . . Hiyo, Quilp.' Fytton chanted the greeting in a slow, rhythmic way as he walked along the row of cells, lightly tapping each cell door as he shuffled by. His massive fist made the steel door chime as if it were a cathedral bell being gently struck by a muffled hammer. 'Hiyo, Quilp.'

Quilp, of course, was his colleagues' nickname for 'prey'. Fytton had loved the Quilp hunts when he was stationed with fellow mercenaries in Africa or the Far East. He missed the adrenalin rush when he'd chase locals through bamboo reeds to the paddy fields where he'd blast them with his AK-47. Twenty rounds into the back of a guy could turn a hundred square feet of vegetation a bright and very stick crimson. That was for fun, of course. Occasionally, rascals from a nearby township became a nuisance when they stole tools from a quarry he was guarding, for instance, and then killing civilians became part of the job. His team would find a spot overlooking the township then use sniper rifles to pick off those rascals for a day or two. Naturally, Fytton and his colleagues had no way of knowing if they targeted the actual wrongdoers. Not to worry; random slaughter is a powerful way to drive the 'no thieving' message home. Sadly, this wasn't the great outdoors any more. Fytton would have enjoyed using a shotgun on the cells' occupants. He grinned. *That would be fun. Make me buzz all over.* But Turrock got weird when it came to abusing the prisoners. For some reason it made him angry. *Shit, he doesn't even let me call them names through da door.* But now the boss was off duty in his cabin, and Fytton could have a little entertainment. He shuffled to the table in the middle of the pod. The double doors to the car deck were locked behind him. In front of him, the horseshoe curve of the steel wall where ten doors led to cells lined in yet more steel. *No way them bastards can claw out of that hole.* He hunched over the computer to tap its keys. Images of cell interiors flitted across the screen. *There's bleach girl. Not dead yet, then.* His eyebrows scrunched into spiny tufts as he scowled at the picture. The woman had a delicate frame; very slim – maybe a dancer in the past? He pictured her on stage in clothes that were near see-through. That stirred him inside. There was something erotic in imagining her as a dancer rather than the reality of seeing her sitting cross-legged – and completely naked – on the bunk. She ran her fingers up through her hair, teasing blonde spikes. Should he have some fun with this one? Fytton chuckled. Turrock said there was something wrong with her brain. That she couldn't feel pain. Fytton wanted to test that statement. He could make her experience absolute agony. That's a certainty. His breathing quickened as he stared at the naked woman on screen. Why not get in, do some crazy stuff to her, then be out in twenty minutes? That'd be long before Turrock made his inspection round. She was bruised to hell and back anyway. Nobody would notice if Fytton added a few more bruises to the flesh.

'So many bruises she look like a freaking Dalmatian dog.' He sniffed. 'They gave you da whole bottle, didn't they?' Along with the sharpness of the bleach in his nostrils he detected the prisoners' odor. A subtle difference marked them out from the normals in the outside world. For some reason, these people they shipped overseas secreted different body odors. It wasn't a dirty, unwashed smell; it was as if these individuals also had a diverse biology. It wasn't even an unpleasant odor. When Fytton caught it on the warm air it reminded him of the sweet, delicate scent of a puppy he once owned.

'They got different natures to us,' he told himself, satisfied by his intellectual insight. 'If scientists invented a powerful microscope – really, really powerful – they would see these things aren't human.' He smiled as from his belt he drew a pistol-shaped instrument. Made of black plastic, it had a nozzle protruding from the muzzle.

'Is it going to be you, bleach girl?' His disfigured lips gave his face a cherub appearance, albeit a cherub with a scarred face. The triangular marks glistened red against his olive skin. The anticipation of tangling with a prisoner always had that effect. Air hissed through his nostrils; his skin flushed; his heartbeat quickened; palms grew slick. *I want this. I want this now. Gimme Quilp . . .* His hand hovered over the key that would release the electronic lock. This would give him access to bleach girl, the one spiking her blonde hair. *Very naked on da bed she is,* he thought with pleasure. *Good pointy breasts. Look at da nipples.* He closed his eyes as he imagined battening his mouth on to the dark nipple. *Get a bite on them. Bite hard. Listen to da kind of noise she make then.* Fytton's thick sweaty finger prodded the key. In ten seconds he'd walk in, say, 'Hiyo, Quilp,' then playtime would begin. He couldn't wait. Blood raced through his veins. He tapped the key again. *Damn, what's wrong? Maybe need to reboot da computer. It's always doing that. Piece of crap.* When he hit the key a third time he saw a box appear on screen, overlaying the woman's naked form. In the box was a succinct text: *Code holder access only.*

'Turrock, you piece of turd. Why you done this? Why put a code on da lock?' During Turrock's hours sealed away in here, before even the prisoners arrived, he'd clearly been tinkering with the computer. He'd introduced a new password system to the electronic locks. Now only Turrock could open the cells. 'Damn you, boss. Dirty trick you played on your old friend. What you got planned? Something secret, uh?'

Fytton couldn't hold it in any longer. Gripping the butt of the pistol-shaped instrument he strode across the naked expanse of red floor to the nearest cell. He flipped open the letterbox-shaped shutter. It gave him a six-by-three-inch view of the interior. Inside a man sat watching a children's cartoon on the TV. He'd dressed himself in the only permitted clothing – the white paper coverall. Fytton would have traded with the devil for a tangle with the blonde, but he knew deep down his boss would pay close attention to her, after he'd fought so hard to save her life. Boss would be angry if Fytton messed with her.

Fytton would have to make do with this instead. Inside the

cell the man that resembled a toad turned his big flat face to where his guard stared in through the narrow slot. The man's huge round eyes bulged, but not with fear. Fytton guessed the man had been born like that: a pair of big, round glassy balls for eyes forever ballooning out from their sockets. According to the file the prisoner in this cell was stateless. In fact, police forces worldwide had failed to identify him, so add nameless to stateless. The police had dubbed him 'The Toad'. Not since arrest, or during the trial – or, come to that, any occasion since – had he uttered a word. Fytton peered through the slot at the thing inside. Fytton saw that the prisoner's arms and legs were unnaturally short. The torso had a pumped-up appearance until the chest stretched the coverall so tight it must have been in danger of bursting. If the man's hands were tiny then his face was disturbingly wide, but then it had to be to accommodate huge eyes and a mouth that looked broad enough to fit a dinner plate. Fytton suspected if you watched the man long enough he'd extend a foot-long tongue to lick his entire face clean. Fytton had to close his own eyes for a moment to expunge the mental picture of the prisoner extending a slick tongue to polish each protruding eyeball in turn.

'Hiyo, Quilp,' Fytton murmured. He anticipated the pleasurable sensation of release when he pulled the trigger. 'Quilp's going to sing for his supper.' He chuckled.

In his hand Fytton held a stun gun. Although a copy of a Taser, it weighed nearly twice as much at twelve ounces. In the underside of the muzzle clunked an ugly battery that delivered a beefy 300,000 volts through a stream of salt water droplets. These were discharged in the form of a tightly focused aerosol spray from the muzzle. In most stun guns the high voltage would snap along a pair of wires that terminated in darts embedded into the target's skin, but with this system the water droplets left no trace once they'd dried – or mingled with the victim's urine.

'Quilp. You speak English?' Fytton's question provoked no response other than a toady stare. *Worth a try.* The second the green light blinked on the breech, Fytton fired at the monster. Something like a blue lightning bolt shot through the jet of white vapor streaming from the muzzle. The man sitting on the bunk barely flinched as the electricity discharged into his face. He gulped, the eyes blinked slowly.

'Damn, monster,' Fytton spat. 'You, Toad, feel this! This is da big one. OK!' A one-second blast should reduce a human to a quaking mess as the gun dumped electrical energy into the target's muscles. Not this brute though. Then these things in the cells weren't human, were they? You only had to read the files to see what they'd done. The Toad here might have kept his victims in a closet then drained them of their body fluids in order to turn himself gorgeous. When the green light winked again Fytton squirted for three seconds. A blue fire crackled through the stream of atomized water droplets. Shockingly loud, it sounded like brittle plastic cartons being crushed violently under foot; the torrent of noise made even his teeth hurt. The duration of 300,000 volts cavorting through the Toad's muscles should have induced a crazy fandango of spasms. Loss of balance, disorientation, evacuation of bowel, bladder and stomach. All that should happen in glorious fountains of color that would have Fytton applauding with glee.

But the Toad erupted in an altogether different way. With uncanny speed he bounced on his stumpy legs across the cell floor to the door. With a weird snarl that sounded more like a prolonged burp he thrust his arm out to grab the stun gun.

Fytton blasted again. He all but discharged the entire battery at point-blank range into the prisoner's face. One second, two seconds, three . . . The stumpy arm scythed the air trying to swipe at the gun's muzzle poking through the door slot. Four seconds, five . . . The belching roar became a howl. Six, seven . . . On the eighth second the arm went rigid. After that it swung loosely by his side.

'Got you, Quilp. You don't mess with Fytton!'

Even though the guy should have been unconscious after such a hosing in electricity he glared at Fytton with his two bulging eyes. Fytton knew full well the threat in that bulging stare.

'Yeah, in your dreams, toad man.' A final shot of electricity unbalanced the prisoner. With his nervous system disrupted by a torrent of high-voltage pulses, the Toad fell back to the floor. The impact of the heavy body filled the pod with metallic thunder. 'You've had too much, old friend. You need to sleep it off.' Fytton laughed as he closed the hatch on the cell door. No real harm done; the Toad would be back to whatever was normal for him inside twenty minutes. Fytton returned to the computer, sweating but satisfied – well, partly satisfied. He'd have preferred attending to the naked blonde. Now he'd wait until they were further into the voyage before enjoying himself in that particular cell.

Fytton checked that the cell camera had captured the action. He watched it back on the computer half a dozen times. Impressive the way the Toad dressed in his white coverall had steamed through the lightning blast of the stun gun like it wasn't there. Hell, this is more rewarding than knocking prisoners down like skittles with a stun pistol. Just for a moment Fytton had become the warrior hero. He'd fought the monster and won. He couldn't resist watching the video of him blasting the prisoner one more time. Then he uploaded the two-minute film to his favorite website. That done, he went to the pod's galley to make himself a hot chocolate. As a treat for winning such a decisive victory he took an extra spoonful of sugar. As he stirred the steaming liquid he smiled. 'Blonde girl. As soon as I can, you're next. For you I'm going to come up with something special . . .'

Ten

In the lounge Philip played a slow waltz on the piano but nobody graced the dance floor. Meanwhile, the exotic-looking woman fiercely held on to Tanya Rhone's arm as she implored her to come to her cabin.

Tanya thought: *I don't care if she knows where King Solomon's gold is buried. I'm not going with her.*

'Please.' The woman fixed her with those dark, almond-shaped eyes. 'Hear what I have to say. But it must be in private.'

Tanya's face grew hot with nothing less than shame as she tried to pull free of the woman's grip. So far no one had noticed the silent struggle. Lights were low and people were absorbed in their own conversations.

'My name is Isis Malaika.' The woman's regal glare bore

into Tanya. 'I know you will keep my secret to yourself. You will help me. You have to.'

'I don't know you, do I?' Tanya contemplated pushing the woman off her seat if she didn't move soon.

'I've seen you make this crossing before. In the summer. What's your name?'

Tanya glared back but said nothing.

'Something happened to me when I made the crossing in July. You spent your time on deck reading. I saw you often. Now I need someone I can trust with a secret.'

'I think you've got the wrong person. You're mistaken.' Tanya's whisper had become a growl. 'Now let go of my arm.' *Surely someone's seen this stupid struggle by now. Why am I a magnet for lunatics?* Tanya glanced across at the bar. The barman served drinks to a pair of women in their twenties. They were dressed ready for a party. *On this damn ghost ship? They'll be lucky.* Then, as one turned to check out the bar for any potential party animals, Tanya felt a rush of recognition. 'Milly?' The name spurted out louder than she intended. A group in business suits that were clustered round a blueprint of some industrial machinery briefly glanced up but as quickly turned back to scrutinizing the plans.

Tanya calling out Milly's name deflected Isis from dragging Tanya bodily out of the bar. The woman let go of Tanya's arm then sat back on the sofa, arms folded; she scowled at the glass of tomato juice as if the power of her stare could ignite it.

Milly turned to the other woman at the bar. 'Kate, look, it's Tanya.'

'Tanya!' Kate cried the name like she'd struck gold. 'Tanya Rhone!' In her tight little dress she ran across the lounge to throw her arms round Tanya's neck. 'We didn't know you were making the trip.'

More soberly, Milly added, 'We didn't know we'd be making it, either. Until the last minute when we were told that all leave had been cancelled.'

'Awful, isn't it?' Kate took a large swallow of white wine as she sat down in the chair opposite. 'Hmm, needed that. Now, did you hear what happened? The mine flooded. They've broken into an underground river, get that! Not just a spring but an entire flipping river.'

Milly and Kate pitched alternate sentences to complete the picture.

'Production's been halted for weeks.'

'This is supposed to be a mercy cruise to reunite families at Christmas—'

'But in reality they've added this extra sailing because of the pump.'

'Pump?' Tanya echoed.

'Apparently it's one of the most powerful pumps in the world. The king of pumps. More powerful than engines on a jumbo.'

'It can draw tens of thousands of gallons per hour.'

'Without it the company can't meet the annual extraction quota.'

'And if that happens—'

'I know,' Tanya said. 'The company goes bust.'

'*I am Isis.*'

Milly and Kate stared at the Armenian woman as if they'd only just noticed her.

'Isis Malaika,' she introduced herself. 'You have husbands at the mine?'

They nodded, wary at her forthright way of speaking. Milly glanced quizzically at Tanya.

Tanya cleared her throat. 'Isis and I have just met. She's—'

'This is a business trip.' Isis glared. 'It is, of course, confidential.'

'Confidential?' Kate raised her glass. 'Sounds just like a secret mission. Here's to us.'

'To us,' Tanya echoed Milly.

Isis didn't respond. She merely eyed the newcomers.

'Come on, Isis.' Kate sipped her wine. 'You're not feeling seasick yet, are you? We haven't left the dock.' The floor trembled beneath them.

Isis announced, 'Those are the engines. We're leaving now.'

'In snow, too.' Milly shivered. 'Not a nice night for crossing the sea, is it?'

'I've got crystallized ginger if anyone needs it.' Kate reached for her silver purse. 'Ginger is guaranteed to stop you getting seasick.' Beyond the windows the dockside lights crept by.

'What is it with this dock?' Milly sighed. 'It always takes forever for the ship to get out of the thing.'

'Drink up, Milly. Another couple of those and you'll forget you're even on this tub. Now, who's for a piece of ginger?' Kate drew a plastic bag from her purse.

Isis spoke coldly. 'I despise ginger.'

'It stops you getting seasick.'

'I never get seasick.'

'Oh? Good for you,' Kate said light-heartedly.

Isis is acting as if Kate and Milly have intruded. If we keep chatting long enough then maybe Isis will take the hint and leave.

Tanya sipped her drink. 'I wonder if Philip's noticed that no one's dancing yet?'

'Just wait until later.' Milly gave a mock shudder. 'When he starts playing his own songs . . .'

Kate set down her empty glass. 'And then he tells everyone that if it wasn't for his sick mother he'd have been a superstar.'

'He tells everyone he was close enough to the big time to almost taste it.' Tanya nodded. 'Hit records, Hollywood mansions, private jets. I've made this trip enough times to know his sob stories off by heart.'

'And do you remember the time the sea was so rough that Philip had to play with one hand while he held on to the piano with the other?' Kate snorted with laughter. 'This glass of beer just flew off a table into his lap. You should've seen his face!'

Kate joined in. 'All the time he kept saying to the audience, 'Thank you for staying to listen. You're not quitters.' And he was trying to wipe the beer from his pants and the stain got bigger and bigger.'

Tanya joined Milly and Kate to chorus Philip's catchphrase, 'You're my kind of people'. At that moment Tanya felt a wicked glee in the certainty she was being mean to Isis. By indulging in shared memories the three friends were excluding her. The woman sat there in her red headscarf with an expression like stone. Clearly she'd expected Tanya to be enthralled by being taken into a confidence. *Well, I'm not interested in your secret, Isis. You're arrogant and have worse manners than a mule. Take the hint – go! Find someone else to play your I've-got-a-big-secret game.* Tanya sipped her drink.

Isis moved forward on the sofa, but instead of leaving, she

announced, 'The female line of my family is psychic. I have it, too. I can tell your future.'

'What?' Feeling the wine's magic, Kate grinned. 'Fortune teller? Really?'

'That's amazing.' Milly knocked back the rest of her glass. 'You must have Gypsy blood.'

'Not at all.' Isis touched her own glass of tomato juice, but didn't pick it up. 'I'm Armenian. Our female line can be traced back to the priestess class of Persia. My ancestors were custodians of the most important fire temple in the empire.'

'Really?' Kate sounded impressed. 'And what empire is this?'

Isis surged on. As she talked her voice became lighter. She smiled. Kate and Milly smiled too. All too obviously they warmed to her. *Oh, don't be taken in,* Tanya fumed. *She's faking it. If that's a genuine smile I'll eat the captain's hat.*

Kate extended a hand. 'Tell me my fortune, then.' She gave a tipsy giggle.

'I don't read palms. That's inaccurate. It's all in the eye.'

'Pardon?'

Milly beamed. 'Eye? How?'

Isis spoke gently. 'I see the future in your eyes.'

'Funny. I've not heard that one before. Palms, tarot, tea leaves – never eyes.'

Isis smiled. 'Here, Kate, let me show you. Come closer.'

Kate giggled, her face flushing pink. 'I don't know if I want—'

'Sure you do. Everyone wants to know what will happen to them. My ancestors predicted the fortunes of the emperors of Persia. Even Alexander the Great consulted the priestess at the fire temple.'

'I don't think this is a good idea.' But the two women didn't hear Tanya. They laughed and joked about divining lottery numbers.

'That's it.' Isis smiled brightly. 'Kate, come closer. Let me move your glass so you can rest your arms on the table . . . Relax, don't tense . . . Now . . .' Isis leaned forward until her face was level with Kate's. 'Imagine my eyes are a mirror. Look into them just as you look into a mirror at home.'

'Come on, you're teasing.'

'No, Kate. I can predict your future. Look into my eyes.'

Tanya realized Kate had had enough wine to stop her from feeling overly self-conscious. She tried to break the spell with a joke. 'It looks like you're having an eye examination.'

'Tanya,' Milly scolded, 'don't interrupt.'

'Pardon me.' Tanya shook her head. 'But I don't think it's wise.'

Both Milly and Kate shushed her.

Isis explained, 'What I do is wait until I see my reflection in your eyes. In the black center, the pupil. Got that?'

'Fire away.'

'Now, it's ready. Ask me a question.'

'Any question?'

'Only one that you truly want answering.'

'I'm getting the shivers down my spine. Uhm . . . right. Will I have children?'

Isis answered without hesitation. 'Yes, a big family.'

'Money?'

'You will have that, too.'

'Stability and happiness?'

'Oh, yes, without doubt.'

Milly frowned. 'But how does it work? What do you see in her eyes?'

Isis didn't break eye contact with Kate. 'I wait until I see my face reflected in the iris. Then the subject asks a question. If my reflection shrinks in the iris it means "no". If it expands then that's a "yes". The bigger my reflection grows in your eye then the bigger your good fortune. You follow?'

Good grief. What utter nonsense. Tanya shook her head. If only Kate hadn't drunk so much wine earlier then she'd see how silly it all looked as she stared into the crazy woman's eyes.

'My turn.' Milly grinned. 'You won't tell me anything awful, will you? Nothing to do with doom and destruction.' A pensive expression replaced Milly's grin. The question she asked was clearly heartfelt. 'Will Joe and me go back to Cincinnati?'

Isis considered for a moment as she peered into the woman's eyes. 'Hmm. The reflection is growing.'

'That's good, isn't it? That must mean yes.'

'You will return to Cincinnati but the reflection of my face didn't change in size for a moment, so you won't go home just yet.'

'That's OK; Joe's contract has another eighteen months to run.' Milly sounded delighted.

My God, she really believes what Isis is telling her. Tanya wasn't embarrassed by her friend's gullibility, instead she sensed unease. 'Another drink, anyone?' she asked in an attempt to break the spell. Even Philip's piano playing had become somber. Notes took on a chilling aspect as they ghosted through the air of the lounge that seemed so utterly distant from civilization, even though dock lights still burned through the falling snow.

Milly asked another question. 'Will we be rich?'

Isis studied her own reflection in the pupils of Milly's eyes. 'There's no change. Neither larger nor smaller.'

'So that means we stay as we are, financially?'

Isis gave a single nod.

Kate patted Milly on the arm. 'Never mind, true love is worth more than money. And you're going home to Cincinnati. That's what you've wanted for years.'

Milly's face shone with pure gratitude.

Isis asked, 'Anything else before we stop?'

'I've always kinda wanted to own my own beauty salon. Will I ever do that?'

Isis gave a sympathetic smile. 'Marked reduction in size, I'm afraid. You will never own a beauty salon, Milly.'

'Oh, never mind.' She gave a smile that suggested she knew she'd asked a foolish question. 'Just a silly little dream I had, that's all.'

Isis sat back. 'Happy with the reading?'

'Very happy.' Milly smiled. 'Let me buy you another drink. Bloody Mary?'

'Just tomato juice. Thank you.'

Kate went with Milly to the bar, both laughing as they talked. They were excited by the predictions. Isis had made them happy.

Tanya could stand it no more. This time she was the one to grab an arm. She tugged Isis so they were nose to nose. 'That was some show you put on.' Tanya pushed her face forward to intimidate the woman rather than replicate what the others had done. 'What future do you see for me? Will I live a long and fruitful life?'

'You don't want to know.'

'Don't I? Go on.' Anger burned now. 'Tell me what you see in my eyes. Tell me if I'll live until I'm a hundred in a mansion with dozens of grandchildren.'

'Tanya.' Isis regarded her coldly. 'I don't see my reflection in your eyes. It simply isn't there. Be warned: as far as the future is concerned you are already dead.'

Eleven

Tanya Rhone swept through the mini-mall of the *Volsparr*. The stores, hair salon and beautician had long since closed. Through locked glass doors there was only darkness. Tanya glanced out of a window. Dock lights were shrinking. The ship had slipped into the River Humber now, a vast stretch of choppy water that fed into the North Sea some ten miles away. Out here, midnight was dark and lonesome. Snow no longer appeared to be white. Flakes resembled weird black petals as they tumbled from the sky. From the north came the shriek of storm winds.

When Isis Malaika had made her prediction that Tanya would die young it had been the final straw. As Kate and Milly bought drinks at the bar Tanya had marched out. *The woman's not right in the head, is she?* The way she wanted to rush on to the ship before the crew had begun boarding passengers. The way she'd all but cornered Tanya in the bar to reveal *her* life story, and *her* ancestors' life stories. Hell, she'd even sung in Armenian – or what she claimed to be Armenian. *The clincher is that look in her eye. She has crazy eyes.* The ship heaved. A rolling swell struck the bows hard enough to make the vessel shudder. *We're sailing into a storm – great, just great.*

'Tanya. Tell me what happened to you?'

Anger struck her with scalding intensity. As Isis moved toward her along the corridor, Tanya backed away. 'You've played your joke on me. Good for you. I'm sure you're enjoying yourself immensely. Now, goodnight.' She turned with the intention of hurrying to her cabin. *Bloody woman can't follow me in there.*

But Isis did follow. Tanya became acutely conscious of her footsteps getting closer. At this time of night the mall was deserted. Suddenly, Tanya felt vulnerable, and moved faster. At the end of the mall an elevator would take her down to cabin level.

'Tanya. An event in your life hurt you. It damaged you so much it took your fight. You don't even want to live a long life . . .'

'Isis, I'm going to my cabin. Goodbye.'

'Listen to what I have to say.'

'No.'

'I'm going to share a secret with you, Tanya. You will help me. Then that will help you. It will heal your spirit.'

'Me, help you?' She reached the elevator. 'Then I suppose you'll be able to see your reflection in my eyes.'

'If you do good deeds for others your appetite for life will return.'

Tanya punched the elevator call button. The woman in the headscarf moved uncomfortably close. Her dark eyes looked at her searchingly. 'I knew I'd found someone I could share my secret with. It's you, Tanya. We're two people who've suffered. We can help each other.'

Thank you, Lord. The elevator door slid open. Coldly she said, 'Don't follow me, Isis.'

Isis began to speak in a soft, matter-of-fact voice. She told her secret there and then as Tanya stepped into the elevator. The ship bucked as it ran into a headwind. Engines suddenly grew louder as if forces tested them to divine if they could stand the imminent storm.

Tanya stared at Isis, half-wondering if she'd imagined what the woman had just said.

Isis continued. 'I made the crossing the same time as you in July. You would sit out on deck to read. Sometimes we said hello to each other. I looked different then. I didn't wear this.' She tugged off the red headscarf. 'Now you know why I wear it. Look at the side of my head.'

Tanya had every intention of pressing the button that would take her to the cabin deck. Now she saw what the woman pointed at. Her glossy hair wasn't as perfect as it seemed. Above her right ear naked patches of skin gleamed in the elevator lights.

'At night I tear at my hair in my sleep. I started to do this after your friend the piano player raped me.'

'Philip? He'd never do that.' Tanya's blood ran cold. 'He's annoying but . . .' She couldn't finish the sentence.

'It was the night of a party. You were with friends – a big, big group of them. You were very happy. Drunk too much champagne, I guess. You went out on to the deck with Philip. I thought you were lovers.'

'No. I hardly even know him.' Tanya's throat tightened.

'I was so envious. I felt . . .' She paused as a ship's officer in an immaculate white uniform hurried past with a clipboard. When he'd gone she continued, 'I felt excluded. Lonely. I don't make friends easily. I'm always on the outside looking in. I take these trips to the mine alone; I never manage to make conversation with other passengers; I keep myself to myself.'

Tanya wanted to interrupt this confessional but she couldn't find the right moment, especially after the astounding accusation about Philip.

Isis leaned closer until Tanya could feel the woman's breath. 'Tanya. That time, five months ago, after you'd left the bar I stayed. I did what lonely people are apt to do. They find a glass of wine helps dull the isolation. Philip played those songs of his. Then he came across to me. He asked if I'd like a drink. You don't know what loneliness is like, Tanya. Sometimes it's like having this enormous rock crushing you. You can't bear it any more. I told myself I'd chat with Philip for a while. I didn't find him attractive but if I went back to my cabin after talking to someone I'd feel that bit happier. So I accepted the drink.' She gave a little shrug. 'He must have put something into the wine. I remember my body going heavy. I tried to tell him something was wrong but my tongue just didn't work. All I remember then was seeing him laughing at me, as if I amused him in some way. After that . . .' Another shrug; this time her eyes were lost, frightened, as if memory dragged her back to a terrible place, somewhere she didn't want to go but was powerless to resist. 'In the morning I woke up in my bunk. I was in pain. My thighs were bloody.'

'Are you sure that—?'

'Yes, Philip raped me. I'm certain. For days afterwards I couldn't remember anything about that night. It was only later that memories started to return. Date-rape drugs do that to you. They wipe memory – or at least they seem to. Then sometimes you begin to remember when it's too late for the police to collect evidence.'

'I'm sorry.' Any thought of pushing the button to take her to the cabin deck had vanished. This revelation stunned her. *It's impossible*, she thought. *Philip wouldn't do that to a woman. But what was he saying to me earlier? He made out that we'd had a relationship that had gone further than that kiss on deck. Wait a minute . . .* Fear struck her with the suddenness of a punch. Had he ever bought her a drink? *Are there any nights when I couldn't remember what happened? Any blackouts? Was there a morning when I woke up alone but still had the sensation I'd recently had sex?* The moisture in Tanya's mouth evaporated. She tried to swallow but couldn't. Almost desperately she said, 'Isis, Philip can be a nuisance. But he wouldn't rape a woman. I'm sure—'

'Are you?'

'Oh, God.' Tanya wanted a shower. A hot, scalding shower. Her mind raced until she felt giddy She recalled his peculiar suggestions earlier. Could there be more to it than his tasteless sense of humor?

'He drugged me, he fucked me.' Isis held Tanya's gaze in hers. 'I bled inside. Later I realized that he'd made me pregnant.'

'Oh, God.'

Outside gales screeched through the superstructure. Snowflakes oozed across the windows. Images spat through Tanya's head. *Philip drugs the wine. Then walks me out of the bar. He jokes with other passengers that I've downed too much booze and he's helping me back to the cabin. After he's done whatever he wants to me, because I'm too addled to know any better, he simply returns to his own cabin. I wake up suspecting something odd's happened but not sure what.*

Meanwhile, Isis continued to explain how her life had been ripped apart since that night in July. 'When I learned that the man had put a child inside of me I fought to make the right decision. Then it came to me. Like a slap in the face. I would keep the baby – no abortion, no adoption. I'd keep my son or my daughter. The child would be loved by me as hard as I could. I'd fight with all my strength to make good out of bad. Do you follow? The child would be my triumph over that man's evil act.' She took a breath. Her eyes were hypnotic. 'Last month I lost my baby. Since then I tear at my hair while I'm asleep. I must wear this.' She crushed the headscarf in her fist. The bald patch in the side of her scalp gleamed. 'Today I saw you on the ship. I knew you would help me.'

'But what are you asking me to do?'

'Philip De Fray raped me. I became pregnant. The trauma of the attack grew worse as I remembered what he'd done. The stress killed my baby. Now, you will come with me to confront Philip. For now, he doesn't recognize me because of the scarf; my face is much thinner, too.'

Tanya's insides moved as if they'd turned to liquid. Coldness spread down through the trunk of her body into her legs. She could barely move; come to that it was a struggle to breathe.

'Help me, Tanya. And heal yourself, too. Put life back into your eyes again.'

'I'm sorry, Isis. I'm not the person you think I am.' Her thumb stabbed the elevator button.

'Tanya, you will help me.'

'Speak to a counselor.' The elevator door slid shut. Before it passed in front of Isis standing in the corridor, Tanya added, 'You need professional help. I can't—' The door shut. A second later the steel canister descended into the bowels of the ship.

Twelve

The elevator descended smoothly. With the relief of leaving Isis behind Tanya couldn't help but wonder if she'd misjudged the woman. Clearly, her behavior had been odd – even downright ill-mannered – but if what she said was true . . .

How would I react? If it had been me that Phillip had raped, had made pregnant and then caused me to miscarry? I might be the one ripping out handfuls of hair in my sleep . . . Just imagine the nightmares. Again, Tanya experienced vertigo brought on by uncertainty.

'Stop this,' she hissed. 'Stop this right now. You're letting your imagination run away . . .' She blinked. 'What have I done?' The numbers on the elevator's control panel scrolled backwards. 4 . . . 3 . . . *I must have pressed the wrong button. Damn, I've missed the cabin deck. Come on, pull yourself together.*

The elevator stopped. Text on the screen flashed: *Car Deck 2.* Tanya sighed. The door slid open to reveal a gloomy hallway. Clearly, this wasn't a part of the ship intended to be frequented by passengers at sea. Here the engines were much louder. A heartbeat of sound. One so low that it was felt in the chest as much as heard. She expected to see fire doors to the car deck. Instead, a pair of heavy-duty steel gates sealed off the entrance to another corridor that extended in front of her. A sign attached to the bars warned:

STRICTLY NO ADMITTANCE
CHOIR-MOORE ABSTRACTS PERSONNEL ONLY
TRESPASS IS PUNISHABLE BY CIVIL AND CRIMINAL LAW

Tanya had never heard of Choir-Moore Abstracts. But she would soon enough.

What mattered was returning to her cabin for a hot shower, bed and, God willing, a nightmare-free sleep until morning. This time she hit the right button. As the door slid shut a hushed voice shimmered through the locked gates: '*You are all mine now . . . I own you . . . think about it . . . give me what I need . . .*'

The elevator door *snicked* shut. Tanya stiffened. The way the voice ghosted from the gloom sent ice down her spine. She shook her head. As days went this had been an ugly monster of one. What she longed for was bed, to close her eyes on an awful, harrowing evening. But she knew she couldn't get that strange woman out of her head, or her revelation.

'Damn you, Isis.' Cursing her wouldn't rid Tanya of her dilemma. *I can't hide from this*, she told herself. *I'm going to have to do something about it.*

'*You are all mine now . . . I own you . . . think about it . . . give me what I need . . .*'

Even though Turrock's shift didn't start for another four hours he couldn't wait. He told Fytton to finish his watch early. Fytton didn't mind. He shrugged, then shuffled back to his cabin.

Turrock checked the monitor to make sure the prisoners – his trophies – hadn't harmed themselves during his absence. Attempted suicide during transit was a given. Once the prisoners felt the ship in motion they realized that this was for keeps. A one-way trip beyond the pale. Once he'd satisfied himself that his charges were fine – especially the blonde he'd saved from poisoning – he patrolled the cell area. Just thinking about the blonde made him restless. He prowled from door to door. Tenderly, he rested his palm on the steel panel. Anyone else would feel a flat, hard surface, neither warm nor cool to the skin. Turrock, however, sensed a vibration trickling through the door. Something like electricity. It warmed him.

'That's power,' he said out loud. 'That's the power of you.' He licked his lips. 'You do realize . . .' His voice rose as he addressed the occupants. 'That between you, you've killed more than fifty people. And the things you did to those people . . .' His heart beat faster. 'Your lawyers still have nightmares, don't they?' He pictured the naked blonde sitting on the bunk;

the mental image of her nude seared his nerve endings. 'I've never had one like you before,' he sighed. 'Did you enjoy the show I gave you? What did you think to my girlfriend, uhm?' Turrock moved on, taking pleasure from touching each door in turn. He arrived on duty feeling like a spent battery. Being in the presence of his prisoners recharged him. His own sense of power grew. These creatures – and knowing the extraordinary acts they'd committed – nourished him emotionally. His back straightened. He stood taller. That new sense of vigor transmuted a mere walk into a magisterial stride.

Turrock decided to use the bunk in the guards' rest area. He'd tell Fytton that he'd maintain a suicide watch. Turrock loved being here . . . Come to that, he was *in love* with being here in the pod.

The phone chirped. If that was Fytton with some irritating problem . . . He picked up. 'Fytton?'

'Do I sound like Fytton?'

'Suzanne?'

'Listen. I've decided to stay on board. I want us to spend Christmas together.'

Thirteen

After breakfast Tanya Rhone searched for Isis. That allegation of Philip raping Isis had robbed Tanya of her sleep. *This is something I can't ignore*, she told herself as she walked the deck outside. *Isis can't expect me to help her extract retribution on Philip. For heaven's sake, I don't know the woman. She might be crazy; the allegation could be pure invention.* The morning air felt like ice. It numbed her nose in seconds. Flurries of snow raced over an iron-gray sea. The massive ship surged northward. Information monitors set up in corridors revealed that they were halfway across the North Sea between England and Denmark. In a few hours the colossal form of the *Volsparr* would slip through the narrow channel between Denmark and Scandinavia then enter the Baltic. Beyond those straits Russia would be waiting to receive them.

Tanya retreated before the gales roaring down at her from the Arctic Circle. *Instead of wandering round the ship in the hope I bump into Isis by chance, I should find her cabin number from the purser's office.* However, the moment she heaved open the deck door against the barrage of cold air she found what she'd been searching for. Isis, in her trademark red headscarf, marched along the corridor that led from the shopping mall. This time she wasn't alone. With her expression set to one of grim determination she dragged a child by the hand. It was the same girl Isis had knocked down the day before. Tanya guessed her to be aged around six. Now her blonde hair stood on end as if she'd been hauled along the floor. An expression of shock widened her eyes.

'Isis! What are you doing?'

'I must speak with you, Tanya. It's important.'

Tanya stared at the woman as she dragged the child along. 'Good God, Isis. Let go of the girl.'

'We'll go to my cabin.' It was a command rather than a request. 'We can talk freely there.'

'Isis, I don't know what you're thinking of, but let go of the little girl. You're going to break her wrist.'

'If I do she runs.'

'Let her run, then. She's not yours; she's nothing to do with you.' Tanya's blood ran hot. Passengers walked by; all they saw was a mother having trouble keeping her kid under control. But Tanya saw only kidnap.

'Girl, you must not pull.' Isis yanked her arm to encourage her to walk properly.

'Isis, life hasn't been easy for you, but if you don't let go of the child I'll report you to the captain.'

'The captain? What are you talking about?'

'Stop this,' Tanya warned. At that moment she knew she'd physically restrain Isis from dragging the girl away. The woman was clearly deranged. 'Isis. This is your last chance.'

Before she could lunge at the lunatic a woman emerged from the ladies' just paces away. She wiped at a damp patch on her cream jacket. Tanya remembered that this was the girl's mother. *What will she say when she sees Isis hauling her child away with a mad gleam in her eye?*

The woman looked at Isis, then said what Tanya least expected. 'I'm sorry, Isis. I couldn't get the hand dryer to work. Jo's not been any trouble, has she?'

Isis smiled. 'She wanted to play in the children's ball pool. But I daren't let her in case these are her best clothes.'

'They are. But knowing Jo they won't be for long.' The mother smiled. 'Thank you so much for looking after her.' She smiled at Tanya, figuring she and Isis were friends. 'I'd bought a hot chocolate, only I haven't got my sea legs yet. I spilt it all down my jacket. Isis rushed to my rescue.' She laughed, but with a hint of nervousness. 'I think I've saved it.' She dabbed the damp patch.

Isis nodded. 'You've got the worst out. If I were you, though, I'd take it to the laundry room.' She awarded Tanya a cool glance. 'I had to have a dress of mine cleaned on a crossing once. It was in a very bad mess.'

After another flurry of 'thank you's the woman led her daughter away. Jo still shot frightened glances back at Isis as she went.

Isis folded her arms. 'Tanya. You thought I stole that child from her mother, didn't you? Did you expect me to throw her into the ocean?'

'It looked . . .' Tanya sighed; she realized she'd made a prize chump of herself. 'Seeing you with the little girl took me by surprise.'

'Stick around, you can watch me pan-fry babies next. They're delicious.'

'Isis, I didn't—'

'And then I dip puppy dogs in honey. Very sweet, yet so good for you.'

'OK, OK. I apologize.' Tanya turned to Isis, intending to stare her down if she planned on turning nasty. Instead, she saw the woman's lips soften into a smile.

'Did you know I own a company that supplies the mine with dynamite?' Tanya stared. 'No, you didn't, did you? Come along. Buy me a coffee. I'll tell you about it.'

Turrock opened the cell-pod door to admit Suzanne. Then he stood back, which allowed him to appreciate her whip-thin figure, her taut muscular waist. He noticed she'd applied make-up to conceal the scar that ran from ear to jawbone.

This morning she wore a tight shirt with equally tight blue jeans.

'I'm flattered you decided to spend Christmas with me,' he told her. 'But you do know that we'll have to spend the holiday on the ship? There's nothing at the mining camp.'

'Being with you is all that matters.' She shot him one of those slow-burn erotic smiles. 'I told you last night, I love you. It's not fair that we have to spend so much time apart.'

'Then we'll make the most of being together.'

She ran her fingertips along one of the cell doors.

As he watched her he added, 'Won't your employer be annoyed when you don't turn up for work tomorrow?'

'It's all fixed.' Her attention turned to the computer screen that bore images of the prisoners in their cells. 'I'm owed leave. Besides, the boss daren't fire me. I'm the only one who really understands the transport schedules.' The cycle of images now revealed the blonde who'd nearly died from bleach poisoning. She lay on her back on the bunk, the bruises on her breasts still vivid. Turrock's colleagues always delivered expert beatings. 'Why are some of them still naked?'

'They're on suicide watch. If we allowed them clothes they'd try to choke themselves.'

'They choke themselves? How?'

'One way is to take a sleeve, then pack it down into their throats until it blocks the airway.'

'My God, that'll take some doing.'

'Believe me.' He smiled. 'These men and women are extraordinary. You wouldn't believe what they can accomplish once they make up their minds.'

'And you never ever let them out?'

She's frightened of them. I can see her gooseflesh. 'Not while they're on board. To them I'm life and death. They're fed through those chutes. Energy bars, cookies, fruit. Soft foodstuffs. I don't permit them cutlery.' Turrock nodded at the cells. 'Those people in there could devise a way to kill you with a paper cup.' He enjoyed the way she shuddered. Lightly, he brushed her dark hair from her cheek. His flesh tingled as he recalled the way she'd sat astride him last night then slowly rocked her way into total bliss. She kissed his fingers.

'Hmm,' she whispered. 'I can still smell me on you.'

'My favorite souvenir.' He kissed her on the mouth.

She touched her face. 'Where's the guy with the . . . ?' Her finger drew triangular scars.

'Fytton's off shift. He'll be taking a walk out on deck.'

'What happened to him? Did he argue with a tiger?'

'Faulty grenade.'

'Lucky he didn't lose his head.'

Turrock grinned. 'We're not going to spend all morning discussing Fytton's complexion, are we?'

'Oh?' She kissed him again. 'Anything else you want to do?'

As she stripped for him Turrock once more tapped the keyboard. 'I'm just sealing the doors to the ship. We don't want Fytton getting a free show, do we?'

She slipped of her shirt. 'A free show? You must be planning something extra special.'

'Just you wait and see.' As he picked up her naked form she wrapped her legs around him. Easily he carried her to the wall so her back would be supported by the vertical slab of steel. He glanced at the computer screen. His prisoners no longer watched the ship's information program but had a perfect view as their master, John Turrock, pressed the woman up against the wall, and penetrated her for their entertainment.

Turrock closed his eyes at the blissful sensation. Ten pairs of eyes would be fixed on ten TV screens. *I hope you find this as stimulating as I do. Just you wait and see what I do to her. You're not going to believe your little psychopathic eyes . . .*

Tanya Rhone thought: *I've lost control of my life. This is one ride I want to get off but I can't.* Because she felt embarrassed at all but accusing Isis of kidnapping the girl, when she was, in fact, only helping the mother, she had accepted the invitation. Ten minutes later she sipped her cappuccino in the lounge bar on the upper deck of the *Volsparr*. At this time of the morning the piano was draped in purple velvet. Philip was nowhere to be seen. *Thank God.* In groups of threes and fours, passengers occupied sofas and armchairs as they sipped coffees. All were wrapped in a conversation that could be described as earnest. They leaned forward, fingertips pressed together, brows furrowed; either they talked in low, serious tones, or they listened with equally serious expressions. Tanya picked up a variety of accents – American, Canadian, English, Irish, Australian, South African. This was no pleasure cruise. They'd sacrificed their Christmas holiday in order to undertake a rescue mission for Boson Eumericas. Big business is dog eat dog.

Tanya listened to Isis talk about her trade in dynamite.

'I never touch the stuff, of course.' She patted the side of her headscarf. Tanya tried not to stare. Isis continued, 'I'm wholesale. I buy dynamite from the manufacturer then sell to Boson. Once the Chief Mining Engineer tried to cut me out by negotiating directly with the explosives company, but I still managed to undercut by buying in bulk.' Then she added lightly, 'I made so much money I need never work again. I could buy a Caribbean island and live as I please.'

Tanya listened patiently to Isis talk about the dynamite industry. Surely, this was a preamble to explaining in more detail what happened that night in July when Philip attacked her. *Is Isis completely sane? Had she invented the whole thing?* Isis smiled as she talked, yet her manner did seem odd. Although her eyes darted in a lively, even vivacious way, they reinforced Tanya's notion that this woman in the red headscarf might be an oddball, to say the least.

Tanya sipped her coffee. She nodded, feigning interest as Isis told her that the mine consumed a hundred tons of dynamite every twenty-four hours. 'Listen. They blast the rock face by night, then dig out the ore during the day. Seven days a week, fifty-two weeks a year. It is unceasing. Until the mine flooded, that is. Now this ship sails just before Christmas to deliver the pump. If they fail to deal with the water and meet the extraction deadline they lose the lease. Pffft!' She made a falling gesture with her arms. 'Then everything collapses. Boson Eumericas goes bankrupt. They own this ship, you know that? They lose this, too. All these people here and at the mine lose their jobs.'

'And you lose your contract to supply dynamite?' Tanya said with a tingle of revelation. So Isis has a vested interest in this rescue mission. If the pump fails to clear the mine, then will she be bankrupted too? 'Does the company owe you money?'

Isis blinked, maybe a little surprised at being asked so

directly. 'Not that much. If they meet the deadline and survive then they will expand operations. Copper is in greater demand now. In twenty years electric cars will begin to replace the internal combustion powered vehicle. Copper is needed for electric motors.'

'So the company will need more dynamite – *your* dynamite?'

Isis looked Tanya in the eye as if reassessing her earlier impressions. The insight into Isis being here to sell more dynamite impressed her.

Tanya suddenly shivered. *Isis plans to sell more dynamite to Boson Eumericas. That's why she's here. But she also told me she'd made this voyage especially so she could confront her attacker, Philip De Fray . . .* She felt a shiver as she guessed what Isis planned. *My God. She's going to use the rape allegation as a bargaining tool. She'll meet the mine personnel to negotiate the dynamite deal. Then she'll make the same revelation that one of their employees, albeit a musician on their ship, had raped a passenger.* Tanya could imagine Isis sitting there in the buyer's office. The company's in a precarious state. To avoid bad publicity they'd make a deal with Isis, even if it meant the equivalent of paying her hush money. *If this woman isn't insane she's truly monstrous.*

Tanya withdrew emotionally into a protective shell. Despite her suspicions about the woman chatting so casually to her over coffee, she'd still allowed herself to become involved. *Isis is manipulating me. She thinks she can use me to get what she wants. And what she wants is money, lots of money.* Through the windows Tanya could see the North Sea. Streaked with foam from the winds, it heaved itself upward into hillocks of gray brine. The big ship rose with the waves. Through the gloom of the winter morning she glimpsed one of the rigs that pumped oil from beneath the seabed. A bright yellow flame revealed the burn-off of flammable gases.

On TV screens set on walls around the bar an information film played. Now that Tanya had decided to distance herself from Isis's toxic personality she picked up on the narration. *'At this moment, midway between the British Isles and Denmark, the ship on which you are traveling is passing over the North Sea's very own Atlantis. Six thousand years ago you would have seen no ocean. Beneath your feet would have been the open prairies of what is known as Doggerland. There, Neolithic people hunted woolly mammoth while keeping a watchful eye on the prowling saber-toothed tiger.* Tanya glanced across at a screen peeping out from above a Christmas tree. With the commentary were animated images of hunters clad in animal skins. Armed with spears they stood beside a tent constructed from the rib bones of a mammoth and covered with its skin. *'Beneath our vessel, as it carries us in safety and comfort across the ocean, are the contours of hills, valleys, and the ghostly courses of mighty rivers. When the ice age ended five thousand years ago, rising sea levels inundated the land. The flood separated Great Britain from mainland Europe. Yet even today fishermen's nets haul up the great bones of mammoth from the ocean floor almost a thousand feet beneath our keel . . .'*

'We've only just started to talk,' Isis announced. 'I'll order more coffee.' She strode across the room to the bar; other passengers were forced to step aside as she walked as if marching to war.

I'll make one more attempt to persuade her to get counseling for the attack, Tanya promised herself. *Then I will have done all I can for her. I'm under no obligation to be her friend.*

The aroma of coffee filled the air. With it came a sense of tension. Most of the men and women here were on a mission to rescue the company. To do that the pump that the *Volsparr* carried must be delivered to the mine. Then it had to be installed so it could pump out the flooded workings. When Tanya caught snatches of conversation from those grave-faced technicians she divined the single topic of conversation: The Pump.

The occupants of the bar had formed themselves into clusters of anything between two and five individuals. Two women pored over a blueprint of the pump on the next table. They took it in turns to smooth out the blue-gray sheet so they could examine the detailed plan of the mechanism. Although Tanya couldn't make out any other words of the conversation, the word 'pump' leapt out as if the speaker's anxiety over it gave the word more force. The more she listened the more convinced she became that this pump had such a special

place in these people's lives as to be regarded as not only
the savior of the mining company but also their livelihoods.
The employees' financial security depended on the pump that
lay like a sleeping giant in the bottom of the ship. She'd
noticed it on the quayside prior to loading. The thing had
been bigger than a gas truck. The pump had the power to
save. But only if they treated it with respect – no, more than
that; the pump must be *revered*. It had to be spoken of with
awe. Every aspect of the pump – every valve, pipe, motor,
drive coupling, electronic sensor, data monitor – had to be
studied in such detail that it had become an act of near-
worship.

Tanya could imagine what these technicians were thinking.
'Please God, let it work. There's Jenny's school fees. Think
of the overdraft. What about the pension plan?' A big man of
around sixty with gold-rimmed glasses smoothed out another
copy of the blueprint. His fears seemed to float around him
like a dark mist. 'This has got to work. If the pump can't
clear the flood then I'll be out of a job. At my age I'll never
get hired again . . .' His large hands were scrupulously clean,
the nails perfectly trimmed. Even so Tanya knew he'd get
them dirty and bloody heaving the pump into position if that's
what it took.

From time to time one of the technicians that formed the
pump's entourage would disappear for a while. Tanya envis-
aged them taking it in turns to ride the elevator down into the
hold. There they'd respectfully approach the pump with heads
bowed as true believers approach a church altar. The braver
ones – or those with the most to lose if the pump failed to
suck the flood from the mine – would approach the truck-sized
machine, gently stroke its steel flank and murmur encourage-
ment. The pump would defeat the invading water. Mining
would resume. Quotas would be met. Livelihoods would be
saved, homes spared, credit-card debts repaid. But everything
depended on the pump.

'I said be careful. You'll spill.'

'Sorry. I was miles away.' Tanya accepted the cup of
steaming coffee from Isis. The heat through the ceramic stung
her fingers to dispel her reverie. The rocking motion of the
ship had almost lulled her into a doze. She glanced round.
The pump technicians still huddled close. Apprehension

mingled with blind faith in their eyes. They only had one shot at this to succeed.

Outside the Arctic gale screamed across an ocean where the bones of extinct beasts lay in cold depths of absolute darkness.

THIRD TRACT
Fourteen

Tanya lay in her bunk, dead to the world. When she opened her eyes, the clock on the bunk-side table told her she'd slept solidly until 9.15. She yawned. The bunk was snugly warm. *There's no reason to rush,* she told herself. *If I'm up by ten I'll still catch breakfast.* The light beneath the door revealed little, other than the blocky shadows of the closet, the empty bunk at the other side of the cabin, and the doorway to the bathroom that was little larger than an upright coffin in the corner of the room.

Yesterday afternoon Tanya had spent a couple of hours in the ship's cinema watching *It's A Wonderful Life.* A great movie to see with family and friends but watching it alone made Tanya homesick. Once more she questioned why she'd decided to make this voyage just before Christmas to a barren Russian island that played host to a mining camp. If it wasn't for Jack . . . She tried to not to think ahead to the meeting and the ultimatum. She'd had enough of playing the distant girl-friend. Either he came home to find work locally or she'd tell him that the relationship couldn't continue. She loved him. But this constant estrangement had become nothing less than torture. Now she had to endure what had become a tortuous sea voyage. Hell, Isis had made the trip tortuous. Tanya had escaped her for the afternoon by hiding in the cinema. Then last night she'd queued for the canteen-style dinner (normal waiter service had been suspended; this was an emergency sailing and most of the catering staff would be home for the holidays by now). Isis had cut in line beside her, which sent a murmur of annoyance along the queue of pump technicians.

'Eat this fish.'

'Isis, I don't like pickled herring; it's—'

Isis hadn't listened. She'd insisted on loading Tanya's plate with food she detested. *Dear God*, she'd marveled, *I really have lost control of my life. Isis now decides what I eat.* Tanya kept her mouth shut, but she'd longed to yell, *Isis, mind your own business. Leave me alone. And don't even try talking to me again!* Tanya shook her head as she lay there in the bunk. *I genuinely sympathized with Isis when she told me how Philip had assaulted her. But the woman would make a saint curse. I bet she's got a home to die for but nobody to share it with. So she travels all the time, pretends it's necessary for her business, only it's a way of never having to admit to herself that in truth she's lonely. So she imposes herself on the first person who shows her even a smidgen of kindness. To even think about her makes my blood boil. I'm supposed to be enjoying a lie-in. All I can do is get angry . . .*

She slipped out from under the blankets and stretched with another heartfelt yawn. In the gloom of the cabin she couldn't make out the nearest light switch so she flipped open a blind that covered the porthole instead. Beyond the thick glass lay a gray realm. She rubbed sleep from her eyes as she gazed out.

'So much for a sea view,' she murmured. 'At least I won't need my sun hat today.'

A thick gray fog had settled over the ocean. Not only had the sea become calm, she saw that ice had formed on its surface. This was the characteristic ice of the Baltic, which told her they must have passed through the straits between Scandinavia and Denmark sometime during the night as she slept. Now the ship appeared to wallow at a standstill. Then again that wasn't unusual. The area where the North Sea merged with the Baltic became so busy with maritime traffic that vessels were often held in queues before being allowed to proceed into the required shipping lane.

She shivered, and as she peered through the porthole she felt the coldness of that icy world reach into her to lay its deathly fingertips on her heart. The Baltic Sea was little more than a grave – one very large, very sodden, very wet grave. Hundreds of wrecked ships lay rotting on the seabed. Aircraft by the score had plunged into it, never to be seen again. Legends say that in 1867 a clipper carrying money from the United States to buy Alaska from Russia foundered here.

In the twentieth century alone the Baltic had drowned tens of thousands of men, woman and children. In World War 2 this had been a raging battleground. Warships had clashed with explosive ferocity. Submarines sent cargo vessels to the bottom. In 1945 the RAF mistakenly bombed ships that carried concentration camp survivors to safety. Thousands of innocents were burned alive. In this mass of brackish water rusted the *Wilhelm Gustloff*, a passenger liner that holds the macabre record for the worst ever loss of life. When Soviet torpedoes struck it one bitter January night in 1945, nine thousand civilian refugees and wounded German troops died. Sometimes Tanya had nightmares when she made this crossing, imagining she was one of the poor souls who had perished that night.

The Baltic Sea exhaled an atmosphere of menace. An Arctic chill always clung to it, even on summer crossings. Tanya often lay in her bunk where she saw in her mind's eye the ferry passing over this graveyard for ships. Rotting vessels trapped in the mud at the bottom of the sea. In hulks, engulfed by fearsomely cold water, would be the corpses. Thousands of them. Bulbous eyes staring into the face of eternity. The hair of the dead would fan out as currents tugged the bodies through submerged passageways of the ships; the dead would ghost through drowned rooms. Fish would gnaw at fingers. Bones would thrust out from decaying clothes. The screams of the drowning would be locked into the very atoms of the iron hull. Maybe they waited for science or a supernatural act to free the caged sounds so human ears could hear the agonized cries of the dying.

The ominous prophecies of Isis rose like poison through her body. A sense of danger throbbed like a red light inside of her. A bleak warning of menace that lurked just ahead of them in the future.

Tanya didn't focus her gaze on the skull-white ice on the sea; instead she stared at her reflection in the porthole glass. Her eyes had become unnaturally round, more like the sockets in the face of an ancient corpse. Now she searched for her own reflection in her iris, that pinpoint of liquid darkness in the center of the eye.

'*Damn you, Isis. How did you get inside my head?*' She slammed her hand against the cabin wall then whirled away to the bathroom, determined to take a shower hot enough to sear away those morbid thoughts that haunted her.

Fifteen

Tanya made it to the restaurant by 9.50. Usually, it would be busy at breakfast time as employees of Boson Eumericas enjoyed a leisurely meal from the self-serve counter. Now, however, there was more evidence that this was an emergency sailing with a skeleton crew. Tanya couldn't smell bacon – nor detect the welcoming aroma of coffee, come to that. Half a dozen people were dotted among the thirty or so tables. Talk about silence. This could be a library or a church. The few breakfasters nibbled at toast. Instead of coffee cups there were glasses of orange juice. Frankly, it was a miserable sight. Tanya had been in the mood to enjoy a breakfast that would bring a gleam to a truck driver's eye. On the walk from her cabin she'd imagined heaping golden-brown strips of bacon on to her plate. One good thing, though: there was no sign of Isis Malaika. What's more, in around ten hours from now they'd be docking. Then there would be the twenty-minute transfer by bus to the mining camp where she'd find Jack. They could make the most of the holiday, but there was an issue to resolve, too.

She headed for the self-service counter. Beyond the observation windows gray mist blanked out the world. There was no movement; the ferry must still be held back in a queue of vessels waiting to join their shipping lane. Pre-Christmas traffic must have made the Baltic routes exceptionally busy. Usually the engines were an ever-present bass sound, a muscular throb that pulsed up through the steelwork, but today she could not hear even them. Tanya cast a puzzled glance across the self-serve counter. No hot food, just trays of pastries stacked at random. She wrinkled her nose. So much for her bacon binge.

There were clean glasses beneath sheets of tissue paper, so she took one then found a juice dispenser. At that moment a door to the kitchen swung open. Instead of a member of serving staff she recognized the big, silver-haired man as one of the engineers who'd been poring over the blue print yesterday morning.

'We're going to be late with the pump. They've got to get this crate on the move. Now!' His steely blue eyes focused on her face; maybe he realized he'd mistaken her for one of the pump entourage. 'The galley staff were thin on the ground yesterday, now I can't find one.' He lifted a plate above the level of the counter so she could see. 'I heated a batch of beans myself. They're in the back there, if you want some?'

'I'll pass, thanks.'

'You sure? They're warm if nothing else.'

'I'll be fine with the pastry.'

'I'd have made coffee but all I could find were kegs of prune juice and, believe me, after that vodka last night that's one thing I don't need. Did you know they mix it up by the jug load with chilies and raw garlic?'

One subject pressed her more than the man's choice of cocktails. 'But where is everybody?'

He found a loaf of bread behind the counter, sniffed it, nodded then said, 'They're sailing with a skeleton crew. Last night there was barely any restaurant staff. But they still managed to hire a damn pianist.' He paused, maybe seeing concern in her expression. 'The waiters and the kitchen jocks will be sleeping off a hangover. That vodka is pure rocket fuel. See you around.' The man headed across to where a couple of his colleagues sat with the pump blueprint spread in front of them.

Tanya filled her glass with orange juice. The TV screen fixed on the wall showed a mass of gray with darker shapes beneath. She figured that must be a view from the bridge CCTV. The shapes must be raised parts of the deck. With the shipping lanes being so busy, perhaps the navigator didn't trust the radar to get them safely through this murk. She took her pastry and juice to one of the few tables that wasn't littered with dirty crocks. *Surely, the captain would be outraged to see his ship in such a filthy state? And if it's true that every ship has rats then how long before they scuttle out to enjoy the leftovers?* Tanya sat by herself to eat the pastry. In the vastness of the restaurant where hundreds normally dined she felt alone. Her muscles grew tense; she couldn't explain why the sensation gripped her the way it did, yet here she'd become such a lonesome soul. She'd never felt so vulnerable and exposed in her life.

Sixteen

Suzanne Lynch stared at her boyfriend. He lay face down on the floor in the center of the cell pod. Trickles of blood formed long lines on the red surface, which had been so painted to reduce the visual impact of such a spill.

She had slept soundly after a long evening of unadulterated joy. By ten a.m. she'd decided to find Turrock. He should have finished his shift a couple of hours before that. He'd promised to meet her at the cabin when his shift ended, then they could go up to the restaurant level for breakfast, leaving Fytton in charge. Turrock hadn't arrived. She'd waited some more; maybe one of his prisoners had tried to end it all before they arrived at the port. She knew these stateless murderers were en route to be dumped in some foreign jail. Even Turrock didn't know which country would play host, just that it would probably be a former Soviet state that needed Dollars, Sterling and Euros more than it needed human rights legislation. Just as whole stars vanished into cosmic holes, never to be seen again in this universe, so the ten convicts being transported on the compact onboard jail would vanish for ever.

Just minutes after ten that morning Suzanne Lynch had stepped out of the elevator on to the ferry's modified car deck to be greeted by the sign warning against trespass. But the gate was wide open. For Suzanne this had been as menacing as seeing the open jaws of a shark looming through the sea. With waves of hot and cold surging through her she had raced along the corridor into the cell pod, but had come to a dead stop. The force of what she saw rocked her back. For a moment

it seemed as if the heavens had fallen on her. She was so
shocked by what greeted her eyes she could barely stand.

There was her lover, lying with his eyes shut, motionless,
arms flung out. Blood streamed from his head across the floor.
The cell doors – every single one of them – were wide open,
revealing empty rooms. The cell TV screens carried a picture
of the ship's deck. Beyond that was fog and an ocean covered
with ice.

Suzanne blinked at the vacant cells. She knelt beside her
lover so she could cradle his bloody head in her arms.

Seventeen

Tanya made short work of her meager breakfast. She didn't
recognize anyone else in the restaurant, so it seemed
absurd to sit there amid a mass of empty tables. The ship
always hummed, either with people talking or the engines far
below decks, but this silence rubbed along her nerves in such
an unpleasant way that she couldn't keep still for long. She
headed to the mall. A browse of the magazines might dispel
her morbid mood. But when she got there she found that the
entire complement of mall units were closed, doors firmly
locked, shutters down. Christmas decorations sagged from the
ceiling like they'd died from a lack of seasonal spirit. There
were no people here at all.

Tanya walked faster. She passed through bars, lounges, the
coffee shop, casino, but didn't see a soul. The sense of oddness
about the place became a kind of mental itch. When she noticed
it first it didn't seem much, but now it grew more intrusive.
*Where is everybody? It's nearly eleven in the morning. Surely
not everyone's in their cabins with a hangover.* For the first
time she found herself thinking it wouldn't be so bad bumping
into Isis. The sense of isolation drove her outside on to the
open deck. Cold bit through her clothes like a set of ice teeth.
She grunted as her flesh shriveled before the onslaught of

Arctic chill. Shivering, she approached a guardrail. Fog buried everything from sight. A skin of ice had formed round the ship. Every so often a slight swell would deform it; then black water would well up through the fractures. The air smelled of stagnant ditch water, as the Baltic wasn't particularly saline. Rivers from Poland, Finland, Germany and Russia fed it with the muddy run-off from countless hills that would be shrouded in black forest. To stave off the unease that had stalked her all morning she walked quickly along the deck. Mist reduced visibility to a few paces. A figure moved in front of her.

'Good morning,' she began. 'Awful fog, isn't . . .' A dark shape lumbered toward her, stifling the words in her throat. She stiffened; they were going to charge straight at her. Then before they emerged fully from the murk they loped off at a tangent. Moments later she heard the clatter of feet as they climbed steps to the top deck.

Probably crew, she reassured herself. *This weather is giving them problems.* By now her shoulders shook; the cold had even found its way into her teeth to make them ache. *Maybe this walk on deck isn't a good idea. All I need to do is slip on some ice and I'll wind up with a broken wrist.* The holidays didn't promise a lot of cheer at this moment; to spend them in the mining camp with a cast on her arm would be downright woeful. Behind her a door led into the ship. She took one more look over the guardrail to check if the mist had begun to thin. The surface of the ocean lay far beneath her. *A lovely way to end it all,* she told herself with a morbid grin. If the leap into icy water didn't finish you, freezing temperatures would dispatch you into the hereafter before you had time to drown.

Lifting her head, she stared into the wall of gray. Visibility couldn't be much more than a couple of hundred feet. Yet, just for a moment, she thought she saw a dark mass through the mist. A hulking great thing that didn't possess the regular geometry of another ship. Then it was gone, buried in the mist. *Of course it must have been a ship,* she reasoned. The irregular shape would be an effect of this murk. Tanya folded her arms tight against her body. Her face had grown numb. Her legs ached from sheer cold. *OK, you've had enough. Go indoors. Get warm before you catch pneumonia.* The instant she turned she saw another figure. It ghosted from the mist toward her, raising its arm as it did so.

'Tanya.'

'Isis?' Tanya made out the trademark headscarf.

'Come inside. I have bad news.'

'If it's about Philip—'

'No, not him.' She waited until Tanya drew closer. 'Listen. Don't speak until I've finished. I have to tell you something shocking.' She fixed her with grave, dark eyes. 'The crew have gone. We're alone on the ship.'

Eighteen

Naked as sin, she walked along the corridor. It seemed subterranean to her. This steel-lined passageway might, if she didn't know better, run deep into the earth. She understood she was aboard the ship, only the engines had stopped; an absolute silence engulfed this enclosed world.

She paused. Her body looked surreally white beneath the lights. A thing made of bone rather than skin. Even the bruises the guards inflicted didn't appear as dark mottling any more; they'd paled. She ran her fingertips over her bare stomach. The bruises tingled pleasantly to her. The guards couldn't understand why she hadn't screamed in pain when they beat her and poured bleach down her throat. But then they were as mystified as the men who'd punched her around in the past. She'd once looked up the word 'pain' in the dictionary. Its definition had been a mystery.

The ship had a stillness about it too. For some mysterious reason it had stopped dead. Even the waves had died because it did not rock. Her hands ran up her body, exploring it for more wounds. An indentation in one naked breast. A guard had become so excited he'd sunk his teeth into the soft flesh above one nipple. The wound had a fizzy sensation, like it would feel if you poured an effervescent liquid on to bare skin. Champagne perhaps. Standing straight she sucked in her stomach as she inhaled deeply.

So, this is freedom. Kind of freedom. Anyway, I'm not in the cell. But why did they let me out?

She licked her lips. They were roughened from bleach burns. No pain though; only a cooling sensation as if she'd been recently kissed. *Why aren't there people?* The last few hours had been an utter mystery. She'd woken in her cell to find it open. The other cell doors were open, too. The only other person in the vicinity had been a man lying on the floor unconscious, his head bleeding. Within seconds she'd found all the security gates were ajar. All she need do was stroll out of the jail area to the elevator. She'd taken that up one level; a sign warned that this was the crew's quarters only. Now she walked along a corridor with dozens of open cabin doors. Nobody occupied them. Bedding on some bunks had been ripped off. Blankets were strewn in doorways. A woman's sandal lay in the center of this corridor.

Where two corridors intersected she glanced to her left. Twenty paces away a hefty man stood in the corridor facing her. He wore the white paper coverall of a prisoner. For him nothing else mattered in the universe apart from what he ate. A sticky black mass occupied one hand. He devoured it with a dreamy expression of bliss. This individual she knew. He had a massive head, throat and torso. In comparison his arms and legs were small. His eyes bulged. Every so often he would blink very slowly as if hypnotized by the flavor of the treat he devoured. He might have seen her standing there, the light making her nude body shine. If he did, he didn't care. The chocolate cake occupied all his senses. This must be the Toad, a name she'd heard in the cell pod. He stood there without moving any part of his body other than hand, tongue and jaw. Cake was everything. The world beyond it, nothing.

The empty corridor stretched away. Coins lay scattered. A watch sat against the wall; its glass had shattered, the bracelet snapped. It glittered with a golden light. The next cabin boasted an occupant. A young man lay on the bunk with his head hanging over the edge. His throat had been carved open. His upside-down face regarded hers. She leaned forward to sniff it. Tobacco odors. He'd been a smoker.

In the next cabin she saw four bunks. On a rail hung four neat uniforms. Four crisp white blouses, four pleated tartan skirts, four matching tartan ties. On entering the cabin she

noticed her reflection in a wall mirror. Her nude body possessed
a fragile slimness; a slender reed of femininity. Her blonde
hair had become ruffled, something she detested. For a moment
its ugliness made her glare at it in absolute rage. Then she
noticed four toilet bags hanging on pegs. Each one contained
a hairbrush. For a while she tidied her hair with each brush
in turn. The one with steel bristles suited her best. Now she
smiled at her reflection – humanity flowed back into her.

I'm free, she thought. *I should explore.* Once more she
noticed her nudity. Then her eyes flicked back to the four
uniforms hanging smartly in a row.

Fytton sat in his cabin, the door locked. This turn of events
didn't frighten him. It was bad, of course. A disaster. There'd
be internal inquiries, demands for sackings, payments of
compensation. All that legal stuff. But he, himself, was exhil-
arated. How it happened he didn't know. The prisoners had
escaped. Boss was dead or as good as. Methodically, he
removed weapons from a steel locker, checked the loaded
magazines, and then tested the action of a machine gun
before adding a drop of oil to ease the movement. That done
he unplugged his digital camera from the mains, checked
the battery, then switched it from still mode to 'movie
capture'.

Fytton must do the right thing. Crisis management. That
entailed finding the prisoners, then killing every single one.
Today he would enjoy a good old-fashioned Quilp hunt. He'd
make a movie of it, too.

She finished brushing her short blonde hair then ran a mirror
check. White blouse, above-the-knee skirt, which was made
of the same tartan as the tie knotted loosely around her neck.
Four women must share the cabin; all the uniforms were
different sizes. The smallest, however, fitted her own petite
frame perfectly. From the cosmetics set out on the dressing
table she used foundation to conceal the scratches the guards
had inflicted two days ago. A bright red lipstick hid the bleach
burns on her lips. As she brushed specks of bedding fluff from
the blouse her fingers clipped a badge pinned just above her
breast. *Moonlit Bay Lounge* it said, and beneath that, stamped
in gold, *Maya.* The name pleased her.

A pair of hands seized her shoulders. As they dragged her backwards she glanced into the mirror. She half expected to see the webbed paws of the man she knew as the Toad. Only there was no white paper coverall cladding the arms. A pair of muscular hands covered in black tattoos emerged from beneath denim shirt cuffs. A moment later her attacker began to crush her throat. It didn't hurt, but then she never felt pain. A sensation of a warming hug oozed into her brain. A pleasant feeling; a good feeling. Even though she knew that in three minutes she'd be dead.

Isis insisted on walking in front of Tanya as they passed through the mall, its locked doors underscoring the fact that something had gone very wrong with the voyage

Isis cast phrases back over her shoulder as if Tanya was some lowly hired hand. 'These units never opened this morning . . . Notice the ship's engines aren't running . . . Lights might operate from battery power or a secondary power plant . . . We've entered the Baltic . . . There's no information about our position on the monitors. We need to rectify that . . .'

Tanya's exasperation notched up a level. 'Isis, wait. How can the crew have gone? Crews don't just *go* in the middle of the night.'

'Those on the *Volsparr* have.'

'That's impossible!'

'Impossible? People embark, disembark.'

'In port. Not in the middle of an ocean.'

'On the first night I heard a helicopter. When I asked the steward what was wrong he told me that one of the crew had fallen sick. They were airlifted to hospital from the deck.'

'Are you telling me the entire crew were spirited away by helicopter in the middle of the night?'

'No.'

'So they've all deserted?'

'No, no, no.' Isis sailed along the passageway with Tanya trailing. 'I'm not saying I know *how* the crew left; I'm saying it is a matter of verifiable fact that they *have* left.'

Tanya stopped as suddenly as if she'd hit a glass wall. 'The crew must number over a hundred. They've *all* gone?' Her voice rose. 'Isis, stand still, will you? Tell me how a hundred men and women vanish from a ship of this size?'

Isis breezed along the passageway. 'We must act. This could be the most dangerous day of our lives.'

'Isis? What on earth do you mean, 'Act?' *Isis*?'

Fear. Pain. Danger. Those trigger a flood of adrenaline through the body. The blonde woman now being strangled experienced neither pain, nor fear, nor sensed danger at an instinctive level. Instead, she knew intellectually that this man intended to kill her. It would take moments now; mere moments. Already a black fog crept inward from the periphery of her vision; it left her a dwindling view of the cabin bunk where three waitress uniforms hung in a row.

A big enough shot of adrenaline can lead to panic. That delivers so much disorientation that the victim of an attack dies because they are too confused to remain lucid and consider their options in a logical manner. With no adrenalin in her blood, her thoughts, for the moment, remained ordered. That state wouldn't last long. Oxygen starvation was mere heartbeats away. Her attacker would expect her either to fight or struggle to escape. So she decided to do what he least expected. Lightly, sensually, she ran her fingers up and down his back. She continued to stroke him; the fabric of his shirt was taut across muscle. During the attack he'd turned her to face him so he could expertly exert pressure on her carotid artery with his thumb.

A second figure appeared at the door to address her murderer. 'Make it snappy. We're ready for the next phase.'

'Give me five minutes,' snapped her attacker. 'Collect the others.'

The second man left, leaving her alone with the one who crushed her throat. She stroked his back again. Then her hand rubbed his thigh.

He stopped. 'You want to do a trade.' No smile, only an expression of hard determination. 'If I get enough of what I like I'll let you live.' He lifted the badge on her breast to read the name. 'Maya.'

She was under no illusions. *He'll use me, then kill me.* When he released his grip she kissed him on the lips. He returned the kiss. The next time she stretched up to meet his mouth she bit him on the lip.

'A live wire.' He bit her back on the top lip. She tasted blood.

Now he grinned. Her bite excited him. Breathing hard, he worked her breast with his thick fingers. The animal scent of his male sweat glands spiked her nostrils. Mid-thirties, she figured. Shaved head, stubbled jaw. Muscular. He must train hard. A no-nonsense expression. This could be a soldier on a mission, though he wore a blue shirt and jeans as if ready for a night out.

As he thrust his hands up her tartan skirt she noticed he'd laid a sub-machine gun on one of the bunks. He must have done that before he seized her. Unfortunately the gun lay beyond her reach. When he rubbed her sex she took the opportunity to stroke his back again. This time she felt the hilt of a knife slotted into a sheath on the belt.

He panted. 'You like this, eh? You damn well love it!'

Swiftly, he picked her up as if light as a doll, then set her on the lower bunk so he could take her there; already he'd unbuckled his belt.

'Blast.' The bunk above him bumped against his head. The ship bunks were hinged to save space. With one hand he slammed it upright, so it fitted flush and vertical with the steel wall. 'Now let's finish what we started, eh?'

He'd begun to unbutton his jeans when she struck. She eased out the knife from his belt sheath. With him lying above her she wouldn't be able to stab him through the chest or back. She simply wouldn't have the strength. Instead she waited until he closed his eyes in bliss as he pushed his loins against her. Then she jabbed the knife point into the underside of his jaw. The tip pierced the skin between jaw bone and Adam's apple. Even then it only entered by half an inch. She lacked the muscle power to drive it any further.

Instead of pushing she waited until he recoiled from the pain, and made to kneel up on the bunk so as to draw away from her. He was fast, powerful. His strength drew her up with him as she encircled his neck with one arm; with her free hand she slapped the lever that released the upper bunk. When the heavy steel frame dropped she gripped the hilt of the knife. She pushed upward hard as the bunk slammed on to her attacker's head. The concussion knocked his head downward; the knife blade went in deeper, a full two inches up the blade. Grunting, he rolled off the bunk to the floor. There he

lay on his back, stunned more by the audacity of her attack
than any significant injury.

She leapt up so she could stand on his chest. Using the two
upper bunks to steady her balance, as if they were a gymnast's
parallel bars, she used her body weight to keep him flat. But
he was strong. It wouldn't take much effort on his part to flip
her off as she stood there, her bare feet pressing down on his
ribs.

'You are dead.' The knife handle quivered as his throat
muscles shook it.

She lifted her left foot then placed the heel on the flattened
end of the hilt.

Now his eyes widened in shock. 'You wouldn't dare.'

Shifting her balance, she applied more of her body weight
to the foot that pressed down on the hilt, and in turn the blade
sank another half inch into his flesh.

He gritted his teeth. 'You win. Get out of here. I'll let you
live.'

She looked down into his eyes. 'What do you know?'

'You want information too?' He grimaced. 'So who are you,
really? You're not a little waitress . . .'

She pressed harder with her heel. 'What do you know?'
Her voice came as a burned whisper.

'What do I know? Hah . . .' Blood oozed through his lips.
The tip of the blade had punctured the lining of his throat.

'What do you know?' Her whisper was relaxed, almost
conversational.

'I know everyone on this ship is dead. So if you want to
live, come with me.'

'What do you know?' she repeated.

'That's all I'm saying, you bitch.'

She applied more pressure with her foot to the knife's hilt.
A little deeper. He grunted. A tear ran from the corner of one
eye as he lay there on his back between the two bunks. A
figure appeared in the doorway. The Toad. Still dressed in his
white coverall he licked the remains of chocolate cake from
his fingers. With an expression of complete indifference he
regarded this odd couple for a moment. After sucking his
thumb clean of cream he moved away along the corridor. She
heard him sigh. Finishing the last of the cake must have been
a moment of deep sadness for him.

'*What do you know?*'

'OK, I'll fucking tell you.' Fear itself seemed to bleed from his eyes. 'This is what'll happen. Thirty-six hours from now, this ship will be gone. Not just to the bottom of the sea but *gone*. Vaporized. Got that? Now, I've told you everything.'

'Everything?' *But I want to know how the blade feels. I want you to describe the pain. What is agony? Why does it have the power to make people shout? I don't want to know about the ship. I'm not interested.* 'You've nothing else to tell me?'

'You know everything I know.'

She lifted her right foot from his chest so all her weight was transferred to the left. The knife blade slid smoothly into his throat, all the way to the handle. His eyes flared in horror; his spine arched as agony blazed through him.

As he lay dying in a lake of his own blood she checked herself in the mirror. It took a moment to straighten her uniform. There wasn't so much as a speck of the man's blood on her crisp white blouse. She liked what she saw. And she loved her name badge. Maya. A glance at the man told her that life had abandoned him. His brown eyes had already begun to grow dull. Smartly dressed, and with a new name, she left the cabin to find an elevator.

Nineteen

Isis headed to the Moonlit Bay Lounge. During the day it served as a café where passengers chatted over coffee and employees of Boson Eumericas held informal meetings. When Tanya followed Isis into the place that morning she saw engineers huddled round tables with blueprints of the pump. Their faces had adopted universal expressions of concern. They were worried about getting the pump to the island in time.

Isis shot Tanya a hard glance. 'They haven't realized yet, the fools.'

'Isis, you don't know for a fact that the crew have left the ship.'

'Normally the bar staff would be here to serve coffee. Where are they? Why haven't there been any announcements over the PA? Do you hear the engines?'

'There's fog. Obviously, the weather forced them to—'

'See any crew? Any stewards?'

Her eyes raked the bar area. The place could accommodate a couple of hundred people. This morning there were a couple of dozen at most, mainly technicians.

Isis marched across to the grand piano, pulled back the velvet cover, flipped the lid, then smashed her fist down on to the center keys. Everyone flinched at the clang of discordant notes.

'Now I have everyone's attention,' Isis began, 'has anyone noticed that the crew have abandoned ship?'

The silver-haired engineer Tanya had spoken with earlier smiled to his colleagues first as if to say, *Just what we need, a hysterical woman.* Clearing his throat, he addressed not only Isis but everyone in the bar. 'The *Volsparr*'s operating with a skeleton crew. This is an emergency sailing. You can't expect the same level of service at a time like this.'

'Take a look round.' Isis spoke coldly. 'Have you seen any crew today? The ship is drifting without power.'

'That's nonsense, young lady.' The gray-haired man spoke as if Isis was simple. 'Where would the crew go? We're as frustrated by the delay as you are but have you seen the fog? Visibility's near zero. The entrance to the Baltic is busy with other shipping. Clearly they're—'

Isis slammed the piano keys again, an explosion of notes.

'Young lady, that's an expensive musical instrument; I wouldn't keep—'

'Listen. The crew have gone. I don't know how or where . . .' Her eyes raked the assembled people. 'But don't you understand? We are in danger. We are adrift in treacherous waters. Other ships might collide with us. We could be beached.'

The boy with the toy dart gun was standing in the lounge with his mother. 'Is the lady saying we're gonna die?'

This triggered the mother into action. 'Look here, whoever you are. You're scaring my son. I suggest you speak to the captain. You've got yourself into a panic, and—'

'Do I look panicked?' Isis spoke evenly, controlling every syllable with icy calm. 'We must search the ship to confirm that there are no members of crew left. If they have vanished we need to send a distress call from the bridge.'

The mother of Billy advanced on Isis. 'Stop that right now. I don't know if you're saying all this to make yourself feel important but you're being foolish. And you're frightening my son.'

Billy fired the gun at Isis. The orange dart bounced off her chest. With a slash of her hand she grabbed the pistol and flung it to the far side of the bar. 'This isn't the time for toys.'

'Hey!'

The mother started forward. Isis shoved the woman so hard she bounced down on to one of the sofas. 'Sit there. Listen to me.' She grabbed Billy and shoved him into his mother's arms as she sat there, stunned by the violence of Isis's action. The other passengers began to protest.

'My name is Isis Malaika.' Isis spoke over the chorus of criticism, her voice clear as a bell. 'Don't you get it? We are in danger. You're too blind to see it.'

The silver-haired engineer shot his colleagues a meaningful glance. 'You've got yourself all upset. We'll take you some-where quiet. You can rest, gather your thoughts.' He nodded to a couple of men. 'John, Eric. Lend a hand, won't you?'

Tanya had taken an instant dislike to Isis, but now she found herself coming to the woman's defense. 'My name is Tanya Rhone. I don't know about being in danger, but we should hear Isis out.'

One of the technicians laughed. 'Very noble to side with your friend but clearly she's talking crap. We're at sea, for God's sake; the crew couldn't just stroll off in the middle of the night.'

'They might not have strolled.' Darkness filled Isis's voice. 'They might have been thrown.'

'You mean piracy?'

The mood changed as another man laughed. 'Yo-ho-ho and a bottle of rum.' He called to the gray-haired guy. 'Listen to that, Gus. Pirates made the crew walk the plank.'

Adopting a pack mentality, passengers fell in behind Gus, who'd assumed authority.

A moment later Isis slammed her hand on the piano keys again. This time the passengers didn't fall silent.

Isis pounded again. 'Listen.'

They didn't listen. Gus told her to calm down, that he would take her for a little stroll. Somewhere quiet, to get things in perspective. No more scaremongering. Isis replied by bashing the keys with both hands.

Philip appeared at the bar. He stared with horror at his piano being abused. 'Excuse me, madam. Passengers aren't allowed to play the piano. The tuning is very sensitive . . .'

Tanya took the moment to check Philip's expression. Clearly, he hadn't recognized Isis. Did that mean Isis's claim that he'd drugged her and then raped her was a fabrication? At that instant he was simply wracked with woe over the abuse of his musical instrument. Meanwhile, the men took hold of Isis by her arms. Gus spoke in what he believed to be a calming way. Billy had dashed away to find his dart gun. The mother wagged her finger in Isis's face as she vented anger. The din of people shouting grew louder and louder until even Billy put his hands over his ears.

Tanya herself winced as the hullabaloo assaulted her ears. It echoed around the lounge until she craved to run out on to the deck where there would be only cold stillness. The clamor made her nauseous. There was an undercurrent of violence in the way the men dragged Isis away. Meanwhile, Philip had reached the piano and went through each note in turn, a strained look on his face as he checked whether the assault on his instrument had knocked the strings out of tune.

Then suddenly the din began to fade. The shouting eased. Billy stood still as granite with his mouth open. Philip even stopped testing his precious piano. He turned to stare at something behind Tanya.

The others stared in the same direction. They neither moved nor made a sound. Whatever it was that caught their attention gripped them to the point of shocked fascination. Even as Tanya turned to look behind her a flood of icy shivers cascaded down her spine. Isis's expression was the worst. All too vividly it said: *I told you so.*

Standing there beside the Christmas tree, a figure stared at the passengers in the bar. Tanya saw that the woman, who'd appeared with phantom-like silence, was tall and lean. Her jeans and shirt were drenched in blood. More blood covered her hands. One side of her face had been smeared in the stuff, a sticky, red-brown mess.

The sudden quiet almost hurt Tanya's ears as much as the shouting of just a moment ago.

For a while the woman stood there; it seemed as if she desperately wanted to convey some important message but for the life of her she couldn't get the words out. Then the emotional barrier collapsed, and she voiced the words that must have burned inside of her. 'The guard's been attacked . . . God help us. They've all got out!'

Twenty

The blonde woman moved along the corridor of the apparently deserted deck that housed the crew's quarters. So far, there were two corpses. Of course, that left the man who'd told her attacker to hurry. He'd intimated there were more of them. The situation appeared odd – the killers, the lack of crew – but it didn't intimidate her. Her whole life had been spent out of step with the world. This wasn't really any different.

'Hello. I know you, don't I?'

She looked through an open cabin door to see the man who'd spoken lacing a pair of black leather shoes. He wore a jersey with blue and white hoops. With that he'd chosen cream-colored cargo pants. When he stood up to test the comfort of the shoes she noticed the white paper coverall lying on the bunk. *One of us.*

'My name's Sami.' He smiled, then nodded at the shoes. 'Good fit.' He gave her an appraising look. 'You've got really nice eyelashes.'

She glanced along the corridor. Halfway along it was an elevator. Sami followed her gaze.

'You're planning to explore?' When she didn't answer he

smiled. 'Me too. I don't know what we'll find. I woke up to
find the cell door open. The guard lay flat out. Blood every-
where.' When he stepped out into the corridor he examined
her face more closely. 'Astounding eyelashes. Really amazing.
I saw you when they brought you into the holding bay at the
dock.' His expression became sympathetic. 'I heard them
hurting you, too. Did they beat you because they were bored?
The guards do that a lot. If you ask me, most of them should
be behind bars, not us. I mean, what did I do? I discovered
something that could help the world. I cured myself of malaria.
I wanted to share the cure with everyone, but the pharmaceutical industry has friends in the government, and they run
the judiciary. See where I'm going with this? They framed
me because I've discovered a way to cure disease without
pumping chemicals into your body.' He paused. 'You do speak
English, don't you?'

She didn't reply. Instead she shot glances along the corridor.
*Where's the other man? He had a gun as well. It might not
be safe to stay here.*

'I'm Sami.' He repeated the name, perhaps thinking she
hadn't heard first time round. 'What's your name?'

She remembered the badge on her blouse. 'Maya.'

'So you do speak English?' He shrugged. 'I guess wher-
ever we're being shipped English won't be of much use. I'm
sorry they hurt you. Are you in pain?'

Maya – yes, she'd stick with that name – shook her head.

'Are you sure? I noticed some painkillers back there.'

'I'm not feeling any pain,' she told him truthfully.

He held out his hand. 'Sami Voss; pleased to meet you, Maya.'

She stared at the hand for a moment then shook it. At that
moment came a series of muffled snaps. They sounded faint
yet she sensed the threat in the sound.

Sami knew. 'Gunfire,' he told her. 'I grew up hearing
shooting. Every time I heard it I knew people were dying.'

'The elevator.' She nodded toward the steel doors twenty
paces away.

'Good idea, Maya. After you.'

The gunfire sounded again; this time much closer.

'Hiyo, Quilp!' Fytton sighed the words as he moved along
the corridor. He'd taken the service ladder up from the deck

that hosted the cells to the crew's accommodation deck. Now he realized the problem was far bigger than he imagined. Not only had the cell doors been opened to release the prisoners and his boss been clubbed, but the cabins here had the appearance of being abandoned at breakneck speed. Shoes dotted the corridor, bedding torn from bunks, money lay scattered in a bathroom. Then there was the dead guy with the knife rammed into his throat. *So where's the crew? Where are the prisoners?*

Fytton nosed into another cabin. Chef's whites hung from a peg. The mirror revealed him as the hunter once more. The reflection brought a grin to Fytton's scarred face. This is how it should be. No longer a butt wipe for psycho prisoners, but the hero again. There he was, a sub-machine gun in one hand. In the other he carried his camera. He could film the kills he made, then upload them to the Quilp site that was a Choir-Moore staff favorite.

'Hiyo, Quilp.' At the end of the corridor he saw the Toad. He stood there simply watching in a disinterested way as Fytton emerged from the cabin. At thirty paces this would be an easy kill with the machine gun, even one-handed as he held the camera in the other. The Toad, however, stepped back along another branch of the corridor. 'Come back, Toad. You need to go back to da cell.'

The Toad wasn't falling for it. Oh well, it wouldn't be a proper hunt if the quarry didn't try to escape. He moved quickly along the corridor. Then he paused. In a cabin to his right a balding man sat on a bunk. He wore the regulation paper coverall unzipped to his waist to reveal thick chest hair.

The man looked up at Fytton with large gray eyes. 'I want to give myself up,' he said in Hispanic tones. 'I won't fight.'

'If that's what you want,' Fytton told him. He thumbed the record button on the camera. On its display screen he saw a miniature image of the prisoner.

The prisoner appeared troubled. 'It's not safe.'

'It isn't, you're right,' Fytton agreed. He raised the muzzle of the gun.

'There's been a big fight on the ship. The crew have gone.' A tear rolled down the man's cheek. 'And I want to live. I so much want to live.'

'I know,' Fytton sympathized. When he'd centered the man on the camera screen he shot him through the face. One round would have killed him stone dead. Those six bullets tore his head to pieces.

By the time the woman had been taken to a sofa in the lounge the two men had let go of Isis. People gawped at the blood-stained figure.

A guy of around twenty-five who'd been with Gus's group now gestured, utterly baffled. 'First that woman,' he nodded at Isis, 'tells us the crew have deserted the ship. Now this one is saying that a bunch of prisoners have escaped. What prisoners? There are no prisoners.'

Gus ran his fingers through his silver hair. 'They do say that hysteria is contagious.'

The blood-stained woman clenched her fists. 'I'm not—'

'Miss, you are on the *Volsparr*. It belongs to the mining company Boson Eumericas. We're shipping a pump to Russia. We don't carry prisoners.'

The woman tried again. 'Listen, my name is Suzanne Lynch. I know perfectly well what the *Volsparr* carries. I work in the port's shipping office. This vessel—'

'It's a ferry, not a prison hulk. Don't be—'

'Hey! For God's sake let the woman speak!' Isis blasted the words at Gus with enough force to make him flinch. 'She knows *something*. You know *nothing*! Use your eyes. Blood! Proof there is trouble!' Her accent grew stronger the angrier she became. 'Give her a moment to speak, then act. You might save your lives.'

Tanya realized the final statement found its mark. The twenty or so people assembled there no longer appeared so sure of themselves. Tanya took advantage of the lull by saying gently, 'Go on, Suzanne. Nobody will interrupt.'

Suzanne took a deep breath. 'I decided to make this voyage at the last minute because my boyfriend is the chief guard. This is his blood. I've left him in a cabin. I don't know if he's still alive.' Her calm voice became a hypnotic litany of matter-of-fact statements. Tanya wondered if she'd have even a shred of the woman's equilibrium if the same happened to her. 'There's a complex of ten prison cells on a converted car deck four levels below this one. The *Volsparr* sailed from

England with ten prisoners. During the night my boyfriend was attacked: the cell doors were opened. All the cells are empty. The prisoners are free.'

'Unless they left with the crew.' Isis frowned.

Suzanne's eyes widened. 'Pardon? The crew have left? How?'

'It's connected,' Isis announced. 'The crew vanish, now this.'

Gus gave a deep sigh. 'Personally, I think this is a hoax. The *Volsparr* serves a mine in the Baltic. It doesn't export convicts to Russia.'

Another man spoke up. 'If there were prisoners on board, I'd know. I'm the cargo manager.'

Suzanne stared at him. 'Nobody knows. Only the guards on the ship and senior members of crew. And executives at Boson Eumericas, of course. The company charges plenty to carry them.'

Isis said, 'We should find the prisoners.'

Suzanne grimaced. 'You might not want to do that.'

'Why?' Gus asked in his slow, gravelly voice. 'They could be trouble.'

'Exactly, they're big trouble. Between them they've killed more people than are in this room.'

The passengers exchanged uneasy glances.

'But prisoners?' Gus doubted. 'On this ship?'

'In America it costs thirty thousand dollars a year to keep a maximum security prisoner in jail. If they have prisoners who are stateless, or can't be identified, it's cheaper to ship them overseas and let someone else keep them under lock and key.'

'You mean Russia?'

'Russia's only one stage of the journey. My guess is the prisoners are shipped to former Soviet states in the south.' She grimaced again. 'There you'll get more bang-up for your buck.'

'OK.' Gus rubbed his jaw. 'I'll buy it. We need to alert the crew—'

'Don't you hear? There are no crew left on board.' Isis looked as if she could spit with rage.

Gus took it in his stride. 'In the unlikely event that the crew have gone, we need to muster all our people. Suzanne, can you call on the other guards? We'll help them round up the prisoners.'

Suzanne swallowed. 'There is only one other guard. He's vanished.'

This information sparked anxious whispering. Billy's mother screeched, 'You mean there's a bunch of killers running around the ship? And no one to catch them?'

'Yes. Exactly that.' Suzanne began to shiver.

Isis digested the statement. 'Then we must capture them ourselves. You'll help us.'

'I'd try . . . Only there's a big problem.' Suzanne's expression grew even more unhappy. 'Nobody knows what the prisoners look like. They might be mingling with the passengers already.' She stared at Isis. 'For all we know you might be one of them.'

On the deck that contained the crew's quarters Sami reacted to the snap of gunfire.

'Maya, that's a lot closer. We need to get away from here.' Sami stabbed the elevator call button. A green arrow pointing upward told them it wasn't heading in their direction yet. He gave the woman in the waitress uniform a grim smile.

Sami could tell a lot from the sound of gunfire. He could tell direction, type of weapon, and distance. Where he grew up lives depended on such knowledge. On a ship like this, with steel bulkheads and thick floors, a gun shot would have to be very close to be heard at all.

He hit the call button again. 'Please. We need you, elevator. Come quickly.'

Fytton reached a T-junction in the corridors. To his right a corridor led to more cabins. To his left, twenty yards away, a man and a woman stood at the elevator doors. The man in the striped jersey wasn't familiar. The blonde woman was, even though she was no longer naked.

'Hiyo, Quilp.' He stepped out so they could see him.

The man froze when he saw Fytton with the machine gun. The woman appeared bizarrely nonchalant.

'Come here,' Fytton ordered. 'Time to go to your cells.'

By way of reply the man pressed the elevator button.

'OK. I warned you.' In one hand he held the pistol grip of the lightweight machine gun; in the other hand he held his camera. He pointed both at the couple; the red spot on the camera's screen told him it was recording. Perfect.

The man slammed his hand into the elevator door in frustration.

Fytton murmured, 'Three, two, one, f—'

A figure stepped out from the junction of another corridor beyond the pair at the elevator, blocking Fytton's line of fire

There was something about the man who'd suddenly appeared. He wore a pale blue shirt and jeans. Fytton didn't have to see what he drew from his belt. Experience told him that was the body language of a man with a gun. A second later he saw the black automatic in the man's hand. He didn't seem particularly interested in Fytton's escaped prisoners. Instead he raised the gun to aim it directly at Fytton.

The elevator still hadn't arrived. The blonde woman saw that two men with guns faced each other. Despite being such a fragile build she grabbed her companion then hauled him out of danger, both disappearing into a cabin opposite the elevator. Calmly, the man fired. Fytton ducked back into the other corridor. A dimple appeared in the steel wall where the handgun's bullet had struck it. Fytton knew a professional when he saw one, and decided to display his expertise too. When he looked round the corner into the main corridor he did so at a low crouch. Simultaneously, he thrust the muzzle of the machine gun outward. The man in blue spotted Fytton's superior weaponry and darted back out of sight.

'Here's proof I mean business,' Fytton muttered. Before his opponent could even think about loosing off another shot, Fytton emptied the entire magazine of fifteen rounds into the wall at the end of the corridor, just feet from where the guy must be hiding himself. *Hey, I might get lucky with a ricochet.* Bullets slammed into the steel wall, leaving pockmarks that smoldered with the heat of the rounds. Fytton ducked back to where he'd be safe to replace the ammo magazine. When he risked looking again he saw the two prisoners run across the corridor and into the waiting elevator.

Before he could snap off a shot the doors had closed. A green arrow showed the elevator had begun its ascent.

Fytton's scarred face formed such a delighted smile that it revealed his big yellow teeth. The Quilp hunt had just got interesting.

FOURTH TRACT

Twenty-One

The elevator hummed. Maya hadn't seen such trappings of comfort in years. Her world had been strictly utilitarian. Concrete floors, walls made of concrete blocks, a lot of dull gray steel bars, doors and off-white handrails that swooped up and down stairs built of yet more concrete. The only color in the maximum-security jail had emanated from TV screens. Now this elevator had become a little canister of luxury. It boasted a plush tartan carpet that shared the same pattern as her tartan skirt. Its walls were covered in soft red leather. This elevator even smelled nice.

Sami listened as they ascended. 'Shooting,' he announced. 'Someone's fighting a war down there.'

'They let us leave the cells.'

'Yeah, but why?' He pulled a grim smile. 'There's never a free lunch. They opened the cell doors for a reason. And it wasn't unconditional love.' His nostrils flared as he considered. 'It could be pirates. That's what the ship owners claim anyway. That pirates board at night, overpower the crew then take the ship and rename it. Of course, they collude with the ship owners. The owners get the insurance pay-out and a share of the sale price. It happens all the time . . . Maya? Do you feel any movement?'

'No.'

'There's no engine sound, either. If we're moored in a port we'll leave the ship.'

'What will you do then?' she asked.

He smiled. 'I'm going to continue my work. Only this time somewhere where the pharmaceutical industry can't victimize me.' The elevator slowed. 'OK, this is our stop. If you see guys with guns, *run.*'

*   *   *

Ten prisoners had boarded the ship. Fytton had killed one so far. Now for the final nine. For the first time in months he felt alive. His blood powered through his veins. The fittings on the ship were somehow brighter, more vibrant; his senses were suddenly attuned to every scent, image, sound; even the touch of the air on his face had become more real. How he'd missed front-line action! A stupid accident with a grenade had left him with few choices. The best option had been guarding prisoners. *It turned me into a zombie.* But now his boss lay dead – or as good as. Everyone's safety on the ship depended on him hunting the prisoners. Nobody would grumble about their deaths. Fytton would have the satisfaction of gunning the psychos down. *I'll be a hero.* Of course, there were complications. The escaped prisoners had several hours' start. They couldn't, however, escape the ship. When Fytton glanced out of a porthole he saw ice on the water. None of the prisoners would try swimming for freedom in those conditions. However, if they'd reached the crew's accommodation deck then they'd be able to change into ordinary clothes. It would be difficult to differentiate them from the other passengers. Apart from the Toad, and the naked blonde, he'd not even bothered to look at the faces of the other prisoners. They'd been non-descript bodies in cells when he'd glanced at the CCTV earlier.

'Hiyo,' he breathed. The Toad crossed the corridor ahead of him. With luck, he could increase his kills to two. Once he'd blasted this one right in his toady eyes he'd move to the upper decks to find the pair that had just evaded him.

In the lounge Gus Hammond, the engineer with the abundant silver hair, was taking charge. He was apparently the chief engineer in charge of installing the mine pump, and his team of technicians and assistants already accepted his role as leader without question.

Isis fumed. 'Cell phones won't work so far out to sea. We must break into the bridge. Then we can use the radio to make a distress call.'

'You're running before you've learnt to walk, miss.' Gus shook his head. 'Instead of breaking in anywhere we need to ascertain if the crew have left the ship.'

'Of course they have, you fool.'

'Hysterics won't help, either.'

'I'm not hysterical.' Isis kept her cool, although her eyes blazed with anger. 'I'm trying to make you understand that we are in danger – imminent danger. We have to act now!'

The blood-stained woman jumped to her feet.

'Suzanne.' Gus spoke with calm authority. 'Please sit down. You've had a shock—'

'Blast the shock. I don't know if my boyfriend is alive or dead. I'm going back to him.'

'You can't go alone. The prisoners—'

'I know all about the prisoners,' Suzanne snapped. 'If my boyfriend's still alive he'll need help and all you do is talk.'

Isis sniffed. 'Hear, hear.'

'We do this properly – that means calmly, sensibly. OK?' Gus held up a finger; his blue eyes scanned the twenty people, challenging them to disagree. 'A man has been hurt. We need to find medical help.'

A woman came forward. 'I've trained in first aid.'

'Thank you, ma'am.' Gus nodded. 'I'll make a mental note of that but we need to follow protocol and call the ship's doctor. You don't want to be on the wrong end of a lawsuit if . . .' He noticed that Suzanne listened intently so he abandoned the sentence with a shrug. 'I'll take a look-see with a couple of my people. The rest stay here.' He indicated a middle-aged man in a leather jacket. 'That's Jerry Lopez. He's in charge until I get back with the doctor.'

'You'll find no doctor,' Isis uttered, monotone. 'You'll find no crew. But will you ever listen to me?' She shrugged. Nevertheless, she walked alongside Gus and his two assistants as they crossed the lounge.

'All right,' Gus rumbled. 'You can come, too. Once you see the bridge is manned it'll put your mind at ease.'

'I don't need your permission to go with you.' Isis glanced back. 'Tanya, come with me. I don't want us to be separated until we are safe.'

'Welcome to the search party, Tanya.' Gus didn't restrain his patronizing tone. 'The bridge is located on the deck above this one. Everyone stick close.'

When they left the lounge a set of stairs took them up to the next deck. There they found a line of offices, all empty of personnel.

Gus noticed Isis's expression. 'The *Volsparr*'s running with a skeleton crew. These haven't been manned since we left port.'

Another door was marked: 'Surgery – Doctor Ntabbi'. Gus tried it. 'Locked. We'll go straight to the bridge. That's manned twenty-four hours a day. Relax, everything's going to be fine.'

Twenty-Two

S ami and Maya stepped out of the elevator. The sight that met their eyes made Sami instinctively reach for the blonde woman's hand. She looked into his eyes as she gave his hand an answering squeeze of reassurance.

Before them stretched a small, onboard mall. Sami hadn't seen a hairdresser's or coffee bar or grocery store in more than five years. For half a decade his life had been confined to a narrow cell, concrete hallways and an exercise yard hemmed in by thirty-foot walls. Now, Christmas decorations dangled from the ceiling. There were gambling slot machines along one section of wall.

'That's a pity,' he breathed as he hung on to the security of Maya's hand. 'The stores are shut. I'd have loved to pick up a newspaper again.'

Maya stared through the observation window. 'Fog . . . Ice . . .' Maybe she'd been in solitary for so long she'd lost the speech habit. Then again, it might have been her way. Sami didn't mind. In the last few minutes he'd grown fond of the woman.

'So we're still at sea. I hoped we'd be in port. If I can only get away I know I'd be able to start my work again. Millions of lives could be saved. It's all so simple but all those busy-bodies refuse to listen. They *daren't* listen. Because what I can teach them would rip their world apart . . .' He breathed deeply.

'What is your work?'

'You really want to know?'

She nodded.

A young woman walked along the mall with her arm around

a little girl's shoulders. The woman's face was drawn; her eyes anxiously scanned the deserted mall. For a moment she appeared ready to speak to Sami and Maya but her nerve deserted her. Sami recognized her timidity. It held her captive just as much as the prison had confined him. He tried to reassure her with a smile but she turned back the way she'd come. The mall made Sami feel vulnerable, too. A guard might appear at any moment.

'We should find somewhere quiet. We're exposed here.' Although he heard voices coming from some way off he didn't see any other passengers. 'Looks like a good omen.' He indicated the door to the ship's cinema. A board announced:

SHOWING THIS VOYAGE: *IT'S A WONDERFUL LIFE.*

Sami held the door open for Maya to enter the cinema. Velvet drapes covered the screen. He liked the theater's coziness, the deep purple walls, the carpets. The room accommodated around fifty seats in rows of ten. He and Maya settled into the front row where he told her his story.

In every life there's a moment of revelation that shapes all your actions and dreams thereafter. For him it was Gordon. When he was eleven years old the schoolteacher had sat Gordon next to Sami in class. Everybody hated Gordon. He couldn't run properly. For some reason he kept his knees locked when he moved. It made his legs as stiff as chopsticks, and he could only run extremely slowly. Gordon wasn't very bright either. When the teacher asked Gordon a question he'd begin the answer with a long series of 'Ah . . . hooms'. This irritated the other kids. One punched Gordon as he sat beside Sami. The sound of flesh breaking before the force of the blow made Sami want to be sick. Violence disgusted him. Yet he wasn't powerful enough to tackle the bully. Instead, Sami set out to find a remedy for Gordon's peculiar gait.

Sami coached Gordon after school. In the park he'd tell Gordon to run, then he'd call out, 'Bend your legs, Gordon. Bend your legs!'

It worked. Sami still got warm feelings at the memory of Gordon's eyes shining with delight as he ran, this time at a fair old speed, his knees bending like they ought to. Gordon didn't become the most popular boy in school, and he didn't win any races, but he rarely came last, either. Gordon's confidence grew. His grades improved. He made other friends. Within a few weeks the kids had stopped picking on him.

I'm a healer, Sami told himself. The lesson he learnt reinforced an instinct that his remedies wouldn't follow traditional medical routes.

How it happened he still didn't really know. In his early twenties he spent months in a kind of coma of the mind. He still held down work at the factory, and the regular day-to-day stuff of washing, shaving and running his home worked out all right. Only he didn't connect with the world as he'd done in the past. At the time it didn't bother him; he just got on with life. But now he recognized the problem. His body worked, but his mind sort of froze up – simple as that. In childhood he'd contracted malaria in Central America. Every six months or so he'd be struck down by a flare-up of fever. Then he'd have to spend forty-eight hours in bed, sweating from every pore, his energy zero. When his body shivered his teeth would snap together so hard he'd draw blood from his tongue. The malaria, he decided later, brought on the mind coma. He was sure of it. Somehow through this he began abducting people. Always he chose young men and women. They needed to have the right kind of look. Sami picked the ones with gentle voices, who tended to be shy, even timid. He'd follow them, listen to their cell phone conversations. Meticulously, he cultivated a relationship – a one-sided one, of course – and they never knew he existed at all.

During the mind coma he worked on autopilot to convert a room in a deserted farmhouse way out in the woods. Every few months he donned a black cotton bag with eye-holes that covered his head and face. Then he put the chosen man or woman into the back of his truck. He never used violence but he was forced to pretend to threaten violence. For a week he kept them locked in the farmhouse. He took pains to provide food, drink, a radio, books. He even spent good money installing a gas heater.

Then came the next revelation. Sami found it difficult to put into words – he was still working on the mechanics of it – but he found he could milk his captives of energy. That's the term he always found himself using. *I'm going to milk you today. I won't hurt you. Don't be frightened.* He secured his special guest venue with a steel gate. This allowed him to sit on a stool outside the locked room and talk to his chosen man or woman inside. Through the eye-holes in his hood he'd watch their eyes. They said they were certain he would kill them. Their eyes would become huge disks that radiated fear. Sami would reassure them. The hope that shone in those eyes became the milk of human energy that warmed him from head to toe.

Soon he realized that the outbreaks of malaria fever had gone. He'd cured himself. He now filmed his discussions with his captives, carefully making notes. Once the week was up a tired emptiness filled his guest's eyes. 'All milked out,' he'd tell himself. They'd nothing left to give. Keeping them any longer would be futile.

So he released them. The process was simple. He hooded them with a pillow case then drove them to the suburbs where he'd quietly drop them off. He'd taped the pillow case around their necks so it would take them a few minutes to get their head free. By that time he was long gone. Nobody was hurt. Sami could continue his work, which filled him with so much joy. The mind coma evaporated. He was so excited at the prospect of helping humanity cure itself of so many lethal illnesses. All he needed to do was identify the milked energy. The milk of human kindness, a warming plasma that infused every fiber of one's body with the power to heal.

Then came his big mistake. To amplify the process he took two people in one day. A man and a woman. Hooding them as they walked home on a winter's night, then bundling them into the truck and taking them to the remote farm had been straightforward. He left them locked in the room with plenty of food. The gas fire kept them comfortable. However, he'd only kept single captives before. These two colluded. They didn't cooperate when he tried to chat through the gate to the room. If they weren't ignoring him they became aggressive as their initial timidity evaporated.

Sami persisted, hoping for a breakthrough. In the end it led to more of a breakdown than a breakthrough. Their constant demands to be released were tiresome. Sami made stupid mistakes. He'd park the car in bushes where it couldn't be seen from the road. Only he'd forget the groceries then have to tramp through the winter rain to the car, then all the way back to the farmhouse. He scraped the skin from his knuckles trying to shut the pantry where he stored the food. When he got ready to lock up the farmhouse he realized he'd mislaid the padlock key. It took two hours to find it. All the time the pair in the room nagged. The rain fell harder, turning the dirt track into a swamp. Sami had to push the car before he could drive it.

He found that when he tried to form that all-important relationship with the pair, which would allow them to express their 'milk', that healing plasma, he failed miserably. Then fever flared as the malaria returned. That night he'd been forced to stay in a motel. He was too sick even to drive back to the farmhouse.

What those two in the locked room did he didn't exactly know. He figured they'd somehow tried to find a way out through the big chimney. In doing so they'd broken the gas fire. The next day some hunters had followed a wounded stag. By chance it led them to the farm where they stumbled on a pair of bodies. The damaged gas fire had leaked carbon monoxide into the room. The man and woman lay dead by the window where they'd been trying to lever off the bars with a table leg.

Police descended. They took casts of footprints, tire tracks. A grocery bag that Sami had forgotten to dump elsewhere contained a receipt which pinpointed time and place of purchases to a mini-mart. CCTV recordings did the rest.

Within twelve hours Sami had been deprived of his liberty and his life's work. Only now, five years later, had he regained freedom.

'I never intended to hurt those two people,' he told Maya. 'They did it to themselves when they bust the gas fire. It leaked poison fumes into the room.' He began to pace the front of the cinema. 'Even though it was an accident, even though I had every intention of releasing the pair, just as I'd released all the others without harming them, the prosecutor insisted I'd planned to kill them.' He ran his fingers through his hair as indignation took hold. 'Of course, they pinned the deaths on me as murder. The judiciary is in cahoots with the pharmaceutical industry. They want to keep selling expensive drugs. And they jailed me to silence me. Now they've declared me a non-national, like you, and they're shipping us to an overseas jail that will be nothing more than a trash can.' His body shook at the injustice. 'You see, Maya, money is truly the root of all evil. Big industry bosses want to stay rich, so even though they can make oil from coal the petro-chemical industry pretends that the techniques have been lost since World War Two. Now I discover that the secret of healing lies inside us. So what do they do? They sneer at me. I'm treated like a criminal. The trial lawyer told me my research was garbage. Even my defense lawyer insisted that I suffered from delusion.' Anguished, Sami dropped into one of the cinema seats where he buried his face in his hands. 'All I want to do is help people.'

Maya rested her hand on his shoulder. 'I understand.'

'Really?' He wiped his eyes. 'Will you help me in my work?'

Her mouth tightened into an odd, broken smile. 'Sami, I *will* help. Maybe we can make a start now?'

Twenty-Three

'This can't be right.' Gus stared through the glass-panelled door to the bridge. It was locked, bolted, impenetrable, bullet-proof. 'This is most definitely not right,' murmured the gray-haired man.

Isis allowed herself a flash of triumph. 'Haven't I been telling you that?'

'But it's mandatory to keep personnel on the bridge when a vessel is at sea. This flies in the face of maritime law – not to mention common sense.'

One of Gus's assistants uttered the blindingly obvious. 'Then there really is no crew. If there's nobody on the bridge we're adrift. We could be hit by other ships.'

Isis groaned with frustration. 'Welcome to the real world. I told you we're in danger. We must radio for help.'

'There's an axe back there in a glass case. I'll get it.'

'Don't bother, John.' Gus slapped the steel door that formed the barrier between them and the bridge. 'This'd need dynamite to shift it.'

'Fetch the axe anyway.' Tanya shivered. 'Those prisoners, remember?'

Gus appeared troubled. 'We should find weapons. From what the woman said those people from the lock-up were killers.'

Isis added, 'Suzanne also pointed out another problem. How do we recognize them? They won't be shackled to a ball and chain.'

'Prison uniforms,' suggested one of Gus's men.

Even Gus shrugged that suggestion away. 'If they're even remotely sensible they'll ditch prison wear for regular clothes.'

'What now?' Tanya asked. 'We can't just wait it out.'

Isis looked suspiciously pleased with herself. 'Tanya's right. What now, Gus?'

'Well . . .' He rubbed his smoothly shaved jaw. Answers now eluded him. Come to that, so did speech.

'I know little about ships.' Isis spoke confidently now she'd undermined Gus's authority. 'However, logic dictates that there'll be more than one radio transmitter. If there's one on the bridge, where's the back-up?'

Tanya spoke up. 'And don't the coastguards monitor shipping? If their radar shows we've stopped dead they'll send out someone to check.'

Gus tried to recover his status as self-appointed leader. 'They might know we're in trouble already. Only that damned fog . . .' He nodded at the all-engulfing gray. 'Weather conditions might force them to sit back for a while.'

'Not too long, I hope.' Isis gazed through the bullet-proof glass into the abandoned bridge where banks of illuminated monitors streamed information that would never be seen. 'The crew have gone. We've heard that violent convicts have escaped from their cells. Are you going to tell me, Gus, that it's all a coincidence?'

The man who'd taken the shot at Fytton was the same one who'd watched his comrade strangling Maya. He continued his thorough search of the crew's cabins. He'd half expected the prison guard to show. After all, the guard's sense of duty would dictate he search for the escaped convicts. The man recognized ex-military when he saw one. The guard with the scarred face handled the sub-machine gun well. In other circumstances he'd make an ideal recruit to the team. However, the guard had to be considered as the enemy. If the man saw the guard he'd kill him.

It was now past midday. He needed to rejoin his team, then pick up a dozen or so passengers. After all, it was part of the grand plan that the world would hear about the ship's fate. The *Volsparr* and its owner, Boson Eumericas, would become the bad news story of the week. TV across the globe would carry footage of its destruction. Some extremely nasty video clips of the carnage on the *Volsparr* would appear on the internet. School kids would share them with their friends via cell phones. The man could almost hear the kids' wicked chuckles already. He smiled.

Handgun drawn, he checked the cabins again. Bootman had taken too long over the blonde woman. A moment later he stared down at his colleague as he lay dead on the floor between the bunks. Blood oozed from a neat entry wound in the neck. *The little waitress isn't what she seems. Bootman wouldn't be an easy victim.*

In a store room that contained what looked like a whole platoon of vacuum cleaners he found two men in kitchen whites hiding under a table. They clamored in a language he didn't understand. Coolly, he returned his handgun to the holster. That done he unclipped a grenade from his belt, popped out the pin, then lobbed the bomb over the assembled vacuum cleaners into the lap of one of the kitchen porters. They both howled in terror.

The man closed the door on them. A second later the explosion deformed the steel panels. With his ears tingling from the force of the detonation he checked his handiwork. Neat rows of vacuum cleaners had been replaced by a mess of torn bags, cables and hoses. Dust turned the air white. Satisfied, he closed the door on the corpses, then resumed his search for the waitress.

They headed back to the Moonlit Bay Lounge, but Gus lacked the purposeful stride of old.

One of his assistants stopped dead. 'Did you hear that?'

Tanya tilted her head. 'A thud. It seemed to come from below.'

'Someone slamming a hatch.' Gus strived for a note of authority.

Isis listened. 'I heard it, too. These floors are solid steel. It must have been extremely loud.'

The technician with the axe gripped the handle tighter. 'It might be one of the prisoners?'

'Or the ship hitting a reef?' suggested a second man.

'We're not moving,' Tanya said. 'How can we run into anything?'

'But something can collide with us.'

'A hatch slamming,' Gus reiterated. 'That's all. We'll go back to the lounge and talk through what we do next.'

When he walked on with his colleagues Isis gripped Tanya by the arm. 'Stay here,' she hissed. 'Gus and his guys don't know what to do.'

Tanya grimaced. 'Do we?'

Isis nodded at one of the offices. 'See that? The one marked "Studio".'

'Sure. It's where they broadcast weather bulletins and passenger announcements over the ship's TV system. I doubt if there'll be a radio transmitter—'

'No, there won't, but look.' She nodded at a monitor bolted to the wall. It revealed a shot from a camera fixed high on the ship's exterior. Through the fog they could just make out the dark point of the prow. 'Might they not control the CCTV from there?'

'I guess.'

'Then we could search the entire ship without leaving that room.'

Tanya began to say that they should inform Gus but Isis marched to the door. Pleased with herself, she pushed open the door. 'Very remiss. The studio manager forgot to lock up.'

Tanya peered inside. A woman's shoe lay on the carpet. 'There's something horribly suggestive about a discarded shoe, isn't there?'

'Absolutely. You might drop your keys and not notice. But a shoe . . .' Isis became serious. 'I'll check inside. Stay here.' After ducking her head through she turned back to Tanya. 'Nothing else to worry about.' She kicked the shoe aside.

'Something's happened here, hasn't it? The crew didn't stroll away, did they? They fled, or they . . .' Her mouth dried as grim images flooded her head. 'Do you think the crew might have—?'

'Tanya.' Isis nodded along the hallway. 'There's a waitress. She might be able to tell us where to find the back-up radio.'

A man in a hooped sweater walked alongside a blonde woman in the uniform of the Moonlit Bay Lounge.

Tanya frowned. 'I don't know if bar staff would know much about—'

'Wait in the studio. I'll be back in a moment.'

It was strange, really, how quickly Tanya felt so suddenly alone. Gus and his colleagues had already vanished. The couple disappeared as they turned a corner. Isis followed at a run. A second later she'd gone, too. Tanya couldn't even hear footsteps.

Beyond the windows fog swirled. The hallway lay deserted. For a moment she stood in the doorway to the studio. The proximity of the discarded shoe continued to whisper its own ominous prediction. *What happened to its owner? Only in abnormal situations do you shed a shoe, like if you're running in panic.* The emptiness of the hallway became threatening. A sinister figure could so easily stroll along it to find her standing here. Her vulnerability became intolerable. It sent tremors of panic flitting through her. *Damn you, Isis. Why did you leave me here?* It occurred to her to follow Isis. But if she tried to catch Isis, or even make her way to the lounge on the next deck, who might she meet round the next corner? One of the escaped prisoners could appear at any moment.

Tanya Rhone's heart thudded in her chest. Carefully, she backed into the office then eased the door shut without a sound.

Philip De Fray spent some time after the departure of Gus and his team carefully running through scales on his piano. The woman in the red headscarf could have knocked the strings out of tune with her rough handling. He'd woken late with a fully ripe hangover. What he'd seen in the lounge hadn't made a lot of sense. The abuse of his piano had infuriated him though. Now he'd heard a wild rumor that the crew had abandoned ship.

Philip resented the fact that there were no bar staff to serve him black coffee. The dry mouth collaborated with a headache to give him hell. Philip wasn't an outdoors kind of person. Nevertheless, he realized that without coffee the best thing to help dispel a wretched hangover was fresh air. He reaped it in abundance when he tottered on to the outside deck. Sub-zero temperatures sank ice teeth into his skin.

'Oh, hell,' he grunted. Fog concealed the world beyond the ship. Chilled air hurt his lungs. The headache graduated from a blunt throbbing to a sharp stab through his skull. *Endure it until the count of ten then get back inside. One, two, three* . . . He peered over the guardrail with immense distaste. *It's the Baltic all right. Ice skin on the water. Four, five, six* . . . Drinking vodka with cloves of garlic in it didn't prevent hang-overs as lovers of that particular spirit claim. Then again, he had polished off a bottle of merlot after he'd finished playing the piano last night. *Damn, forgetting to count. There's ice forming on my eyelashes. Seven, eight* . . . A breath of winter air stirred the fog. Not enough to dispel it. Yet wraiths swirled. A gap opened to reveal a stretch of fractured ice sheet; a second later the mist closed in and the white crust vanished. The air movement came again. Hardly a breeze; it stirred the vapor though.

'Now that's odd . . .' Philip stared hard into the fog. 'What on earth's that?'

He found himself leaning forwards as he searched the wall of gray until his eyes watered. Another breath of air. The fog bank rolled. He started back when he saw dark shapes protruding from the ocean. His mouth gaped open. Instinctively he retreated.

'Oh, God,' he gasped, his chest hurting from shock. 'The lunatics . . . look at what they've gone and done.'

Twenty-Four

With the studio door closed Tanya took in her surroundings. It was a slick, if compact, operation. The dimensions of the studio were no more than ten feet by ten feet. Here the presenter read news items, gave weather bulletins, issued advice to the seasick, or simply reminded passengers when stores closed or bars opened. As well as the live feed to monitors in public areas and TV sets in cabins, the studio also piped recorded programs through the closed-circuit system. When Tanya sat at the desk she saw a rack of discs. She read the labels. *Shipwrecks of the Baltic*. 'In dubious taste,' she murmured. *Wildlife of the Baltic*. Boson Eumericas had also added its own promotional video, *From Mining to Midas Touch*.

Tanya now studied the computer screen. The upper half revealed the same shot that had graced the public monitors all morning. A view of the ship's prow wreathed in fog. Beneath that were three rows of postage-stamp-size images. These revealed different aspects of the ship both inside and outside. Experimentally, she touched one of the miniature images beneath the main one. The large view of the prow melted away to be replaced by one of the deserted shopping mall.

'Ah ha.' Triumphant, she went to the studio door, eased it open, then checked the monitor on the corridor wall. The mall occupied its screen now. 'Success.' Tanya smiled as she closed the door. *You were right, Isis. We can search from the comfort of our swivel chairs.* Tanya returned to the desk. She touched more of the thumbnail images. Cabin decks, exterior decks, bridge interior, corridors – all deserted. Once more a chill ran down her backbone.

'But why is the ship so empty? Where's the crew?'

She touched another thumbnail. The legend at the top of the screen announced CAR DECK, but only blackness filled the screen. Another black screen described itself as CARGO

HOLD. Clearly, there would be no need for those parts of the ship to be lit during the voyage. She murmured darkly, 'At least it doesn't show sea water flooding in.'

Another image revealed a human face in close-up. The way the face loomed toward the camera made her flinch. She steeled herself for a shock as she touched the thumbnail. There was a face all right; it filled the screen. What surprised her most was that it was *her* face. *No way.* A green light appeared above the camera lens. Damn it. Her face appeared unflatteringly as a puffy ball as she leaned forward; it even revealed a yellow spot breaking through the center of her chin. By accident she had not only filmed herself but had broadcast her image throughout the ship.

'Damn,' she hissed, then clamped her mouth shut as she noticed another green light, this time on a microphone extending from the desktop. At random she stabbed one of the thumbnails. Mercifully, the close-up of her face, complete with its new zit, vanished. Replacing it was a view of the corridor that led to the bridge. Tanya could even see the broken glass cabinet that had contained the fire ax. What made her clench her fists in shock was the appearance of a figure.

In a white, shapeless overall it waddled into view. Short arms hung by its side, yet the face appeared enormous. The man paused to take in his surroundings, not that he appeared to be interested; he searched in a random way that lacked energy and with only the barest amount of motivation. For a second his bulging eyes regarded the fog outside the windows. He licked his fingers. When he swallowed whatever had been smeared there it made his throat gulp oddly. It struck Tanya that the motion of the throat seemed reptile-like – no, make that toad-like. Then Tanya stiffened. She'd been watching the man as if he performed on a TV show beamed from hundreds of miles away. Only this man in his utilitarian paper suit stood just fifty paces from the studio. Her eyes flicked to the door. She could almost hear the man's footsteps outside.

'I know who you are,' she hissed. 'You're one of the prisoners.'

At that moment he walked off camera. The pulpy white figure vanished.

He's walking this way. Her eyes swept to the door again. Any second it might open to reveal the over-large face with its bulging eyes. Maximum-security prisoners, Suzanne had explained: killers, kidnappers, rapists, cannibals . . .

If she opened the door she risked drawing attention to herself. But if he waited in the corridor she'd be trapped here. She returned to the computer screen. Quickly, she tapped another thumbnail. It revealed a stretch of corridor where the pianist, Philip, jogged along. That was the deck below this one. The next CCTV camera she tried was fixed on the wall outside the studio. Its oddly distorted image showed the corridor with slewed angles. Onscreen was a door bearing the word 'Studio'. As Tanya stared at the deserted area of carpet, feet appeared. No shoes, they were each covered by a baggy white sheath of paper. They began to shuffle forward.

Then they paused. Another shuffle. The full figure came so slowly into the camera's view it appeared to ooze with reptilian slowness. The man noticed the studio door. He turned to look directly into the camera. Then he turned back to the studio. He'd made the connection, too. The studio controlled the CCTV. For some reason that information was important to him. He took shuffling steps toward the studio. Tanya stared at the door. Any moment it would open. Panic rose through her, a hot liquid feeling that felt as if it would burst through her skull.

What now? She scanned the room. Nothing would serve as a weapon. Where could she hide? Apart from a desk, a chair and the DVD rack there was nothing. The door. But where was the key? She scanned it for a bolt. *Damn it, how do you lock the door!*

Then she saw a small brass button set into the door knob. Silently, she flew across the room, even shedding a sandal in her need for speed. She had to get this right first time.

The door knob quivered as if pressure had been applied at the other side. The door wasn't as sturdy as she would have hoped. The man on the other side must be glancing along the corridor to check he was alone before entering the studio.

Tanya pressed the button that locked the door from the inside during broadcasts. A slight click. The handle rotated part way then clunked to a stop. The toad guy tried again. The brass knob turned a fraction then stopped. He pushed as he turned, but the door stayed shut.

Tanya backed across the room until she could see the desktop monitor. It revealed the man as he tried to enter the studio. His bulging eyes rolled as if some dark emotion threatened to get the better of him. Then, licking his lips, he shuffled away.

Tanya sat heavily on the swivel chair. Her hands shook. A tight band seemed to encircle her chest. Tremors ran through her. Until that moment 'danger' had only been a word that Isis had fired at the passengers. Now 'danger' had become an emotion. It defied her ability to deal with it logically, to mentally digest it. It invaded her body; it squeezed her heart; it made her limbs shake, her mouth go dry.

She wanted to run, to find other passengers – safety in numbers. But she needed to check the way was clear. She punched up CCTV images onscreen. Empty decks shrouded in fog. Lonely stairwells. A corridor with a discarded jacket. Bank notes covered the floor like leaves in the fall. Then she brought up a view of the Moonlit Bay Lounge. Gus appeared to be giving a speech to a group of around thirty passengers. At that moment he stopped in mid-sentence. A figure raced into the bar waving its arms.

When Tanya looked closer she saw it was Philip. He appeared to have something to say that just wouldn't wait.

Philip De Fray's calf muscles ached from the unaccustomed run from the deck to the lounge. Thirty or so passengers had assembled there. The woman with the red headscarf stood by the piano as a tall gray-haired man gave a speech. Philip grimaced with the pain of catching his breath.

Gus stopped speaking as Philip lurched into the center of the lounge. At last he managed to claw in enough air to shout at the people who stared at him.

'Idiots!' He drew another breath. 'They've gone and run us into the Fiezeler Convoy.' He sucked more oxygen through his burning throat. 'We're right in the middle of them! God help us!'

The people gawped as if he babbled in a language that not one of them understood.

'The Fiezeler Convoy,' he repeated in exasperation. 'German captains scuttled a convoy of ships at the end of World War Two.' Again blank looks. Philip slammed his hand down on to the piano. 'Three munitions ships, full of torpedo warheads. Five thousand tons of them. If we smash into those wrecks the world's going to hear the biggest explosion since Hiroshima!'

FIFTH TRACT
Twenty-Five

Tanya Rhone reached the bar as around thirty people surged to peer out the picture windows. Today visibility was nil. Nevertheless, men and women hurried to the windows as if they expected an astonishing spectacle.

Maybe it's a rescue ship. Tanya felt hope swell. *Or at least a helicopter?*

Gus Hammond scowled. 'I don't see a thing.'

Philip paced behind him, agitated. 'It's there all right. The Fiezeler Convoy.'

'Are you certain?'

'Wait until the mist lifts, then you'll see.'

'To be more precise,' Gus rumbled, 'why are you certain?'

'Because I've seen all about the convoy on that.' Philip stabbed his finger toward the TV monitor. '*Shipwrecks of the Baltic*. A documentary they used to show until the captain suggested that it was hardly likely to make passengers rest easy in their bunks. Listen, there are thousands of boats lying at the bottom of the Baltic.'

'Really?' Evidently, Gus didn't like the musician's prissy hand gestures.

'Philip's right about the film,' Tanya broke in. 'I've just seen a copy of the disk in the studio. But what's this about a convoy?'

Isis explained in her customary cold tones. 'The Fiezeler Convoy. At the end of World War 2 the German crews scuttled munitions boats. Philip tells us that we're just about to ram them and blow ourselves to kingdom come.'

'I'm not joking.' Philip's hand shook. 'There were three ships. They carried torpedo warheads destined for the U-boats. The Nazis surrendered so the convoy's commander ordered the boats be scuttled by their own crews to prevent the weapons being taken by the Russians.'

'You know the film off by heart,' ventured one of the technicians knowingly.

Philip hissed in exasperation. 'I'm the ship's freaking pianist. How much time do you think I have on my hands between shows? I've seen every DVD on this tub.'

'But how did you see the ammo ships outside? If they were sunk they'll be underwater.'

'They were scuttled in the shallows. The superstructure and funnels are still above the surface. I've seen film of them. I know what they look like. Three ships close together, poking their funnels out of the water.'

'But there will be an exclusion zone,' Gus began. 'Every sailor would know to steer wide of them.'

'There is a quarantine area.' Philip stared through the glass. 'No ship is allowed to come within twenty miles of them.'

'We'd hardly drift that—'

'We haven't drifted.' Isis moved to the window. 'The crew were taken. Dangerous prisoners released from their cells. The ship has been sailed here for a purpose.' She stared into the fog.

'Bang. Big bang.' Philip's face started to twitch.

Gus gestured in frustration. 'But why on earth would people do this?'

'Just think about it.' A chill crept up Tanya's spine. 'What's so important that your company ordered a special sailing just before Christmas?'

Gus's eyes widened as the revelation struck. 'The pump.' The big man bunched his fists. 'Someone's trying to sabotage the operation!'

A technician ran his fingers through his hair in near panic. 'If the pump doesn't reach the mine by the end of the week it will be a disaster. We won't fulfill the quota. The lease will be will be void; the mine repossessed.'

'To hell with the pump.' Philip pointed. 'That's what we should worry about.'

The mist had thinned. Growing out of the sea, as if the Baltic had developed a dark crust of a scab, was the superstructure of a ship. Through rust violating the funnel were the crooked arms of a grimly familiar symbol.

'There . . .' Philip nodded, grim faced. 'See the swastika? What you can't see is that the ship is full of explosive. But trust me; it's there.'

Most of the passengers stared through the window, thinking the same thing. *All those warheads . . . thousands of tons of them . . . lying in wrecked ships . . . corrosive sea water flooding cargo holds.* Through the funnel's rust the black swastika made its presence felt so intensely it seemed to burn its way into Tanya's brain.

Isis broke the spell. 'I'm going to check the lifeboats.' With that she pushed open the door to an outside deck. Air colder than Tanya had ever known flooded over her.

Twenty-Six

Toads love stillness. After he failed to enter the studio, the Toad shuffled to the stairs and slowly descended to the halfway point.

A boy appeared. He ran downstairs, crying hard. In one hand he clutched a toy gun; in the other, orange darts with suckers on the end. The boy stopped. Even though he wept with passion he understood this was peculiar. Men in paper suits don't crouch in stairwells.

The Toad rolled his bulging eyes so he could study the boy's wet face. Possibilities occurred to the Toad. In that sluggish way of his he realized he had an option here. He pushed himself to his feet. The boy remained there, frozen. Now the Toad towered above him. The enormous face with its bulging eyes loomed closer.

The boy didn't make a sound now. Wide-eyed he stared up into those ugly features. The Toad leaned closer. He studied the boy's horror-struck face. Paralysis gripped the child. The Toad gave a belch of disappointment. This didn't have what he wanted. With another belching grunt he rejected the boy with a sluggish push. As the man descended the stairs a woman's voice echoed down the stairwell. It quivered with fear as if she was close to losing her mind.

'Billy! Come back . . . I told you not to run. Billy? Can you hear me?'

'*Mom!*' Billy's shout came with the explosive abruptness of a sneeze. Then, when he could make his legs work, he ran to find his mother.

The Toad met the young businessman in the reception area on the passenger cabin deck.

Smiling, the man rubbed his neck. 'That'll teach me. I didn't hit the pillow until five a.m.' In an affable way he patted his jacket pocket. 'I had to resort to a hair of the dog from the old hipflask. One nip to nail the headache. Two nips to feel human again.' He pressed the elevator call button. 'With luck, I'll just make lunch.'

The Toad struck. Bemused, the man muttered, 'Pardon me,' as if he were the one at fault. The Toad locked his short muscular arms around the man's neck. It took a while but at last his victim stopped breathing. Then he waited for the part he liked: the moment when the convulsions started. It pleased the Toad to feel the man's body butting against his as the torso shook. The Toad licked his lips. Death spasms were good ones; richly satisfying. The Toad grunted, his heart thudding against his ribs. A moment later the man hung limp in his arms. His killer sighed with regret. Over too quickly . . . always too quickly.

Never mind. With sluggish movements the Toad dragged the man to his cabin. *Now, the best is yet to come . . .*

'Don't touch any metal,' Gus warned as people spilled out on to the deck to stare at the part-submerged ships. 'It's so cold your skin will stick. You don't want to know what it feels like when you have to rip it off.'

'Three of them.' Isis stared. 'You are certain these are the ones, Philip?'

'Trust me.' Those three hillocks of rusting metal thrusting darkly out of the ice locked Philip in their thrall. 'Those wrecks are packed with explosive.'

Tanya stepped up to the guardrail. 'But why didn't the authorities remove the bombs from the ships?'

'They'll be too unstable,' Gus replied. 'No UXB man in his right mind would lay a finger on that lot.'

'In that case they should detonate the warheads rather than leave them to get more unstable.'

'There's an island about six miles from here,' Philip said. 'If that lot goes up it takes the town there with it.'

Gus agreed with the musician for once. 'The SS *Montgomery* sank with fourteen hundred tons of bombs in World War Two. It lies close to the British town of Sheerness. Scientists calculate if the cargo detonates it will throw what's left of the ship more than two miles. The shockwave would blast Sheerness clean off its foundations.' He rubbed his jaw. 'Over there we have the equivalent of three SS *Montgomery*s all within the space of half a mile.'

'Then get us off the damn ship.' Philip turned to the others. 'We've got to get away before we run into them.'

'That's not going to happen,' Isis told him.

'Oh, excuse me, did you see it in your crystal ball?'

'I don't have a crystal ball, Philip. I saw it when I looked over the rail.' She took satisfaction from his alarm. 'Look for yourselves. The ship is at anchor. It cannot move.'

The Toad didn't move quickly, but he was methodical. And creative.

After hauling the dead businessman back to the cabin, he laid the body on the bunk. Then with tireless attention to detail, and acting entirely on instinct, he set to work on the corpse. Carefully, he positioned the corpse so it sat propped up on pillows. Then he placed a cell phone in one dead hand, a pen in the other. For the next hour he dressed the cabin to match his inner vision. Sometimes he had to break into neighboring cabins for what he required. Soon, however, he added photographs of families to the bedside table. The Toad wanted those children to be the dead man's offspring. He adjusted lighting to create the perfect mood. After that he found the right shade of lipstick in the cabin next door. He returned to the corpse and added three pink ovals to the side of the dead man's face. The three marks matched the three pink blemishes on the Toad's cheek. That done, a sense of rightness filled the Toad. He'd completed his work. Gently, he eased himself on to the bunk beside his victim. From there the Toad could see both of them reflected in the mirror. The man looked like the Toad now. He had the three pink marks on his cheek. *Gosh, we're so alike.*

Inside, the Toad normally felt cold, always cold. Now a heat spread out from his chest into his big, wide face. He licked his lips as he felt his blood come alive inside of him. *Time to go . . .* Moving fast, he raced along the corridor to search the cabins. Soon he found shoes that fit him – glossy black loafers. He ditched the white coverall in favor of an orange tracksuit. A crisp white T-shirt arranged around his neck, with the ends tucked inside the tracksuit jacket, resembled a cravat. He darted back along the corridor. Excitement blazed inside. Laughter roared from him like a force of nature.

Eventually he managed to control the outburst. Even so, he bounced toward the stairs as if itching to break into a dance. Cheerful, animated, in love with the world, the Toad climbed the stairs in search of his fellow passengers.

Twenty-Seven

The Toad didn't find bizarre situations troubling. The upper, public areas of the ship were deserted. The *Volsparr*, itself, appeared to be moored near three wrecked ships. The only people he encountered were behaving strangely in the Moonlit Bar Lounge. He watched them surge in through a door from an outside deck. They weren't dressed for winter in their lightweight indoors clothes. Some passengers cursed as they stamped their feet to restore circulation.

When he caught the eye of a man who leaned against the piano, the Toad repeated the words of his victim. He even rubbed his neck above the makeshift cravat just as he'd seen his victim do before pouncing.

'That'll teach me,' chuckled the Toad. 'I didn't hit the pillow until five a.m.' In an affable way he patted his jacket pocket. 'I had to resort to a hair of the dog from the old hipflask.' He leaned against the piano too. 'One nip to nail the headache. Two nips to feel human again.' He lifted a strand of lint from his orange sleeve. 'With luck, I'll just make lunch.'

The man stared. 'You mean you don't know?'

'Know what?'

Then the Toad listened with great care as the man told him about the crisis that had befallen them this morning.

Meanwhile, Tanya took the opportunity to confront Isis.

'Isis, why did you leave me in the studio? There was a man—'

'I tried to catch up with the waitress.' She breezed over Tanya's anger as if it meant nothing. 'They went downstairs into the restaurant. I lost them after that. Then I arrived to find that we've been anchored next to those ships full of bombs.'

Isis was infuriating, but in the light of recent developments Tanya's alarm at being left alone in the studio seemed trivial. Vaguely, she noticed a newcomer to the lounge. Sporting a bright orange tracksuit, he leaned against the piano as he chatted to one of the technicians. She might have paid him more attention, only the passengers had been so shaken by seeing the munitions wrecks that they either sat in stunned silence or became agitated. Her attention was diverted to Gus Hammond who paced as he debated the situation with his assistants. Philip had perched himself on a bar stool. One man had climbed over the bar's counter where he now served tumblers of brandy.

She heard Philip announce, 'They'll never get the pump to the mine on time now. Face it; everyone employed by Boson will lose their jobs, so why worry? This way, we'll be home for Christmas. I've saved some money. I'm going to book a recording studio, then record my own songs. Whoever's spirited the crew away have done me a favor.' He downed the brandy in one.

The Toad radiated charisma. He charmed the man into chatting with him as if he were an old pal. In his teens the Toad had always liked to wear odd shoes. Usually a boot on one foot, a sneaker on the other. He chose footwear that didn't match because it reflected his state of mind. He had the knack of being in two places at once: the real world, and an imaginary realm. In the imaginary world lived an idealized version of himself. In reality the Toad was stolid, sluggish and ugly.

In that imaginary realm the replica of himself moved lightly on his feet. Everyone he met became his friend. By the time the Toad hit twenty he learnt he could be like his imaginary counterpart. All he need do was turn another human being into him. Just an hour ago he'd done exactly that.

Now, as the Toad enthralled the young man with his amusing conversation, he also saw in his mind's eye his duplicate lying on the bunk – the one that held the pen and the cell phone, and who now bore the same pink marks on his face. This system had worked so well for years. He'd offer lodgings to a lonely young man down on his luck, then the Toad would undertake that conversion process. The ugly creature the Toad saw in the mirror vanished. The reflection became handsome; he no longer shuffled but walked lightly with the poise of a dancer. Where he'd been unemployable now he had the pick of well-paid jobs. As long as he could revisit the duplicate of himself, which he'd fashioned from the corpse, then that was enough to keep the magic flowing happily. Five years ago, however, the stench from a dark fluid leaking through a party wall had prompted his neighbor, a retired mortuary assistant, to telephone the police.

The Toad chuckled pleasantly as the young man showed him photographs of his family. All those years in jail belong to the past. *I'm a free man now.*

Tanya realized that Gus now thought of Isis as part of his team, as he came across to discuss a problem with her. Meanwhile Philip, along with a couple of his barfly amigos, binged on expensive brandies.

Gus's face broadcast concern. 'It's industrial sabotage. Has to be.'

Isis nodded. 'It adds up. Your company has a rival. It wants to get its hands on the mine. The easiest way is to delay the arrival of the pump. That way your employer can't meet their extraction quota.'

'I know,' Gus growled. 'Then it'll be in breach of the terms of its lease so it will have to surrender the mine to the landowner.'

'Who, no doubt, has a new tenant waiting to take over operations.'

'For a heap of kick-backs, bribes and million-dollar sweeteners.'

Tanya stared as they discussed it so matter-of-factly. 'A rival company would really put our lives in danger for a mine on some godforsaken island?'

'That godforsaken island generates a billion dollars per year.' He gave a grim smile. 'You hear about thugs who pound old ladies for the price of a fix? Well, there are some industry bosses with morals so rotten they make those old ladykillers look like saints.'

Isis agreed. 'And those news reports of guerillas blowing up oil pipelines in Africa, or bandits causing trouble for plantation owners? Well, often the bad guys are in the pay of companies who want to buy out rivals at dirt-cheap prices.'

'And they often get their way.' Gus sighed. 'Once a plantation owner has had family members butchered, they're soon willing to sell for next to nothing.'

Tanya grimaced. 'So where does that leave us?'

'It leaves us in a bad place.' Gus dropped his voice. 'They haven't parked us alongside those things for nothing.' He glanced out at the three mounds of rusting metal that were surrounded by a bleak expanse of fractured ice. Slowly it began to deform as a swell ran through the hitherto placid ocean. 'That's an explosion waiting to happen.'

Tanya stared at the three menacing shapes. The mist had thinned to allow her to see an object that simply shouldn't be there. 'Isis . . .' she began.

At that moment the mother of little Billy hurried over to them.

'Listen to this,' the woman cried. 'My cabin has been broken into. They've tipped my make-up all over the bunk.'

Isis flared. 'What do you expect us to do, you ridiculous woman? We are the victims of a highly organized attack—'

'Isis.' Tanya didn't take her eyes from what occupied the water alongside the nearest shipwreck. 'Isis, look at—'

'I'm not ridiculous,' bleated the woman. 'While you've been gossiping, a thief has been ransacking our cabins.'

Tanya turned to Gus. 'Look outside. Over—'

Isis put her hands on her hips as she faced the woman. 'If we are the victims of such a precise strategy, then we must assume our enemy hasn't finished with us yet.' She glared. 'We must conclude we face an even greater crisis.'

Gus spoke to one of his team. 'We should check the pump. If it's industrial sabotage then they might have damaged—'

'My cabin,' the woman howled. 'It's been trashed!'

Tanya turned away from the window and what the thinning mist revealed. Something as disturbing as it was unexpected. *Will these people ever shut up and let me tell them what's out there!*

Frustration propelled Tanya's words with so much force that everyone stopped talking. 'Just listen to me!' She pointed at the window. 'Out by the wreck. There's a boat!'

'Thank God for that,' one of the technicians muttered. 'They've finally got round to rescuing us.'

'You mean the other two wrecks?' Isis frowned.

'No, *another* boat.' Tanya nearly howled with frustration. 'It was there a minute ago.'

'I don't see one now.' Gus turned to his team. 'Anyone else see it?'

They shook their heads. A couple made faces that suggested Tanya had imagined it.

'I saw a boat,' Tanya insisted.

'What did it look like?' Isis went to the window. 'Big, small?'

'Very small. An inflatable with an outboard motor.'

'Then it might be a rescue craft?' This hopeful suggestion came from one of the technicians.

'No . . .' Philip spoke in theatrical tones as he waved his brandy tumbler. 'It's the ferry of the dead. Ladies and gentlemen, it has come to collect your souls.'

Gus disapproved. 'You've had too much liquor. Go lie down for a while.'

'I will keep drinking, sir. Until I can no longer see those three bomb boats. Cheers.'

Tanya slammed her palm against the glass. 'No, it wasn't a rescue boat. There were three people on board; they didn't even bother looking in our direction.'

'Are you sure you really saw a—'

'Gus, I saw the damn boat! It wasn't a rescue boat because it was painted in a camouflage pattern. I only noticed it because it showed up dark against the ice. It must have circled round the far side of the wreck. There's a line of broken ice.' Tanya pointed it out for them. 'It's only thin; an inflatable could have left that as it broke a way through.'

Gus grunted. 'But you'll notice a swell getting up. The

natural movement of the sea could have done that easily. As you say, the ice is thin . . .'

'There was a boat,' Tanya insisted. 'It's hiding behind the wreck.'

'I believe you,' Isis told her.

'I'm not so sure.' Gus appeared even more troubled. 'But I am convinced that somebody has deliberately sabotaged delivery of the pump. What's more, they might damage it to make doubly sure the mine doesn't meet its quota – if by some miracle we get the machine there on time.'

The pump technicians spoke of the apparatus as if it was a newborn baby. As soon as Gus suggested that it might be harmed they glanced at one another with expressions of deep anxiety.

'We should check that it's OK,' said one and they all nodded.

'I'll take a couple of my team down to take a look-see.' Gus cracked his knuckles. 'Everyone else stay here. Stick together. We're not out of the woods yet.'

Twenty-Eight

Facts presented themselves with absolute clarity to Fytton. He'd garnered ten years' experience as a mercenary, and before that he'd served in the army. He knew an operation conducted with military precision when he saw one. Fytton eased his head through the doorway of a storage room to see the damage the grenade had wrought. Two bloody corpses lay amid the shattered wreckage of a dozen vacuum cleaners. Though the uniforms were now a sticky crimson he recognized these as kitchen-staff whites.

Fytton's search on the crew's accommodation deck revealed half a dozen bodies. A cautious investigation of the upper decks proved to him the crew had vanished. The ship lay at anchor; he'd glimpsed three partly submerged vessels nearby. Why the ship had been taken there was a mystery. However, the wrecks would conceal the ship's presence to radar operators on other craft, while the mist would effectively make the *Volsparr* vanish from the ocean for the time being. He already knew that the prison cells had been opened to free the prisoners. But that wasn't the goal of the attackers, surely? The prisoners were garbage. Their only value was the revenue that could be generated for the overseas prison-owner who would house them until the day they died. Therefore, the strategy of releasing the prisoners must be to create panic among the passengers. If he could hunt the prisoners down that would solve one issue. The big problem, he figured, was that a squad of trained killers had taken control of the ship, even though they currently remained out of sight for reasons known only to themselves.

He'd found the passengers huddled together in the Moonlit Bay Lounge. But, rather than explaining why he carried a sub-machine gun in his hands, and pistols and an electric stun gun fixed to his belt, he returned to the lower decks without being seen.

On the way he'd checked cabins where the doors were unlocked. He'd counted seven of the white paper coveralls. Another fact presented itself with shining clarity. There had been ten prisoners. He'd killed one. He'd seen the blonde girl who had been fed bleach and was now wearing a waitress uniform. Another prisoner had been with her – a guy in his late twenties in a sweater with a blue hoop design. That meant that seven other prisoners were on the run, having swapped paper coveralls for regular clothes. And that left a big conundrum: he didn't know what the other jailbirds looked like. He'd not bothered to even check their files.

Who's to say that those psychopathic killers weren't already mingling with the passengers in the piano lounge? Any moment now all hell might be let loose.

Maya and Sami kept away from the other passengers. Briefly, a woman in a red headscarf had followed them but they'd slipped away down a staircase to the restaurant area. From there they moved into the kitchen with its labyrinth of steel preparation tables. By now a craving gripped Sami.

'We could begin work here,' he told Maya. She registered no surprise at his suggestion. 'Maya, look, my hands are starting to shake.'

'Is that your malaria? It must hurt. What does pain feel like?'

Tremors ran through his body. 'It happens every six months or so. The malaria takes hold again. I get the shakes. Fever . . . really bad fever. There's nothing I can do normally but go to bed . . . sweat it out.'

'Normally?'

He managed a smile despite the way the malaria made his veins burn. 'When I was in jail I'd take to my bunk during a flare-up. Now I'm free.' His smile broadened. 'I can heal myself. All I need is the right person.' A spasm ran through his fingers. 'But we need to move quickly. In another couple of hours I'll be so sick I won't be able to stand on my own two feet.'

She'll help me, he thought with the same kind of desperation a heroin addict has when they hit the streets in search of a dealer. *Maya's going to do whatever it takes. Maya believes in me. We'll work together as a team . . .*

She stared at him with those deep brown eyes. 'Pain. When your body hurts does it drown your mind in sensation?'

'Yes.' The malaria had come roaring back with a vengeance. 'Help me find a subject. If your inability to feel pain . . .' His voice wavered as the fever took hold. 'If your inability to feel pain is the result of an underlying medical condition then my procedure will heal it.' *There, I sound like a scientist again. I will prove the doctors wrong. The world will welcome me as a hero.* Gently, he took her hand. 'Maya, is that what you want? To be able to feel the pain?'

A strange serenity smoothed her features. 'I know until I feel pain I am not human. I want to be human. Then I can be part of this world.'

He grinned. 'Careful, what you wish for.'

'What do we need to do now?'

'Find a subject. Then contain them. We must have tranquil surroundings in order to establish a rapport with them.' He squeezed her hand warmly. 'Then just wait until you make contact – that flood of power through your body; you feel like you're being carried by angels.'

Through the open door to the restaurant he glimpsed a man of around twenty in sweat pants and a fleece. He carried a flashlight in each hand; his face wore an expression of anxiety.

'We don't have much time.' A fever sweat broke out through Sami's forehead. 'That's the guy we'll use.'

*   *   *

From the guards' rest area that formed an annex to the cell pod came murmuring. 'Hiyo, Quilp,' Fytton whispered. There must be at least two people there. Maybe some of the prisoners didn't relish freedom after all. Had they returned to give themselves up? Perfectly understandable if they'd been pursued by the guy with the gun, who'd taken a shot at Fytton. He curled his finger around the trigger of the machine gun as he stepped over his boss's blood. A short burst from the weapon would finish the prisoners, pronto. 'Hiyo, Quilp.' Fytton pushed open the door to the guards' room.

Fytton wasn't particularly fazed by what he saw. 'Hello, boss. How ya doing?'

Turrock sat in an armchair. His girl, Suzanne, had been in the process of bandaging his head; blood still oozed from the scalp wound.

'Suzanne,' Turrock grunted. 'You've met Fytton before.'

She nodded. 'I'd prefer it if you didn't point that thing at us.'

Turrock smiled. 'He's just being careful.' He lightly touched his bandaged head. 'Fytton, tell me what you know. We need to formulate a plan.' Soldier speak. His boss was back in action.

It didn't go how Sami intended. From a distance the guy appeared slightly built, but when Sami tried to grab him from behind he discovered that his victim had a wiry physique with a formidable strength.

'What the hell are you trying to do?' the guy spat as he slammed Sami back against the restaurant's picture window. The reinforced glass thundered at the shock.

Sami said the first thing that came into his head. 'The captain wants to speak with you . . . there's a problem.'

'Liar.' The guy in the fleece had no hesitation in striking Sami's head with one of the flashlights. 'The crew have gone. Who are you? What were you trying to do to me?'

The flare-up of malaria weakened Sami as much as the blows to the head. His knees buckled as the man hit him again, the plastic case of the flashlight cracking under the impact.

'I though you could help me.' Waves of nausea ran through him. Malaria, blows, shock . . . *I can't last much longer.* 'I'm sick . . .'

'You creep, you tried to jump me. Who sent you?' The guy

raised the flashlight for the next strike. 'If you don't tell me, I'm going to bash you until you do.'

The sound of the blow came as a crunch; a suggestion of a hard surface collapsing, fibers splitting.

Suddenly the man's face changed from blazing aggression to one of bewilderment. As he sank to his knees Sami noticed the V-shaped wound in the top of his head. Blood gushed from it with a surreal power all of its own. Behind him, Maya stood with a steel cleaver. Gore dripped from its keen edge.

With a calm expression she stared at the dying man. 'Tell me what you know.' Maya's eyes burned at her victim. 'What's it like? Tell me what you know.'

'I'm hurt . . .' His eyes slipped out of focus and he sank to the floor.

Sami climbed to his feet. The fever sweat soaked his clothes now. It made his back itch so much he wanted to claw the jersey from his torso.

The death of the man saddened him. Sami despised violence. 'It's OK, Maya.' He glanced round to make sure the restaurant was still deserted. 'You're not to blame. The man attacked me. You saved my life. He forced you to hit him. He's the guilty one, not you.'

Quickly, Sami dragged the body under one of the tables, then arranged the chairs so they hid the body. Unless someone searched the place the body wouldn't be found – not yet, anyway. Not that Sami could be concerned about it now. Tremors jolted his body. Fever cranked up the heat. Desperation drove him.

'Maya, come with me.' He took her by the hand and led her away. He must find another subject – soon.

In the guards' room Turrock, Suzanne and Fytton realized they were faced with a near insurmountable problem.

'I don't know how we'll recognize the majority of the prisoners.' Turrock managed to stand, but he was still unsteady on his feet. 'I can ID the blonde woman – the one our colleagues tried to poison.'

'I know da Toad guy,' Fytton added.

'But it's the others,' Suzanne said. 'We can't differentiate between them and the passengers.'

'Exactly.'

Suzanne rubbed her forehead. 'Surely there are files?'

'There are, complete with photographs of the prisoners.' Turrock balanced himself by resting his hand against the door frame. The debilitating effect of the head injury still made itself felt. 'Only whoever sprang the prisoners also smashed the computer. That contained our only copy of the file.'

Suzanne shivered. 'So all we know for certain is that there are nine convicted murderers roaming the ship.'

Fytton grunted. 'If it was only murder then it wouldn't be so bad. Those things are psychopaths, monsters . . . What they'll do to da passengers God alone knows.'

Gus checked his watch. 'Three p.m. Where's John with those flashlights?'

'I can go look for him,' one of the technicians offered.

Isis stood up. 'The moment you start looking, then John will come back and we'll have to send someone to search for you.'

The man flushed. 'You're not in charge of—'

'Isis is correct, Mike. We'll waste the entire afternoon looking for one another. How many flashlights did we get hold of?'

Mike didn't like being corrected in front of Isis. Sullen, he answered, 'Five. There's probably more flashlights at the emergency muster stations, but that means more of us going off – and getting ourselves lost.'

'Thank you, Mike.' Gus gave his assistant a look that spoke volumes. 'OK, team, is everyone ready?'

The man in the orange tracksuit chipped in perkily. 'If you need another pair of safe hands I'm more than happy to come?'

'Thank you, sir.' Gus appeared to notice the man for the first time, and frowned as if trying to recall if he'd seen that distinctive face before. 'But if you would stay here to guard the women and children. That goes for the other men who aren't coming with me to check on the pump.'

Isis glared at Gus's implication that women are weaklings.

Meanwhile, the man with the over-large face beamed with that extraordinary mouth. 'Whatever you say. I'm at your disposal, absolutely.' Then to those remaining behind he beckoned as he exuded a winning charisma. 'Gather round, everyone. We can entertain ourselves by confessing our deepest, most mysterious secrets.'

'Is that one of the ship's entertainers?' Mike appeared puzzled. 'I haven't seen him before. Perhaps he's the comedy act?'

'Does it really matter?' Gus rumbled. 'We need to check that the pump hasn't been wrecked.'

Isis folded her arms. 'I take it you don't require any of the "fairer sex" to accompany you?'

'Miss, I'd prefer it if you stay here where you'll be safe.'

'OK, but you do realize we're no nearer finding the back-up transmitter so we can send out a distress call?'

'We'll redress that as soon as we're back.' He motioned to his assistants as they checked the flashlights. 'Right, we'll head out. We should be back in twenty minutes.'

How wrong he was.

Twenty-Nine

Ten minutes after Gus's departure some of the passengers complained they were hungry. They began to head for the stairs that would take them to the restaurant level; there they could forage the kitchens for food.

The man in the orange suit held out his arms as if stopping kindergarten tots running out of class. 'You should all stay here where I can keep my eyes on you.'

'My son needs to eat.' Billy's mother yanked the boy along by the arm. For some reason he appeared paralyzed with fear. But then he'd have heard about the munitions ships crammed to the rusty hatches with high explosive warheads. No wonder he was petrified. When the woman made to bypass the tangerine-clad man she complained bitterly, 'We haven't had so much as a bite all day. If Billy doesn't eat soon he'll be ill.'

The man in orange held out a short, stumpy arm to the boy. 'Come with me. I'll find you something nice to eat.'

Billy grunted; his eyes locked on to the man's face as if they sprouted tentacles.

'We all need food,' the woman insisted.

'But you heard Gus.' The man beamed as if taking part in a parlor game. 'We must stay here. It wouldn't do to wander; it would not do at all.'

Isis spoke up. 'This gentleman is right. We need to remain together.'

The mother advanced in a determined way, towing her son by the arm. 'I'm going to get food. Can't you see my boy's on the point of fainting?'

'Wait!' Isis's voice came with the abruptness of a thunder clap.

'Don't you tell me—'

'I have a solution,' Isis interrupted. 'Tanya and I will fetch the food. I'm sure we can find bread, cold meats and pastries.'

'Oh dear, miss.' The man in orange reacted with a dismay that was almost pantomime in its intensity. 'Don't go alone. Please let me come with you.'

Isis breezed through with a thanks-but-no-thanks answer. Tanya thought that when it came to carrying supplies he might be handy. *I'm sure I've seen him before. Where though?* But then with today's pandemonium Santa Claus could have danced through here and she wouldn't have noticed.

Diplomatically, Isis added, 'Perhaps you would stay here and entertain the passengers as you suggested?'

'My pleasure, dear.' His jolly face beamed. 'We'll have so much fun. I'm brimming with inventive possibilities already.' He ruffled the boy's hair with a set of stumpy fingers. 'You're game for adventure, aren't you?'

'I'm feeling fine,' Turrock insisted. 'Once we have the prisoners back in their cells, then I'll rest.' He touched the back of his head where it throbbed from the blow. *I still look a bloody mess*, he told himself as he opened the gun cabinet. The loss of his prize prisoners left an aching emptiness inside of him.

'Are you sure you're all right?' Suzanne asked him. 'You're very pale.'

He forced a grim smile. 'I've got a job to do. We always feel good when we've got a mission. That right, Fytton?'

'That's right, boss.'

Turrock took a sub-machine gun from the rack, the same

model as the one Fytton sported. 'You best take more ammunition clips. You've got Mace?'

'Sure, Boss. And da stun gun and sidearm.'

'Good choice.' Turrock was reassured to have a fellow professional by his side. 'Suzanne, I'd offer you a gun . . .'

'I don't want one,' Suzanne said firmly.

'That's also a wise choice, but for your own protection take the Tazer. It's non-lethal if you should plug either Fytton or myself.' He donned a leather belt with clips from which he could hang weapons and a pouch for spare ammo clips. When he spoke he fell back into the tones he used to instruct new recruits. 'Suzanne, if you need to use the Tazer, point and shoot. Darts will fly out the muzzle, dragging thin wires behind them. When the darts embed in your target the battery in the pistol will deliver a hundred thousand volts.'

'You said they weren't lethal. A hundred thousand volts will fry their face off.'

'It won't. It'll give the bad guy a big enough jolt to knock him off his feet. He'll stay like that for a minute or so, giving you time to retreat or alert one of us.' He hefted his sub-machine gun. 'Ready?'

Suzanne and Fytton nodded. Easing back the bolt of the gun, he led the way down a stark corridor that ran into the heart of the ship.

Sami knew they'd blown it. The fever had weakened him; he was no longer up to wrestling a victim away into captivity. On the passenger cabin deck he'd pounced on a guy dressed in a blue shirt and denim jeans. His intended subject had pulled a handgun from his belt. *How could I have not seen that?* Sami thought. But then the malaria flare-up turned the screws. He found it hard to keep his eyes in focus. The fever-sweat drenched his clothes. The man shoved him backward. Sami stumbled into a crouch against the corridor wall. Smoothly, with no sign of stress on the man's part, he raised the gun, aiming into the center of Sami's face.

Sami blinked. He realized the man wore the same kind of clothes as the gunman who'd traded shots with the prison guard. The blue jeans and blue shirt were like a uniform. The face wasn't familiar though; this wasn't the same man. He

blinked again; a black balaclava mask hung from the jeans'
pocket. What was happening here?

Just as the man tightened his finger on the trigger Maya
stood between gunman and intended target.

'Move,' grunted the man.

The blonde stood her ground. Calmly she met the man's
gaze. Casually, he slapped her aside. She recovered her balance
and he slapped again. The force of the blow rocked her sideways, yet she regained the same stance in a second. Again,
Sami detected an otherworldly serenity about the woman. The
blows hadn't fazed her one iota. The gunman could have been
slapping stone.

The gunman shook his head. 'What the hell's wrong with
you?'

She didn't reply. Instead, she met his angry stare with those
brown eyes, amber tints glowing. 'You must tell me what I
need to know,' she said in a calm voice.

'What?'

'You are here to tell me something.'

The man's baffled expression cleared. 'Damn it, why didn't
you identify yourself? I could have killed you.'

'Tell me what you know.' Her voice was softly insistent.

The guy glanced back along the corridor. 'We can't be seen
by the passengers just yet. We need to keep some of them
alive for this to work.'

'You haven't told me.'

'We're in control of the ship and it's been moored by the
Fiezeler Convoy. But I'm not sure what else you need to know.
And who's this guy?'

For the first time that afternoon Sami got lucky. Maya had
distracted the gunman. When he spoke he allowed his head to
drop a little. This allowed Sami one good shot. He punched
as hard as he could under the man's chin; his eyes dulled as
his blood pressure dropped from the shock of the blow. The
gun fell from his fingers.

A second later Sami and Maya, pulling hard together, hauled
him into one of the vacant luxury suites. There was plenty of
room for what Sami needed to do next.

Thirty

Isis took Tanya to one side. 'Gus promised he'd be back by three twenty. He needed twenty minutes to check the pump in the hold. It's now almost four. So, what do we do now?'

Tanya had just finished helping hand out sandwiches to the passengers assembled in the Moonlit Bay Lounge. She'd never even been aware of the time. If anything, the part-submerged munitions ships with their swastikas still exerted a powerful grip on Tanya's imagination. Repeatedly, she glanced out the window in case the inflatable boat returned. But the only thing to return had been the mist. It thickened again, transforming the wrecks into monstrous phantom shapes that menaced the *Volsparr* from the ice-covered sea.

'Tanya, did you hear me? I asked—'

'I know. I heard. Gus and his team are late. We can't go searching for them.'

'That's exactly what we must do.'

'But you heard Suzanne. She told us the prisoners had escaped. We don't want to run into those.'

'Safety in numbers?' Isis's cold gaze roved across the assembled passengers – more had chosen to sink brandies at the bar. 'You think we have sufficient numbers to be safe, Tanya?'

'It's better than roaming the corridors. I told you I saw this guy earlier. A weird-looking guy dressed in a white coverall.'

Isis clicked her tongue in frustration. 'I hate doing nothing.'

'We're feeding ourselves and biding our time until help arrives. That's what we're doing.'

'When will help arrive?' Isis gripped Tanya's elbow. 'When? Look out there: thick fog, ice. Can helicopters search in that? Visibility is little more than a hundred yards. Those shipwrecks will probably mask our position on radar.'

Tanya pulled her arm out of Isis's grasp. 'Do you really

think we should hoist up the anchor and simply steam out of here? You'd be crazy to—'

'Ladies, ladies, can I be of help?' The man with the bulging eyes approached them in his exotic orange sportswear. 'I've got the drinks machine working behind the bar.' He beamed with delight. 'I can offer hot beverages – tea, coffee, drinking chocolate . . .'

'We need Gus here,' Isis insisted, 'then we have to find a transmitter.'

'Lovely idea,' the man chirped. 'Normally, I'd offer to come with you.' His smile lost its sparkle. 'But I do really need to go downstairs to recharge my batteries. I'm feeling my age.'

Tanya glanced at the staircase entrance as if it led to hell. 'You should stay up here. It won't be safe to go off by yourself.'

'Oh, I'll be fine, my dear.' His features sagged as the energy drained out of him. 'There might be fearsome chappies down there, but will they look any more fearsome than yours truly? Cheerio, my dears.' A little while ago he'd danced on tiptoe despite his curiously bulky body; now he shuffled to the stairs as if he'd aged forty years in a matter of moments.

'That's why we need Gus.' Isis gave a sigh that revealed she couldn't shoulder all these responsibilities by herself. 'Gus might be annoyingly old-fashioned in his attitudes but it's better if he's here.'

Tanya's gaze was drawn to the yawning pit of the stairwell. 'Then we've no alternative. We bring back Gus and his men.'

'Absolutely.'

'My God. That's strange.'

Isis turned to the window as if expecting to see some change. 'What is it? The inflatable boat?'

'Look at the TV screen.'

Isis studied the screen fixed to the wall. 'It's just the name of the ship, the *Volsparr*.'

'But I know what that is. It's the backdrop in the studio. Someone's changed the camera feed.' With a tingle running up her spine she added, 'Before it showed a view of the open deck.'

'It might be automatic – a timed cycle of different views.'

'No. When I was in the studio a couple of hours ago I figured out how it worked. I changed the feeds myself. Before I left I locked it on to the deck shot.'

'Gus might be in the studio now,' Isis suggested. 'It would be a fast way to check the ship via CCTV.'

'Then why isn't the view changing? It's as if somebody's about to broadcast to us from the studio.'

'OK.' Isis's air of resolve hardened. 'We find Gus now. Circumstances are changing.'

Within moments Isis had pressed a couple of the pump technicians into accompanying them – two of the most muscular guys. Tanya hoped that wasn't an indication that Isis anticipated trouble deep in the underbelly of the ship. Tanya had no time to prepare herself to leave the relative safety of the lounge; soon she found herself descending those stairs that now held all the charm of the entrance to hell. Cool air swept up them. She caught the tang of brine on the draught. It didn't bode well. As her feet took her down into that exhalation of ice-cold air she shivered. *I'm not going to like what I find down there . . . I'm not going to like it one little bit.*

The Toad had exhausted himself. His arms hung limp; all definition had gone from his face. The energy that had bubbled up so warmly inside to transform him into a jovial raconteur had vanished. Now there was only a neutrality of emotion. Neither sad nor elated. A blankness settle over him. *Recharge . . . back to home cabin . . . rest.* His stumpy fingers managed to ease the key card from his pocket. He unlocked the cabin door.

'I missed you,' he murmured to the corpse that lay on the bunk. 'I missed you lots.'

Entering the cabin, he locked the door behind him.

Turrock didn't rush. Carefully negotiating the corridors on the crew's accommodation deck, he and Fytton checked the cabins. Fytton had seen the bodies before, of course. Turrock ensured that Suzanne didn't see the butchered remains.

'Professional work,' he murmured to Fytton as he appraised the guy with his throat slit. 'Our prisoners didn't kill these. It was people like us.'

Sami finished tying the man to the chair. He'd been thorough. Not only had the man been bound so he couldn't move so much as a finger, he'd also been gagged to prevent him shouting out.

Sami had left the eyes clear though. Before the man regained
consciousness, Sami couldn't stop himself from lightly touching
the eyelashes. They had a springy resilience, a latent power,
like a coil waiting for release.

Sami wiped the sweat from his face. The malaria outbreak
raged in his blood. Fever robbed him of saliva; his tongue felt
like a dried sponge that had been rammed into his mouth.
Through blurring vision he could make out Maya standing
there in her little tartan skirt. Normally, she didn't move much.
Now, however, she ran her fingers through her blonde hair
from roots to tip, spiking it above her head. Her respiration
quickened.

'I'll do it soon.' Tremors made his voice waver. 'Just wait
until he wakes, then you can watch me work on him . . .'

Ten minutes after entering the cabin he'd made home for
himself and his fantasy twin, the Toad left it again. The corpse
he'd carefully made up to resemble himself lay propped up
on pillows so it could gaze at the mirror with lifeless eyes.

The Toad had a spring in his step. Good as new. Batteries
recharged. Fingers fizzing with energy. Happy again. A sound
of murmuring came from the luxury suite at the end of the
corridor. *Must take a little peep! Oh, what fun might be there.*

Tanya descended the staircase. The two pump technicians knew
the way. They'd checked the precious cargo immediately after
it had been loaded on the ship at Hull. Isis carried a flashlight they'd found at a muster point. One of the men had
armed himself with a fire axe.

The Moonlit Bay Lounge sat perched on an upper deck.
Beneath that were two passenger decks, including the deck
for the cabins; below those everything became decidedly
grimmer. The carpet vanished to be replaced by steel floors.
Now feet made a ringing sound on bare metal risers. The place
had the starkness of a morgue. The temperature dropped with
every flight of stairs descended.

'Maybe we should have taken the elevator?' she ventured.

One of the technicians, a burly red-haired man with tattooed
forearms, grunted, 'Elevator doesn't run down to the cargo
hold. This is the only way I know.'

'How much further?'

'Apart from the engine room the cargo hold's as far as you can go before you get your feet wet.'

If that's what passes for a technician's sense of humor, remember never to date one. An odd thought, she realized. Because she planned marrying her fiancé, Jack. If everything worked out, that is. Only now, the Baltic mining town where they were headed seemed part of a different world. Somehow it, and the rest of planet Earth, belonged to the realm of living people. Here, the *Volsparr* and its passengers had sailed into its own iced-up, fog-shrouded universe; a realm of the dead. And beyond their ship lay the bitter waters of the Baltic Sea. Just a couple of hundred yards across the ice were the humped forms of the Nazi munitions ships that rose like the ugly heads of primeval sea monsters. The accumulation of anxieties and fears weighed down on her. Here they were, venturing lower into the ship, probably getting close to the ocean's surface. Its cold reached through the skin of the vessel to slide across *her* skin. The cold of an Arctic tomb. Her breath came in ghost-white forms.

This seemed like the kind of secret abyss that could swallow Gus and his team into oblivion. The hushed world of the cargo deck stole sound from the air. It had the power to distort reality until shadows at the bottom of the staircase appeared to assume noxious forms. Nobody talked. Now even the lounge many feet above their heads could have been as remote as another planet. Nothing was smooth or refined here. The corridor had been braced with huge steel girders that thrust from the walls with a power that appeared brutal. Rivets bulged with the cold roundness of dead eyes. Down here the steel hull waged eternal war with the relentless forces of the sea. Metal beams fought against the crushing downward force of all that iron above their heads. Through the walls ran grossly thick pipes; enlarged arteries that carried whatever fluids this monstrosity of a ship required. There were no windows; no decorations to ease the severity of vicious angles.

Grim-faced the red-haired guy pointed to twin doors. Lettering in a glaring yellow read: MAIN HOLD. DANGER! DO NOT ENTER AT SEA. Then, to savagely beat home the point: DANGER OF ASPHYXIATION. DANGER OF CRUSHING.

'Danger of crushing?' Isis murmured the words as if she decoded a curse.

The second technician whispered, 'Cargos can shift in heavy seas. The first stage of the crossing was a rough one. We shouldn't be here.'

'The sooner we find Gus then, the better.'

Isis gripped the handle of one door while the red-haired man took hold of the other. At that moment the lights went out. And, for Tanya, nothing in her life would prepare her for what happened next. Her world would never be the same again.

SIXTH TRACT
Thirty-One

Within a second of the lights dying Isis hit the flashlight button. It blazed in the confines of the entrance vestibule to the hold.

Tanya saw the faces of the technicians were luminous in the flashlight's glare, their eyes unnaturally large. The red-haired man and Isis finished what they started; they hauled open the twin doors to the cargo hold.

What emerged Tanya couldn't say. All she saw were an avalanche of shadows that erupted from the cavernous void. The two guys that accompanied them yelled that they were armed (they weren't, of course, but gambled on a bluff to save their lives). However, it did nothing to stop this torrent of forms that sped from the hold. In the first moment Tanya had been knocked back against the wall. One of the upright girders smashed into her spine; the air exploded from her lungs. In the second moment the flashlight whirled upwards as if it flew in terror from the assault. Then the flashlight blinked out. Darkness engulfed her. No voices now, only a scrabble of movements, wild movements like a mass of creatures had stampeded. Tanya felt solid objects crash into her.

'Stop.' Winded, she panted the word again. 'Stop.' Another impact as something or someone collided with her. In this windowless place the darkness imposed a total blackout. It left her blinded, confused. 'Isis?' No answer. 'Isis, are you there?' A succession of grunts became audible. *How similar the sounds of sex and pain . . .* The grunts faded.

'Is anyone there?' Tanya blundered forward. *'Anyone!'* No answer.

Even though she couldn't see a thing, she realized she'd entered the cavernous hold. The sound of her respiration altered;

the air turned even more icy. Odors of engine grease sank into her hair; they crept over her face to slide into her nose as if they'd evolved into a parasitic life form. Meanwhile, the din receded. *Go forward*, she told herself. *Get away from them.* That tornado of movement had driven her into a panic. Collisions of people running in the dark had hurt her; she could hardly breathe after being smacked into the girder. She licked her lips, tasted blood. Not that she could feel a wound; had a flailing arm given her a bloody nose? *Get me out of here . . . get me out of here . . . get me out!* The plea bleated through her head. But now she blundered through the cargo hold in absolute darkness. She saw nothing. This dark could have been an evil force pouring through her eye sockets to fill her head with yet more darkness; it confused her judgment. She had no sense of direction, no knowing what lay just ahead.

Tanya forced herself to keep walking forward, convinced that she'd trip. Or bang her head. Or blunder into exposed machinery with whirling gears. Her imagination turned on her with the relentless savagery that comes with panic. One moment Tanya was convinced cold water flooded around her ankles, the next: *Someone's got hold of me.* She whirled away through pitch black to find that the floor had vanished under her feet. *A hole. I'll fall through.* She pictured an open hatch. She'd plummet twenty feet into the engine room.

No! She gripped hold of a metal spar or pipe – she couldn't identify it in the darkness. *Take control. Stop panicking.* She breathed deeply to quell the riot of nerve impulses snapping through her brain. *The ship isn't sinking. That's cold air you can feel on your legs, not water. A stranger hadn't grabbed you, it was dangling cable. You aren't falling; panic's making you lose your balance. Get light, that's what you need. Find a switch.* She went groping her way along the wall. Beneath her fingertips slid bulging rivet heads, cables, pipes, welded seams. Then she bumped her face against a vertical structure. A ladder? Yes, she was sure of it, a ladder bolted to the wall. What might you find at the bottom of a ladder? Her fingers searched the wall.

Suddenly she made the discovery. Seconds later, Tanya knew that there are gods – or demons, or evil spirits, call them what you will – that really are devoted to making human beings suffer.

Click.

Light.

The cargo hold.

Filled with brilliant radiance.

And all around, in heaped mounds, death. *And such death . . .*

Tanya's hand flew to her mouth. Her lips stretched so tight that skin cracked open; she wanted to scream. Only nothing came.

She stared at what occupied the cargo hold. Inside the void, which was the size of a church, the pump rose up proud in its timber traveling case. Lying slumped around the walls were dozens of corpses. Most wore uniforms. The mystery of the crew's disappearance had been solved in one brutal blast of light. Drips of cold liquid fell on Tanya. She looked up. Through the steel grill of the walkway above her head one of the pump technicians who accompanied Gus gazed down. From the gaping wound in his throat blood still migrated from his body. The drops had a stinging iciness to them. Tanya wiped her face. Now she understood that the blood that had run into her mouth moments before hadn't come from her own nose; it had trickled down from above. The entire length of the upper walkway contained butchered human beings. She didn't want to know how many bodies were there. An old habit of counting items tried to compel her to make a gruesome tally. Even though she resisted the impulse she knew there were dozens.

Get out of here. Get out. Stay out. She forced her line of sight away from the mutilated bodies. *And for God's sake, don't look at the faces.* Yet she glimpsed bullet holes in foreheads. A woman in an officer's uniform lay with a broken neck. The back of her head lay between her own shoulder blades. Its eyes stared in horror; they captured the last agonized seconds of life.

In all those still figures there was another one, a moving one. A man in a business suit.

Tanya wiped her face; blood had fallen like rain. 'Have you seen what they've done?' The words roared out.

The man nodded, then smiled warmly. A second later he advanced, flexing muscular hands as he did so.

Thirty-Two

In the luxury suite Sami had been working on his subject for thirty minutes. After the guy recovered consciousness Sami pulled up a stool right in front of where the subject sat bound to a chair. At this stage it would be too risky to remove the gag.

But, dear heaven, he needed to work quickly. The fever had turned his innards into a furnace. Perspiration bled from his skin; it even dripped from his earlobes. Spasms shook him. His back ached. Speech became near impossible; it stammered from his lips in fractured sentences. Sami was ill, really ill. He longed to climb into bed. But if he persisted? Oh, God, if he persisted then maybe he could make the process work again. He could milk his subject of that energy that healed all ills. Before he'd been jailed he'd made it happen time and time again. He would take a man or woman captive, keep them hidden away, then begin that exotic milking process. Every human being is a power house of the life force. A flesh and blood generator.

He, Sami, had made the breakthrough. The force could be siphoned off into the sick person. Despite what the doctors, psychiatrists and even his own lawyers told him, he was not deluded. *I know I can do this*, he told himself as he shivered on the stool. *This flare-up of malaria fever is curable my way.* And so Sami worked on his precious subject. Maya stood beside him. She didn't speak or move, but he knew she willed him to succeed.

This is the process. Talk to subject. Maintain eye contact. Keep speaking, open up the pathway that links the two individuals. It's all through the conduit of the eye. Those eyes ... that delicate structure of the eyelashes. The lashes on the lids are important ... Sami's head lolled. A dizzy spell seized him. His mouth grew as dry as asphalt on a hot summer day.

'I need you to cooperate, because . . . all this . . . you'll understand. It won't hurt . . . you won't be harmed . . .' Sami gulped as he tried to expel the words.

Maya gazed dispassionately at the subject.

'There is a kind of power . . .' His teeth clicked as body tremors struck. 'A milking process . . . a siphoning of surplus energies . . . heal the sick . . . uh, this fever is . . . Now . . .' All of a sudden his voice quickened; speech became fluid. 'I want you to allow your eyes to feel as if they've opened again; as if there is a second eyelid that has snapped back. Open your eyes for the second time. Link with mine.' The fever agitated him. He glanced back. Another figure had entered the room. Sami had seen the wide face with its bulging eyes before. He recalled the white-clad figure being referred to as the Toad by the guards.

Now the Toad witnessed Sami establish a rapport with his subject, a man in blue, sat bound to the chair with stockings retrieved from neighboring cabins. His mouth gag consisted of a sleeve torn from a silk shirt. *Ottoman princes were strangled with a silk noose.* Bizarre thoughts slid through Sami's head as fever raged. At one point he even believed himself back in court again as the judge delivered his judgment. *'Yours is a despicable crime. You have repeatedly kidnapped innocent people to gratify your own perverse compulsions. On the latest occasion you deliberately asphyxiated a young man and a woman who had become troublesome to you. Psychiatrists are divided about the state of your mental health. While they agree you are fixated by the notion that you can somehow extract a psychological electricity, as it were, from your victim, the experts cannot agree whether or not you are clinically insane as defined by the laws of the land. Therefore, I will not make an order for your detainment in a psychiatric hospital. Instead, I will sentence you to a term in prison. One that will be for the whole of your life. Do you understand? You will spend the rest of your life in captivity . . .'*

Sami blinked through the tears. The judge in the courtroom melted away to be replaced by the man in blue. His eyes met Sami's with a cool hostility. *This isn't working. I'm not establishing a rapport with the subject . . .*

Beside him stood Maya. By the door was the Toad. Both watched him at work. *They've placed their trust in me. I can help them both if I can demonstrate the miraculous power of this process.* Sami positioned himself on the stool so he could lean forward to establish eye contact with the subject. 'Listen to me. I have invented a revolutionary process. There is a way to cure people with the most dangerous illnesses imaginable. And it doesn't require surgery or drugs. In fact, it's the pharmaceutical companies that conspired with the government.' He swallowed. The fever produced agonizing muscle spasms in his back. 'Work with me. Help me prove this process is the greatest discovery of the century.'

With a glare of contempt the man in blue kicked out both feet. The blow caught Sami in the chest, sending him tumbling backwards off the stool.

After that, fever overwhelmed Sami. Vertigo caught him up in a psychological tidal wave to sweep him away. The Toad and Maya didn't react when he raced round the luxury suite to yank open drawers. A strange force appeared to reach into him from outside his head. It compelled him to run into the neighboring cabins to widen the search. Then a calm settled over him. When he came round he thought he must have fallen asleep. Yet the moment he opened his eyes he realized where he was.

He knelt on his subject's chest as he lay flat on the floor, still tied to the chair. His subject screamed loudly. For a moment this confused and frightened Sami.

Then he saw the reason for his subject's huge braying yells. Sami had found a pair of nail scissors in one of the cabins. With these he had proceeded to quite neatly, and extremely accurately, snip away the man's eyelids.

The moment the man smiled in the midst of all that slaughter Tanya Rhone knew that she might be only heartbeats away from joining the corpses in their long final sleep. She darted along the steel vault of the cargo hold. To one side of her the monster pump towered. At the other side the ribs of the vessel soared upward. The space she passed through resembled a deep canyon. At either side of it lay bloody bodies still in uniform. Chefs, waiters, waitresses, ship's officers, engineers, stewards; nobody had been spared. Sometime during the night there had been a massacre here. Thick steel floors had prevented sounds of the killing reaching passengers as they slept three decks above this one. As Tanya ran she glanced back. The man in the business suit merely strolled. His smile grew larger. Wolfish.

In the luxury suite they'd started laughing. The Toad had chuckled first. Nothing much, just a gentle quiver of the shoulders as he watched Sami remove the man's eyelids with the nail scissors.

Sami had been distraught. The suffering of others distressed him to the point of nausea. *What have I done! This wasn't meant to happen. I only wanted to start the process. Now this cruel laughter.*

'I'm sorry,' he blurted. 'I don't know what happened . . . I had no intention of hurting you.'

The Toad's giggles grew louder. Maya's face twitched. With no eyelids the subject wore a perpetual expression of astonishment. Still screaming, he looked from Sami, to Maya, to the Toad in quick succession. Now the blood that gushed from the wounds became a veritable river. It smeared his eyeballs with a wash of pink. But he had no eyelids to blink it away. Crimson torrents ran down his cheeks. His expression of wide-eyed astonishment grew.

Maya picked up the giggle from the Toad. Her shoulders shook. Sami felt his own face quiver; the spasm generated a pronounced wink. This tickled the Toad, whose chuckle became laugher. Maya giggled louder. Sami intended to cry out to them to stop laughing at this poor victim's suffering, but it emerged as a squeal of hilarity. This in turn goaded Maya to open her pink lips to release a whole gale of laughter. Sami tried to stop laughing but it became a source of energy now.

'I'm well again!' Sami yelled with delight. The fever had vanished. He was strong. He longed to share his gift with the world. 'Come on!' he shouted.

After replacing the gag all three tumbled out of the suite. The subject stared at their departure in wide and bloody-eyed astonishment. Together they raced for the stairs to join the rest of the passengers.

Thirty-Three

Tanya Rhone knew one stark fact right then: *If the man catches me, he'll kill me.*

The cargo hold that contained the pump also contained its own oozing cargo of butchered men and women – the crew of the *Volsparr*. The man behind her upped his pace, a brisk, all too purposeful walk. Tanya ran along the narrow canyon formed by the high flank of the pump casing on one side and the hold's wall on the other. Beneath brutal electric light corpses lay in lines. Faces blown away, bullet-riddled torsos, gashed throats, missing hands, intestines hanging through ripped bellies.

Spilt blood is slippery as grease on a kitchen floor. More than once her feet skittered out from under. Down she'd fall with a jolt that flashed agony through every limb. Blood daubed her as she splashed into yet another pool of congealing crimson.

The man in the business suit bore down. His silver hair had been so severely cut his scalp gleamed through it. When he was barely twenty paces away he uttered, 'Don't run . . . there's no point . . . don't run, lady.'

An ominous quality in his voice propelled her back to her feet. And then Tanya did run. She belted along the walkway between the pump and the sides of the hold. Her bloody hand painted a line of red along the steel wall. Straight ahead, a door. *Don't be locked . . . please don't be locked . . .* With the man little more than a dozen paces away she wrenched at the handle, but her hands were so slick with blood they slid off. *Please don't be locked.* She encircled the handle with her fingers then made them rigid as a hook. She pulled again. The door swung open. She half tumbled through.

Beyond the door lay a service corridor. Doors led off it – storerooms perhaps. If only she could find an elevator.

The moment she ran the door behind her swung shut with a bang, and the moment it shut Tanya was plunged into darkness. The only light in the corridor had fallen through the doorway from the hold.

There's no time to find a light switch, she told herself. *Run!*

With her hands held in front of her she raced along the corridor. Absolute darkness. She could see nothing. An attacker could step through one of the doorways. She'd never even know they were there until she slammed into them.

Suddenly there was light. The man who pursued her opened the door to the corridor. He slipped through, then the spring shut the door. Darkness flooded back.

Tanya's trajectory resembled that of a human pinball. She glanced off the corridor wall as she ran in the dark. *Don't stumble. Keep your balance. For God's sake don't panic. Focus on getting away.*

Once more the man uttered, 'Don't run, lady. Stand still. Running will do you no good.'

She ricocheted off a wall, and fell sprawling. Fear drove her to stand. A second later her feet drummed the steel floor. Tanya seemed to fly through the darkness.

Dear God. When she reached out sideways to steady herself the wall vanished. Instead her fingers clawed air. Another concussion knocked the air from her lungs. A wall or pillar made its presence felt all too painfully. This time when she pushed herself upright she realized her hands pressed down on the risers of a staircase. As quietly as possible, and on all fours, she climbed. Beneath her the stairwell was a black fog of darkness.

Praying that her pursuer would miss the stairs in the dark, she scaled them. Seconds later she reached a turn in the stairs. A closed door offered an exit point. *What now? Keep climbing the stairs? They might take me to the passengers in the lounge. Or quit them now for this deck?* Holding her breath, she listened carefully. A clump, clump of heavy feet ascending. *Damn it; he knows I've used the stairs.* At that moment her legs felt weak; she knew she couldn't climb fast enough to outrun him. *The door it is, then.* She exited into another utilitarian corridor. At least here there were lights. Blinking against the dazzling glare, she blundered away from the stairwell.

Tanya staggered as she walked. Her mind became strangely

numb. Even her thought process appeared too exhausted to continue operating normally. Bizarre ideas streamed into her head for reasons she couldn't fathom. *If I make it upstairs the passengers won't believe me. They thought I'd imagined the inflatable boat. But it was there. It scooted out of sight behind the shipwreck. It's there though. Hiding. It's connected with the bodies in the cargo hold. They did it. They'll do the same to us. Get proof. Make the passengers believe you.*

But how do you prove a massacre without producing corpses? Take them down into the hold? Show them? No way; psychotic killers are roaming. That woman . . . Suzanne. Yes, yes, Suzanne Lynch. She told them about the prisoners escaping. Wait . . . what if Suzanne lied? What if she's one of the prisoners? Trust no one, Tanya . . . trust absolutely no one.

She walked unsteadily along the corridor. A gate bore the warning sign: *Choir-Moore Abstracts: No Admittance.* She struggled to draw in enough oxygen. The chase had been hard. She limped; her calf muscle hurt with every step. She wanted to creep into her cabin, then slide into bed. *No, not yet. Get proof.* The passengers must know she's telling the truth about the massacre. All those poor men and women in the hold. They'd been slaughtered like rats. The apparent casualness of the killings appalled her. Tears blurred her vision.

Proof . . .

But what evidence would satisfy the passengers that this wasn't a hysterical delusion on her part? *I'm covered with blood.* Would that persuade them? Might some sneer that she'd rubbed raw meat from the kitchen over her face and clothes? Tanya could imagine the accusations. *Proof. Show them something they can't deny.* She lurched along the iron-gray labyrinth. Where's her pursuer? He didn't seem the kind to give up so easily. *I've got a camera phone*, she told herself. *It's in the cabin. I could fetch that then . . . But that means having to return to the hold to take photographs . . .* Walking became impossible. *I need to lie down. I'm exhausted. I can hardly stand . . .*

She heard footsteps – stealthy ones. Groggy, she half turned to gauge if the sound came from ahead or behind. Her attacker? *From the look in his eyes he won't be satisfied with killing me first. He's one of the psychopaths. He'll torture me . . . Won't he want me down on my knees begging for my life?*

Tanya drove herself forward. Running wasn't an option. All she could manage was to put one foot in front of another. The world had become dream-like. A monster pursued her; he'd have killed people in a manner that was sadistic beyond imagination – and yet she couldn't run. In fact, her pace slowed. It was as if she walked through thick mud that sucked her feet down.

'Get proof of what you saw,' she murmured.

The footsteps grew louder.

'Proof.'

With blood-caked fingers she pushed open doors to storerooms. Racks full of equipment, plastic boxes, cables. Then in one room a body. A body positioned three feet from its head. Without blinking, she stared dumbly at a naked female that sat with its back to the wall. A sign commanded: *No Firefighting Equipment To Be Removed Without Permission.* The nude corpse sat beneath fire-proof suits hanging from pegs.

'Hello, head.' Tanya didn't know why she'd said that. Horror vied with a sudden hilarity. The head lay on its side. Its long hair flowed out across the tiled floor. One eyelid had slid back part way as if the dead woman gave a drowsy blink. For some reason the other eyeball had been slit with a knife. Into the wound had been thrust the end of a gold neck chain. About a foot of delicate gold links trailed from the ruined eye to the floor tiles.

'Proof.' Tanya nodded with satisfaction at solving her problem. It took two attempts to pick up the head. Heads, once they're removed from their bodies, are far heavier than they seem. Eight pounds of compact muscle, cerebral tissue, elaborate sensory organs together with a bone helmet designed by Mother Nature herself. Tears ran down Tanya's face, and all the while she laughed – only it was laughter generated by an overload of panic, terror, exertion, pain. Her senses were scrambled. Heaven, hell or a walk through the carnival, they all seemed the same right now. For one crazy moment Tanya though it was her own head she tried to raise from the floor. It belonged to someone of her own age, build and coloring. Only with much longer hair. The blood on her hand made the hair slip through her fingers when she tried to lift this ruddy lump with a face.

'Try, try again,' she sang as she swayed. This time she wound the long hair round her fingers a couple of times before lifting the head.

When she stepped out of the firefighter's room a group of three people stood with their backs to her. Two men she didn't recognize . . . and Suzanne Lynch. For some reason they were armed. The men carried sub-machine guns. Suzanne carried a Tazer. The men whirled round. The shorter one had old scars covering his face. The taller guy wore a new bandage round his head.

'Get down,' he shouted to Suzanne as he raised his weapon.

Suzanne protested, 'No, it's—'

'No, she's one of the prisoners. Look at what's she's carrying.'

Tanya gazed down at the head she carried by the hair as if it was a purse hanging by its strap. Tanya even swung it gently backwards and forwards. *Did I really pick that up?*

'Please don't shoot her.'

'We can't waste time trying to capture them alive.'

In that dazed state the voices seemed to reach Tanya as if they echoed down a long, long tunnel. As the man pressed down on Suzanne's shoulder to make her duck he still couldn't aim the gun properly. Tanya grabbed her chance. She went whirling away. The head swung as she gripped it by the hair. It thudded against the wall when she ran. Any second now . . . She could almost feel the machine gun bullets that would crash into her spine. He'd be aiming, squeezing the trigger.

Crossroads! The main corridor ran straight ahead. But narrower ones ran to her left and right. Through blurred eyes she made out the doors to an elevator. She ran for her life.

Then miracle and nightmare happened at the same time. Miracle: the doors lay open, inviting her to hop lightly aboard. Nightmare: the silver-haired stranger in the business suit stood waiting for her. If she paused the gunmen would round the corner then slay her. The only remaining option would be to ride the elevator with the psychopath. Even in her dazed state she didn't doubt for a moment he'd take great pleasure in killing her. The lift door began to slide shut. He reached out his hand to stop the door closing. A slow smile spread across his face.

'I do beg your pardon.' He spoke softly. 'I hadn't realized

that you were one of us.' Smiling even more warmly, he nodded down at the head she carried in her right hand. Blood dripped from the open-ended neck. 'Which floor?'

As if in a dream she stepped into the elevator. From the corridor came the sound of running feet. A shot rang out.

But that deck now belonged to the past. Right now, she rode the car back to the lounge with its piano, waiting passengers and ocean views.

'This is me.' The elevator stopped. With a bright smile the man touched his eyebrow in a leisurely kind of salute then stepped out. As the doors slid shut he nodded with approval at the head she carried; its gold chain still hung twinkling from the eye.

The elevator hummed as it obediently delivered her to her companions. In a distant, dream-like way she wondered what their reaction would be to her stepping out of the elevator with her blood-dripping eight-pound burden.

Thirty-Four

Maya led Sami and the Toad upstairs to the Moonlit Bay Lounge. Sami had recovered from his malaria flare-up. The fever had gone. He radiated health. Without doubt doctors would claim that his earlier symptoms of malaria were all psychosomatic, that he hadn't really cured himself using his innovative technique, and that both the fever and return to health were all part of his delusion. *But I know differently, don't I? All you so-called medical experts, what will you say when I deliver proof of my cure to the world?* As he climbed the stairs he enthused about developing his drug-free technique. The man's eyelids he carried in a little plastic wallet in his pocket. He didn't mention them. Nor did he mention the man who would have screamed the ship to blazes if it wasn't for the massive gag they'd applied to his mouth.

For a moment they had to wait just outside the lounge on the top deck to make sure the last of the giggles had abated. At last, with a final exchange of elated grins, the Toad opened the door to the lounge where the passengers were gathered. Maya and Sami entered. The man with the broad smiling face followed. There they melted into a group that clustered at the bar, downing free liquor.

Thirty-Five

Tanya Rhone's entrance to the Moonlit Bay Lounge couldn't have had a greater effect than if she'd detonated fifty pounds of gunpowder under the grand piano.

When the passengers saw what she carried in her hand it created an emotional shockwave. People flinched backwards in such a way she saw a ripple of movement run from the person nearest to her to those at the bar.

She advanced toward the room's center. Some detached fragment of her noted that fog still shrouded the wrecked ships.

Tanya lifted the head so they could all see. All the doubters.

'This is proof.' Her voice rang out with a power she couldn't have believed. 'In the cargo hold, with your precious pump, you'll find what's left of the crew.'

Isis emerged from a knot of people. 'Tanya. Put that thing down. Then come with me. I'll get you cleaned up. You can change your clothes in—'

'Isis, for once in your life, shut up. Listen to someone else for a change.'

'You're in a state of shock. Let me—'

'Obviously, you came back up here when we were split up. You fled like rabbits. You haven't seen what's down there. It's a massacre. In all likelihood we will be next. Understand? If you don't believe me, feast your eyes on this.' Tanya raised the head even higher. Pendulum-like, it swung gently from side to side. The open wound plopped blood on to the carpet.

The gold chain that some sadist had rammed into the eye dangled down the cheek as if the head wept a single line of yellow tears.

Tanya noticed what played on the TV screens on the wall. A burst of laughter erupted from her mouth. Inappropriate, evil laughter, but unstoppable, shocking, a force of nature in its own right.

Through her laughter she announced to her dumbstruck audience: 'I didn't need to bring this as proof, did I?' She shook the head by its bloody hair. 'Just look at the TV screen. That's all the proof you need!'

SEVENTH TRACT
Thirty-Six

The Moonlit Bay Lounge is located on an upper deck of the *Volsparr*. Comfortably appointed; sofas with big squashy cushions; low tables in dark wood, deep carpets. There is a bar adorned with polished brass, stocked with tempting drinks. There are mirrors, soft lighting, framed prints of steam ships. In the center of the room, a grand piano. All in all, quintessential sophistication.

Now this.

Tanya stood holding the woman's head as it leaked crimson on to the luxury carpet; the gold chain inexplicably dangled from a dead eye. With her other arm outstretched she pointed at the TV screen on the wall beside a Christmas tree.

'Do you know what you're seeing?' she demanded of her shocked audience. 'Do you know?'

'Tanya . . .' Isis began.

'Watch.' Laughter burst from her lips, a harsh, nerve-stripping sound. 'Whoever did this,' she twitched the head by its hair, 'has been considerate enough to film it for you.'

The passengers were drawn to watch what unfolded on the screen. In utter silence a series of camcorder shots revealed a massacre. Horrified faces loomed into view; a second later gunfire exploded heads. A ship's officer lunged toward the camera's operator, only a handgun appeared in shot. Its bullet punched a hole in his throat. The officer flopped down lifeless.

It lasted perhaps two minutes, a compilation of savage little scenes that recorded the murder of the crew in the ship's cargo hold. From the back of the lounge area Gus emerged from a doorway. With him were a couple of his assistants who had gone to check on the pump. Blood smeared their clothes; whether their own or someone else's wasn't clear. Their expressions reflected the horror they'd witnessed on the lower deck. Now they saw footage of the massacre as it occurred.

On screen, a waiter begged for his life as a masked figure showed him an axe. A second later the axe blade opened up the waiter's rib cage in a torrent of blood that carried internal organs with it.

Gus walked stiffly, his eyes fixed on the screen. 'I can understand that all those poor people were killed.' His voice came as a feeble croak. 'But why film it? What on earth would compel a human being to record such abominable . . .' Words failed him.

'Oh, there's a reason all right.' Isis nodded. 'The massacre. Releasing the prisoners. Anchoring the ship near the munitions wrecks. Believe me, this is all part of someone's master plan.' She turned back to the screen where masked men fired sub-machine guns into a line of crew members. They screamed – silently, as no sound accompanied the footage. Blood atomized by the impacts spray-painted the very air crimson. Even this image didn't prevent Isis from coolly asking, 'The question is, what do they plan to do to us?'

Maya had the instinct to melt into crowds. She merged with the group by the bar. Probably nobody would notice her, especially at that moment when they stared at TV screens replaying footage of the crew's execution. If, however, one of the passengers did notice her they'd describe the slightly built woman with the blonde, spiked hair as having a shy demeanor, as being somehow insubstantial. Maya had read that individuals labeled 'psychopaths' have the ability to merge with their surroundings. They are human chameleons. In their home towns and workplaces they don't stand out at all. Crocodiles conceal themselves from their intended victims by submerging themselves in muddy water. Psychopaths conceal themselves by submerging their true, monstrous natures beneath masks of restraint and quiet affability. They don't roam the streets bellowing and raging and attacking people at random. The psychopath patiently waits 'submerged', until the time is right.

Maya gazed dispassionately at the mayhem on the TV screen; beside her, men and women gasped in horror. The Toad made gasps of horror, too, although when he caught Maya's eye he gave an impish wink. Sami appeared to sag as he stared at the screen. She knew he felt genuine horror.

He hated violence. The idea of suffering made him sick to his stomach. Sami would fantasize he could save the crew who lay dying from gunshot wounds in the cargo hold. She smiled at him and wanted to hold his hand. But now wasn't the time. The woman who carried a gooey head seemed to be the catalyst for that promise of transformation that lingered in the air.

Soon everything on this ship would change. In Maya's blood she felt it coming.

Tanya had lost her grip on time. Even reality had a greasy quality that constantly slipped away from her. *Am I really standing here, holding the head of a corpse in my hand? Those TV screens, do they really show the crew being murdered?* Her shoulder throbbed where she'd collided with walls in that crazed dash through the darkness.

On screen the waiter fell as the axe man struck him down. His lung sagged through a gash in his chest . . . *It's on a loop. The same scenes are repeated. The film has got a hold of the passengers. Nobody can move . . .* She'd no sooner thought that when the screen crashed to black. A moment after that the head of a figure appeared on screen. Behind it was the formidable bulk of the pump. The figure wore a blue shirt. On its head was a black balaclava mask with a pair of holes to reveal cold gray eyes. The figure raised a hand to reveal it carried a heavy-duty revolver.

'Listen to me.' The voice possessed a tone that was as neutral as it was professional. 'We have the *Volsparr*. You know what happened to the crew. You know where the ship has been anchored. Those wrecks you've seen contain unstable warheads. Demolition charges have been set there. Our demands have been delivered to your governments. If they are not met, the explosive charges will be detonated on the wrecks precisely twenty-four hours from now. There are five thousand tons of munitions. They will destroy this vessel and all onboard.' He paused, but not to gather his thoughts. Instead, he hauled a young sailor by his shirt collar into view. He placed the gun muzzle at the side of the man's head. Already the sailor's eyes were dulled by trauma.

'Oh, my dear God,' Gus whispered.

The masked figure continued. 'Passengers of the *Volsparr*, listen to instructions. Obey them to the letter. Do not leave the lounge. We know you're assembled there. Do not attempt to leave the ship. Do not contact anyone outside the ship. This is your world now. If you want to live, do not cause trouble.' He gave the sailor a shake with one muscular arm. The young man appeared more bewildered than frightened. The masked man spoke louder. 'Your governments have twenty-four hours.' He squeezed the trigger. The round smashed through the sailor's skull to exit the temple in a jet of blood.

The screen crashed to black. Then silver numerals appeared.
24:00:00
23:59:59.

Isis breathed, 'This is it. The countdown's begun.'

Thirty-Seven

Twenty-three hours until zero hour. Monitors throughout the ship carried the vivid numerals scrolling relentlessly downwards. The screen had been split into four quarters. One quarter showed the countdown. Another had looped footage of the massacre. The third quarter showed CCTV of the passengers in the Moonlit Bay Lounge. The last quarter contained a close-up of the masked man, also on a loop, endlessly repeating his demands.

Tanya shivered. She'd been staring through the windows at the wrecks. Mist swirled round them. In her imagination she could even hear the clanking as waves jostled them. Meanwhile, the monstrous hooked cross of the Nazi swastika awarded her a baleful stare through the murk.

'It knows we're here . . . it can see us . . .' Tanya uttered the words in a daze. 'This is what it wants. It's been waiting for this so it can kill us all . . .'

Isis pushed a tumbler into her hand. 'Drink this. You're in shock.'

Tanya's eyes swiveled to her hand that until recently had held the corpse's head. 'Where is it?'

'I got rid of it.'

Tanya stared at her hands. There had been so much blood . . . 'I'm clean,' she whispered.

'I took care of you,' Isis said firmly. 'You are my friend, Tanya. I will look after you. Drink. All of it.'

Tanya drank from the tumbler. It must have been a spirit of sorts but at that moment Tanya's senses were in shutdown. The liquor tasted of nothing.

'Better?' Isis asked.

'No. I never will be. Did you see the eye? Why did they ram a chain into it? What was the point?'

'There's every point. Whoever's doing this has a plan. This is carefully orchestrated violence, not random killing for the fun of it.'

Gus limped across the lounge to join them. Just hours ago he had been the silver-haired alpha male – strong, resourceful, a leader of men. Now he seemed so old, stumbling over simple words. 'Ah . . . hmm. I see the clo— clock. There on the . . . uhm . . . TV.'

Isis spoke crisply. 'Whoever has taken us hostage has begun a countdown. If their demands aren't met by our governments they'll detonate the munitions on those wrecks. We'll go sky high.'

'Yes, I . . . I'd gathered that . . . Uhm, so there was a boat –out there in the uhm . . .' A finger pointed vaguely in the direction of the Nazi convoy.

'An inflatable. I saw it distinctly, but nobody believed me.' To Tanya's surprise her self-control returned. She licked her lips. The brandy's strength tingled across her tongue. Her sense of taste came back in a snap. She watched Gus Hammond as he struggled to remain on his feet. He could have been a faded photograph of his former self. His eyes roved in a fearful way. Even small sounds made him flinch.

Two thoughts struck Tanya. First: she felt sorry that he'd been reduced to this shambling, inferior version of himself. The second: *I can't rely on him to help me. I've got to save myself.* Immediately, she shifted to self-preservation mode.

'Just over twenty-two hours now. Then they flip the switch . . .' His lips were gray. 'We have to obey them. Best make use of the bar . . . uhm . . . there's plenty . . . it'll get us through the hard part.'

Tanya fired up mental connections. 'Gus, they locked you in the hold, didn't they?'

'Yes, with all those . . . that mess . . . red mess . . . bloody . . .'

'And then they turned out the lights.'

He nodded. Tremors ran across his face.

Tanya turned to Isis. 'Then when we opened the doors to the hold Gus and his team ran. They stampeded over us in the process.'

'I must sit down now.' There was no impression of strength in his limbs. 'I need to get myself together . . .' He tottered away.

'Isis, we're on our own.' Tanya tilted her head at the growing throng at the bar. Bottles clinked. Someone shouted for whiskey. 'They're not going to fight for their lives.'

Isis had been thinking. 'There will be radios in the lifeboats. If one of us can reach one we can at least speak to the outside world.'

Tanya shook her head. 'We've been told to stay here. Surely they'll be watching us?'

Isis snorted. 'We don't have the luxury of doing nothing. Nor the luxury of getting drunk.' She glared at people downing liquor. 'That's the fool's way. They're signing their own death warrants.'

Before Tanya could comment the masked man returned to the TV screen. This time the backdrop suggested the man was now ensconced in the ship's studio. There he made a stark order that turned their blood cold.

'Listen to me.' The volume rattled glasses on the tables. Everyone turned to the screen. 'This is an address to the man in the green fleece top. You, standing at the bar.'

They turned to look at the middle-aged man in the green fleece. And everyone must have thought the same: *Thank God they didn't pick me.* The man froze; his face became suddenly bloodless. His eyes locked on to the screen; for him it could have been the opening to his tomb.

The masked figure on TV continued, 'I see you all via the camera mounted in the lounge. Man in the green top, indicate that you can hear me.'

Very reluctantly, the man raised his hand.

'Everybody remain in the lounge. You in green, take the stairs down to the restaurant.'

The man's expression clearly displayed his horror.

The masked man had anticipated the response. 'You will obey. Go to the restaurant. We need to speak with you.'

Not one passenger made eye contact with him, let alone persuaded him to disobey the command.

'Go to hell,' yelled the man in green to his fellow passengers. 'Just wait until it's your time. Can't you understand? I'm only the first!'

The voice rumbled, 'Proceed to the restaurant. *Now*.'

Thirty-Eight

The man in the green fleece took the downward steps slowly. In the back of his mind he wanted to rip off the fleece then fling it from him. He'd begun to sweat with fear. An unbearable itch had started between his shoulder blades. His imagination went wild. God, he wanted rid of the fleece, only he'd been ordered down to the restaurant to meet the hijackers. He passed a TV monitor at the exit of the staircase. It showed the recording of crew members being shot.

Neville West had once saved a boy from drowning. For some reason he remembered that so clearly as he took those tentative steps across the restaurant. Tables bore clean linen. Cutlery gleamed in the overhead lights. They boy had fallen into a river where Neville kept his boat. He'd told his wife to stay with their baby daughter as he dived in to save the boy. The mayor awarded him a certificate. Local TV news interviewed him. Neville West, hero of the day.

Now why did it seem his insides were liquid? Why did he want to cry for his wife? The fleece top stuck to his skin as the fear-sweat oozed.

'Hello?'

A masked figure appeared. For some reason, instead of a gun it carried a camcorder, which he aimed at Neville. A second figure appeared. In its hands was an AK-47 with its characteristic crescent moon ammunition clip protruding from the bottom. When the figure pulled off his mask Neville knew it was over. He'd seen the man's face. He could identify him. That meant one thing . . .

RUN!

Instinct carried him away on pounding feet. Running was all that mattered. Running was his universe. Even so, he yearned to shout that he'd once saved a boy from drowning. His selfless act of humanity might be enough to make the hijackers change their mind about killing him.

Behind him, one guy said to the other, 'Get as much as you can of this on film. Command needs more.'

Command needs more. More of what, Neville West did not want to know. Even so, he could guess. As he ran he saw the footage on the monitor set above a Christmas tree. Thankful to be away from the horror unfolding in vivid splashes of crimson on the monitor, Neville ran toward the restaurant exit. This led into the shopping mall. A huge screen hanging from the high ceiling revealed to him just how they'd cut off the woman's head with a fire axe. Behind him the door to the restaurant burst open.

The man with the machine gun didn't even have to shout. 'You've nowhere to run.'

Neville pelted by locked stores. Ahead the cinema door lay partly ajar. A leg cut off from the knee down revealed why it hadn't closed properly on its spring.

'Stop, or I'll fire.'

Damn it. He wouldn't give them the satisfaction. He'd leap over the rail into the sea first. Through the windows he saw the open deck with frost sheathing the cables. Beyond that, night had laid a dark blanket over the ocean.

A shot rang out. The bullet whined past him to scythe through decorations strung across the mall ceiling. Gold angels floated down to the floor.

'Don't run. There's no point.'

Neville ducked through a room full of video games that pulsed with lights. He knew the room had two entrances. The one opposite would take him into the corridor that ran along the port side of the ship. If only he could find a stairwell. Beneath this deck there was a whole labyrinth of corridors that served the cabins. This would be the place to hide.

By now he heard the sound of running feet. They were no longer so leisurely in their pursuit. At any moment the guy with the AK-47 might turn a corner to unleash high-velocity rounds into his belly.

'I saved a boy from drowning,' Neville panted as he fled. 'I don't deserve this. Please God, I don't deserve this.'

To his right lay a children's play area. Toddler slides, a mini-carousel . . . and a ball pool! He stared at the brightly colored balls, which occupied a cage six-feet deep. It could be accessed via a chunky plastic ladder that lead to a plummet platform where children could enjoy the two-foot drop into the surface of the multi-colored balls. Fixed to the cage bars were cartoon pictures of clowns sailing on funny caricatures of the *Volsparr*.

A plan evolved in Neville's mind. He raced past the carousel, then leapt head first through the aperture in the cage to bounce on to the platform. Driving the ache in his ribs from his mind, he slithered off it into the cool mass of plastic balls. There he buried himself deep inside the ball pool. He worked hard to reach the bottom. A moment later he lay there with a layer of plastic balls four feet above his face. Darkness surrounded him. With all his willpower he forced himself to take shallow, noiseless breaths, although he longed to gasp huge lungfuls of air. The itch returned to the center of his back.

He waited.

No sound reached him other than his respiration. Sweat tickled the skin of his neck. He longed to wipe it away. Moments crawled by. He seemed to have been lying there for whole minutes. But how long? He couldn't risk looking at his watch. In his mind's eye he saw the placid surface of the balls that shone beneath the lights.

A click came from faraway. It seemed nothing to do with Neville or his hiding place. But then the balls started to flow of their own accord, and a light appeared above him, growing brighter. A moment later there were no balls above him. He clenched his fists. Someone had removed one of the mesh walls; the balls poured out into the play area.

With a plunging sense of disappointment he lifted his head. The gunman stood beside the cameraman.

'Nice try.' The gunman then turned to his pal. 'Get in close for this. Make sure you get the clown pictures at the back. Also I want the guy's head dead center.'

'Bastard!' Neville flung a ball at the gunman. It pinged off his chest.

The gunman laughed at the use of such a flimsy weapon. Then, pausing only to check that his companion was filming, he raised the gun and blew Neville's face away.

Thirty-Nine

Twenty-one hours to Zero Hour. Tanya followed Isis out on to the deck. Philip leaned against the guardrail in the darkness. So much brandy had gone down his throat in the last three hours that he no longer felt the bitter Arctic air. Little could be seen beyond the guardrail other than a wall of fog illuminated by the ship's lights.

Philip gave a boozy smile. 'Hello, ladies. In there . . .' He gestured with a bottle of brandy that he clutched. 'They're all being killed, aren't they?'

Isis glared. 'It won't be the first time a crime's been committed on this ship.'

'Really?' He took a swig from the bottle. 'No, you're right, I agree . . . Those slot machines are rigged. Nobody's ever won a jackpot. Not one.' He chuckled. 'The croupiers are crooked as well . . .'

Isis advanced until she stood five paces from him. 'Don't you remember me?'

Tanya couldn't believe her ears. 'Isis, not now. Wait until—'

'Wait until we're blown sky high, Tanya? Have you forgotten we're moored next to five thousand tons of explosive?' Isis whirled from Tanya to face Philip.

'The lady's right,' Philip waved his arm theatrically. 'Declare what we feel in our hearts right now. Because tomorrow . . . Boom.'

Isis tugged off her headscarf. 'Remember me now, Philip?'

He tilted his head as he examined her face under the deck

lamps. He noticed bare patches in her scalp, caused by Isis tugging out clumps of her hair when she slept.

Coldly she said, 'My name is Isis Malaika. Anything coming back to you now?'

He gave a drunken shake of the head; his expression puzzled.

'Come, come, Philip. I made this trip last July. You plied me with drinks. Then you raped me.'

His eyelids yanked back in absolute horror. 'No!' he protested. 'Never . . . never. I couldn't—'

'Raped me. Made me pregnant.'

He choked out his disbelief. 'I-I'd never . . . why are you accusing me?'

'You remember me now, don't you?'

'Yes, of course, but I—'

'I carried your child. I decided to keep it but then I got sick. I lost your baby son.'

'Oh, God . . .' Philip could barely stand.

Tanya had been going to beg Isis to return to the lounge, to wait for a better time to confront him. *But then, what other time is there? Isis might not survive this. She's every right to seize the chance.*

Philip sagged against the rail, the brandy bottle hugged to his chest. He kept stammering denials. 'I-I didn't do anything to hurt you. I wouldn't attack you, Isis. I do remember we met and we talked until late. Then we went to your cabin. We were both drunk. But you consented. I didn't do anything that—'

'Liar.'

Tanya couldn't stop herself. 'Philip. Tell the truth. Did you drug her?'

'Drugs? No way. Never. We were both lonely and . . . and, yes, we downed the booze. I had a hell of a hangover, but I'm telling you God's honest truth. I did not make Isis do anything against her will. And there was a child?' The man's hands shook. 'Oh, God, a child? I'm so sorry. I don't know what to—'

'Isis,' Tanya interrupted. 'Could Philip be right?'

'Even if there were no drugs, he plied me with alcohol. He must have realized I was drunk, then he took advantage of me.'

'No, I wouldn't.' Tears filled his eyes. 'I'm sorry. I'd do anything to make you believe me.'

'Liar.' Her eyes blazed with the intensity of laser beams. 'How many more victims have you attacked?'

'I'm not like that. I was fond of you.' He pressed his hand to his mouth as if he'd wretch. 'I even tried to find your phone number. I wouldn't do that if—'

'Liar.'

Tanya stepped forward ready to grab Isis if she attacked the man. But at that moment Isis stopped stabbing him with her finger. Taking a step back, she touched the side of her head. 'Ever since I lost my baby I do this at night. Grab a handful in my sleep then rip hair straight out of my scalp.'

'Sorry. You can't believe how much I regret—'

'See those bald patches? But that's nothing to holding my son in my arms in the hospital. Have you any idea how much that hurt?'

Philip shook his head; he tried to speak but shock robbed him of the words.

'Isis, he's had enough. Leave him.'

'Yeah sure, Tanya. This bastard gets away with it. He can't lose, can he? If the ship explodes nobody will ever hear the truth of what he did to me. If he survives he'll keep denying it. What proof do I have?'

He took a deep breath. 'We made love. I did not force you to do anything.'

'So I'll just have to live with the hurt, won't I?'

'I'd do anything to prove to you that I'm a good person. I'm not the evil man you think I am.'

Isis wrapped her arms around herself. A tear rolled down her cheek.

Tanya said gently, 'You'll freeze out here. Come inside.'

Isis shook her head.

Philip had sobered up a great deal in the last five minutes. His eyes cleared as he dropped the bottle of brandy over the side. 'There must be a way I can prove to you that I'm a good person.'

Again she shook her head.

'Isis. If there's something I could do to make it up to you . . . I mean, if it's money you need . . . Or if we could meet after all this is over?'

Isis gave a toss of her head. 'All this is over? You think we'll escape with our lives?'

'Of course we will. The government will give these men what they want.'

'But that isn't guaranteed. We're pawns in their game. They'll kill more of us to prove to the authorities they mean business.'

Tanya eyed Isis in surprise. The woman had suddenly become more self-assured. A moment ago she verged on nervous collapse.

Isis sighed; white vapor issued from her red lips. 'If only we had some way of protecting ourselves.'

Quickly, Philip said, 'I'd do anything to protect you. *Anything*. I just want to prove to you I would never hurt you.'

'You want to prove that?' Her eyes glistened as she held his gaze.

'Of course, Isis. Anything.'

'The lifeboats.'

Philip appeared startled by her sudden change of subject. No doubt he thought the shock had confused her in some way. He blinked. 'Lifeboats?'

Isis spoke firmly. 'A lifeboat might be our last chance. If one of us could sneak into one of the lifeboats without the hijackers noticing, we could find out how the winch mechanism works. Then lie low in the lifeboat cabin. If the hijackers plan to blow up those munitions wrecks – and us with them – they'll need to leave here in plenty of time in their own boat. That will give us the opportunity to board a lifeboat, lower it into the sea, then get clear.'

Tanya noticed Philip's surprise. Isis had delivered this little speech about the lifeboat as if she'd rehearsed it.

'It's freezing,' Tanya said. 'No one would survive in the lifeboat overnight.'

'Tanya, whoever is courageous enough to hide in the lifeboat won't launch it yet.' Isis sounded her old imperious self. 'If you'd been observant you'd have noticed that each lifeboat has its own cabin. They are stuffed with life-saving equipment – flares, radios, blankets, food, water. All one need do is enter the lifeboat cabin, figure out how to deploy the boat, then be ready for us to join them, if need be.'

'But if the hijackers see one of us going down to the lower decks to—'

Philip butted in. 'I'll do it. I'm going to prove to you I'm not some kind of rat that attacks women.'

Isis nodded, then added curtly, 'Take the stairways on the outside of the ship. Use the lifeboat nearest the stern. Got that?'

'You can count on me.' Determination drove Philip. 'Come as soon as the hijackers leave. Bring everyone with you. I'll have everything ready.'

The man hurried to the steps that led down to the next deck, his breath trailing a ghostly white behind him.

'You're cold,' Isis said to Tanya. 'Come back into the warmth.'

Tanya lunged at Isis. 'You bitch.' This time she lost her self-control. Tanya delivered a full-blooded slap into the woman's face. 'I can't believe what you just did. You never intended confronting Philip to find out the truth. You did it to force him to risk his life so he could save your skin.' Once more rage took hold. Tanya wrestled Isis back against the rail, then slapped her again. If anything, the slap pained Tanya more than the woman she struck. The palm of her hand stung with a ferocity that made her gasp. And yet there was something so satisfying about the sensation. With the pain came a gushing sense of release. All that irritation she'd built up since she met this infuriating woman discharged in that full-blooded strike to her cheek.

'Feel better for that, Tanya?' Isis registered no emotion. 'I can see it did you good, so why not hit me again? You'll feel a million dollars.'

'I don't know if Philip did rape you or not, but right from the start you've planned to use this allegation to get exactly what you want. I'm ashamed; every woman would be. You're heartless.'

Isis pushed Tanya back. With her headscarf she wiped away a spot of blood from her lips. 'What I did there might save our lives. Now take a deep breath, forget all about sentimentality for the next few hours, and do what must be done.' Then she said something that made Tanya's blood run cold. 'The lifeboat might not be the means of survival. You should prepare yourself for seducing one of the hijackers.'

On the lower deck Turrock, Suzanne and Fytton were still pinned down by a gunman. Turrock knew they couldn't move out of the corridor that ran into the prow of the ship. However, their firepower matched that of the gunman. He wouldn't risk charging along the corridor to break through Turrock's barricade. That would be suicide. So this is it for now: stalemate.

Tanya followed Isis back into the lounge. *Have I heard right? Does Isis plan to pimp me to the hijackers?*

The woman strode purposefully across the lounge. This time she hadn't bothered replacing the headscarf. But the passengers were so wrapped up in their own fears they wouldn't notice anyway. Tanya had slapped Isis out on the deck. Now she planned on beating her down to the floor with her fists. On wall-mounted monitors the brutal film played of the crew being butchered. The clock counted down to zero hour.

'Wait, just one moment.' Tanya grabbed the nearest part of Isis that came to hand. It was the remaining long strands of hair at the back of her head. 'I'm not offering myself to the hijackers. No way!'

'Oh, you'll do it. If it's a question of surviving.'

'*Listen.*' The male voice roared from the ship's PA. '*There is a woman amongst you with a child. It's a girl of about five.*'

Tanya shuddered. It was the same voice that demanded that the man in the green fleece go to the restaurant.

'*The child's mother must take her to cabin number forty-five on D deck.*'

The mother screamed as she clutched the little girl to her. 'I won't do it! I won't!'

The man in the fleece hasn't returned. We've seen what happened to the crew. Now what did the hijackers have planned for the little girl?

Forty

Twenty hours to Zero Hour. *More footage. Lots more footage.* The order came through from the very top of the command structure.

'More footage, Camera,' called Axe Man as he stood above the ship's engineer, who lay howling on the generator room floor.

Camera barked back as the masked man raised the axe. 'Not yet! On my count. Three . . .'

'Please.' The engineer pushed himself into a semi-sitting position with one hand. The other hand he held up in a 'stay back' gesture. This hand had already parried one axe blow. The blade had run down between the first and index finger, along the hand's metacarpals, until it encountered the barrier of wrist bones. Now the hunk of flesh with the finger and the thumb attached to it hung down alongside the guy's forearm, connected by a shred of skin. Blood streamed over the metal floor.

The hijacker known as Camera ended the countdown. 'Two . . . one . . . go.'

With expert timing Axe Man lopped off the guy's arm at the shoulder. Then with a good, meaty chop he sheared the legs away. Axe Man kicked the severed limbs across the floor. The foot on one leg twitched. The engineer's eyes locked on the bloody members. He howled in dismay as much as agony.

Axe Man lopped away the remaining arm. The engineer waggled his stumps; this time he screamed that he wanted to die.

Camera laughed. It's how she dealt with scenes like this. What's more, she felt good. And she was getting plenty more footage. Axe Man pointed where he'd strike next with his weapon. She zoomed in on the dying man's groin.

If Camera peered up the chain of command she saw

'Foreman' above her, and then 'Control' above him. No doubt there were many other commanders above 'Control' but Camera never saw him, or her. She didn't know names, nationalities or whether she worked for a government agency or a private security company that rented out gunmen for the right price. No questions asked. No repercussions in high places.

None of the men and women in the Squad knew one another by their real names. They were ordered to keep their personal lives canned. If they mentioned so much as their child's birthday or mother's home town they were re-assigned to guard some gas pipeline in the wilderness for a year or two at least. Resigning from Squad is not permitted.

As was customary for the Squad's employees in the front-line, they eschewed their names. Instead, they referred to each other by their profession or anonymous nickname. The guy in command was Control. Second in command: Foreman. Others need no explanation: Sniper, Radio, The Executioner, Axe Man, Knife Man (a woman, but then the Squad imposed a sexual neutrality on its team members – gender isn't important; what is important is their professionalism). Camera knew the *Volsparr* job was the biggest ever. Control called it their 'gold strike'. The reputation they earned from successfully completing this operation would keep them in lucrative assignments for years to come. But HQ wanted to be sure. So they repeatedly demanded more footage. This wasn't home-movie stuff for the resident sadist; this was résumé material. This was film to present to new clients. They'd prove the Squad is brutally effective. Some would find its way on to the internet, and that was fine. *Power is back where it belongs. In the blood-stained hands of the modern warrior. This trophy footage proves it.*

Camera followed Axe Man across the engine room. Foreman's blue eyes locked on to hers through the holes in the black mask. 'Five more, then get the footage up to the studio. All major news channels are carrying this story. HQ wants your footage uploaded tonight.'

She felt a warming glow of pride. Camera had been one of the most accomplished snipers for hire. Over the years she'd developed the technique of entering a trance so she could remain immobile for hours. That way she could stay undetected in undergrowth as she picked off plantation workers from half a mile away. Lately she'd developed a talent for shooting film that equaled her talent for shooting crop pickers. In four hours people the world over would sit down at their computer, maybe after a boring day at school or at work, and in a few moments they could watch the final breath of the *Volsparr*'s engineer. Or the latest victim . . .

The chosen subject wore the uniform of a wine waiter from the ship's restaurant: dark trousers, white shirt, bow tie and a claret-hued jacket with a silver badge depicting a wine bottle on his lapel. He was one of the five. The other four stood handcuffed to a guardrail that protected the drive shaft.

'Filming,' she said, as a signal to the rest of the team to keep quiet.

Foreman nodded to Knife Man. There's an old method of execution called 'death by a thousand cuts'. Not *literally* that many, but it was dozens. The waiter gurgled prayers as he received cut after cut – arms, hands, face, neck, chest – but nonetheless he managed to remain alive for a full five minutes.

Then it was time to deal with victim number two. They took the steward to a hatch set just twenty feet above the waterline. When Foreman opened the hatch it admitted the Arctic air. Victim Two wore only pajamas. He moaned as the cold scythed through the material.

In a French accent he asked, 'What are you going to do to me?' When they taped a hand grenade to his face using gaffer tape he understood.

Axe Man and Knife Man worked together. One held the hand grenade to his cheek so it pressed against the side of the steward's nose. Then they looped the shiny black tape around his head until it formed a black band between mouth and eyes. His eyes remained uncovered so he could still see. The mouth stayed unfettered too.

'Do it,' he told them. 'Quickly. Do you hear? Quickly.'

The grenade beneath its strips of sticky tape formed an ugly bulge on his face.

Camera filmed with due diligence. Foreman held the steward by his elbows then guided him toward the open hatch where he shivered in his pajamas. Outside, night had descended. Darkness concealed the shipwrecks with their brooding cargoes. All Camera could see of the sea was a few square yards of ice lit by the ship's lights. Cold bit them to the bone. Their breath billowed white. Foreman maneuvered the steward forward. The Frenchman shivered. She filmed his face as the fear left him and his features became smooth. Foreman placed his hand between the man's shoulder blades. He nodded to Camera to get closer so she could film everything.

Axe Man pulled the pin from the grenade that bulged with tumescent vulgarity from the Frenchman's face. Instead of losing his self-control, in a clear voice he called out across the frozen ocean, '*J'arrive . . . Madeline! J'arrive.*'

Such joy in the voice. This was a man calling to a long-lost love; they would be reunited very soon.

Foreman pushed. The man tumbled out. Camera kept the falling man in shot. A second later he struck. His legs pierced the white crust. The top half of his body remained above the ice.

'*Madeline! J'arrive!*' The triumph pealing through those words sent a shiver down Camera's spine as she translated the joyous call. *Madeline. I'm coming.*

The grenade detonated. The head and much of the torso dashed a crimson flume across the whiteness of the ice.

For victim number three they must be quick. This footage had to hit the internet by midnight.

Just then, new orders came through. 'Leave the crew members for now. They're bringing a child down to cabin forty-five. Camera, rendezvous with the team there. I want powerful, memorable footage of what The Executioner does to the little girl.'

And on the monitors throughout the *Volsparr* the clock relentlessly continued its countdown toward zero hour.

Forty-One

The Toad sighed. 'I want to go home.'

Sami gave a sympathetic shrug. 'I wish there was a way.'

'I'm very tired, Sami. I'd like to go home now.'

Maya watched this exchange take place between the two men in the corner of the Moonlit Bay Lounge as a storm of emotion broke in its center. A male voice had announced over the ship's PA that a girl of about five must be taken down to the lower deck by her mother.

Those standing at the bar exchanged uneasy glances.

'Don't let them take my daughter!' the mother screamed. 'You can't let them do it. You know what they'll do, don't you? You've seen the TV!'

The Toad rested his stumpy hand on Maya's forearm. 'Maya. I'm so very tired. I need to go home right now.'

Maya realized that home for the Toad was the cabin where he'd placed the corpse in a tableau.

'You can't go now,' she whispered. 'There are men with guns. We've been told to stay here.'

'Nevertheless,' he murmured. 'Nevertheless.'

The sparkle abandoned the man as he stood there in his orange tracksuit. His shoulders sagged. A few minutes ago that uncannily broad face of his with its toad-like mouth had been fascinating, somehow radiating a magnetic charisma that had enchanted the other passengers before the crisis had occurred. Now the once-mobile face had stilled; his eyes were dull.

'Sami,' he mumbled, 'will you take me home, please?'

A tremor started in Sami's cheek. 'I wish . . . I wish I could help these people,' he breathed. 'They're good people but the violence on this ship is a sickness. I can heal all sickness. I know I can.' He licked his lips. 'All I need is more subjects.

Then I can employ my techniques.' He reached into his pocket to extract the cellophane envelope. He held it up to regard two bloody eyelids lying inside. Two red slivers of soft flesh. 'I need more.'

Trouble was brewing. The Toad needed to recharge his batteries in the only way he knew how. Sami craved to stop the violence. He hated violence. Now he saw it as an illness that could be cured. If only he could apply his special technique.

In the center of the room the woman clutched the five-year-old child. 'I won't let them take her. I won't!'

The little girl's blue eyes were open wide. She didn't cry. Suddenly her once safe world had become an emotional inferno. People wept. Others shouted. Men drank at the bar until they became silly.

The mother hung fiercely to the child. *'I won't let them take Jo; I won't let them take her. I won't!'*

One of Gus Hammond's assistants lunged forward; he reeked of whiskey. 'You gotta. See what's on TV? That's what'll happen to us if you don't send the kid.'

He grabbed Jo by the arm then tried to separate her from her mother.

'Please help us,' the mother begged the passengers who stood fixed in horror, unable to take their eyes from the tragedy unfolding in front of them.

Gus Hammond stumbled forward, not drunk but sick-looking. 'Don't worry,' he gasped. 'I'll take her to them. I won't let them hurt her.'

'What the hell can you do to stop them?' cried the woman. 'You're an old man!'

The guy struggling with the woman tugged harder at Jo. The child's sobs made passengers flinch.

'Do you know what they'll do to her?' The woman's eyes blazed. 'You do, don't you! They'll hurt her and they'll film it all, and they'll show it up there, because they're *torturing* us.'

'Lady, let me have the—'

The mother raked his face with her nails.

'Bitch.' He lunged at her but Gus grabbed the man. 'Stop it, Lou. The woman's right. They'll hurt the child.'

'No, they won't.' Isis's voice cut across the noise with the sharpness of a blade. Everyone fell silent. 'I'll take the girl to the cabin and I'll speak to the hijackers.'

The mother gazed at this woman with tufts of hair missing from the side of her head as if she were a strange apparition.

'No. I'm not letting my daughter go. They'll hurt her. I know it.'

'They'll hurt us all if we don't obey.' Isis nodded across to a TV that revealed one of the ship's officers being bludgeoned with a hammer by a masked figure. 'See? We must do as they say. I'll do what I can to protect your daughter.'

A pair of Gus's assistants took the opportunity to seize the mother and draw her back to a chair, where they forced her to sit. She tried to stand again but they held her. Absolute fear for her daughter's safety struck her voiceless. Her mouth opened but no sound came out.

The girl sobbed softly as Isis held her by the hand. A man darted forward. He wore a hooped jersey and was so concerned for the child's well-being that tears welled up in his own eyes.

'There, there,' he whispered as he crouched in front of Jo. 'What lovely eyelashes you have.' He dabbed her eyes with a tissue. 'Lovely and long they are. Special.' He gently dabbed again. 'My name is Sami,' he told her. 'I'll come with you and this nice lady.'

'It's OK,' Isis said. 'I'll take Jo. My friend Tanya will come too.' Then in a low voice that nobody else but Tanya heard she whispered. 'When we go downstairs use your lipstick. This is your chance to meet the hijackers.'

Tanya stared at the woman. Her heart thudded. Then she glanced down at the girl clad in bright pink. *Isis will take the child to the hijackers anyway. I've got no choice, have I? For the little girl's sake I've got to go. And I'll offer myself so they won't hurt her.*

More footage. HQ's imperative rang in Camera's ears. *It's excellent footage but we need more. Much more. And we need it transmitted by midnight.* The problem now was that they didn't have enough victims. What's more, killing crew members would become repetitive. Massacres can bore. *What HQ needs is fresh blood.* It had to be passengers now. *And now they'd summoned a child.* Camera and the others in the team – the

Executioner, Knife Man, Axe Man and the rest – had heard the command boom from the ship's PA system.

Now the PA spat out another announcement, this one for the team. '*Required personnel go to cabin forty-five.*'

That's us. Camera motioned The Executioner to follow.

'Maya . . . Maya . . .' The Toad became a washed-out image of his former self. His dull eyes held hers. 'Maya, I'm very tired. I need to go home. Please take me there.'

Sami frowned. 'Home?'

'He means the cabin,' she explained. 'The one where he keeps the man.'

'Why?'

'If he can spend time there it will make him strong again.'

Sami glanced round the lounge. After the departure of Isis, Tanya and the little girl the emotional charge had dissipated. Passengers sat around as if they'd been drained, too. The mother stared at the staircase that had claimed her daughter. It wasn't so very hard to imagine what thoughts dominated her now. *What will happen to my baby? What will they do to her?*

Camera and The Executioner reached the passenger deck. On the way to cabin forty-five they pushed open doors to check that there weren't any occupants. Camera still required subjects for her films. She smiled, eager to shoot more footage. *This is good; this is the best work I've ever done.* Such a skill would increase her earning power three-fold. *Now for the child. I've got to make this the best ever.*

The Executioner pushed open more cabin doors. They revealed bunks, jackets hanging on coat hangers. Make-up on dressing tables. The next door opened on a man apparently dozing on a bunk. The Executioner eased his knife from the sheath.

Camera touched her watch. 'No time. Do something quick . . . OK, recording.' She tracked him on the viewfinder. Swiftly, he unclipped a hand grenade from his belt, pulled the pin, then tossed the steel ball packed with high explosive into the cabin and shut the door. Three seconds later the explosion buckled the door. Its steel panel instantly acquired a raised stipple effect as shrapnel battered it from the other side.

'He never even woke,' commented the masked Executioner. 'Must have been sleeping like a baby.'

Quickly, she grabbed a shot of the aftermath. Through the smoky interior she could see the place had been wrecked. Bunks had been mangled, a mattress flung through the bathroom door. Chairs smashed. Streaks of soot violated the walls; the ripped up remains of the man hurled on to the floor.

The Executioner patted her shoulder. 'Good work. It's time for the kid.'

They heard the detonation all the way up in the piano lounge. A muffled boom of a sound. Some even ran to the window to see if the munitions ships had detonated. But out there was only fog.

The mother of the now absent child began a soft, heartbroken weeping. She sat hunched on the sofa, her eyes locked on to the carpet. If the steelwork became magically transparent she would have seen two hooded figures, one holding a camcorder, moving quickly along the accommodation deck to cabin forty-five where Torture awaited with the tools of his trade. If she'd seen the assortment of blades and hooks and steel spikes in his briefcase, the mother would have done anything in her power to reach her daughter.

Meanwhile, if the entire ship had become see-through, the woman would view yet more corpses lying on the lower decks. Also, there would be two prison guards and a woman besieged by a pair of masked men armed with sub-machine guns. They squeezed off solitary shots at one another but this was clearly a battle at stalemate. Far below her, in the lower cargo hold, were yet more bodies; the dead crew adorned the place like Christmas decorations crafted from raw flesh. Here, alongside the pump, one of Turrock's prisoners ambled happily, poking at the dead while cooing to himself. Beneath the cargo hold living members of crew were shackled to a rail in the engine room.

Even if the whole ship were invisible, there was a figure she might have missed: a lone figure on the lowest of the outside decks. In sub-zero temperatures it crept through darkness to a lifeboat. The *Volsparr*'s lifeboats weren't row boats but motor launches. Sixty feet long with a roomy cabin for passengers, they hung from steel derricks, waiting to be slung out then lowered into the ocean if disaster should strike. The figure, which she might have recognized as the ship's pianist, hauled himself aboard the lifeboat. Repeatedly, he had to blow on to his frozen hands. The metal ladder he gripped wore a rime of thick frost. Once inside the vessel's cabin he unhooked a bright yellow survival suit, then proceeded to wriggle into the all-in-one garment.

Thankfully, there has been no transformation of the decks to render them as see-through as glass. So the mother is spared having to witness what happens next . . .

Forty-Two

Nineteen hours to Zero Hour. 'So this is what made the noise.' Isis stood with her hands on her hips in the first-class cabin.

Tanya put her hand over the child's eyes. Then she turned her away, sat her in an armchair, a figure no bigger than a doll clad in shouting pinks. Tanya whispered that she must be a good girl, do as she's told, but on no account was she to peep back at the man.

'Who is it?' he rasped. 'Tell Control. I need the medic. Look what they've done to my eyes!'

Isis stared. 'My God . . .'

'Who's there? You've got to help me.'

Tanya stepped closer. The man had been gagged; somehow he'd managed to work it free so the stockings that formed a blood-stained loop hung loose around his neck. He hadn't been able to wriggle free of the bonds that held him in the straight-backed chair.

'Someone's cut away his eyelids,' Tanya breathed. 'Look, he can't close his eyes.'

From smears of congealed blood that formed a dark, sticky mass a pair of blue eyes stared at them. Almost panda eyes; they were circled black. But what might have been make-up soon revealed itself as bruising. The blue eyes stared into hers, but . . .

Tanya whispered, 'He's blind. Look how the eyeballs have dried out.'

'Did the hijackers do this to you?' Isis asked the man.

Tanya caught her by the elbow. 'Look at the holster. And this.' She dragged a black hood from where it had been tucked into his belt. 'He's one of them.'

'Then who'd . . . Ah.' Isis nodded. 'We've our friends the prisoners to thank for this. The hijackers were stupid enough to release them from the cells. A case of biter bit I think. Tanya, what are you doing? Leave him.'

'Help me.' She grabbed hold of the back of the chair frame. 'Drag him through into the bedroom. Away from . . .' She nodded to the armchair where Jo sat out of sight.

'Dear God, Tanya.' Isis paled. 'I know what you're going to do.'

'You said anything goes. That we must do whatever it takes to survive.'

'But we've been ordered to take the child to the cabin.'

'You know they'll kill her; film it as they cut her to pieces. You've seen what they did to the crew. Grab the chair; start pulling.'

Together they hauled the chair with the man still sitting on it. He groaned in pain. 'My eyes . . . fetch the medic.' His head lolled like he'd downed a bottle of vodka. Those unblinking eyes had begun to wrinkle.

Panting, Isis and Tanya reached the bedroom, then, after reassuring the girl and telling her to stay in the chair for just a moment, they returned to their captive.

'They tied him up good and tight.' Isis checked his hands. 'See? The flesh has gone black. No circulation. His hands are dying.'

His head rolled forward. Tanya pushed it back. 'Listen. What's your name?'

'Gunner.'

'That your real name?'

'Gunner. That's all. Get the medic,' grunted the man. 'I'm in pain.'

'Not until you tell me what I need to know. Are you one of the hijackers?'

He'd been dazed; his speech had been slurred, but instinct kicked in. His expression hardened.

Isis murmured. 'We'll have to leave him. He's not talking.'

'Oh, he's going to tell us everything.' Tanya scanned the first-class cabin. It was a luxurious confection of gleaming brass, polished walnut and Queen Anne style furnishings. 'This is how the executives travel. But no matter how rich you are everyone needs a toilet.'

'Tanya? Have you gone insane?'

'And it'll be en suite.' She headed for the door with gold scrollwork.

'Tanya, if we don't take the child to the cabin they'll start killing the passengers.'

Tanya paused at the bathroom door. 'I know what you've planned, Isis. You were going to use me as currency to buy your life from the hijackers.'

'Face reality. That will save us.'

'I *am* facing reality. And now *you* are just about to face the biggest dose of reality in your life. Grab that cushion and shove it against the guy's mouth.'

The man snapped. 'Get a medic. Do that, and I can save you.'

Tanya ducked into the bathroom. She emerged with a bright purple plastic bottle. 'Hold his head as hard as you can. Make sure the pillow's clamped to his mouth. This is going to hurt him a lot.'

'Toilet cleaner.'

'Concentrated bleach.' Tanya squirted the powerful smelling liquid into one of his eyes. It would have been bad enough for anyone. Only this man could not blink.

The Toad couldn't stand it any more. 'I want to go home. I'm so tired. I'll come alive again if I can only spend time at home.' If only the Toad could spend a few moments there. That's where this man with the bizarre anatomy nourished his soul. 'Home' is where his dream world and reality merge in a way that only the Toad could understand. There, weariness would vanish. He'd become young again. He'd return to the lounge in his orange leisure suit, a light-footed dandy, exuding charisma. *I'll be amazing!*

Not now though. Now he'd become comatose. A zombie

. . . I'm a toad made from clay. He'd been told by Maya to remain in the passenger lounge. Some words about danger. But danger meant nothing to the Toad. He must go home. That's all that mattered now.

'OK! I'll tell!'

It had taken some minutes to reach this point. Tanya had squirted the thick jet of bleach on to the man's naked eyeball. The astringent fluid melted the scab that had formed where the eyelids had been sliced away. The detergent then burned its way into the nerve endings. It created such a tidal wave of agony the man had screamed himself into unconsciousness. Luckily, they'd remembered to use the cushion.

Tanya rinsed his eyes with water. When he'd woken she'd said very softly into his ear, 'In moment I'll take the cushion from your mouth. You won't shout, you won't make any noise, other than telling me what your people's plans are for the ship and the passengers. If you don't talk I'll pour bleach in both your eyes and we'll leave you here – and remember, your hands are tied. And you cannot blink.'

Tanya nodded to Isis to remove the cushion; bile and blood painted dirty streaks on cream velvet.

'Talk,' she whispered.

And this time he told them everything he knew. 'The ship's dead – as good as. When the clock on the TV monitor reaches zero those ammunition wrecks are going to explode. Five thousand tons of warheads. *Bang.* Wreckage from this ship will be blown ten miles. The blast will scoop out a crater in the seabed a thousand feet wide. Stockholm will hear the detonation.'

'How will the passengers be evacuated?'

'They won't.'

Isis shuddered. 'My God.'

Tanya's hand tightened around the bleach bottle. 'But if the government meets the hijackers demands then—'

'Hey, don't you get it, stupid?' As he chuckled a brown liquid streamed from his wounded eye. 'The demands aren't real. It's all part of the strategy. We've demanded that terrorists are released from US and European jails. The governments will play for time but they won't comply. Or they'll fake a release of the terrorists. Or they'll storm the ship with special forces. Any way the authorities play it is win-win for us. We'll be long gone by the time they act. Those terrorists rotting away in the jails mean nothing to us. My team even helped put some of them there.'

'So Gus Hammond was right,' Tanya said. 'This is all about the mine and delaying the arrival of the pump.'

'Ah, the beautiful, beautiful pump. That won't be delayed.' The man chuckled again. A drunk sound; pain had addled his mind. 'In a few hours parts of it will be hurtling into outer space.'

'Your plans are to interfere with the mining operation.'

'Yes, damn it. Haven't you put the pieces of the jigsaw together yet? My team has been employed by rivals of Boson Eumericas to make sure the miners don't meet their deadline. If they fail to meet the deadline—'

'Then the mining lease is cancelled.'

'Of course. But let me explain the master stroke. This operation is the model for future operations. My employer can use this model to destroy multi-national companies or make governments change certain policies that might be . . . ahm . . . unpalatable for us or anyone who buys our services.'

Tanya frowned. 'Then you are terrorists?'

'We might be viewed as that this year. But next year we could be working for your government. Whoever can afford us buys the ability to wield enormous power.'

'And who are you exactly?'

'I'm not saying.'

'Isis, hold his head. I'm going to squirt this into both eyes.'

He stiffened. 'I'm not saying because I don't know. I don't even know the real identities of my colleagues. As far as I know, I'm employed by a phantom and work with ghosts.' Again he made that groggy chuckle. 'And no, I don't get a payslip or written employment contract. My wages arrive in grocery bags.'

Isis glanced at her watch. 'We must be moving, Tanya.'

'Moving? You might as well make the most of your last hours on earth.' The man rolled his head. 'Now, if you were told you had twenty hours before you were blown over half of Europe, how would you spend it? One of those dilemmas we talked about as kids, isn't it? If you could save either your Ma or your Pa, which one would it be?' The chuckle became a giggle.

'Keep talking. Don't go to sleep.' Tanya shook his shoulder.

Isis nodded at his hands. 'His fingers are black,' she whispered. 'Could be blood poisoning.'

'Then we might not have time to find out what—'

'We've got no time at all,' Isis hissed. 'We're supposed to take the girl to them.'

Tanya rounded on her. 'We're not taking Jo. You heard him; they're going to kill all of us in the end.'

'Then thank your lucky stars I sent Philip to prepare the lifeboat.'

'Ah, dilemma, dilemma,' the man murmured. 'You see, we need some living witnesses. They have to tell the world what bad, bad boys we've been. Five passengers will be selected. One American, one British, one Canadian, you know where this is going. I don't have to draw little pictures, do I? It's a known fact that people in, say, Britain only want to know details about a plane crash if there's fellow Brits on board. That goes for other nationalities, too . . .'

'Your people will save five passengers?'

'Yes. That's right. Absolutely.' Saliva crawled out of his mouth. Lucidity had begun to creep away from him. 'Spot on. Five will be saved. Five will prosper. Five will take tea with the queen.'

Tanya fumed. 'He's going to pieces.'

Isis tossed her head. 'So would you if— God, Tanya, don't!'

'Desperate times.' She squirted bleach into his eye.

Rather than experiencing agony it seemed to rouse him. When he spoke the words were distinct – faster, too. 'You've heard the strategy. Do you understand how each component interlocks? Do you appreciate its beauty?' He grinned. His eyes must have felt like two pits of fire in his head, yet he spoke with a surprising eloquence. 'It's more than making sure Boson Eumericas forfeits the mine. After what happens to their workforce on this ship, its shares will hit rock bottom. The company's value will tumble. Its executives will resign, some will face negligence lawsuits. Its security staff will be scorned as incompetents. Listen, in a few weeks nobody will trust Boson Eumericas to run so much as a candy stall. After all, if they can lose an entire ship, crew, passengers . . .' He squealed with glee. 'Shareholders will panic. In three months Boson will sell itself to the highest bidder. But who will want it?

I get the feeling that the company that employed us will do the charitable thing and buy it out. For a tiny fraction of what it's worth today, of course.'

'It's true then,' Tanya murmured. 'Money is the root of all evil.'

The man's blind eyes searched in vain for Tanya. 'Coins have two faces, of course. Imagine one is evil, as you say, but the other isn't just good; it is *God*. Money created civilization.' He laughed. 'Without commerce you'd still be giving birth to your babies under a bush.'

Isis tapped her watch again, her face appeared drawn.

'Just five more minutes,' Tanya insisted.

'No.'

'You're worried about time,' the man's eyes had begun to melt as the corrosive chemicals ate the flesh. 'Damn right you should be. Tick, tick, tick . . . At zero hour all this goes boom.' Then he added craftily, 'Unless you can persuade my guys that you should be the ones to be saved.' He gave a spluttering laugh that sprayed saliva into Tanya's face. 'If you're pretty, be *nice* to them.'

Isis upped the pressure on Tanya. 'We have to go. The child will be frightened.'

Tanya shook her head.

'You won't learn anything else. Look at him, he's lost his mind.'

'But we need to learn facts we can use to save ourselves.'

'You heard him, Tanya; they'll take five passengers with them when they go. The hijackers want five survivors who will bear witness to what they've done here. It all fits now. They didn't just kill the crew; they tortured them and violated the bodies in bizarre ways, so the outrages committed on the *Volsparr* will be remembered. They'll sear this nightmare of bloodshed and slaughter into the mind of the public.'

Tanya recalled the woman with the gold chain in her eye. These monsters had been imaginative for a purpose. 'You're right. Hence the footage of the killings on TV monitors.'

'Vietnam.' The man beamed as he sat tied to the chair, his strangled hands slowly turning black as the cells died. 'When the Viet Cong suspected someone of treachery they didn't just kill them, or their family. They would send a death squad to the house, kill everyone in it, and then they would kill the family's pets. Even goldfish were scooped out of their bowls, thrown on the floor, stomped on. Then everyone in the village would be made to walk through the house to see the carnage. Isn't that the consummate lesson? Don't double cross the Viet Cong. Now, my team. When we're at work nobody will dare interfere with us.'

'Governments will track you down and destroy you.'

'Destroy us? They'll end up hiring us!'

'OK.' Tanya wanted to vomit. 'I've had enough.'

'My hands,' the man whined. 'Call the medic.'

Tanya wiped her mouth. 'Leave him.'

Isis couldn't believe what Tanya had just said. 'Leave him tied up? With his eyes still swimming in bleach?'

Tanya walked to the bedroom door.

The man choked with mad laughter. 'Best of all, there's something you don't know. Something *huge*. You will be shocked, amazed, you won't know whether to laugh or cry.' Spit bubbled from his lips.

'You've told us that the ship will be blown to pieces in twenty hours.'

'No . . . no . . .' His voice became a hiss. The blind eyes bulged until they were in danger of bursting. 'No, this is the genius of it all. What you see on the monitors – all those big screens fixed around the ship – all that footage is sent to the internet.' His voice rose. 'That's right. All around the world millions are watching it.' He rocked as a lunatic mirth gripped him. 'Wait! It gets better. We're also transmitting images from the closed-circuit cameras. The world is watching the passengers up in the lounge. The world watched you walk down here. *That's right, girls, you're the biggest show on earth!'*

Tanya closed the bedroom door behind them. His deranged monologue continued.

'You're going to fetch help?' Isis asked.

'Like hell I am.' Tanya crossed the lounge to the armchair where they'd left Jo. 'Thank goodness she hasn't wandered off.'

Though Jo couldn't be seen as the armchair had its high back to them, they could hear the child singing softly.

'I'm sorry we took so long, sweetheart,' Tanya said. Then she saw what the girl held in her hands. 'Oh, my good God. Where did she get *that* from?'

The little girl sang contentedly as she cupped an object in both hands. 'Look at this.' Jo sounded bright as a new penny. 'I found a metal tennis ball.'

Tanya stared as the girl played catch with a dull green hand grenade.

EIGHTH TRACT

Forty-Three

Eighteen hours until Zero Hour. *'Catch!'* The girl lobbed the hand grenade. Of course, it was heavier than the children's balls she was accustomed to. The five-year-old's throw fell short of Tanya's outstretched hand.

In her mind's eye Tanya saw the green hand grenade striking the floor of the first-class cabin then bursting into a thousand high-velocity fragments that would rip them to shreds. Tanya Rhone flung herself forward, hand outstretched, and thumped on to the carpet so forcefully she thought she'd snapped a rib. Despite the pain stabbing her chest she kept her cupped hand extended. The grenade slapped into her palm.

She lay there on her chest, panting, her eyes locked on to the apple-sized bomb. *The pin . . . where is the pin?*

Isis plucked the grenade from Tanya's palm. 'Nice work, my dear.' She held the grenade in front of Tanya's face. 'Pin still in place. You've saved our lives.'

Jo held out her hands. 'Throw back to me, please.'

'Ah, no. It's not a toy, I'm afraid.' Isis gave Jo a tight smile. 'You might break it.'

Jo's face dropped.

'We'll find you something else to play with soon.' Then to Tanya as she pulled herself to her feet, 'I'm impressed. You're stronger than I thought you were. You tortured the gentleman in there until he talked. Now you've proved you can catch.' Isis bounced the grenade on her palm.

Tanya eyed it. 'I'd feel happier if you put that down.'

'What? And leave behind our only weapon? This is ours now.' She'd brought the man's black balaclava with her. She dropped the hand grenade into it. 'It might come in useful.'

'Yeah, to blow ourselves up,' Tanya added darkly. 'Come on,

we need to take Jo to her mother. Then we've got news to pass on to the rest of the passengers.'

'They'll go to pieces. They won't be able to handle it.'

'We'll take that risk.' Tanya rubbed her aching ribs. 'If the hijackers are going to destroy the ship we need to leave as quickly as possible.'

'So? Are you ready to credit me for encouraging Philip to ready the lifeboat?'

'You're still a bitch,' Tanya told her. 'But maybe that's why you're so successful.'

'I'll take that as a compliment.'

They left the cabin. Ahead lay the reception area. Tanya noticed the CCTV camera fixed to the wall; it filmed the area around the receptionist's desk.

'Don't forget,' Tanya whispered, 'they might be able to see us.'

'And they'll already know that we're not taking the child to them.'

'I want my mom.' The girl's voice cut across their whispers so loudly they flinched.

'We're going there now.' Tanya took the girl's hand. 'But someone's asleep in that cabin so we must be very, very quiet. OK?'

The girl nodded, then added loudly, 'OK.'

They approached the stairwell that would take them up to the Moonlit Bay Lounge. Tanya drew Isis's attention to a TV screen behind reception. It showed the final moments of the man in the green fleece. 'I wonder what they're making of this in the outside world.'

And above that image the silver numerals of the clock counted down.

Isis murmured, 'Less than eighteen hours until zero hour.'

Tanya's imagination flew to the half-sunken munitions ships where explosive charges must nestle amongst tons of torpedo warheads. *When it comes, will we even have time to hear the bang?*

In the lifeboat cabin Philip kept busy. The craft was more sophisticated than the old rowboat-style lifeboats that graced the likes of the *Titanic*. The vessels that hung from derricks on the lowest external deck area of the *Volsparr* had room for sixty people. Rugged fiberglass cabins were weatherproof. Motors would propel survivors to safety. In watertight cupboards were food rations, drinking water, lifejackets, first-aid kits, thermal blankets, flares and the craft's instruction manuals.

Even though Philip had only served as ship's pianist he'd received basic training in emergency procedure. He knew cold to be a ruthlessly efficient killer, and he'd already donned one of the bright yellow survival suits. These were one-piece water-proofs, complete with integral mitts and shoes. Clipped to the suit were a whistle, flashlight and two flares. Into the vast pocket of the survival suit he stuffed a Very pistol flare together with half a dozen cartridges.

The injustice of the rape allegation made by Isis drove him. Blood surged through his veins. His face burned with anger. Oh, he'd prove to her that he wasn't some low-life rat. When they had tumbled into bed it was consensual. As he readied the boat his mind whirled. He'd seen what happened to the crew on the TV screens; the footage had been explicit enough. When he glanced out into the night he could see the pale expanse of sea ice. He prayed it wouldn't impede the lifeboat when it was time to flee. *And let that be soon. The clock's ticking. If we don't put some distance between us and the munitions ships when they go up, we'll be blown off the face of the earth.* Philip couldn't delay the preparations. He must begin disconnecting the chains that secured the lifeboat to the ship. As soon as passengers stepped on board he needed to throw the lever that would set the winch in motion. In moments that would lower them to the sea, and maybe – if they were lucky – *safety.*

Isis led the way up the staircase towards the restaurant deck. Tanya followed, the little girl holding her hand.

Isis stopped dead. 'Back,' she hissed.

'What?'

'Back down to the cabin deck. There's someone coming.'

Tanya didn't need to be told twice. She heard the plod of heavy feet descending.

'If it's one of the hijackers we've had it.' That might be an unnecessary comment on the part of Isis but Tanya wasn't about to quibble. She scooped Jo into her arms then flew down

the stair. *Don't trip,* she thought, *for heaven's sake, don't trip.*
Isis ran alongside, the grenade swinging weightily in the
makeshift pouch of the hijacker's balaclava. When they hit
the cabin deck Isis sped towards the suite they'd just left.

'No,' Tanya hissed. 'Get into the reception area.' She pushed
open the hinged gate that separated the public area from that
of the receptionist. 'Under the desk.'

Both Isis and Tanya hunkered underneath. Jo opened her
mouth to protest. Tanya clamped her hand over it. The girl's
eyes went huge.

'Shush, it's all right,' Tanya whispered. 'This is a game . . .
if we're not found we win the prize.'

Isis hissed, 'A lovely prize. Chocolate, lots of chocolate.'

From Tanya's cramped corner beneath the desk she still had
a view of the monstrous images on the TV monitor.

'It's just a game,' Tanya repeated softly, 'just a funny little
game.'

The Toad clumped downstairs to the reception area. All his
energy gone, and with it the verve. Even if someone spoke
to him now he doubted if he could reply. He wanted to go
home.

Slowly, he dragged his feet through reception. A near
reptilian instinct for self-preservation had allowed him to evade
the police for years. Now, it reached up from the core of his
brain to warn him that people hid behind the reception desk.
It might be subtle sounds of respiration. He didn't know, but
he sensed their presence. He shuffled toward the desk, stumpy
arms swinging. He stared at the desk where he knew someone
hid themselves. Why do that? Were they planning on hurting
him? Would prison guards hide?

Home . . . that's all that mattered. Dimly, he realized he
wasn't supposed to leave the lounge but the craving for home
overwhelmed him. *Why am I staring at the desk? I need to
be home . . .* He stared with bulging eyes that were dull now.
Spark gone. Wearily, he turned his back on the reception area
then trudged towards his home cabin.

'I'm home.' The words came as a faint rasp. 'Be happy in
there. I'm home.' He pushed open the cabin door. Blinked.
His long tongue emerged. He licked his lips like this when
trying to fathom a conundrum. The Toad had left the cabin

in perfect order. It had been his idealized image of home. The man on the bunk was the embodiment of the Toad's imaginary twin. He'd arranged it all. It had been perfect. The man had been holding the cell phone. Photographs carefully arranged on the bedside table. The Toad had applied make-up to the face to echo his own birthmarks. And now this . . .

'Oh, my gosh.' The quirky expression of surprise caught something of his earlier cheeriness when the Toad felt full of life. The expression now mutated into a growl. 'Gosh, oh gosh . . .' A sibilant expression of rage.

His eyes bulged yet further. Purple veins pushed into the whites, pupils shrank to fierce black dots. The tongue emerged to snap from side to side across his lips, as if lashing at an object of hatred. The Toad stared into the cabin. Walls blackened with soot. Furniture hurled about. Bedding strewn. Much, much worse – his other 'self' lay on the floor. Some cruel force had devastated it. The face hung by fleshy strands. One of its arms had been ripped away. In a manner that would be inexplicable to the most gifted psychiatrist this devastation also devastated the Toad's mental equilibrium. A sense of loss, bafflement, violation and grief morphed into pure, unalloyed rage. The Toad reached out to the despoiled figure that meant everything to him. Trembling, he caressed the ruined face.

Then he moved. The energy returned to his limbs, but this time it wasn't one that elevated him into a charismatic figure that had skipped lightly into the lounge. This time, a dark, baleful energy powered his movements. Grunting, he burst from the cabin into the corridor. His stumpy legs carried him in a full-blooded run to the receptionist's desk. The people hiding there – were they responsible for the desecration?

Snarling, he launched himself upward then slammed chest-down on to the desk and thrust his head over to look into the space beneath. He'd make them suffer! His broad face turned from side to side as he searched the void beneath the desk. *Empty.* With a furious energy he raced back across the reception area to the nearest cabin. *Somebody in there. Can feel it.* They were hiding; no doubt laughing at him. He shoved open the door to the first-class suite. A voice came through the bedroom door. The Toad rushed at it. Inside the bedroom a man sat on a chair, a dislodged gag beneath his chin. His eyelids had been torn away.

'I knew you'd come back,' giggled the bound man. 'You need me. Because soon this ship will be blown to kingdom come. I'm going to hurt you, oh, lots and lots, but I'll let you live.' His head rolled. 'But you're going to have to be very nice to me . . .' His head jerked upward. 'So, who's there? Who is it?'

The Toad growled. *'Spoilt.'*

The visitor wasn't the one the hijacker expected. 'Don't touch me,' he shouted, 'don't you dare!'

The Toad advanced. Those eyes. There was something disgusting about those eyes that had no eyelids. They could have been made from bright red glass – like red marbles bulging from the sockets. The Toad lunged. He thrust his thumbs into the two red eyes. Those hateful things must be destroyed. And when they were the Toad took hold of the screaming man by the throat then squeezed until he screamed no more.

Forty-Four

When the owner of the trudging feet vanished into one of the cabins, Tanya, Isis and Jo exited their hideaway under the reception desk. The plan had been to take the stairs to the piano lounge. However, another cabin door had banged so they'd darted into a linen store. Tanya had expected the child to cry in fear but she'd burst into a fit of giggles. Clearly, she still thought all this was a game.

Through a tiny gap in the storeroom door Tanya and Isis watched the man in orange leisure wear come racing down the corridor. He launched himself halfway across the reception desk. His over-large head had ducked over the edge as he searched beneath it.

Isis breathed, 'He knew we were there all along.'

Tanya watched the man as he pushed himself back from the desk. The face contorted, the eyes bulged, the sheer maniacal fury: it left her in no doubt at all. 'He's one of the escaped prisoners. But I saw him with the passengers upstairs!'

Isis shook her head. 'After they were freed they must have changed their clothes then mingled with us.'

The little girl chuckled with excitement. Isis hushed her. Tanya was glad that she had. *The man's gone berserk. If he finds us hiding here . . .*

For a moment the man in his bright orange suit stood in the reception area. His chest heaved, the short arms quivered. The over-large face with bulging eyes turned from left to right as if he scoured the place for fresh meat. Tanya recalled him as being charming in a fey, almost foppish, sort of way. Now he'd become something she could only describe as reptilian. A moment later he raced to the first-class cabin. Shortly after that she heard the captive's raised voice, which then evolved into a scream of terror and then one of agony.

'Close the door,' Tanya hissed. 'Before he sees we're here.'

Isis did so. But *not* seeing became a torture in its own right. So they listened at the door; lives depended on it. Tanya couldn't be certain but the crash she heard next could have been the first-class cabin door opening. Following that, a purposeful thud of footsteps approached the storeroom where the three hid. Isis gripped Tanya's forearm as the footsteps grew louder

Jo's voice hit them like a punch. 'Have we won the chocolate yet?'

Tanya whispered, 'Not yet. We must be very, *very* quiet.'

Jo gave an exaggerated to wink to show she understood the rules of the game.

'Spoilt!'

A terrific bang reached the storeroom.

'Tried to keep you safe inside . . . spoilt . . . I'm sorry . . . not my fault!'

The bellow was anger fused with grief. Another bang. Tanya pictured the man in orange punching the wall as he walked.

The way the voice fluxed between a roar and weeping chilled Tanya. She'd not heard anything like that come from a human mouth before. Another thump on the wall, only this time from further away.

Isis sighed. Then she did a stupid thing. She opened the door.

Tanya hissed, 'Not yet!' She could have punched the woman.

Instead she gripped Isis by the same hand that held the door handle so she couldn't open it further. *But if I shut it now the madman will hear the catch click. Isis, you idiot!* Tanya longed to use some choice words right now but she had to be content with giving Isis such a glare of fury that everything she wanted to yell was contained in that searing look.

'Wait,' she whispered. 'We can't go yet.' *Especially not yet.* Though the inch wide gap between door and frame limited her view she saw two armed figures enter the reception area. Both wore blue denim jeans and denim shirts, clearly a kind of uniform. Most noticeable of all were the black balaclava masks.

'Well, someone was shouting.' This, a woman's voice, came from a figure carrying a camcorder. 'It came from down here, I'm sure of it.'

Then a male voice, angry: 'It's probably a passenger or one of the prisoners. They've gone now. Forget it.'

'The passengers were ordered to stay in the upper lounge. If—'

'It doesn't matter. What bothers me now is that they haven't brought the girl. Voice ordered them to deliver her to the cabin nearly ten minutes ago.'

'Voice will have to issue the order again.'

'And that delays everything. Command needs the footage in the studio. The next batch has to be uploaded by midnight. Shit!' The guy slapped his thigh in frustration. 'Axe Man needs to finish off in the engine room. We didn't have enough manpower; we're falling behind schedule.'

'Tell me about it. I'm supposed to join the detail collecting witnesses in precisely four minutes.'

The guy rubbed at his jaw under the black balaclava as if the material had begun to itch. 'Look, if they bring the girl now we'll do it here. It'll take all of twenty seconds. You stand by that wall; film them as they enter the reception area at the foot of the stairs.' He pulled back the bolt of a sub-machine gun. 'I'll just rip them apart with this.' He laughed. 'Trust me. You'll get beautiful film.'

'Call up Voice. Have him tell the shits upstairs to bring the girl now or we'll chuck grenades into the lounge. That'll focus their minds.'

The guy unclipped a radio from his belt. 'You've enough tape left?'

'Have you got enough ammo?' They seemed more inclined to indulge in banter now that they'd found a solution to their problem.

'Twenty-five rounds; more than enough to paint this place red.'

'Tell Voice they have three minutes, or—'

'Change of plan.' The other voice came from out of vision. Tanya watched as a third figure joined them. He wore a black balaclava, too, which covered his entire face and head apart from two circular eyeholes.

'Sapper, we haven't got the child yet. We need footage of—'

'Nope. That's all we need. We're getting out.'

'But—'

'Control's issued revised orders. We're pulling out. Everyone to be off this tub by 0300.'

The woman cursed. 'What's gone wrong?'

'Everything's gone right. Absolutely right. Mission accomplished. We don't need to hang around here.'

'So where now?'

'You two rendezvous with the others in the engine room.'

He patted the machine gun. 'I'm joining Foreman at the top of the stairs. We'll make sure the passengers are contained in the lounge until we're good to go.'

The figures hurried away. The one called Sapper raced up the stairs. The very stairs Tanya had planned to use to return to the Moonlit Bay Lounge.

Isis sighed. 'We'll have to find another way back up there.'

'I want my mom,' Jo announced. She'd seen enough of the masked figures to be unsettled.

'Don't worry,' Isis told her, 'we're going there right now.'

'Chocolate?'

'Yes, there'll be chocolate.'

Tanya gripped Isis by the elbow.

'At least they're leaving, thank God.'

'They are,' Isis allowed, 'but remember they've rigged explosive charges on the munitions wrecks. And the guy in the cabin told us they're going to blow us sky high anyway.'

'They said they're leaving at three in the morning.' Tanya glanced at her watch. 'Five hours from now.'

'As soon as they do we need to leave also – if Philip knows how to lower the damn lifeboats.'

Isis opened the door.

'Careful,' Tanya hissed. 'What about the psycho?'

'With luck the hijackers will shoot him. Ready?'

'OK . . . OK.' Tanya didn't feel fine. Right then she longed to hide away until all this was over.

Then came the Voice. 'Witness Detail, calling Witness Detail. Assemble at muster station A. I remind the passengers they must remain in the lounge. It is dangerous for you to move to any other part of the ship. Stay in the lounge; there you will be safe. Witness Detail assemble muster station A immediately.'

'This is it,' Isis murmured as they moved along the corridor, 'just like the guy told us. They're about to collect some passengers. The ones that can bear witness to what atrocities took place here. Just to add a little more razzmatazz, they're uploading footage of their bloody little films to the internet.' Isis looked her in the eye. 'Tanya, you know we could volunteer our services to join their witnesses? What say you?'

Forty-Five

A board the lifeboat, Philip had a visitor.

'I congratulate you on your foresight.' The man in the black balaclava mask aimed the machine gun at him. 'How did you know we needed an extra boat?'

Even though Philip couldn't see the man's face it was clear he enjoyed Philip's expression of shock.

'Were you going to take off in this all by yourself?'

Philip said nothing.

'Anybody else on board?' The hijacker checked the cabin. 'No. You're sailing solo, aren't you?'

Philip's body locked up tight with fear. He could barely breathe.

'And all suited up.' The man poked the gun's muzzle into Philip's chest. The rubberized survival suit crackled slightly. 'You must know what you're doing. Those things are tricky to put on. Are you crew?'

Philip nodded, then shook his head.

'Either you are or you aren't.'

Philip tried to answer but no sound came out. The man jabbed the gun muzzle into his ribs.

'Entertainment.' Philip heard the waver in his voice.

'Ah, you must be a magician. You've managed to conjure yourself out here past my men.'

'Piano player.'

The man laughed so loud that white vapor jetted through the mask's fabric. 'Don't shoot me; I'm only the piano player. Isn't that a line from a song?' He glanced round the cabin. 'You've spent as much time reading emergency manuals as you have sheet music. Look at this; you've been getting ready to launch this baby, haven't you?'

Don't answer. He's going to kill me anyway. Damn, if only Isis could see me now. She'd know I'm no rat. I gave my life to save her and the passengers. She should watch this and burn with guilt. I didn't rape her, as God is my witness.

The man poked around the lifeboat, checking Philip's preparations. He nodded with approval. *Maybe I can jump him. Get the gun out of his hands.* The hijacker wasn't stupid. As he flicked switches on the lifeboat's control panel he aimed the gun at Philip's chest. 'You're not thinking of doing anything stupid?'

Philip quickly shook his head. He knew he couldn't overpower the man.

'Good, good.' The hijacker appeared satisfied. 'You're nearly ready for launch. Two items for you to digest, though. One: I'm commandeering your vessel, skipper. Two: I'm commandeering *you* to help me launch her.'

'No.'

'No? I've got the gun, remember.'

'Use it then; I'm not helping you.'

'You've got guts. You were wasted tickling the ivories, did you know that?'

'Go to hell.'

The masked man laughed again. 'OK, let's cut a deal. Help me launch this boat. And I'll make sure you reach dry land in one piece.'

'Really? You won't kill me?'

'Nope. I guarantee your safety.' The man's brown eyes

regarded him through the eye-holes of the mask. 'You're going to have to trust me on this.'

Philip nodded. *All I can do is buy time. If the chance comes to knock him down . . .*

The hijacker returned to the control panel. 'Friend, I know you'll be asking yourself questions. *Can I jump him? Can I snatch the gun?* Don't even try. I kill people with my finger-tips. This is just for show.' He waggled the gun. 'Sure it works, but I'm a hands-on kind of person. You follow?' He pointed to a red button on the panel. 'All I need to do to start the engine is press this?'

Philip nodded.

'Looks easy enough. Call me Sparks. And you are?'

'Philip.'

'Philip the pianist.' He nodded. 'OK, Philip, we need to get this lifeboat down into the sea.'

'Now?'

'No time like the present.'

'But they're designed to be lowered fully loaded with passengers and crew.'

'I'm taking it to the other side of the ship. We'll board everybody by ladder.'

'But that means . . .'

'Philip. I'm in charge, remember. Now, get moving.'

Arguing with a guy who took pleasure in killing with his bare hands was futile. Philip saw that. *Just keep biding your time. He'll make a mistake soon.* He shrugged, 'OK, Sparks. We need to remove the pins on the securing chains.'

'Chop, chop, then.'

Outside the bitter cold turned their breath into white clouds. The moon revealed itself as a silver disk through the fog. By this time the ice had become uniform; before it had been riven with black cracks that revealed areas of unfrozen sea. *The ice is thickening. If we don't hurry the lifeboat will get locked in. But I'm sure as hell not going to tell the guy. What I know and what he doesn't might mean the difference between me making it or winding up dead.* As Philip eased out the heavy-duty steel pins that stopped the lifeboat bouncing against the *Volsparr* in rough seas he glanced down at the freezing Baltic. A formidable drop. *If I could only tip the Sparks guy over the guardrail . . .*

The cold tried to chew pieces out of his ears. He pulled up the hood of the survival suit. 'Sparks,' he said, 'one of us needs to stay on deck to operate the hoist.'

'What? You stand up here and wave me goodbye as you lower me down? Not blasted likely.'

'If I—'

'Philip the pianist, you know as well as I do you only have to hit the winch button. These systems are intelligent nowadays. It'll safely lower the boat with *both* of us on board. OK?'

'OK, Sparks.'

'Good, we're working as a team. You hop back on to the lifeboat. No, not the cabin. Stay on the deck. Go to prow; that's the front, if you didn't know. Chop, chop.'

Philip clambered on to the narrow walkway that ran around the bulbous cabin structure, taking care to maintain a tight grip on the safety rail. He took at least small satisfaction that he was comfortably warm in his survival suit while the sub-zero temperatures sapped the thug of his body heat. The man wore a blue denim shirt and jeans. On his hands were thin leather gloves, which did nothing to keep his fingers warm. He constantly had to shift the machine gun from one hand to another in order to flex his fingers to keep the blood flowing. A dusting of ice particles formed on the black mask around his mouth. *Go on, suffer, you bastard.*

Sparks checked that the restraints had been removed. Now all that kept the lifeboat from plunging into the Baltic Sea were a pair of steel cables attached to the crane assembly. When the man was happy that they'd prepped their deployment he jumped from the lifeboat deck to that of the ship, punched the saucer-sized button on the winch control panel, then leapt lightly back on to the lifeboat.

With a wrenching scream moving parts that hadn't actually moved for years began to turn. Philip gripped the hand rail tighter as the craft vibrated. The cable drum started to roll, the winch motor hummed, and a moment later the lifeboat began inching its way downwards.

The Toad hurtled along the corridor. He snarled yet tears of grief ran down his overly wide face. 'Spoilt it . . . spoilt it,' he wailed. A storm had erupted inside his head. He raged at the people who had destroyed his home. But this thing terrified him, too. From childhood a second version of his self had lived inside of him. Normally he liked his other self, especially when he created the representation of it in the cabin. The way it had lain there on the bunk, cell phone in hand, had given the Toad good feelings. If he spent time with that tableau he would emerge from the cabin in high spirits; his world would become a happy one; he'd be in the mood for pleasant conversation; he'd laugh with the sheer joy of life.

Now it had been spoilt. Worse, his twin self had become enraged that the Toad hadn't protected him. In a manner that psychologists would struggle to articulate, the twin had become externalized. He ran alongside the Toad. Angry, he blamed the Toad for failing. Nobody else ever saw the twin. Even the Toad didn't seem him properly; he manifested himself as a body of shadows that writhed like the tentacles of an octopus. The twin became the concentrated essence of rage, hatred and an overwhelming need to hurt, to destroy, to kill.

Philip couldn't say for sure when he knew that Sparks had decided to kill him. They were still twenty feet above the crust of ice covering the sea when the man advanced from the back of the lifeboat toward where Philip stood in the prow.

'These are easier to operate than I thought,' Sparks told him as he approached.

Revelation seared Philip: *You only needed me when you thought you couldn't launch the lifeboat yourself. Now that you can I'm redundant.* Then came the clincher. *He's not brought the gun. And what was that he said about killing with his bare hands?* Puffs of vapor came through the balaclava mask. The man made a pretence of checking their progress as the winch lowered the lifeboat toward the water. Above them the mechanism rumbled, steel cables that supported the craft vibrated, taut as guitar strings. The massive steel flank of the *Volsparr* seemed to slide upwards as they descended. Beyond the vessel, mist swirled in the darkness.

'How's it going up front?' Sparks asked in a matter-of-fact way.

'Good.'

Sparks appraised him, then nonchalantly looked down

between the lifeboat and the ship. By now they were fifteen feet above the sea. The descent was achingly slow.

'This thing itches like hell.' He scratched his face through the fabric of the mask. 'So how're we doing up front?' It was the same question as a moment ago but it was merely to distract Philip from what happened next. At least that's what the guy's intention had been. His hand swept through the air. Philip saw the glitter of the blade. He tried to dodge round the cabin. At least that ten-foot-wide bulge of fiberglass would put some distance between them. But the hijacker was lightning in flesh form. He sped around the walkway to grab Philip by the sleeve of the survival suit. Philip struck out at the hand that clasped the knife rather than the guy's head. Guys like that took punches from guys like Philip without blinking. But if his hands really are as cold as they seem . . .

Philip's heavy-duty mitt clunked into Sparks' wrist. The knife slipped from his fingers; they must be so numbed with cold that he could barely grasp the handle of the weapon. It rattled on to the walkway. Philip's heart pounded in his chest; for a split-second exhilaration energized him. He swung a punch at the man's jaw. Sparks slipped a flashlight from his belt and brought it down on Philip's head. Despite the padded hood it felt as if the instrument had parted his skull down the middle. He sagged back against the cabin.

'Bad news, Philip,' hissed the man. 'I'm dissolving our partnership.' He raised the flashlight again. Its steel casing turned it into an effective baton.

Philip lashed out again at the guy's head. Punching wouldn't work; it had to be something else. He gripped the balaclava mask then yanked it forward; the back of the mask slid forward over the man's eyes, blinding him. He still struck home with the flashlight, however. Philip groaned with pain.

Now Sparks decided to finish the job. Nothing fancy; just get rid of the troublemaker. One-handed he shoved the ship's pianist off the lifeboat's narrow walkway.

'You're coming with me, too!' Fine words from Philip, only it didn't work like that. Though he grabbed at the hijacker's arm with the intention of dragging him overboard, the guy held on to the safety rail. Philip's mitt on the survival suit was slippery. His grip only lasted a second before the man jerked himself free and Philip was falling towards the sea.

On the cabin deck the steward congratulated himself. He'd heard the hijackers talking and learnt that they were leaving the ship early. When all hell broke loose a few hours ago, when his colleagues were butchered in their cabins or blasted by machine guns as they'd run down the corridors, the steward had gone to ground. He knew that if you removed the mattress from one of the bunks that folded up against the cabin wall it created a coffin-sized void in which a grown man might conceal himself. The steward did exactly that. He'd lain in the stuffy darkness for nearly a full day. He'd silently mouthed the lyrics to *West Side Story*, *Cabaret* and *Cats* to distract him from the screams of men and women being slaughtered. Now, thank heaven, the murderers were leaving. As soon as it fell silent he crawled out of the void. Even so, he'd taken peeps out of the cabin door to make sure the coast was clear, before he mustered the courage to leave. And even then he made use of the bathroom first. That twelve-hour hideaway had done untold mischief to his bladder.

From the announcements over the PA he knew the passengers were assembled in the Moonlit Bay Lounge. *Time to find some company.* He'd taken ten paces along the corridor when a figure lunged into view at the far end. An odd, dumpy man dressed in bright orange. When he saw the steward he let out a bark of rage then started running towards him. The steward spun on his heel, then ran as fast as he could in the other direction. At that moment he felt a sudden urge to go to the bathroom again. Only he knew that this was one call of nature that would, for the time being, have to remain unanswered.

Philip dropped the remaining fifteen feet to the ocean's surface. He braced himself for being immersed. Even at that moment, with his skull aching like fury from the blows, he knew that the shock of sub-zero salt water could kill him.

A jarring concussion knocked the air from his body. Screwing his eyes tight shut, he tried to hold his breath, so he didn't inhale brine, but the jolt left him gasping. He kicked his legs against water; beneath him would be fathoms of darkness stretching down to the seabed. But when he moved his arms to swim he realized they slid over a hard, flat surface. He opened his eyes. Above him the lifeboat's keel descended. Now it was little more than ten feet away from crushing him. In surprise he looked down at his bottom half. His legs had smashed through the ice skin; they kicked freely in the brine, but above his hips he remained dry. He lay face down on the ice; so close he could see a powdery frost. A strand of green weed had been locked into the crystalline surface. A tang of salt air filled his nostrils, chasing the dizziness out of his head. He rolled his eyes up at the boat as it descended. Its rudder and single propeller were clearly visible in the moonlight. Philip should have been visible to the hijacker (and an easy target for his gun); however, when he'd briefly hung on to the guy's arm the action had made him swing pendulum-like. When he'd fallen he'd still been swinging so his fall had deposited him directly under the lifeboat and out of sight. So where would the hijacker be right now? *In the stern, at the lifeboat's controls. He'll figure I've gone through the ice and I'm already dead – or as good as.* Philip hauled his legs out of the hole. Without the survival suit that kept him dry he really would be as good as dead. The cold would be as lethal as the hijacker's machine gun. What now? No point in running for the ship; not even a spider could climb that sheer wall of steel. The only alternative would have been too dreadful to contemplate if it wasn't for sheer panic that drove him. Go forwards. Move away in a line directly in front of the lifeboat. The bulk of the cabin would interrupt Sparks' view.

With the keel of the lifeboat just inches above his head Philip loped away. Under him the ice groaned. At times it sagged, more than once his foot went through it with a crunch; black waters welled up through the hole he left. *Just keep moving*, he told himself. *Get away from the ship. Right now, I'm an easy target.*

Pain from blows to the head and the fall mated with panic, driving him to keep running. At that moment his course of action didn't seem like the act of madness it was. Doggedly, he jogged into darkness and mist; the only sounds his respiration and the creak of ice. Soon the ship faded away until it could have been nothing more than a ghostly image of its former self. Ahead, three hillocks of dark, mangled ironwork rose out of a white plain. Through the evil murk drifting on the cold, night air he caught sight of a rusted funnel that still bore the black swastika. Deep, resonant notes reached him; a fugue for lost souls.

The steward raced along the corridor. He passed monitors that still showed footage of his colleagues being murdered. An onscreen clock counted down to zero hour. The strange-looking man in the orange leisure suit was following him. His eyes bulged from his head, while his unnaturally wide mouth that resembled a frog's gaped open as if ready to bite. The steward reached an intersection in the passageways. He took a left, which opened into a small lounge area with sofas. In one corner a vending machine shone its amber light through bottles of cola. *The man chasing me is short. If I can get into a place that's high enough he won't be able to see me.* Despite being over fifty the steward athletically bounded on to a sofa then scrambled on top of the vending machine. The area was smaller than a desk top yet it was enclosed by a raised section of paneling that carried the names of the drinks. In this shallow depression the steward curled into a fetal position. And waited.

Running feet came. Running feet went. Then there was silence apart from the hum of the refrigerator motor.

The steward opened his eyes. The corridor ceiling just lay a foot above him. When he was confident that his pursuer must be long gone he turned his head to look out into the lounge area.

From a distance of ten inches a huge face looked into his. Eyes bulged in sheer rage. The steward bawled out in shock. A pair of hands seized him, but they didn't pull him from his hiding place. The toad-faced man hauled himself on top of the vending machine to join the steward on his little plateau six feet from the floor.

Forty-Six

Seventeen hours until Zero Hour. Philip ran across the ice. Above him, the moon blazed as a silver disk. Surrounding him was a frozen sea. Perfectly flat, it had become surprisingly easy to traverse. The grips on the boots that were welded to the survival suit had great traction. Behind him, the *Volsparr* could have become a ghost ship. Its lights burned faintly from the silhouette. Compounding the eeriness of the scene were bodies frozen into the ice. The hijackers must have thrown corpses of the crew overboard. Now faces with mouths that yawned wide were embedded into the semi-transparent crust.

Ahead, the remains of the ill-fated Fiezeler Convoy rose out of the ocean. The swastika fixed on him, an evil eye, a nexus of hate. Moments ago the munitions wrecks had seemed like hillocks, now they were *mountains* of rusted metal, each one crammed with high explosive. He sensed their explosive potential now. The rotting hulks seemed to groan under the pressure from the cargo holds. All those catastrophic forces that had been contained for all these years now wanted to fulfill their destiny. *They wanted out.*

He shook his head. After being under the sentence of certain death just moments ago now he was free. The urge to run and run carried him along at a sprint. *No, think this through. If you keep running you'll get lost in the dark. There are no points of reference. If you head out to sea you're a dead man. Get on board one of the wrecks. There are no tides in this part of the Baltic so there's nothing to break up the ice. Then wait it out until daylight. There's an island just six miles from the wrecks. That's why the authorities couldn't risk blowing up the ammunition on the ships. There's so much TNT it would flatten every house for miles. So, wait until daylight. Then, when you can see the island, just get back on your feet; walk across the ice. You'll be on dry land in a couple of hours. Simple!*

Yet at that moment an eerie, ominous groan reached out to him through the darkness. He sensed all those tons of high explosive longing to burst through the steel casing of the warheads. The harder they fought to escape, the louder the groan.

That groan is real, I'm not imagining it. Then he knew for sure the sound was entirely natural. A crack opened at his feet with the sound of a gunshot. The ice sheet surrounding him gave another pained groan. Seconds later shards of ice lifted into the vertical as he plunged down through it. The hole he fell into had an absolute darkness, the night-time ocean as black as the space between the stars, and its cold just as lethal. As he fell he thrust out his arms at either side of him. If he went under his bare face would be immersed in cold water. The temperature would kill him.

Down he went, slipping smoothly through the pit in the ice where it had been too thin to support his weight. His elbows slammed against a solid block; the muscles in his armpits were yanked hard enough to make him cry out.

Thank God. He hadn't slipped lower than his shoulders. Water splashed his face but he managed to avoid it soaking him, and possibly running in through the collar of the suit. In his mind's eye he saw himself from beneath the ice. A yellow-suited figure kicking its legs in the dark body of water. While just a few yards away the vast bulk of the half-sunken ship lay in the sludge of the ocean bed. A monstrous hulk with ammunition spilling out through holes in the ship's sides.

Grimly, he fought to escape the hole. The danger now was that every time he began to climb out the edge of the ice would collapse. He'd be deposited back into the brine and would have to try again.

He gritted his teeth. 'One, two, three . . .' With a hard kick of the legs he managed to push himself upwards on to the horizontal ice sheet. Around him in the open water were chunks of white. He kicked again. Now he lay half out of the water, his torso, arms and head clear and lying face down on the cold surface. Through it he saw bubbles roll along the underside. *Damn, it must only be a couple of inches thick here. It's almost as clear as glass.* Strands of green kelp drifted.

If he tilted his head he could see through the ice to two under-water blobs of yellow that were his legs. Like he aimed to do a push-up he pressed his hands down on the ice to pull himself forward, inch by inch back on to the ice. The sheet groaned beneath him. A crackling sound; more fissures appeared directly under his face. 'Please don't break, please don't break . . .'

Then two things made his heart lurch. A powerful blow struck his foot as it flailed underwater. The ice lay just six inches beneath his eyes, and beneath that fathoms of cold, black seawater. Yet just for a second a vast shadow slid beneath the ice; a solid form scraped its underside. A suggestion of a fin. Patches of light and dark skin.

He clenched his fists. 'Crawl . . . keep crawling. Spread your weight . . . as big an area as possible. That's it; that's the way; keep going . . .' He kept his torso down flat in an attempt to distribute his weight evenly. Using his feet, he pushed himself forward so he slid chest downwards. His chin buffeted the cold surface; his eyes locked on the ocean depths beneath the semi-transparent layer. It seemed a fog of uniform black but once again the quality of the water changed. He knew a solid shape, instead of liquid, had glided beneath him with preda-tory menace.

'Keep moving.' He used his arms in a breaststroke motion, though there was precious little traction.

Thirty seconds later there was a splash followed by a roar. He risked glancing back through the mist at the hole that was formed when he plunged through the ice crust. Rising from it, a domed object. In a moment of near delirium that made him want to shout, he recognized a glistening snout, a vast mouth, dozens of scalpel sharp teeth. The whale vented air from its blow hole.

Orca. The name sent tremors down his spine. *Killer Whale.* Was he hallucinating? Did Orca hunt in the Baltic? Philip couldn't remember. All he could recall were documentaries showing nine yards of killing machine ripping into seals. How the beasts flung heavy bull seals through the air like they were no heavier than a posy of blossom. Right now Philip slith-ered along the ice, just like a seal. Even his profile glimpsed from beneath the ice would be seal-like. Didn't Orca hunt by sonar, too? One fact he did remember is that these predators had developed a natural version of ultrasound. They not only saw their prey, their senses penetrated the bodies of fish and seals to divine their internal organs. That killer whale might be gazing at the valves of his heart as it pumped blood at a manic rate.

The whale sank back into the water. A second later its rubbery snout vanished. He locked up tight. Moving seemed insane right now. The whale might be homing in on him from a dozen fathoms down. Any second it might charge the ice, smash through it, then close those vast jaws around him. He shuddered. He could imagine those teeth crunching through his survival suit to find his body inside.

Instinct suggested he fight the huge creature in some way. He even reached into the suit pocket for the Very flare. But how the hell do you target something as fast as a killer whale through ice?

No, not *fight*. The key is *flight*. He continued his slow crawl across the ice. Ahead of him rose the mass of twisted steel that formed the bulk of the munitions wreck. Right now, that seemed the safest place on his particular horizon.

As he crawled he heard the ice being smashed. The image came to him of those corpses of crewmembers who had been frozen into the ocean. Oddly inappropriate, but somehow accurate, he had the impression of pieces of fruit sitting in the surface of a cheesecake. The Orca family had found the frozen corpses. Now they were enjoying the flavor of some easy pickings.

'Keep moving,' he murmured, 'just keep moving.'

When the Toad had finished with the steward, he surged on through the ship. His twin wasn't satisfied with one victim, however. He still raged at the Toad for leaving him alone in the home cabin. He craved more retribution, and the Toad knew this would continue all night. He turned a corner to find two masked figures. They were armed but didn't get a chance to raise their guns before he blundered into them. He was smart enough not to tackle two armed men. He contented himself with shouldering through them with so much force he knocked them down, and then he lumbered away before they could recover enough to use their weapons.

*   *   *

Tanya led Jo by the hand. Isis followed; she repeatedly glanced back along the corridor to make sure they were alone.

'I want my mom,' insisted the girl. 'Now.'

'I know, sweetie,' Tanya whispered. 'We're on our way. You'll see her soon.'

But the appearance of the prisoner, then overhearing the hijackers saying they intended to guard the entrance to the piano lounge, meant that Tanya and her companions were forced downwards. Now they walked along a corridor on the deck that housed the crew's accommodation. Anxiety dried Tanya's mouth. Even though it seemed deserted, at any second someone might step out from one of the dozens of cabins. This place resembled a necropolis that comprised dozens of silent tombs. She glanced at Isis who still carried the grenade in the black mask as if it were a purse. At that instant, however, a minor miracle occurred: Tanya had an idea.

Close up, the munitions wreck rose high above him, like a mountain of tangled iron. In the moonlight it was blood red from rust. A surreal vision in crimson, as if metal had morphed into raw beef.

Philip didn't risk standing for fear of plunging through the ice again. It still groaned as he crawled on his belly across it. Instead of climbing to his feet, he found a section of the deck that allowed him to enter, still on his chest. Only when he saw the corroded metalwork beneath him did he risk standing. In his chest his heart hammered like fury. His face oozed perspiration. Knees shook, his ankles weak as water. For a moment he swayed. But, thank God, the mass of blood-red iron on which he stood was solid.

Across the white expanse the *Volsparr* had been reduced to a phantom presence, merely an ethereal outline with lights gleaming like distant stars. All that mayhem, the slaughter, the hijackers; all of that had become distant now. He had taken command of his own vessel. His head swam from exertion and the release of anxiety. At least the killer whales couldn't reach him here. He swayed. *Gotta sit down.* Vertigo nearly toppled him. Exertion, terror, whacks to the head, the fall . . . He found a slab of iron jutting from the tilting deck. It made an ideal stool, so he perched himself. There, in the moonlight, he concentrated on bringing his racing heart under control.

It wouldn't do to faint now. As his breathing eased his eyes re-focused. The rusting iron was a mass of reds and browns, yet as he took in the twisted guardrails, crumpled walls, and the battered winches, he noticed a shiny black cable that appeared brand new. It ran along the remains of the floor to an equally shiny black box. His eye followed the cable in the other direction. It branched off into yet more cables that disappeared through chasms in the deck.

'Ah,' he murmured, light-headed, 'funny thing that. I'd forgotten that they've planted explosive charges here.'

Forty-Seven

From the crew's accommodation deck Tanya realized how vulnerable they were. She stood in the long corridor that ran centrally through the ship like some steel highway and she knew at any moment one of the hijackers would appear. Then there would be nothing they could do to save their lives. She glanced down at Jo, who trustingly held her hand. Isis regarded the way ahead with characteristically cool gaze.

Tanya took a deep breath. 'I've got an idea. Give me the mask.'

Isis handed her the black balaclava with the grenade still weighing it down like there was a brick inside. 'It better be a good idea, Tanya; we won't make it if you foul up.'

'Before I share it with you, will you be honest with me?'

'Fire away.'

'Do you see your reflection in my pupils?'

'Oh.'

'Oh? You've forgotten already? It was only twenty-four hours ago that you said you were psychic. That because you couldn't see your reflection in my eyes it meant I had no future.'

'I remember perfectly, Tanya.'

'So, Isis, do you see it now?' Tanya faced the woman.

'Conjurors manipulate their audiences during the show. People like me have to manipulate everyone that comes into their sphere *all* of the time.'

'You mean you were lying to me, like you lied about Philip assaulting you?'

'Tanya.' She held her head in that haughty way again, the empress addressing her servant. 'This is a competitive, dog-eat-dog world; it always has been.'

Tanya seethed. *The way she does that makes me furious. I want to hit her.*

Isis continued her impromptu lecture. 'One must develop a whole arsenal of weapons to succeed, not only in business, but in life.'

'You are a manipulative bitch. I could punch you.'

'But you won't.'

'No, because I'm not going to waste my anger on you. Anger is one of my weapons. I'm going to use it on those . . .' Jo's proximity encouraged her to modify the sentence. 'I'm going to direct my anger at those *disagreeable* people who have caused us so much trouble.'

'Nicely phrased.' Isis nodded. 'Tell me your plan.'

'I won't tell. I'll show.' She drew the hand grenade from the black mask. Its steel clip allowed her to hang it on to the belt of her jeans. 'Now help me find a denim shirt to replace this.' She touched her white blouse.

Isis awarded her an appraising look, judging her. 'You won't fool the hijackers. They'll know you're just one of the herd upstairs, a passenger who found a mask. They'll kill you.'

'Then you'd better play your part well, hadn't you?'

Isis and Tanya began a search of the cabins. Some contained murdered crew. Isis remained with Jo in the corridor while Tanya opened the closets. In the third cabin Tanya opened a suitcase. 'Bingo.' A moment later she laid a neatly folded denim shirt on the bunk, then began to unbutton her white blouse.

All the hijackers she'd seen had worn a uniform of denim, along with the black balaclava mask, of course. In her teens she'd acted in school plays. *It's time to see if I can give another convincing performance.* Back then if she fluffed lines the audience would only laugh. *This time getting it right is a matter of life and death.*

*   *   *

The stalemate had held them there for hours. Suzanne Lynch had helped Turrock and Fytton build a barricade across the passage that led to the cells on the former car deck. The barricade – tables, chairs, doors from cabinets and steel benches – kept the hijackers at a distance. For the last three hours or so the gunfire had subsided into a solitary shot every fifteen minutes, as if to say: 'Hi, I'm still here, don't forget me.'

The hijackers couldn't reach them, unless they attempted a suicide dash along the corridor to the barricade; neither, however, could the three escape into other parts of the ship. What they could see were the televisions in the now empty cells. They'd seen the atrocities the hijackers had committed; they knew all about their demands. Suzanne had just moments ago seen footage of a guy in green fleece being blasted to death in a kids' ball pool.

Suzanne barely flinched at the report of a pistol from the hijackers. By now it seemed as if the guns chatted to each other, rather than being instruments of death.

Turrock stood behind the barricade; a sub-machine gun rested handily next to him on a chair. His head was still bandaged from the clubbing he'd suffered earlier. Suzanne stood out of the line of fire in the doorway of a cubicle crammed with cables and meters. It smelled of hot plastic as if high voltages were channeled through there. Shoe-horned into the corner of the room was a computer workstation. On screen it showed the same gory footage that played on the TV monitors. A handwritten sign fixed to the wall above it warned: *Secondary Studio Facility. If you don't have the studio officer's permission, do not touch!*

In the long silence between conversational gunshots Turrock gave a grim smile. 'The irony of all this, Suzanne, is that we probably know some of the hijackers. Isn't that right, Fytton?'

Fytton grunted an affirmative as he wiped a sub-machine gun with a rag.

Turrock nodded in the direction of the enemy barricade. 'We probably slept in the same huts, ate at the same tables, as we guarded some pipeline. Funny, huh?'

'Hilarious.' Suzanne grimaced. 'And I thought a Christmas voyage would be fun.'

Fytton held out his camcorder to Suzanne. 'Film me loading da gun.'

'What?' Suzanne rolled her eyes. 'I filmed you doing that five minutes ago.'

'That was da Uzi. I want you to film me loading Agram.'

She whispered to Turrock, 'He must be mad. All Fytton does is nag me to film him loading the gun or firing the damn gun.'

Turrock smiled. 'Do you really believe we'd do this job if we were sane?'

Suzanne groaned. 'Give it here.' She took the camera from Fytton.

'Make sure you get da magazine in da screen's center. Twenty-two rounds. Nice Croatian instrument.' Then to Turrock. 'Hey, boss. 'Dis going to be good Quilp hunt, huh?'

'It's a brilliant Quilp hunt, Fytton. Only this time it's difficult to know which are the Quilp. Them or us?' He slipped the pistol's muzzle through a gap in the barricade and fired off a random shot.

Dear God, she thought as she filmed Fytton loading the machine gun, *I'm going to wind up as crazy these two. I really am.*

The Toad's feet drummed the stairs as he raced up them. 'I'm sorry,' he panted to the twin that nobody else could see. 'They spoilt it, not me.' The twin didn't have it in his heart to be merciful to the Toad, nor anybody else. The steward in the tight little white jacket had felt his wrath. When they reached the top of the stairs the writhing knot of shadows at the Toad's side pointed out the masked man standing by the doors to the Moonlit Bay Lounge. For a moment the guard had his back to the Toad. As he turned the Toad retreated back into the stairwell.

The Toad's face quivered. 'Not that one; he's armed . . . No, don't make me.'

When his twin murmured he had every confidence, the Toad's fear turned into an electrifying sense of elation. He had to push his paw against his mouth to stifle a burst of giggles. 'Gosh, aren't we wicked?' A quick peep revealed the man to be armed with a shotgun; however, he carried this on his shoulder by a strap. Instead, he favored a long-handled axe, which he let dangle in one gloved fist.

The Toad took another glimpse of the setting where the

hijacker stood. Nearby were sofas. Beside the guy was a Christmas tree. Above him, swaying in air currents, were plastic angels. They hung from the ceiling; each one by a wire connected to the wing tips then the wire looped over a small adhesive hook. The Toad's bulging eyeballs swiveled down to the guard again as he calculated distances.

He ducked back into the staircase. 'Not looking good, I'm afraid. We should find someone else.' The twin's anger loomed over him like a storm cloud. 'Oh, my gosh,' the Toad breathed, 'you're going to make me go through with this, aren't you?'

And the moment he remembered the devastation of the home cabin, anger blazed once more. Now he could not stop himself from attacking, although he realized it might be his final act on this earth. He readied himself for the charge. As he did so he heard a door slam. A woman's voice rose in protest but a male voice crashed over it, drowning it.

The Toad stepped out. 'Gosh.'

A woman had exited the lounge. She tried to argue with the hijacker, but he'd grabbed her by the hair.

'I warned you,' he boomed. 'You had your chance. But no more.'

The masked man dragged her by the hair as she yelled in terror. Efficiently he pulled her across the sofa so the back acted as a chopping block. She writhed. The yell rose into a scream. In the other hand he held the axe, which he raised above his head; the sharp blade glittered beneath angels that floated on wires.

They must have heard the screams inside the lounge; the passengers, however, were too frightened to investigate. This woman would be decapitated away from their gaze.

'You might as well make it easy for yourself,' warned the Axe Man. He pulled her head down over the sofa back. Her bare neck formed a rounded arc of flesh.

The Toad would have charged anyway. He couldn't stop himself. He raced from his hiding place, leapt on to the sofa, then bounced upwards to grab at an angel. With a kind of grace he unhooked the wire and on the downward drop he swung the loop down over the hijacker's head. Gripping the wire itself would have carved the flesh from the Toad's stubby fingers; instead he gripped the plastic angel in both hands. He lifted his feet; body weight should be sufficient.

The hijacker managed to dropped the axe then get his fingers between his own throat and the wire to prevent it strangling him.

The weight of the Toad's bulk snapped the wire tight. The man's fingers presented no serious obstacle, and the fine wire sliced through them; bloody digits dropped on to the sofa cushion. He managed a gasp as he understood that after all this killing his own death would come next. Then like wire parting cheese the angel wire glided through his throat. With the trachea and arteries severed the hijacker slumped downward to the floor.

The Toad fell with him. By the time he climbed to his own feet the woman had scrambled away, unscathed. She raced into the lounge shouting to startled passengers that a hero in an orange suit had miraculously appeared to save them.

Tanya walked along the corridor. Behind her Isis followed hand in hand with Jo. Tanya wore the black balaclava mask. It itched her face; she smelled its previous owner and she longed to hurl it from her. As she walked the hand grenade jiggled against her thigh.

'OK,' Isis whispered, 'where now?'

'We're going outside.'

'But I want my mom.' Jo sounded close to tears. 'I want Mom now. I'm not playing the game any more.'

'You'll see her soon.'

'And take that mask off. It's silly.'

'All part of the game,' Tanya whispered. 'It'll make your mom laugh, too.'

They passed a cabin where a man lay on the bunk, his throat cut.

'Exactly where outside?' Isis asked.

'The lifeboat. We've no choice. We've got to leave the ship.'

'And the rest of the passengers?'

All Tanya could do by way of answer was give an emphatic shrug.

NINTH TRACT
Forty-Eight

Sixteen hours until Zero Hour. In the hold of the wartime munitions vessel Philip could see a small fraction of the consignment of torpedo warheads. He shone the flashlight into the void. The sea moved in and out of a gash in the ship's side, a movement sluggish enough to suggest something sickly about the slow pulse of water. *My God*, he thought, *those things look new.* Philip had expected the cylindrical forms of the warheads to be corroded but they were rust-free, even shiny in the radiance of the flashlight. Due to the chafing action of surf mixed with sand? It didn't take a close examination to discern that the warheads were intact. *So scrub any thought of the sea water wetting the volatile stuff inside. Those things look primed and ready to blow.* All that high explosive down there made Philip's head spin. Another pulse of water crept inside with a hiss. It tugged at cables linking the detonation charges. And then he saw them: plastic packages in a dull green that must contain the explosives intended to trigger what would be a catastrophic eruption of munitions.

In homes and offices across the world millions watched the man in the orange leisurewear march along the corridor in a ship called the *Volsparr*. A strange frog-like face, with bulging eyes and short arms that were ill-matched to his powerful torso. Conspiracy theories bounced around the globe: he was the product of an inhuman experiment. Or that there were more like him swimming in the Baltic. Amphibian hybrids. Everyone knew the story now. TV and radio news revealed that negotiations with the hijackers were going well. That soon a deal would be reached, hostages released, then tearful homecomings. They didn't know that negotiations were only a delaying tactic, and that when the clock in another section of their screens reached zero then the images they watched so intently would dramatically, and extremely violently, stop.

Tanya, along with Isis and tiny Jo, made their way to a door that would take them out on to the lifeboat deck. If Philip really did know what he was doing they'd soon be leaving the ship to its fate. Tanya still wore the black balaclava mask. When she glimpsed herself in mirrors through open cabin doors she saw her passable imitation of a hijacker: the denim jeans and shirt echoed their uniform, and then the clincher – the hand grenade clipped to her belt.

'Nearly there,' Tanya whispered.

Isis scowled. 'Just pray that Philip hasn't taken off without us.'

'I'm fed up!' Jo screeched. 'I'm going to Mom!'

Before Tanya could react she ran for an elevator that stood with its doors open. Tanya knew she could catch the child before she could press the button then coax her to the lifeboat. But it didn't work out like that. The elevator had been called from elsewhere. The doors began to slide shut before Jo even reached them. If it wasn't for the five-year-old being so tiny she wouldn't have made it through the gap as the doors hummed to meet each other.

'My God.' Tanya couldn't believe her eyes. The doors had closed on the child. A second later the elevator motor purred.

Isis stabbed the call button. 'Too late. It's gone.'

Tanya looked at the illuminated arrow. 'It's going down.' A sense of panic gripped her; the little girl was all alone. 'What's below this level?'

'The car deck, and below that the cargo hold. There's the engine room beneath that but I doubt if the elevator goes that far.'

'We should be able to beat the elevator if we run.'

Isis hesitated. 'The hijackers will be—'

'Come on!' Tanya bounded down the stairwell. Isis followed.

After twenty steps she reached the corridor on the former car deck. She noticed the sign: *Choir-Moore Abstracts. Strictly No Admittance.*

'I've been here before,' she whispered to Isis.

At the same time she heard the elevator doors hum shut.

Jo stood in the center of the corridor ten paces from her. Only thirty paces beyond the child was a sight that made her blood run cold. Tables and cabin doors had been piled across the corridor to form a barricade. At this side of it two figures sat on stools. At their feet were cartons of apple pies, while water bottles stood like bowling pins along one wall. Hijackers for sure. Same denim uniform, same black balaclava masks. They both cradled sub-machine guns across their laps. They noticed Jo instantly, of course. It's possible she had called out as she exited the elevator. Tanya also stood in plain view. *Do they see me as a colleague, or am I really so obviously a passenger in a mask?* Tanya glanced back. Isis remained out of sight in the stairwell; she must have noticed from Tanya's body language that she'd been discovered. One of the hijackers slid their hand towards the machine gun.

Tanya realized that her freezing up with shock might be taken as nonchalance by the two killers. What's more, they couldn't see her face. She pointed at Jo, who'd frozen in shock, too.

Tanya tried to sound calm. 'The kid ran away. I'll take her back upstairs.'

'Isn't that the one The Executioner's supposed to be taking care of?'

Tanya swallowed. 'Sure. I've got her now.'

The pair exchanged glances.

This isn't going well. They suspect. She walked toward Jo. *Just grab her by the hand then leave.*

The other killer held up a hand. 'Wait.'

Maybe it was the harsh voice that did it, but Jo ran. The route she chose was a second passageway opposite the elevator doors. Clearly the two men terrified Jo, but she'd also had enough of Tanya. The kid was escaping *all* adults. Tanya followed.

'Hey!' shouted the men.

Jo's escape route was a bad choice. Just ten paces along the corridor a steel gate blocked it. Jo tugged at it in desperation but it was solidly, irrevocably locked.

'Come back here,' called one of the hijackers. 'What's your name?'

Trapped. Damn it. If she fled back along the corridor to the stairwell the killers would have ample time to cut them down.

At that moment Tanya knew she had to save the girl's life. She'd promised her mother to look after her. The emotion came so strongly tears formed in her eyes. She was responsible for Jo. Every instinct screamed that she must protect her. It was as if some program that had hitherto lain dormant suddenly roared into life. The girl would be blasted by the machine guns. The hijackers wouldn't give a damn.

'It's up to me,' Tanya panted. 'It's up to me. I've got to get her out of this.' She put her hands on the little girl's shoulders and pushed her gently towards the gate where she'd be furthest from the junction of the two corridors. Then she pulled the grenade from her belt. *How big an explosion do these things make? In confined spaces the blast is worse. The sound will damage Jo's hearing permanently.* She listened. Awful quiet out there. In her mind's eye she saw one of the hijackers tiptoeing the thirty paces along the corridor from the barricade to the junction. Then they'd only have to raise the weapon to fire at point-blank range. Her attention returned to the grenade. A screw nut protruded from the bottom. Quickly she unscrewed it. With the bolt came a brass cylinder as thick as a pen and perhaps two inches long.

She murmured, 'The fuse . . . has to be.'

'Hello.' A voice echoed along the corridor. 'Your name? We're waiting.'

Hell, they know I'm a phony.

'Tell us your name.'

Tanya pocketed the fuse, then began to replace the bolt. She dropped it.

'Your name.'

'I'm . . .' Isis had told her the hijackers referred to each other by their role only. 'I'm Grenade.' Quickly, she picked up the bolt.

'Come out, Grenade. We've something important to tell you.'

They know, God help me, they know. Tanya worked at the bolt, screwing it tighter into the grenade.

'If you don't come to us, we're going to come to you.'

The other asked, 'Is that Miss Grenade or Mrs Grenade?'

When it came down to it Tanya didn't know for sure whether the brass component she'd removed was a fuse or not. Maybe the bomb would explode the moment she removed the pin. *No other option now. If I don't get this right Jo's going to die, and it'll be my fault.* She hauled the pin out of the grenade then without presenting herself as a target hurled it along the corridor.

The force of her throw sent the grenade hurtling towards the two men; it struck one wall, bounced off, then hit the opposite one with a terrific clatter. The two hijackers lurched back in shock; only the barricade prevented retreat.

'Grenade!' yelled one.

Tanya glanced round the corner. The two men were forced to run towards the grenade. Would it detonate? She'd intended to disable it, but how could she know for sure?

They'd calculated their chances. The pair raced forward maybe ten paces until they could duck into a storeroom where they figured they'd survive the blast. Once they realized the grenade was dud, that's when they'd emerge and kill Tanya and Jo.

'Isis!' she shouted. 'Get back upstairs. I'm bringing Jo!'

Turrock heard the clatter. Then came the yell: *'Grenade!'* Just a second after that had come a woman's voice. *'Isis! Get back upstairs. I'm bringing Jo!'*

Years of front-line experience told him that their chance had arrived.

'Fytton.' He mouthed the word. 'Forward.' As he moved towards the hijackers' barricade in a silent run, with his assistant following, he re-positioned his grip on the machine gun. Five seconds later they reached the barricade that formed a six-foot wall across the passage. Like the barricade Turrock had built it had an opening at eye level, just large enough to accommodate a gun muzzle.

He rammed the gun muzzle through. Much further along the corridor he saw a figure in a black mask carry a little child to a stairwell, then as quickly vanish. Next he saw the grenade on the steel floor, the pin absent. *But no boom.* A second later a pair of masked hijackers emerged from a storeroom.

'You're right,' one said to the other, 'it's a dud. Find the joker with the girl and get rid.'

Turrock had the perfect opportunity. He used it well. A squeeze of the trigger and he emptied the thirty-round magazine into the two men at a distance of a dozen paces. The nearest hijacker dropped instantly, the rounds bursting through the head. The second swung his machine gun. One of Turrock's rounds slammed into the guy's trigger hand, smashing the thumb back flat to the wrist. More rounds ripped into his arm as he whirled away.

'He's in the storeroom.' Turrock began ripping at the barricade with his free hand. 'Help me clear this!'

Turrock had got through the barricade by the time Suzanne reached them. Grim-faced she used the camcorder to capture what happened next. After stepping over the hijacker with brain stuff hanging out of his worthless skull, they approached the storeroom. 'This time, me first, boss.' Fytton snapped a fresh magazine into his weapon. 'Keep filming,' Fytton ordered. 'Miss nothing.'

Turrock watched the man step into the stockroom, gun at the ready. The second hijacker sat with his back to steel laundry racks, one arm shattered by machine-gun rounds, his torn shirt revealed bloodied biceps. A bullet had sliced through his neck. As he sat there he clamped his palm to the wound. Even so, a rich crimson blood poured between his fingers. The man panted.

Turrock watched as the eyes beyond the holes in the mask followed Fytton as he entered. Fytton checked that Suzanne still filmed him. He stepped forward, pulled off the guy's mask.

'I've got you both in shot.'

'Good.' Fytton fired a bullet between the hijacker's eyes.

Forty-Nine

'Excuse me, miss, I think you dropped something.'

Tanya saw the man with the bandaged head hold out an object in his hand. It was the grenade she'd thrown. She, Isis and Jo had crouched down on the stairs when they heard the sound of gunfire. Now at the entrance to the stairwell were two men she didn't recognize, dressed in casual clothes, and a woman she *did* know: Suzanne Lynch, who had stumbled into the lounge all those hours ago to announce that the prisoners had been freed from their cells.

'This is yours, isn't it?' The man with the bandaged head jiggled the grenade as he pointed the machine gun at her.

'Quilp,' the other man added. 'She's damn good Quilp.'

Tanya still clutched the balaclava mask in one hand; she wore the denim uniform of the hijackers. *They think I'm one of killers*.

'Quilp hunt,' claimed the man with a scarred face. He carried a gun, too.

'Wait,' Suzanne lowered the camcorder. 'I know the woman. She's not one of the hijackers, she's a passenger.'

'You sure?'

Isis stood up, her confidence returning. 'Suzanne's correct. This is Tanya, my best friend. We took the mask and the grenade from one of the hijackers.'

The man appeared surprised. 'And he didn't complain?'

Tanya rose. 'By the time we finished with him he didn't mind one way or the other.'

The scarred man whistled, impressed.

'Then claim your spoils of war.' The man held out the grenade.

Tanya gave a grim smile. 'Bombs aren't really my style. Keep it.'

'Thanks, it might come in useful if the bad guys are still here.'

'Oh, they're here.' She pulled a pair of objects from her pocket. 'So you best take these. One's the fuse, the other the pin.'

'You removed the fuse?'

'I sure as hell wasn't going to detonate the grenade.' Tanya spoke with feeling. 'If I'd tried I'd have blown myself up.'

Isis added, 'If we don't move quickly that's what'll happen anyway. The hijackers plan to detonate munitions wrecks. If they go up we go with them.'

'Then we need to leave.'

'Before we go any further,' Isis said, displaying her self-control of old, 'we should introduce ourselves. You know this is Tanya. The little one is Jo. I'm Isis.'

Suzanne stepped forward. 'You know me already. The man with the bandage is Turrock, my boyfriend. And this gentleman is Fytton.'

Tanya nodded at the camcorder. 'What's with the home movies?'

'Quilp hunt,' Fytton explained with satisfaction.

Suzanne rolled her eyes. 'I don't understand, either.'

Turrock smiled. 'We picked up strange habits when we were mercenaries. We film ourselves at work. Then it's posted on the internet for our colleagues to admire.'

'I can imagine what kind of films they are,' Isis commented.

'Yeah, you need a strong stomach.' Fytton sounded pleased.

'What we need do is trade some information here. See the screen on the wall over there, the one showing a ship's officer being bludgeoned. That's on a loop—'

'I know,' Turrock said. 'I've seen it.'

'What you might not know is that clock is counting down to zero hour when the biggest explosion the West has heard in fifty years is going to rip this ship apart.'

Turrock rose to the challenge. 'Then we've got fifteen hours to put this right.'

'And save our necks,' Isis added. 'OK, this is what we know . . .'

The passengers moved freely about the ship now the only guard had been garroted by the Toad. Most gave the body a wide berth but the big silver-haired male, who the others called Gus, searched the body. Soon they took possession of the shotgun and a pair of revolvers.

The Toad watched with bulging eyes. *Gosh, oh my gosh, am I responsible for this? The passengers are breaking free.* The Toad regarded both hijackers and passengers with equal suspicion. One party would kill him, the other would lock him up. He didn't really know what to do now. Normally, he'd find some corner where he could go to sleep. But his nerves were all jangly; he longed to roar out his fury. His twin might be invisible to everybody else but him, but he had the loudest shout of all. He told the Toad he must leave the ship. Obediently, the Toad scampered down to the restaurant level. Passengers headed down there, too. They were frightened. None of them really knew what to do other than escape the piano lounge. He glimpsed Maya and Sami as they strolled towards the kitchen. The Toad might have been tempted to go too, but his twin demanded they should stay away from others.

The Toad was frightened of the twin so he obeyed. Right then, it seemed wise to leave all these people behind. He exited through a door on to one of the outer decks. The darkness beyond the ship was total. No twinkling lights in the distance. In fact all he could see in the moonlight was a few acres of frozen ocean. Beyond that, thick fog obliterated everything.

Out here on the deck he was alone, yet he heard a voice calling. 'Are you ready to board the witnesses yet?'

The Toad leaned over the guardrail. On the deck directly beneath him a figure in blue denim leaned over the rail, too. White vapor jetted through the man's black mask as he called to figures standing on two boats that were moored to the side of the ship. One vessel appeared to be a lifeboat from the ship. In front of that was a chubby fishing boat. But it wasn't fishing now. The hijackers must have used it to transport their squad to the *Volsparr*. The hijacker on the deck still leaned over the rail, clearly waiting for instructions.

'No.' The Toad didn't like what his twin had ordered. 'I can't do it. I'll die.'

But he couldn't refuse the writhing mass of shadows that loomed over him. The Toad obeyed. With the man still leaning over the rail on the lower deck the Toad climbed on to the rail, then jumped. His feet smashed into the back of the masked man's neck. With a grunt he toppled over the rail. The Toad shifted his balance so he thudded down on to the deck. Like lightning, he darted to his feet in time to see the screaming man plunge downward. He struck the ice some ten yards from the boats. There he lay howling in agony. His colleagues produced a pole for him to cling to. The force of the impact had driven his bottom half through the ice. He'd suffer broken bones but he should survive. This angered the twin; the Toad flinched before some harsh words indeed.

Then it all changed for the good. As the Toad stared down at the flailing man he made out a shape beneath the ice. It went from small and fuzzy to huge. A body rose from the depths at tremendous speed. A second later the ice erupted as if a bomb had smashed it. The man in the water flew up through the air, as if he'd cheated gravity. Yet behind him a huge snout opened to reveal jaws lined with needle-sharp teeth. Then like a dog deftly catching a treat in its mouth the killer whale's jaws snapped shut around the screaming man's hips then both predator and prey dropped back into the sea where they vanished beneath its foaming surface.

The man's fellow hijackers shouted. A note of panic entered their voices. The Toad knew they were frightened, even vulnerable. A tingle of anticipation ran down his spine. He liked the timbre of their cries. His huge tongue slapped against his lips. *Gosh. Time to go to work.*

Maya and Sami entered the ship's galley. Massive oven doors gleamed; everything here shone with pristine cleanliness. Out in the restaurant area passengers called to one another. There was a sense of excitement mingling with fear now. These people knew that the balance of power had changed. They'd seen the corpse of the hijacker. It meant their enemy wasn't immune to death. They even spoke of a miracle: a hero, who had arrived from nowhere to save them; a man in a tangerine leisure suit.

'If I can procure a subject,' Sami told Maya, 'I can start my work again. You know, this time I can refine my technique.' He unhooked a meat clever from the wall. 'We'll make fools of the pharmaceutical industry.'

Maya chose a carving knife.

They moved through the kitchen until they reached a hooded man. He stood with his back to them as he peered through the door to where armed passengers swarmed to the stairs.

Maya tested the point of the knife with her fingertip. Then she closed in.

Immediately, the man turned round, aimed the machine gun at them and uttered, 'Don't even think of it.'

They froze.

'Drop the kitchenware,' he ordered, then he took them to the service elevator that carried them down to the ship's cargo deck.

'OK,' Philip addressed the black plastic box on the slab of rusting iron, 'let's be methodical about this.' His breath misted white. 'You must be the power pack and the timer. Yup, the counter is a dead giveaway.' Set into the box top were switches beneath an oblong LED screen no bigger than a postage stamp. It revealed figures scrolling backward, counting down to zero hour. 'So, fourteen hours left until it all goes bang.' Philip glanced across to the ship. As ever, it only appeared as a dim silhouette in the moonlight. Fog obscured most of its details other than lights twinkling through portholes. He could hear nothing. And, infuriatingly, there was no other way of finding

out what unfolded there. The only way to do that would be if
he returned across the ice. Although that would make him an
easy target for any of the hijackers who happened to spot him
trudging back. *Even if I did make it without being seen, how
on earth could I climb back on board? The lowest deck must
be thirty feet above the waterline; those sides are sheer.* So this
must be his priority. He turned to the little box of tricks that
would detonate the charges. Those switches probably termin-
ate the countdown. But which one? And wouldn't it be tamper
proof? Wouldn't he need to enter a code to cancel its program?
That left him with cutting through the cables that led to the
explosives. That should be simple enough. The survival suit
came equipped with a clasp knife. Then again, logic dictated
there'd be some self-protective system. To cut through a cable
on a domestic intruder alarm will trigger it, so cutting through
these wires would cause a massive explosion.

Philip pondered over the clock as it continued its countdown. 'There has to be a way to stop you,' he said aloud.
'There has to be.'

By way of cryptic answer came a spectral groaning. The
ice sheet pressed tighter against the half-sunken ship, yearning
to crush the hull and its evil cargo.

Fifty

The gunman urged Maya and Sami through the cargo hold.
The walkway between the massive pump and the ship's
inner wall held a litter of corpses.

'Hurry,' the hijacker told them, 'this is your lucky day.'

Cold air blew into the hold. Sami saw the reason why.
Moments later they reached an open hatchway. He saw that
the ocean had frozen over. A pair of masked figures stood by
the open hatch.

The man who'd captured Maya and Sami nodded at the
pair. 'A passenger and a waitress from the look of them.'

One of the figures by the door shook his head. 'Is this all you could get?'

'All hell's breaking loose up there. A passenger overpowered Axe Man. They've taken his weapons.'

The man shrugged. 'Fortunes of war. Never mind, we've got two. Anyway, the operational footage is the main thing. Control has the numbers, millions have been watching it. We're Pole to Pole.'

'OK, you two,' their captor told them. 'We'll be taking you somewhere safe. You won't be harmed. The police will question you, then no doubt you'll sell your stories to the media. That suits us fine. We want the world to know just how good we really are. After you, madam.' He chuckled. 'Careful, the steps are icy.'

The gunman prodded the muzzle into Maya's back. She led the way down a dozen steps to where a fishing boat had been moored alongside the *Volsparr*. Sami followed, then after him came the two hijackers.

'Control wants you to leave now with the witnesses.'

One of the masked men paused. 'We've only got four men on board; aren't we waiting for the rest of the Squad?'

'No. You go first, get clear of the ship. The rest of the team are using the lifeboat. We've still to pick up our stragglers.'

'We were undermanned.' Another hijacker descended from the temporary staircase slung against the side of the ship. 'We should have double the manpower.'

Another laughed. 'So, go tell Control that he doesn't know how to conduct an operation. Can't you just picture his smile of delight when you rubbish his planning?'

Sami and Maya were taken below into the fishing boat's living area. They passed half a dozen cabins on the way. Clearly this vessel had been designed to spend weeks at sea. An aroma of coffee floated from the galley. One hijacker remained with them in the lounge as the other three prepared for departure. Sami realized that the boat suffered under-manning problems, too. The hijackers complained amongst themselves that they had difficulty in casting off.

The lone hijacker remaining on the *Volsparr*'s steps watched the fishing boat as its motors rumbled. A loud cracking began as it forged a passage through the ice. It wouldn't be a long trip. In little more than an hour they'd run the vessel into an inlet on the coast then its passengers and crew would vanish into the forest. By tomorrow afternoon the pair of 'witnesses' would be released so they could tell their story to the world.

The sound of snapping ice drowned the pad of footsteps behind him until it was too late. He whirled round to see a strange figure in an orange suit bearing down on him. Eyes bulged from a toad-like face. Then a muscular blow from a wrench shattered his jaw bone. As he fell a second blow exploded the back of his skull.

'Do let me come with,' murmured the Toad. He sprinted down the *Volsparr*'s steps to bound on to the departing fishing boat. The hijacker that remained on the fishing boat's deck struggled with a line dragging in the water. He didn't want it to foul the propeller. As it was, the Toad took care of the mooring line. He looped it round the hijacker's neck so tightly the man's eyes bulged right out through the eye-holes in the mask. Even so, he was still alive when the Toad pitched him overboard. The man couldn't cry out because the noose pulled tight as he was dragged through the freezing waters.

When the killer whale returned for more food it discovered the most convenient of snacks being towed through the water. The Toad watched with satisfaction as the huge pair of jaws bit the hijacker in half. The man's blood painted shards of ice a brilliant red.

With nobody on deck the Toad rubbed his hands. *Chilly . . . most definitely chilly . . .* Then he went in search of company.

Fifty-One

Isis finished telling Turrock what she knew about the hijacking when passengers began to spill down the staircase from the upper deck. Jo's mother had come in search of her daughter, too. When Jo recognized the tearful figure she shouted with delight.

'Mom, we won the chocolate!'

The mother hugged her child until she wailed in protest.

Tanya recognized another individual. 'Gus, what's happening up there?'

The last time she'd seen him he'd been a defeated old man; now his blue eyes twinkled. 'We're getting the better of them. At least one's dead. We got his guns!' He brandished a pistol.

Turrock introduced himself, then added, 'We've got some pretty hefty firepower down here.' He patted the top of his sub-machine gun. 'Do you know how many of the bad guys are left?'

'We've just watched one of the boats leave. They must be pulling out. But we've got more of the bastards boxed in the corridor to the bridge. They got control of some offices and the TV studio but that looks to be it on the top decks.'

'There's another boat down there alongside the steps. If they've got any sense now they'll evacuate.'

Tanya glanced at Isis. 'Philip was supposed to be launching the lifeboat.'

'If it's the same one then I guess he didn't make it.' Isis shrugged. 'So we need to take possession of the lifeboat quickly.'

'Very quickly.' Turrock eyeballed Gus. 'Do you know that when the TV screen clocks hit zero we're going to be blown sky high?'

Gus shook his head. 'Only if our governments don't meet their demands.'

Tanya said, 'Negotiations are a smokescreen. They're going to detonate the charges anyway. We're nothing but a commercial for whoever planned this hijack operation.'

Gus rubbed his jaw. 'So, we're a paragraph in their résumé.'

'Not if I can help it.' Tanya had reached a decision. 'Fytton, have you got some good footage on that camera?'

'Plenty.'

'Of what you did to the hijackers back there?'

He nodded with huge enthusiasm.

Isis angled her head, reassessing her new friend. 'What have you got in mind, Tanya?'

Tanya folded her arms. 'What I'd like to do is pull the footage shot by the hijackers from the screens and replace it with ours.'

'Why?'

'That footage is being beamed worldwide. The whole world

is witnessing what those murderers did to us. We should show the world, and the hijackers' employers, what we managed to do to them.'

'Nice idea,' Isis told her, 'but if the hijackers have control of the studio there's zip all we can do.'

Fytton laughed. 'No problem, lady. We got a studio down on da prison deck. That's how I upload my films to da web.'

'Films?' Gus frowned.

'He's been a mercenary as well as a prison guard,' Suzanne explained. 'As for the film's content, I'm sure you can use your imagination . . .'

'My God.'

'OK,' Turrock said. 'Fytton, show Tanya the studio. We'll continue a downward sweep to locate more hijackers.'

'Not yet.'

They stared at Tanya.

'Suzanne, bring the camera. I want lots more footage. There's a guy in the first-class cabin that's going to model for us first. And another thing.' She paused. 'Do me a favor. Catch one of the hijackers alive. He's going to explain to the world what's happened here, and then he's going to give details about his employers.'

Turrock shook his head. 'Guys like that don't make confessions.'

Isis gave a grim smile. 'Don't underestimate Tanya. She has a knack of making them talk.'

Camera continued to work in the studio as the hijackers' plan began to unravel. She ensured that her footage continued to be transferred via the ship's communication system to both onboard monitors and the internet worldwide. Millions would see their handiwork. Corporations and governments alike would scramble to hire her team.

OK, so the passengers broke out. They'd armed themselves with guns from her fallen comrade. But the Squad had almost completed the operation. Now all that remained was for them to board the lifeboat moored alongside, then leave. Numerals on the monitor told her that just fourteen hours remained until zero hour. Then the charges would automatically detonate munitions on the wrecks. These fifty acres of the Baltic seabed would form a nice deep crater for fish to play in.

Still, there were problems.

Sapper appeared in the doorway. 'We've closed off the corridor to the bridge to prevent passengers coming this way. The bastards have got guns.'

'So?' she snapped. 'That's like giving a monkey a laptop. Take the guns away from them, then kill them.'

'Not so easy. Some of those guys are ex-military. Sparks has just taken a gut shot.'

'Then he wasn't up to the job. Forget him!'

'Are you getting the point? We're the ones under siege now. We can't use the stairs to get down to our boat. We're stranded.'

She took a moment to glance out through the studio doorway. The section of passageway that led towards the Moonlit Bay Lounge had been sealed by her people using one of the steel concertina gates.

She turned to Sapper. 'Tell Control that it's time to send a helicopter.'

Tanya got all the footage she wanted. She took over filming when Suzanne blanched at the sight of the hijacker with the ruined eyes. Somebody had also broken his neck as he'd sat bound to the chair. All in all, it would prove to the world that hijackers are vulnerable animals. Often stupid, too. After that she filmed the corpse outside the lounge doors. Blood formed a crimson halo round the masked head as the guy lay dead on the floor.

'They should have left the prisoners where they were, instead of releasing them to wreak havoc on the passengers.' She poked the hijacker's leg with her foot. 'Your boyfriend's psychopaths have wreaked havoc on the bad guys instead.'

One of Gus's people showed her another hijacker.

'Keep your distance; they can fire at us through the gate.'

This guy still wore the mask. On the other side of the concertina gate he clutched his stomach as he rolled from side to side on the floor.

'The guy didn't realize I had this.' A woman of around seventy held up a revolver. 'I managed to put a round into his stomach at close range.' She clicked her tongue. 'The bad guys are running scared. They haven't got the nerve to even try and rescue one of their own. They're leaving him to bleed to death.'

Tanya raised the camera. She zoomed through the slats of the steel gate to get a good, meaty close-up of the hijacker as he cried for help. Crimson oozed through his fingers as he tried to stem the wound in his stomach.

'That's enough. Get Fytton to upload this.'

Before making a search of the crew's accommodation, Turrock armed more of the passengers with weapons from the guards' private arsenal, an exotic array of handguns and sub-machine guns collected from war zones across the world. Tellingly, the gun stocks had tally notches etched into them.

Gus's jaw dropped. 'This stuff is never legal?'

'It isn't.' Turrock smiled. 'Then, strictly speaking, neither is our little operation. But then who's going to complain about us shipping a bunch of killers overseas so they'll never get the opportunity to strike again? I can recommend the mini-Uzi.' He handed Gus the weapon. 'OK, let's clean up the rest of the boat.'

From the look of things, the hijackers that hadn't left on the boat were stranded in the gated section on the top deck. Turrock admired the way Gus arranged a system of runners to keep information flowing between the guys upstairs keeping the hijackers besieged and the ones making a sweep of the lower decks. Here they found bodies, plenty of bodies. Crew, passengers, but no hijackers. Only when they reached the engine room did they find live crew members shackled to safety rails beside the prop shaft. These were a dozen men and women who were dazed to the point of catatonia. As they were freed Turrock scouted ahead. He soon found the open hatchway just twenty feet above the waterline. A set of collapsible steps that had been deployed through the hatch led down to a lifeboat sat amid the thickening ice. Gus joined him. Turrock nodded. 'We've got our escape route.'

'If the ice doesn't lock us in. I'll put a couple of my men here to guard the boat while we bring the passengers down.'

Turrock continued his search for hijackers in the company of three of Gus's people, who he'd armed with sub-machine guns. Meanwhile, Fytton had returned to the tiny studio beside the cell pod to upload the footage he and Tanya had shot to the internet. Even if they didn't make it to safety the world would know their story.

Indoors proved barren of hijackers, apart from the ones they knew were holding out behind the steel gate on the top deck.

Turrock had an idea. 'Search the lifeboats; some stragglers might have decided to make their own way home.'

It didn't take long to discover his hunch proved right. Out on the freezing decks they spotted a masked figure climbing into a lifeboat. Turrock's three companions emptied their guns at the figure with so much appetite for vengeance that the guy disintegrated as the volley of rounds struck him.

A second hijacker made a run for it.

'Wait,' Turrock hissed as his team raised their guns. 'This one we take alive.'

'Pipe the webcams out, too,' she told Fytton as he tapped at the keyboard. The screen in front of him divided into quarters. In one it showed the main studio where a pair of hijackers sat by the door with their guns. In the second quarter played the footage they'd shot earlier – the dying hijacker behind the gate, the guy minus eyelids, the moment when Fytton dragged the mask off the wounded man, then shot him between the eyes.

'Good Quilp hunt,' Fytton murmured with satisfaction.

'Fytton, keep the clock on screen. We need to know how much time is left.'

Now the screen played the webcam footage, plus film she and Suzanne had shot, in one quarter. The second quarter showed the downward scroll of clock numerals. The third quarter of the screen ran CCTV of the studio's interior upstairs. Only the remaining quarter remained blank. At that point the pair of hijackers in the studio upstairs noticed their films had been replaced. One ran to the computer that controlled the studio output. There was no sound but Tanya knew they were desperately trying to prevent her footage being flashed around the world.

'Don't worry,' Fytton told her. 'I can override da main studio from here. They can pull out all da plugs but it won't stop this good stuff shooting out for every man, woman and bambino to see.'

'I wouldn't want any bambino to see this,' Tanya muttered as one quarter of the screen revealed the slash in a dead hijacker's throat. 'The world isn't going to sleep so sweetly tonight.' She checked the clock. 'Especially if five thousand tons of high explosive go bang.'

A knock sounded on the door. A masked figure stood there. Tanya sucked in a lungful of air.

A hand reached from behind to yank the mask off.

'We've brought you a present, Tanya.' Isis pushed the man forward. 'You've got your chat-show guest.'

Fifty-Two

The hijacker wore the hardened face of a man who killed for a living – who would enjoy blooding his knife for nothing, come to that. He scowled at Tanya as Turrock pressed the revolver muzzle into the back of the man's neck.

'Pull the trigger, you little shit. You've lost. We're going to kill you all anyway.'

Tanya pointed into the room containing the electronics. 'In there is a TV camera. You're going to confess to what you've done.'

'I'll start confessing now, if you like.' He smirked. 'Just last month I was in the Congo. I showed a bunch of pilgrims what I could do with meat hooks. Then I doused them in kerosene.' He laughed at the expression of anger on Tanya's face. 'But I'll say nothing to the camera.'

'You will confess,' Tanya hissed. 'And I'm going to prove to the world your kind are cowards.'

He blew her a kiss. 'Let's go to one of the cabins. Then I can whisper into your pretty little ear all the interesting things I've done to creatures like you.'

She whirled to Fytton. 'Switch on the studio camera. I want you to put me on air now.'

He nodded as he swiftly tapped at the computer keyboard. The top right segment of the screen, which had been blank, now went live as Fytton activated the studio camera; it captured a bright-lit image of an empty chair.

Tanya nodded to Turrock. 'Hold our guest out in the corridor until I've finished.' Then to Fytton: 'The camera's carrying live output?'

'Whoever sits in da chair will be seen by everyone on da ship including da bad guys upstairs.' He smiled. 'Even better it's blazing across da web. It can be seen all over. We're global.'

'Good,' she said firmly as she sat in the chair. The top right hand square of the monitor played a video image of herself. Dark crescents had formed beneath her eyes. Her hair badly needed the mercy of a brush. Yet she saw a strength of determination in her expression. Her eyes shone with a clear light of certainty. *So how many are watching me in the outside world? Tens of thousands? Tens of millions? Here I am, Tanya Rhone, on a ship stranded in the Baltic Sea. Surrounded by death. With less than fourteen hours to go until we're swept into oblivion*. Strangely, the notion didn't frighten her. Instead, she felt a great sense of calm. This was so right. She felt the words rise through her throat to her lips.

And then she addressed a watchful world outside this sphere of hell. 'My name is Tanya Rhone.' Her voice rang with a clear authority. 'This is the *Volsparr*. You've seen what hired killers have done. They've murdered most of the crew. Many passengers have died, too. The hijackers' main aim is to prove to all of you out there that men of violence always win. That if ordinary people like you and me are faced with violence we should immediately surrender. But listen to this. They are mistaken . . . they are wrong . . . they are deluded.' As she gazed into the camera lens she saw her face reflected there. And somehow through that it seemed as if she looked down a long, dark tunnel where thousands upon thousands of people watched her. Worldwide, millions heard her voice; it would be replayed on television for years to come. 'Men and women have confronted those who crave power through violence for centuries. Yet men of violence are always defeated in the end. Every successful society is based on trust and mutual co-operation. Tyrants are, more often than not, destroyed by the people they oppress. Even the most brutal of fathers who dominate their families with their fists eventually grow old, and frail, then they rely on their children for help.' Tanya's blood sang in her veins. Her voice rose. 'So whatever happens now on this ship – if I and my friends die when the clock you see on screen reaches zero – don't turn away with the belief that men of evil always win. No. Tell yourself evil has lost, just as it will always lose. In your heart of hearts believe that. Evil-doers might have guns, bombs, missiles, but we have the most powerful weapon of all: our belief that love and good will triumph.' She smiled. A sense of elation soared through her: she knew the words she'd chosen were the right ones. 'And for any politician watching this who is thinking of hijacking what I've told you for your own benefit, remember this. Presidents and prime ministers might claim to be the most powerful men in their nation, but we, the people, only lend you that power. You don't own the electorate, you serve it. If you forget that, we, the ordinary people, will take all your powers away from you. You will become nothing. Less than nothing.'

Tanya stepped away from the camera. She nodded to Turrock to bring the hijacker in and sit him down. The top-right quadrant of the screen showed the hard-faced killer, a head and shoulders shot as if he was a newsreader. He glared into the lens. Across the world millions gazed into his eyes.

With an air of arrogance he shrugged. 'Well, aren't you going to interrogate me? Knock out some teeth? Work on me with a knife? I'm not giving you any information.'

Tanya stood by the door, arms folded. She held eye contact with him.

With a belligerent grin he nodded at Turrock. 'Hey, when are you going to tell your friend to shoot me? That's what you're going to do, aren't you? Go on then. Give the order. Nice face shot. Billions of people are going to watch my head explode all over the damn wall.' His eyes flicked back at the lens.

'Go on,' he growled. 'Shoot me. Put a bullet right here.' He touched the center of his forehead.

And he really is asking to be killed. He's desperate to escape all this global attention. He'd gladly welcome death right now.

Turrock raised an eyebrow at her. He waited for her to give the signal, so he could squeeze off a round into the guy. Everybody would watch their screens as the hijacker died.

Tanya remained there, arms folded, eyes locked on to the

eyes of hijacker. Nobody moved. No sound. The hijacker licked his dry lips. A bead of sweat trickled down from his fringe.

'Get it over with, you bitch. Tell your monkey here to shoot me in the frigging skull.'

She didn't reply, merely stared.

'You want to spin this out.' He shrugged. 'I can wait until that clock reaches zero hour. Because you know what happens then? We're all going to heaven.' He gave a squeal-like laugh. The tension in it made the hijacker blink.

Tanya kept her eyes locked on his.

'You won't get any information out of me. You can't make me. You haven't . . .' And there his voice broke. Tanya raised an eyebrow as if to say, *My, my, so what happened then?*

He flinched back in the chair. 'You didn't break me. You'll get nothing out of me!' But the hijacker knew that everyone watching had heard that inflection in his voice. That was the moment his nerve gave out. He'd revealed to the world that his bravado had been a false front. It was like looking up at the huge concrete wall of a dam, thinking it could never be breached in a thousand years, then noticing a tell-tale crack that started to leak water. This guy wasn't begging for forgiveness yet, but the cracks showed in his macho facade. Eventually, his spirit would break, then everything the authorities needed to know would come flooding out.

Tanya knew that. The world knew that. *He knew that.*

He screamed, 'Damn you! I'm going to rip you to pieces!'

Tanya smiled. 'Turrock,' she said, 'make sure *this* is the first on the lifeboat. I'm going to be at his trial when he's sentenced to jail. And I'm going to watch him grow old there.'

'Do it!' He jammed his finger against his own head. 'Shoot me. Go on, pull the trigger. *Kill me!*'

'You heard the lady,' Turrock told him. 'All the world's going to enjoy watching you rot in jail.'

The man's face flushed from red to bloodless white. Saliva trickled from the corner of his mouth. More than once he tried to speak. Each time he failed miserably. Together, Turrock and Fytton hauled the hijacker out. Once in the corridor they taped his hands behind him then Gus's people hauled him away to the lifeboat.

Isis drew Tanya's attention to the clock. Barely thirteen hours left. 'These people might have a back-up plan for their bomb. We should be leaving. By the way,' she smiled, 'good work. That guy won't be able to look at his reflection again without hating himself. You broke him.'

Turrock added, 'The people who employed him will have watched it, too. They'll be starting to panic because they know one of their operatives is going to live long enough to reveal their dirty little secrets.'

Fytton winked. 'Hey, boss, we might even end up being da ones to guard him when they ship him out. Think of the fun we'll have.'

'You paint a rosy picture, Fytton.' Smiling, he glanced at his watch. 'Isis is right. Time to abandon ship.' He turned to Gus. 'Can your people get all the passengers and what's left of the crew on to the lifeboat?'

'We're already on it.'

Isis asked, 'How do we stop the hijackers using one of the lifeboats? I'd hate to let them escape.'

'We're on that, too. I've got a couple of guys with axes busting the winch mechanisms. Unless those devils on the top deck grow wings, they're stuck here until the coastguard rescues them.'

Tanya wanted to smile as she descended the stairs. *Smiling is wholly inappropriate*, she told herself, *but I feel we've won a victory here. Evil's taken a beating. We're the ones that delivered the knockout punch. That's something to feel good about, isn't it?* She glanced across at Isis. The woman couldn't stop her own smile, either. She felt that glow of victory, too.

In ten minutes they joined the rest of the survivors on the lifeboat. The cabin had been crammed with men and women – the entire contingent of the *Volsparr*'s surviving passengers and crew; perhaps sixty of them. Jo sat on her mother's knee. The boy that had been there right from the start of it all still held his plastic gun, which he now aimed at his neighbors' faces, deciding which to shoot first. Isis remained on the aft deck, hair fluttering in the icy air as the boat pulled away from the *Volsparr*; she was the image of a Persian empress on her Arab dhow. One of the ship's crew manned the vessel; he gunned the motor, sending the boat crunching through the ice at speed. The *Volsparr* soon fell away in the darkness, its lights throwing yellow smudges across the whiteness of frozen ocean.

The three munitions wrecks formed black hillocks. They could have been ancient burial mounds rising bleakly out of an Arctic landscape.

'Put as much distance as you can between us and that lot,' Tanya told the sailor. 'Lots of distance, and as fast you can.'

In her mind she could almost hear the tick of the time bomb.

Fifty-Three

Zero Hour

Philip studied the problem from all angles. He stared for minutes at a time at the explosive charges in the wreck's cargo hold, which contained the torpedo warheads. Water sluggishly pulsed through a hole in the side to wash over them. Then he examined the cables. After that he returned to the timer. Around the size of a shoe-box in black plastic, it boasted a small control panel and an LED screen that counted down toward the detonation. Twelve hours and three minutes left. More than once he'd been gripped by the urge to simply cut the wires. But at the last second he'd stopped. Inside his bright yellow survival suit perspiration tickled his skin as it ran freely. He clambered about the structure of the wreck to study the explosive charges from different angles in the moonlight. In the distance the *Volsparr* sat there in the mist, its lights burning like stars.

'What if I pull out the charges then drop them over the side?' He ran his fingers across his face. Despite sub-zero temperatures, sweat soaked his brow. 'But won't they have sensors that detect vibration? If I try to pull them up by the wires . . .' His mouth went dry. '*Boom.*' He returned to the black box. There had to be a safety cut-out to halt the countdown. 'I'm a piano player, for heaven's sake,' he hissed. 'So how the hell am I expected to know how to defuse a bomb? Damn it.' Fuming, he rose to his feet on the sloping ironwork which had rusted to the color of blood. The ocean sucked thirstily as the backward action of a wave emptied water through rents in the hull. Because the wreck sat on a sandbank it didn't move. Yet down in the hold torpedo warheads shifted with a clunking sound. A new wave brought an influx of creamy brine. *Twelve hours until this lot explodes. You need to be at least five miles away when it does. It's going to rip one hell of crater into the seabed.*

As he brooded he realized he could hear a motor. He stared in the direction of the *Volsparr*. One of the specks of light began to move. Risky, but he had to do it; he climbed up the mangled superstructure to get a better view. As he stood in front of a swastika painted on to its steel flank he watched the moving light. At that moment he had no way of knowing if it were hijackers or passengers who departed by lifeboat. He saw it accelerate. Luckily for them the ice didn't impede progress. The motor grew louder. The vessel surged through the brittle covering of white. A woman stood on the rear deck of the vessel.

Isis? His eyes watered. But he was sure it was her. He recognized the haughty pose, like an empress who had just conquered the world.

'Isis!' he shouted, although he knew she couldn't hear from this distance. 'See what I've done! I launched the lifeboat. I made it happen, just as I promised! I never ever hurt you! And now I've saved your life!' The words were out. He felt better for it; a powerful emotional release.

The boat plowed through the ice towards open sea. It made sense. The ice should be even thinner there. If that *had* been Isis, that meant the passengers must have escaped somehow.

'OK, Philip,' he breathed. 'You've proved you're a hero. Time to save your own neck.'

He scrambled down the crumbling metalwork. Rust smeared the yellow suit. *Whatever you do, don't rip the thing. You're going to need it watertight if you're going to get away from this. Forget the explosive charges. Just go.* It took only moments to slither off the wreck and back on to the ice. 'Here you are,' he muttered, 'take it easy. Don't fall through again. But in God's name keep moving.'

Behind him the time bomb relentlessly slaughtered seconds until zero hour.

Move. The ice sheet groaned as it struggled to bear his

weight. Gritting his teeth, he marched into white vastness. Behind him were the *Volsparr* and munitions wrecks. In front, the fates willing, was the island. He calculated it would take an hour's steady walk across the frozen sea to reach it. *With luck. With plenty of luck.*

He'd been walking only a couple of minutes when he heard the *thock-thock-thock* of rotors out there in the mist.

Camera called out to her co-hijackers on the top deck of the *Volsparr*: 'When I say go, everyone make for the aft outside deck. That's the *aft* deck. The chopper's approaching now. We're all going to be air-lifted out in twenty minutes. Got that?'

OK, so some of the passengers have escaped. But we've got great footage of our handiwork – and a pair of hostages that will serve as witnesses. This is outstanding work. We'll make a success out of this yet. She stepped over the body of Control. He'd suffered a bout of battlefield psychosis and blundered madly into the field of fire. Camera had seen it before. Men in charge were prone to it. *Now I'm in charge,* Camera thought, pleased. *I can see promotion coming my way. I'm going to be worth my weight in gold.*

Philip saw the big twin-rotor helicopter lumber through the night sky. Its huge rotors churned the mist. One fact Philip didn't take into account was his high visibility: a bright yellow figure against the white ice. In moonlight he glowed like a golden thumbtack on a featureless wall. He'd covered a hundred yards when the helicopter swung round to approach him just twenty feet above the frozen ocean. *At least I don't have to walk.* He saw himself being lifted away to the island where there would be hot coffee, attentive rescue workers. Then home in time for Christmas.

Only the helicopter turned sideways to shuffle crab-like just above the Baltic. A man stood in the open hatchway. The first shot he fired whacked a hole in the ice five feet from Philip. The second smashed through his hip.

With a gasp of surprise Philip slumped backwards. For a second there was numbness, then a bolt of lightning seemed to sear him from hip to head. A guttural roar of pain spurted from his lips. How could he have allowed himself to be such an easy target? What dirty, rotten, stinking bad luck.

The helicopter had to rise in order to make another pass so the sniper could take a body shot. As rotors thudded up into the mist to make the curving turn indignation gripped Philip.

'I'll show you,' he panted. For a moment he dragged himself across the ice; his blood painted it a violent streak of crimson. 'Nothing for it. On your feet. *Run!*'

Often when he played the piano he lost himself to the music, his mind drifting into a world of notes, harmonies, melody. 'Go there now,' he gasped. 'Remember your music. Cut yourself adrift. Immerse . . . disconnect.' He hummed his favorite composition as he walked. As he sang the notes he began to run. The helicopter approached behind him. The pain evaporated from his hip. He left bloody footprints. *Don't think of them. Think only of the music. Beautiful soundscapes. Magic carpets of sound. The melody carries you.*

Philip raced across the ice to the half-sunken munitions ship. The sniper fired. He zigzagged as he ran. A bullet smashed into the ice near his feet. One raked a gash above his elbow. He felt nothing. Nor did he feel the pain in his mangled hip. The music flowed through him, transported him, elevated him; it washed away the pain.

All of a sudden the mountain of rusting metal seemed to rush at him. He clambered on board to scramble over twisted iron rails, then duck under mangled beams. Blood loss distorted perceptions. The bent arms of the swastika seemed to reach out to capture him.

Both the helicopter pilot and the sniper had tougher work now. The vast structure of the wreck meant the pilot couldn't risk his rotors clipping the side of it. Meanwhile, the sniper had to contend with shadows vying with perplexing shades of red, orange and yellow as he scanned the rusted iron work.

On the *Volsparr* a radio message from the helicopter reached Camera. *There's a runaway passenger to take care of out on the ice. Once we've dealt with him we'll land on the helipad. Expect us within five minutes.*

With bullets ricocheting off heaps of metal Philip made it back to the timer. Its LED display told him they had eleven hours until zero hour.

'No, you're mistaken.' Blood bubbled through Philip's teeth. The bullet that smashed his hip had then bounced upward, punching through his intestine to spike his lung. He wrenched a flare from his pocket. Quickly he broke the top to ignite it. For a second he stood there holding the flare aloft as if he were an Olympian presenting the eternal flame to cheering crowds. Blood-red fire crackled from the end.

The helicopter closed in for the final shot. Downdraft from the rotor blades whipped up a blizzard of frost crystals. Smoke streamed from the flare. Its bloody light invested the steel superstructure with the color of raw beef hearts.

Philip smiled. 'To hell with zero hour.' As if the blazing flare had become a sword he plunged it into the timer's plastic shell. The fiery tip of his makeshift weapon burned through the casing; a second later it melted the wiring, the timer. Sparks shot from it. The LED reset to zero.

Philip lifted his face to the helicopter. Those on board might have wondered what he had to smile about.

The device boasted tamper-proof protection. When the electronics realized somebody had tried to mess with it they automatically triggered its detonators. In the hold the plastic explosive blew earlier than planned. That first wave of explosions swept Philip off into eternity.

On board the helicopter the pilot howled as he struggled to ascend. And if it had only been those dozen pounds of gelignite, he'd have made it. But what the torpedo warheads had been biding their time for down through the decades now arrived. This was their destiny. The small modern-day charges detonated tons of vintage high explosive that had been residing in their cylinders all those years.

The pilot reached two thousand feet, rotors chopping the air, still ascending. When the first big blast hit, the helicopter climbed yet faster. Even though its rotors were sheared away by the shockwave, the machine flew upwards like a rocket. When its fuel tanks ignited it became a streak of fire in the night sky.

Camera saw it all. What remained of the helicopter plunged, blazing, into the frozen ocean. She knew they'd reached the end.

Her colleagues ran by her to find a place of safety on the ship. 'Some chance,' she murmured. Just a short distance away exploding torpedoes detonated yet more torpedoes. Nazi munitions shone so brightly they turned night into something more than day. She wished she'd switched on her camera to record this.

The shockwave from the main eruption raced toward the ship. Ice sheets turned black as the concussion shattered them. When the blast struck the *Volsparr* the entire flank of the vessel imploded. Water surged in. Camera managed to hoist herself to her feet as the ship began to list. All around her hijackers scrambled on all fours. Most screamed in terror. Some couldn't. Glass from broken windows had removed faces.

The two remaining munitions wrecks went up in all their fiery glory. Warheads were hurled from the cargo holds and rained down on to the ocean. They exploded, sending up geysers of foam. Other warheads tumbled out of the sky to shatter the *Volsparr*'s decks. Camera saw moonlight shine through the hole in the ceiling. A shiny cylinder had been flung from a wreck to punch through the superstructure. It rolled toward her feet, as big as a garbage can. The time-delay fuse still worked. 1940s engineering had remained sound. When six hundred pounds of high explosive detonated at her feet, all she saw was a fire of the most brilliant silver. Then she was dust.

Fifty-Four

The global population was glued to the television and computer screens. Humankind in its billions. News channels carried live footage beamed by Tanya Rhone. One world leader declaimed, 'If I don't see it on television I won't believe it with my own eyes.' What she did see was CCTV coverage of the hijackers' last moments on earth. Humanity saw the killers screaming in fear as exploding munitions destroyed the *Volsparr*, and them with it.

In the offices of the company that had ordered the piracy in the first place, with the intention of destroying Boson Eumericas, it was eerily silent. Some of its executives had fled in the desperate hope they could evade justice. A couple of them had damaged the sidewalk after they'd stepped out of their windows. The owner of the company strolled into the office of his Development Chief. On the wall was a large map of a certain island in the Baltic. On a computer screen footage of the hijackers' demise played on a loop. His Development Chief lay slumped in the executive chair, his head lolling sideways. The needle of the syringe remained embedded in his naked forearm. A suicide letter addressed to the man's lawyer lay neatly on the desk.

The owner walked back along the corridor. The corporate accountant raced toward the elevator. Normally, the man was immaculately groomed. Now his hair stood on end, he perspired, his suit was dirty. The accountant struggled to carry an armful of incriminating files. For some reason he'd yanked out the hard drive from the computer.

The owner mused on that one. Maybe the accountant believed that all the footage, which would damn him and his colleagues for all time, was confined to his own personal computer and nowhere else. Maybe the accountant couldn't grasp that billions of people had watched it. This particular genie was well and truly free of its bottle.

A moment later the owner reached his lavish office. Outside a hard rain had started to fall. Time to leave . . . He opened the window then stepped outside. City lights burned brightly through the coming storm. When he dropped two hundred feet to the road below the rain rose in volume as if in applause.

Aboard the lifeboat the shockwave from the explosion five miles away made the craft dance on the water. Tanya hung on to a rail in the cabin to prevent herself being hurled across the heads of the seated passengers. More explosions followed but each one was less severe. By this time, one of the ship's crew had made radio contact with the coastguard. The military had been forced to stand off for the duration of hijacking but now they were sending warships to rescue them.

Tanya looked round for Isis. When she couldn't see her she experienced a pang of alarm. The woman had been out on the little deck; perhaps the shockwave from the detonation had swept her into the sea?

Tanya stepped out into the cold night air. In the east a glow on the horizon signaled dawn. Behind them ruddy fires still burned as the *Volsparr* gradually slipped into the eternal embrace of the Baltic. The precious pump went with it to a briny grave. In front of them whales rose through breaks in the ice sheet. A sixth sense had warned them to flee to safety, and now they were out of harm's way they vented white vapor as they made the most of their playground.

Tanya breathed deeply. 'So . . . we made it.'

'Pardon?' Isis had been deep in thought.

Tanya shook her head. 'Didn't you notice? We've just gone and saved our lives.'

Isis grinned. 'Oh, that old thing. That's in the past, Tanya. You should look to the future.'

'I'll do that after I've crawled into bed for a couple of days.'

'Nonsense.' Isis linked arms with her. 'Now that we're the best of friends, why don't we go into business together?'

'You are joking?'

'I never joke about business. Now . . .' Her keen eyes scanned the way ahead. 'I know where there's a copper mine that's going to be sold for next to nothing.'

'You mean Boson Eumericas' mine?'

'Sure. I can design a finance package. We'll get it for a song. I'll be president. You can be vice-president. The future will be wonderful.'

'I don't know how to run a business.'

'If you can beat those evil people back there you are capable of anything, Tanya. So what do you say?'

Suzanne Lynch stood beside Turrock in the lifeboat cabin. 'You lost your prisoners. Do you suppose anyone will grieve for them?'

Smiling, he looked at her. 'They're not dead. At least most of them aren't.'

'Where are they then? Nobody on the ship could have survived the explosion.'

'You're right.' His smile broadened. 'No, my prisoners are right here.' He nodded at the passengers crammed into the cabin. 'Somewhere amongst this lot. They changed their clothes; melted into the crowd. That's what my guys do.'

'How are you going to identify them?'

Still smiling, he shrugged. 'I'll help the authorities. But I guess some will just slip away into the night.' For a moment he scanned the faces of strangers; the ones who appeared the least troubled were the ones that should be suspected the most; however, there was nothing he could do about rounding up the prisoners now. Instead, he nodded at Fytton, who sat beside the aisle.

Fytton grinned back. 'Hiyo, boss.' He still basked in the afterglow of his best Quilp hunt ever.

On board the hijackers' fishing vessel, the Toad sang as he handled the ship's wheel – a jaunty sea shanty that suited his mood. He and his twin were happy again. Why, gosh, in no time at all he'd been able to furnish a home cabin on the fishing boat. One of the hijackers had filled the role of his twin just beautifully. At that moment the hijacker lay on the bunk with a cell phone in his hand. The Toad had used marker pens to replicate the birthmarks that adorned his own broad, smiling face. And the hijacker's dead eyes regarded their reflection in the mirror. *And speaking of eyes . . .*

The Toad ducked his head down through the wheelhouse into the lounge area. 'My darlings,' he sang, 'how're things down there? Progress made? Results achieved? Hmm?'

Sami and Maya stood before the man bound to the chair.

Sami wore a happy smile. He squeezed Maya's hand gently. In his other hand he held a cook's knife.

'This time,' Sami announced with great confidence, 'we're going to make the breakthrough.'

The man tied to the chair turned his pleading eyes to Maya. 'Please . . . don't do this.'

Maya went to hold his head. 'Tell me all about it. Describe pain to me. Explain what it feels like.'

Though the three friends didn't know it at the time, apart from the prisoner on Tanya's vessel, this man was the last surviving hijacker. And he would continue to live for quite a spell yet, although he'd wish that wasn't the case. This time Sami promised himself he'd show the world his miracle cure worked. He took the man's eyelid between his finger and thumb, then positioned the knife blade.

Meanwhile, as the Toad steered the fishing boat he returned to singing the sea shanty with a cheerful gusto that rattled the windows. Down below in the lounge the last but one hijacker made a lot of noise, too. *Oh Gosh. Happy days!*

The way ahead for the Toad's craft lay clear; the ice parted and a virgin shoreline beckoned. What remained of the warheads on the wrecks sacrificed themselves in one final blaze of light. As the fireball bloomed it painted the sky and the moon crimson. Its glare even stained red the faces of escaped prisoners and survivors, alike – a deep, blood red that seemed to linger in the flesh long after the burning shipwrecks crumbled into the waters and disappeared.